THE MAR

Copyright © 201

All rights reserved. No part of this book may be reproduced or transmitted in any form or by any means, electronic or mechanical, including photocopying, recording, scanning, or by any information storage and retrieval system whatsoever, without written permission, except in the case of brief quotations embodied in critical articles and reviews.

This novel is a work of fiction. Any reference to real people, events, establishments, organizations or locales are intended only to give the fiction a sense of reality and authenticity. All of the main characters, organizations, events and incidents in this novel are creations of the authors' imaginations and their resemblance, if any, to actual events or persons, living or dead, is entirely coincidental.

Published by: Celebrity Spotlight Entertainment, LLC
www.celebrityspotlightentertainmentllc.com
FIRST EDITION: 2019
Editor: Porscha N. Dillard

ISBN: 978-1096037866

Library of Congress Cataloguing-in-Publication Data:

Celebrity Spotlight Entertainment, LLC

Printed in the United States of America

DEDICATION

This book is dedicated to the following people:

To Nipsey Hussle, his Queen Lauren London, and his family. The game is going to test you, never fold. Stay ten toes down; it's not on you, it's in you and what's in you they can't take away. The love remains unconditionally in our hearts
The Marathon Continues…..

To all his fans, Thank you for the love you've shown. Let's keep his legacy alive by making a difference in the world. Remember; Drive, Determination and Persistence does not recognize failure.

Sincerely,
Eugene L. Weems

ACKNOWLEDGMENTS

My deepest appreciation and warmest friendship is extended to all the people who have made a positive and productive difference in the world, the urban communities, and or in someone's lives.

You all know who you are.

Eugene L. Weems

DEDICATION	2
ACKNOWLEDGMENTS	3
CHAPTER 1	5
CHAPTER 2	11
CHAPTER 3	13
CHAPTER 4	15
CHAPTER 5	21
CHAPTER 6	27
CHAPTER 7	33
CHAPTER 8	37
CHAPTER 9	47
CHAPTER 10	55
CHAPTER 11	61
CHAPTER 12	73
CHAPTER 13	77
CHAPTER 14	81
CHAPTER 15	97
CHAPTER 16	101
CHAPTER 17	105
CHAPTER 18	121
CHAPTER 19	123
CHAPTER 20	137
CHAPTER 21	145
CHAPTER 22	151
CHAPTER 23	161
CHAPTER 24	169
CHAPTER 25	177
CHAPTER 26	187
CHAPTER 27	191
CHAPTER 28	193
CHAPTER 29	205
CHAPTER 30	209
CHAPTER 31	219
CHAPTER 32	227
CHAPTER 33	231
CHAPTER 34	239
CHAPTER 35	245
CHAPTER 36	253
THE FINAL CHAPTER	259

CHAPTER 1

"Get your ass over here! I'm not gonna be running behind your ass!" Lauren was winding the extension cord around her hand as she was speaking and trying to cut the room off so her son Nipsey couldn't get away.

"Mom, I'm sorry! I won't do it anymore!" Nipsey was terrified. He knew when Lauren got like this it was no telling what she would do.

"Whap! Whap!" The extension cord cut into his skin. He screamed a blood curdling scream.

"I know you not! I'm... sick... of... y'all... asses! Each word was emphasized with every lick he took.

Nipsey Hussle had become accustomed to these types of episodes.

"Now put them clothes on and get in there and clean that room up like I told you the first time!" She was wiping the sweat from her brow as she spoke and lit her cigarette.

"Yes, ma'am." Nipsey was terrified of her. He cowered as he answered.

Lauren was a hard women. She worked to keep a roof over her kid's heads most nights, and slept most days. Derrick, his older brother, was in charge during those times.

"After you get through cleaning that room get your ass downstairs and help your brother and sister clean up! Y'all know I'm having a party tonight! Your ass up here sleeping!"

When she wasn't sleeping or working she was throwing parties.

"Yes, ma'am." He responded, wincing in pain.

He was moving slowly. The cord had tore into his naked flesh leaving welts the size of fingers.

"When you're done downstairs get back up here and get into this tub!" She was going into the bathroom to run some warm water with some Epsom salts to take the soreness out of Nipsey's battered body.

When he got downstairs Derrick was sitting at the bar watching Angel clean up.

Derrick walked over and pushed his head so hard it cracked his neck. "Little punk! Get over there and clean them mirrors!"

"Boy! Don't be doing him like that!" Angel, his little sister, had seen Derrick. She always took up for him when she saw Derrick bullying him. She and Nipsey were always close. Even though Nipsey felt if he was dead everyone would be a lot happier, he knew Angel wouldn't, she was the one bright spot in his life.

"Shut up and mind your business!" He was grilling Angel.

"Make me shut up! You make me sick!" She was rolling her eyes.

"Come on Nipsey, he so stupid!" Nipsey hated Derrick.

He was abusive like Lauren so he was scared of him like his mother. The fear he had of his mother was different from the fear he had of his brother.

Everyone that knew Lauren had thought she was crazy, Nipsey knew she was crazy, and he had the scars to prove it. Deep down he truly believed she would kill him one day. The abuse she inflicted upon him was so severe at times she would have to doctor on him afterwards.

The extension cord was nothing compared to the broken broomsticks she would use that were broken on some part of his body previously and this started as far back as he could remember.

She beat Derrick too, but it was different. It wasn't as severe, and when she beat Angel you would think someone was killing her. He felt she didn't beat Angel like that because her daddy would have probably killed Lauren. She knew how he could get. During their marriage he beat her pretty bad, and he loved his daughter more than anything, and if push came to shove Angel's grandmother would come pack her things and take her back home with her. That was her little Angel, hence the name.

Nipsey and Angel never knew Derrick's dad. He lived in Chicago somewhere and that's where he lived until he was about 14. Then he came to live with Lauren and that's when Derrick began to hurt Nipsey in other ways.

Nipsey was always small in stature, a lot smaller than Derrick, and Derrick was always into some kind of sport; football, swimming, even track.

He used his size and strength to his advantage when he took advantage of Nipsey. It had got to the point where the only way he would stop beating on him was if Angel started screaming and yelling at him threatening to tell on him. At times she really was his Angel as well.

One morning Lauren had come home before Nipsey had gotten up. "Smack! Smack!" She woke him up slapping him across his face.

"Why the fuck them dishes ain't done? Wasn't it your night?" He was scrambling away from her.

"Yes, ma'am." His mouth was bleeding. "I was gonna wash them, but we didn't have no dish soap!"

"Take that shit off! I don't want to hear that shit! It's some washing powder down there right? He was barely listening to the words coming out of her mouth. He was more concerned with what she had in her hand. It was a table leg from the basement.

"I said lay your ass down!" He complied.

"Why you don't know how to listen? What! You dumb or something?" She began berating him. Laying there totally exposed as she did so for ten minutes was torture. Before she even hit him he was in tears anticipating what was to come.

"Whap!" He braced himself for the blow unsuccessfully.

"Whap! Whap!"

"Lay your ass still!" He was squirming, trying to keep her from hitting the same spot.

After six or seven licks his buttocks were swollen and numb. Before she could issue another lick he got up on his hands and knees and crawled across the bed. He made a dash for the door. He had come to realize running around the room to get away from the onslaught of Lauren wasn't working. Before she could get to the room door he was already outside running up the street in the pouring rain.

When he finally stopped running an elderly couple pulled alongside of him.

"Hey, sweetheart. What's the matter? Why are you out here like that? Where's your momma?" The lady on the passenger side of the car asked.

"She was beating me so I ran out of the house. I'm not ever going back!"

She got out of the car. "Aww, baby. Let's get you out of the rain and in some dry clothes, okay?" The concern she had registered in her tone, Nipsey relented. They took him back to their home.

"Here you go sweetheart, put these on. They belong to my grandson, he won't mind." Handing him some sweat pants and a sweatshirt.

"Thank you, ma'am."

"Would you like some cocoa, it'll warm you up?"

"Yes, ma'am. Thank you."

The couple called the police. They didn't know what else to do. When the police arrived they began to question him.

"How's it going young man?"

"Fine."

"How old are you?"

"I'm twelve. I'll be thirteen soon." He was a little more at ease now.

"Oh yeah, how soon?"

"In two months."

"That's great! Well, Mr. and Mrs. Bryant tell us you ran away from home." Nipsey glanced at the Bryants before he responded. The looks on their faces were of discontent.

"Yes sir she was beating me, and I didn't know what to do."

"Why was she beating you?"

"I went to bed without washing the dishes."

"Is the dishes part of your chores?"

"Yes."

"Look son, let's go have a chat with your mom."

"Please don't take me back there, she's gonna kill me!" His expression showed real fear.

"Look Nipsey, your mom loves you. She's not going to kill you."

On the ride back to his house he began to tear up the closer they got. When they got there Lauren was waiting. She put on her best performance for the officers.

"Thank you officers, so much. I was so worried about him. Boy, where you been?" She grabbed him and held onto him.

"Ms. Hussle, your son said you were beating him?"

"I have rules in my home officers, and if you break those rules then there's consequences." She was looking at Nipsey as she spoke. She put on a facade of a doting mother and convinced them that he was exaggerating, and he would be okay if they left him. So, that's what they did.

As soon as she went in the house, she grabbed him by his arm. "Bring your ass on!" Almost dragging him. "Get your ass down them steps motherfucker. What's wrong with you bringing them fucking police to my house?" She shoved him down the basement stairs and locked the door.

Sitting in the dark, Nipsey convinced himself no one really cared for him. He stayed in the basement two days coming out only to eat and take a bath.

"Nipsey! Nipsey!" Angel was calling from the top of the stairs. He was asleep on some dirty clothes.

"Come on Nipsey, she's gone!" He came upstairs squinting from the bright lights of the kitchen. "Here, I got you some cookies and milk!"

"Thanks, sis." Every time Lauren left, Angel would sneak him up into the kitchen for a while and sit and talk to him. "How long she gonna be gone?" Even though she was gone he was still nervous.

"I don't know. Don't worry, we can hear her pull up."

It seemed as if whenever he needed Angel she was always there for him.

He had forgotten how much she loved him.

"Nipsey, don't worry. We're going to get out of here someday for good." "I know. I can't wait either!" He said with conviction.

Nipsey started to become withdrawn. The rest of middle school went by so fast it was like a blur, and when it was time for him to start high school he was ready. But his life was forever changed during his first year.

Derrick was two grades ahead of him and still made Nipsey bend to his will. That year Derrick started to molest him. It took a toll on him physically and mentally. Thoughts of suicide were never too far from his mind, especially since he felt he had no one to turn to. After the third or fourth time (he had lost count), he cried out, "I'm telling mom!" Derrick immediately covered his mouth with his hand so Lauren wouldn't hear in her room.

"Okay, I'll stop," he was saying as he got up off Nipsey. "I'm sorry, I won't do it anymore okay?" Tears were streaming down Nipsey's face. He was fed up. He had never cried so uncontrollably before. That scared Derrick. Nipsey's spirit had been broken. He was tired of being abused, he was tired of feeling alone; he was broken. Nipsey didn't tell, he ran away and didn't come back. When the police found him three days later he was sleeping in one of the many abandoned houses in Detroit.

"Is anyone in here?" The police were cautiously entering the house. Nipsey became alert and didn't make a sound.

"We know you're in here. Come on out slowly!" Still no movement. "The people next door saw you. No one's gonna hurt you! We want to help you!" He saw the flashlights and heard the floor boards creaking as they got closer.

"You don't want to help me, you want to take me back!"

"Take you back where? What's your name?" They didn't know who he was they just got a call of a young child in an abandoned house.

"If you take me back, I'm gonna kill myself! I hate her!"

"Wow, hold on son, everything's gonna be alright. Just come on out and we can talk about it. You don't have any weapons, do you?"

"No, I don't have no weapons. If you promise you won't take me back

I'll come out."

"We promise son. We just want to get you somewhere safe."

They were true to their word. Not long after that he became a ward of the State. He was fourteen.

CHAPTER 2

After Nipsey had become a ward of the State, they sent him to the St. Francis Home for Boys. It was a place for "at risk" emotionally disturbed youth, and for kids who may have been abandoned by their loved ones. It was run by nuns who devoted their lives to helping children.

It was rough for Nipsey when he first arrived, he was an emotional wreck. He'd wake in cold sweats, sometimes screaming, and would toss and turn all night. He didn't associate with the other boys and no one forced him. It was their policy at St. Francis to allow everyone to come out of their shell at their own pace.

In counseling sessions he spoke about his beatings, his sister, not having a father, even how he thought about killing himself, but he never told anyone about being sexually abused. He was scared of how people would view him so he tried to push it to the back of his mind where it never stayed long because those feelings always resurfaced and exhibited themselves in a number of ways, such as: feeling self-conscious about who he was as an individual. He felt being abused in such a manner made him less of a young man, or that maybe now he was gay. It angered him because he was so confused and because of his shame he couldn't tell anyone what he was going through emotionally.

Mass was every Sunday morning and everyone attended. Nipsey found inner peace on those mornings and when he was in the presence of the nuns, he loved how subdued they were at all times. He never heard one raise their voice for any reason, and it intrigued him how one minute he was alone and the next Sister Alicia would be right there. It never ceased to amaze him how he never heard any of them arrive.

Nipsey got the impression that Sister Alicia was the head nun. He liked her because she never bombarded him with prying questions. Sister Alicia liked Nipsey too. Even though he never discussed being molested he exhibited all the signs: withdrawn, anti-social behavior, pent up aggression, distrusting of others of the same sex, self-loathing, and even depression. She had seen it all before. She just prayed it wasn't too late to help Nipsey.

"Sister Alicia, what's a friar?"

"Well Nipsey, he is a brother, like you see the rest of my sisters around here, but they reside in a monastery."

"So, am I gonna be a friar?"

"Well my child, you have to be spiritually led to become a friar. Do you want to become a friar?"

"I thought you said I had to be spiritually led?"

"That is true to become a friar, but not to want to be a friar."

"How do I know when I am being spiritually led?"

"It will be a pressing on your heart, deep down in your soul, a desire only to serve God. Do you understand?"

"I think so. I think that God is calling me to do something else then."

"Why are you so sure my son?" "Cause I feel it deep in my heart." She smiled at his sincerity.

"Oh really, what might that be?" She asked out of pure curiosity.

"I think he wants me to get rid of all the bad people."

"Who are all the bad people?"

"You know, all the bad people that hurt kids, and people who can't take care of themselves."

"My son, you know there will always be bad people."

"Not if I get rid of as many as I can!"

"Well, if that is what God has called you to do my child, then embrace it and God will make a way."

He thought about that for a few moments and went back to cleaning the visitation area. She assumed he wanted to be in Law Enforcement, but that was the furthest thing from his mind. Secretly he prayed God would make a way.

Sister Alicia loved the progress Nipsey had been making. He began to excel in all his studies, in fact, he was at the top of his class. He was well-liked by everyone. He was still a little reluctant to mingle with the other boys, but he still made tremendous strides in the year he had been there.

Though remnants of the abuse Nipsey sustained still showed physically he was still a nice looking young man with his chestnut brown complexion and short wavy hair. His eyes were big and brown and he was beginning to gain a little weight. He wasn't conceited, but you could tell his confidence began to grow.

CHAPTER 3

"Ma! I'm hungry!" Angel was sitting on the floor outside Lauren's room.

"What do you want me to do? Go find something to eat!" Lauren hadn't been out of her room for any real amount of time in the last week.

"There's nothing down there but some bread!" Angel was rubbing her stomach as if trying to rub the hunger away.

"Don't be lying, it's some rice down there too! Get the hell away from my door! You better cook some rice and put some butter and sugar in it!" She sat there and cried.

"Bam, bam, bam!" Someone was knocking at the door.

"Angel!" Lauren yelled from behind the door.

"What!"

"Get the damn door!"

Angel went in her room, slammed the door and locked it. She would try and sleep the hunger off unsuccessfully.

This was Lauren's life now. Since Nipsey had been gone, her life had spiraled out of control. She had become disassociated with anyone she once cared about. For days on end she would disappear behind her room door and get high. Different people came and went all times of the day and night.

"Come in!" The front door remained shut but unlocked. She had a system. She would watch out her bedroom window, so she always knew who was at the door, and since Angel had taken to not even opening the door, she would yell out the window and tell whoever was at the door to come in.

"Little heifer, don't bring your ass out of that room!" She kicked Angel's door on her way to meet whoever it was at the top of the stairs.

Since Derrick had been gone Angel was a lot more fearful of the people that came and went. She would keep her door locked unless she was hungry or was going to the bathroom.

Grandma would come by and bring her money to help her through the weeks. The only reason Angel was still living there was because grandma wanted her to wait for the end of the school year before she went to live with her permanently. Angel knew it was only a matter of time, so she just did what she had to do until then.

On the weekends, when she went to visit, she would take as much as she could. She would leave it at grandma's. She would continue to do this until everything she had was already at grandma's when her time came to leave for good.

Lauren knew it wouldn't be long before Angel left as well. She knew Angel told her grandmother everything and always had, so she knew grandma wouldn't stand for her Angel going without for any reason.

It wasn't that Lauren didn't care, but the total opposite. She did care. She cared more than anyone knew. That was her problem. Her bedroom door wasn't being used to keep her kids out, but to keep her in. It hid her shame from them. She could barely stand to look into their faces without feeling like a failure.

Even though the abuse had stopped since Nipsey had been gone, she had turned to drugs to cope with her own inner demons, the demons that made her who she was today.

Lauren came from a dysfunctional family herself. She had six brothers and five sisters. Her mother was abusive verbally and physically. So abuse was natural to her. It was her way to solve every problem.

When she had her own kids, abusing them was the only way she knew how to raise them. That was the only way she knew how to show she cared about what they did or didn't do.

Lauren loved her kids. She took care of them the best she knew how. She worked and got government assistance. She never relied on a man to take care of her family. No one really knew when things began to go awry. Maybe it was the abuse she suffered at the hands of her husband Lou, or maybe she had been secretly using drugs all along. Whatever it was, it has culminated into something totally out of control. Something no one ever wants to be around. Something everyone began to hate.

CHAPTER 4

While Nipsey was wiping down the confessionals, Sister Burke appeared out of nowhere. He smiled to himself, he loved how they did that.

"What does she want now?" He was thinking to himself. It wasn't that he didn't like Sister Burke, it was just that she asked so many questions and she had a way of looking at him that made him feel like she was reading his mind. It was so unnerving, but the concern she showed for him made him feel loved so he tolerated her prying.

"Nipsey, I have something for you. But first, I'd like to know how's everything going with you. It's Friday and I haven't seen you all week."

"I'm fine Sister Burke, it's just that I've started Advanced Classes this week and Trig is becoming a lot more challenging than I thought it would be. I promise I'll come and see you Monday, is that alright?"

"That's fine my son, just remember Rome wasn't built in a day, and even God rested on the seventh day." She was handing him a letter.

"Yes, Sister Burke." He draped the cloth over his shoulder and went and sat in a pew. He was ecstatic, he hadn't heard from his sister since he had been at St. Francis. It made him feel good to know Angel still thought about him. He missed her immensely.

Dear Nipsey,

Hey boy you thought I wasn't gonna find you, didn't you? I miss you so much. I'm sorry you can't be here with me but you are in my heart.

So let me tell you what's been happening. First off, I don't stay with ma' anymore. My grandma came and got me, so now I live with her for good. Ma' started smoking crack and stayed in her room all the time. She never bought food or anything. When I called grandma and told her I was hungry she came and got all my stuff and now I'm staying with her and daddy.

Daddy is still drinking and he gets on my nerves; plus he's smoking crack too. His girlfriend is smoking crack and they are stealing anything they can. Anyway, Derrick moved out before grandma came and got me. He is freeloading off some girl named Aubrey. They live off Alter Rd. and Mack, I think she's kind of slow but she loves her some Derrick.

Angel went on to tell him how grandma was doing and about

her new boyfriend. And then, before she closed she made sure to let him know she wanted to come visit and if he wanted her to she would talk to grandma and see if he could come and stay with them.

"Just say the word Nipsey, okay?" Was how she put it. Here is grandma's phone number if you can call me: (313) 571-9075.

Love Always,
Your Favorite Sister
Angel

Nipsey was walking on a cloud after reading her letter. He was so happy she had made it out of Lauren's house. "It's good she is with grandma, now I don't have to worry about her," he was thinking to himself.

Grandma owned a big, two-family flat on Cooper, right off Warren Ave. on the Eastside of Detroit in a relatively nice neighborhood considering you're talking about the eastside. Everyone knew everyone on the block, and everyone loved Angel and grandma.

Grandma was a very religious woman. God was the center of her life and Lou, Angel's daddy, who worked for the city before he started getting high.

Nipsey loved grandma. She has come to Nipsey's rescue a number of times while they were staying with her. He thought about one particular time that Lauren flipped because he had eaten the last of her Raisin Bran.

"Nipsey, get your ass over here and stand right here!" She was pointing to a spot on the floor in front of her. "Didn't I tell y'all not to fuck with my shit?"

"Yes ma'am, I didn't see any of our cereal though!" Looking up into her eyes as she stood there with her hands on her hips made him tremble with fear.

"Cause you didn't see none of y'alls don't mean eat mine!" She was pointing her finger in his face. Every time she moved her hand he flinched.

"Smack!" She had caught him glancing in grandma's direction. He fell backwards.

"Get your ass back over here!" He tried to stand a little out of reach. "Right here!" pointing again.

"Smack!" She caught him again before he even had a chance to plant his feet firmly where she indicated. This time when he didn't get up fast enough she went and got part of a branch that was amongst the fire wood and began to unleash a fury of blows.

"Now Lauren, you can't be hitting that child like that, you're gonna really hurt that boy!" Grandma had seen enough.

"This my child, not yours!"

Grandma had made it over to where Lauren had Nipsey. "Look now, this is my house and Lord knows I'll put you out of here right now!" Nipsey saw his chance to get away and hide behind her. "It was only cereal for God's sake!" She grabbed his hand. "Come on baby!" She was ushering him out the door. She took him next door until Lauren calmed down.

She was a good woman, even after Lauren moved out with Angel and Nipsey. She would still let Nipsey come with Angel when she went for weekends. Derrick had yet to come stay with them during these times.

Nipsey was glad that Angel gave him the new number. He could use the phone in Sister Burke's office anytime he wanted as long as he had permission.

Time had been flying by so fast Nipsey didn't realize how fast spring was approaching. He rarely left the grounds and hadn't been anywhere since the beginning of winter. He hadn't gone out on any of the trips because he hated the cold. Winters in Detroit were blistering cold and if he didn't have to go out, he didn't.

Nipsey had recently learned that the next trip would be soon so he was looking forward to getting out. He had been saving all the allowances he received every week. It was only twenty dollars a week. It didn't matter to Nipsey though because he saved every dime anyway. He didn't eat a lot of junk and he didn't have to buy clothes. They had vouchers for that so he was sure he would enjoy wherever they went.

When Monday came around Nipsey was sitting outside Sister Burke's office before class.

"You're early, Nipsey." She caught him off guard. He had been daydreaming.

"Oh, hi Sister Burke, how are you this morning?" She could see he was a lot more upbeat this morning.

"I'm well Nipsey, thanks for asking."

"Sister, do you know where we are going for the next outing?" He had begun to learn to steer conversations the way he wanted them to go so she wouldn't ask so many questions.

"It's supposed to be down at Hart Plaza for the Jazz Festival."

Hart Plaza is downtown Detroit where all summer there's a different ethnic festival every weekend. It usually starts on Friday, and ends on Sunday evening. You have people coming from all around, even Canada, to attend. They have outdoor concerts, different concession stands, and booths for souvenirs and gadgets. Each day it began eleven in the morning until eleven at night.

"So how are you getting along Nipsey?"

"I'm doing good Sister."

"So, how are you and your roommate getting along?"

"He's cool. I like Samuel. Sister, my sister sent me their new number and I was hoping you would let me call?"

"Sure, when would you like to call?"

"Can I call after school?"

"Sure son, that would be perfect, just meet me back here when you're done."

"Thank you, Sister Burke."

"Nipsey, before you go, how would you like to take some self-defense classes?"

"What do you mean, what kind of class is it?" He had an inquisitive look on his face.

"Well, I have a brother who runs a dojo around the corner on Linwood." "What does he teach?" A little more enthusiasm now.

"I think it's Judo." The light in his eyes told her she made the right decision.

"Really? I would love to learn Jujitsu." Sister Burke smiled at his knowledge. The average person doesn't know that Jujitsu was the original name for Judo. "When can I start?"

This was a different side to him she had yet to see. She knew that it was something that he enjoyed to read about because after he gets out of class, instead of watching TV, he would go outside, sit under a tree and read about Kung Fu. She knew cause Sister Constantine who runs all recreational activities, including being out and about on the grounds, keeps tabs on all the boys and their interests. This is how she knew where to find one of the boys if need be. It was a really tedious task but she loved those boys and prided herself on knowing each one.

"Thank you, Sister. That's great!"

"I'll talk to him Thursday and maybe you'll be able to start Monday, but if for some reason your other responsibilities start to slack, then we'll have to ..."

"Don't worry Sister, I'll continue to handle my responsibilities." He cut her off before she could finish. She lifted her brow and nodded her head in approval.

"Being as though it is only around the corner, I thought that maybe you could walk so you won't have to depend on anyone to take you."

"Okay, Sister. Thank you again!"

"Now, do you have any more questions for me?"

"No Sister, that's all."

"Well, don't you think you should be running off to class? Aren't you late? See, you're slacking already!"

"Yes, Sister. Wait, I don't mean 'yes' I am slacking, I mean 'yes' I'm late." He began to make haste. She stopped him as he was leaving.

"I'll see you here after your classes for your phone call, right?"

"Yes, Sister."

CHAPTER 5

Sister Catherine was Nipsey's History teacher. She liked him because he was always very attentive. He asked questions, and when she would put a question to the class if no one else could answer she would count on him as a last resort. She never liked to call on him first because she didn't want to make it appear that he was the teacher's pet, but Nipsey just had a gift for retaining information. He was so intelligent, but you would never know because he was so humble.

Today she noticed something different about him. He seemed preoccupied with whatever was on his mind. He was so deep in thought about how his life was changing he vaguely heard Sister Catherine say something about the Spanish-American War, and when she called on him she got no response.

"Nipsey!" Nothing.

"Nipsey!" Nothing.

She decided to walk over to his desk. She stood there for a second. Then she hit his desk with a three-foot pointer. "Whack!" In that instant he jumped out of his seat knocking his chair over backwards. He took two steps back instinctively. He looked at the pointer and back to her. She looked into his eyes. What she saw was totally unfamiliar to her. It made the hair on the back of her neck stand up.

She started toward him, but when she saw him backpedal while looking at the pointer, she stopped, looked at the pointer, then went and laid it on her desk. She saw how uneasy it made him. Then she spoke in that calm soothing tone that all the sisters spoke in.

"Nipsey, I'm so sorry. I didn't mean to startle you my son. I was just trying to get your attention. Here, let me get that chair." As she started to bend down, so did Nipsey. She placed one hand on his back and one on the chair. She leaned in so the others couldn't hear. "It's okay son, no one here will ever hurt you." A tear formed in his eyes but never fell.

Sister Catherine rubbed his back in a motherly fashion and when he looked at her she winked at him and nodded in a knowingly manner, gestured toward his seat and went back to the blackboard like nothing had happened. When Nipsey sat back down he spoke up. "April 24, 1898."

"Excuse me, Nipsey ?"

"America declared war on Spain, April 24, 1898." "Thank you, son." Another wink and nod.

"You're welcome Sister." A nod and a timid smile.

After class Nipsey did his chores and went outside to his favorite tree. He wasn't reading today and he wasn't going to Sister Burke's office. He did not feel like dealing with her right now. He decided that he would call Angel another time, right now he just needed to think and be alone.

"Why do I feel so ashamed? I thought I had gotten more confident than that. I can't believe I allowed everyone to see me weak. That will be the last time anyone witnesses any of my weaknesses."

"Hello, Nipsey." That startled him and made him angry at the same time.

"Did I scare you?"

"No." She knew he wasn't telling the truth so she just smiled.

"Hi, Sister Alicia, what are you doing out here?"

"I got tired of the air conditioner, so I decided to get some sun by my favorite tree." He knew she was lying so now it was his turn to smile.

"Looks like we have something in common sister because this is my favorite tree too!"

"Oh yeah, Nipsey?"

"Yeah, I love how the sun always shines on it, and I love the way it smells. What kind of tree is this sister?"

"This my dear, is a magnolia tree. It's very distinctive because of the snowy-white flowers and sometimes there are purple or rose colored flowers. If you notice you don't see magnolia trees around here. That's because you mostly see them in the south, like in Mississippi or Louisiana. The flowers are beautiful aren't they?" She was looking up into the tree as she spoke with a far away look in her eyes.

"Yes ma'am, they are."

"Let me tell you something about this tree and why it's my favorite. One day I was driving by a nursery and a young man was getting ready to throw this flimsy, half-dead tree into the chipper. I stopped and asked him if I could buy it from him."

"Sister Alicia, why did you want a half-dead tree?"

"Cause it still had life." The look on his face told her he was intrigued, so she finished. "He just gave me the tree and I brought it back here. My sisters and I dug a hole and planted it. My sisters thought it was a waste of time. They said it would never blossom. I told them, if we nourished it, it would grow to be strong and beautiful. Even after blizzards and thunderstorms it still grew. When termites began attacking it, it continued to thrive. Look at it. Look how majestic it is.

"You see my son, just when everyone thought it wasn't gonna make it, my God's glory shined upon it, as it does all His creation. Just like this tree, if you rest in the Lord when you need him, he will lift you up on eagle's wings. Nothing will tear you down." She knew he understood. "Have a good afternoon my son." Just like that she was gone.

"Nipseysan, you must control your breathing. Focus on inner strength. All power come from inside. Remember, no matter how strong your opponent is physically, if his mind unsteady and weak he will be compelled by emotions. Emotions cloud judgments and become fatal flaws."

Nipsey worked hard with a determination unparalleled. He was astute. When his sensei said "move" or to perform a technique he made sure it was precise. He spent more time at the dojo than any other student. His sensei was pleased and took to Nipsey easily. It was all he thought about. When he wasn't at the dojo and training his body, he was out by his tree studying books about discipline and inner peace as well as styles and techniques. He even made a few friends and came out of his shell more. He still didn't spend much time with the other boys. His confidence had grown so much he even began to speak and carry himself differently.

"Nipseysan, how many times I have to tell you, never take your eyes off your adversary?" Nipsey was bowing in a display of respect, but allowed his eyes to fall to the floor.

"I'm sorry sensei, it won't happen again." He was rubbing the back of his neck from where his sensei locked onto it with his leg before knocking him to the ground.

"Sensei, how do I know who's my adversary?" He asked without taking his eyes off his sensei.

"My son, anyone who is in opposition to you is your adversary. You must learn the difference between; adversary and ally and friend and foe. For instance, when we enter here I am always an adversary and your sensei. It's up to you to understand why. Goodbye Nipseysan." He turned and walked away.

With Nipsey's schedule being so hectic, he rarely got around to seeing Sister Burke every week, but if he saw her he would make sure to stop and speak with her, like today.

"Nipsey, coming from the dojo I see. How's it going?"

"It's going great!" Still pumped, wiping sweat from his face and neck.

"So, I noticed you never showed up to my office last week as we discussed. Any particular reason?" As he thought about that day he realized there were still lingering effects of the shame he felt that day. When she saw it in his eyes she spared him the agony of trying to express himself by saying, "My son, no matter what's in your heart or on your mind, my door is always open and I don't judge."

"Thank you Sister, I know." She smiled with that all too familiar nod.

She knew he had come a long way from a shy, timid boy and was becoming a strong, confident, young man, and it made her job worthwhile.

The first day of summer seemed to creep up on Nipsey and the Jazz Festival was the first weekend in July. Nipsey was so caught up in his training that he had forgotten all about it so he took comfort in knowing he would be getting a well-deserved break.

"Nipsey, what's up?" Nipsey was on his way to his room. Samuel caught up to him.

"Hey Samuel, what's up?" He was always happy to see Samuel. He considered him a real friend.

"What you doing, Nipsey?"

"I was thinking about the Fourth of July weekend and what I was going to wear." He was walking with his hands behind his back casually.

"That's right! The Jazz Festival is on the Fourth. I hope you have fun which is something I don't think you know how to do."

"Why you say that Samuel?"

"Cause you are so serious you need to smoke a joint or something. Matter of fact, when was the last time you did something other than study?"

"I like studying and it is fun to me; learning new things excites me."

"Listen to you, studying is fun. Who says that? Smoke a joint." Nipsey laughed. He couldn't argue with him.

"Samuel, how is it that you smoke so much weed but make straight A's?"

"Cause I smoke so much weed and I study." Now Samuel laughed but he was telling the truth.

He did smoke a lot, but he studied all the time when he was on the grounds of St. Francis, during those times he didn't smoke. Then he was also pretty much a loner.

"So, are you going to the Festival?"

"No, I'm going on a home pass."

A home pass is where your family can come and sign you out for the weekend and bring you back Sunday. Eventually you would be able to go home for good if your weekends were successful. Your day passes play a factor in that as well. You didn't need anyone to sign you out for those.

"So, what are you gonna do?"

"Sabrina and I are going to Cedar Point Amusement Park with my family."

Nipsey had heard him speak about his girlfriend before but they never discussed her in depth.

"I hope you have fun."

"I'm sure we will. Thanks Nipsey."

"Samuel, can I ask you a question?"

"Damn Nipsey, okay, you don't have to twist my arm. You can smoke a joint with me." He had a wily smile on his face.

"I don't think so, but I appreciate the offer. But seriously though; you go home every weekend, your family buys you everything you want, it seems

you have a great relationship, so why are you here?"

"Nipsey, looks can be deceiving, my parents wanted me to be someone other than who I was. They didn't understand me wanting to be different. You see how I dress in all black, and wear black fingernail polish?"

"Yeah."

"Well my family didn't like it. You know anything about Goth?"

"I've read a little about it. I know they don't care much for style or elegance and they're Germanic people. I think they overran the Roman Empire too."

"Damn Nipsey, you need to get out more. You're a real nerd, but anyway I ascribe to their beliefs. My mom is a biologist, my dad works for a bio-research company and I didn't fit into their cookie-cutter lifestyle so I ran away all the time. I would go stay with my favorite uncle Donnie. He understood me and would do anything for me. But my parents found out and they made him promise to start sending me home so I would stay with my friends on the streets. Since we have been in therapy they've come to understand me a lot better now and they understand I'm not gonna go all "Columbine" on anyone. So I should be going home at the beginning of the year after I graduate. Then, I'll go to college in the fall."

Samuel was a jokester and it was rare that he gave you a glimpse into his personal life, but when he did, you knew he felt strongly about his way of life. At one point Nipsey thought he was a devil worshiper or something, but in reality Samuel was really smart and later Nipsey found out that Samuel would be attending Harvard.

"Well, I hope everything works out for you Samuel."

"Thanks. What are you gonna do when you graduate Nipsey?"

"Tell you the truth I hadn't thought about it."

"Don't you graduate next year?"

"Yeah."

"Well, you should start planning for that 'cause you have to leave here when you turn eighteen. You know that, right?"

"I do now."

"Maybe you should talk to Sister Burke about your options."

"I'll do that, thanks Samuel." He hadn't thought about leaving. He was disappointed in himself for not being more prepared, so he decided he would have to go see Sister Burke.

CHAPTER 6

When Fourth of July weekend had arrived Nipsey was ready. He had gotten a haircut earlier that day. He chose a pair of Khaki Polo shorts with a white tank top, a button down cream color silk shirt that he would leave unbuttoned, and since he was going to be doing a lot of walking he grabbed a pair of all-white Nike Air Max. He felt good and he looked good too. He was ready to go. When everyone else was ready they piled into the van. Nipsey got in the back. He felt more comfortable with his back to the door. It wasn't that he was worried about anyone doing anything to him, he just liked to be able to see everyone.

When they got downtown they parked in the Ren Cen parking garage (Ren Cen was short for Renaissance Center). The Ren Cen was like a mall. It had movie theaters, shops, clothing stores, and all sorts of things to see and do, as well as eat. Hart Plaza was right next to it, and all of it was right on the Detroit River.

Hart Plaza had a Riverwalk where you could walk along the water. With the sun shining and the breeze blowing off the river, it made it a beautiful day.

As Nipsey walked onto Hart Plaza he felt good. He heard the music, smelled the different foods and saw all kinds of people. He soaked it all in. Everybody went their own way and had an arranged time to meet back at the van; 10:00 p.m. Nipsey decided to walk around and enjoy the sights and sounds for a while then grab something to eat.

He had been strolling around for about an hour or so. When walking towards the fountain he noticed a group of girls about his age looking at him. He smiled and kept walking. As he reached the other side of the fountain he noticed the same girls. As he started to bear right he saw one of the girls coming towards him, so he stopped walking.

"Excuse me" She said.

She was very pretty. She was a shade lighter than him with a reddish-brown tint to her hair and the biggest dimples he had ever seen. She was a little shorter than he was, and he was 5'8". She had on a pair of thigh high shorts, a little sleeveless tee-shirt that rode low in the front to show a little gold cupid hanging in between her cleavage and an athletic build. The first thing Nipsey noticed was her smile and those dimples.

"You're excused. I think the bathrooms are downstairs there." He gestured towards the stairs where the sign read "Restrooms."

She smiled and put her hands on her hips and said: "Oh, so you think you're cute?"

Now it was his turn to smile before he responded. "I don't know, am I?" He stepped back so she could get a good look.

"My friends think so." Nodding in their direction.

"But you don't think so?"

"You alright."

"Well, I guess I can accept that."

She liked the fact that he wasn't conceited, even though she knew he knew how handsome he was, just by the confidence he exuded.

"What's your name?"

He liked the fact that she wasn't shy and kinda bold.

"I'm Nipsey." He extended his hand for her to shake.

"My name is Sonya." She shook his hand and held it just a few seconds too long before she let go.

"Nice to meet you, Nipsey . Where are you headed?"

"I'm just chillin'. What about you?"

"I'm chillin' too. Can we chill together?"

"Sure. What about your friends?"

"They'll be okay."

They started walking and she started talking. He found out that she went to MLK High School. She graduates next year and planned to go to Wayne State University, so she could stay close to home. She also said she was a cheerleader which would explain her shape. Nipsey didn't divulge too much personal information. He was still very much guarded. He wasn't about to share those parts of his life with just anyone so all he told her was that he graduated next year. He didn't know if he wanted to go to college or the military.

"So, do you have a girlfriend?"

"No, I'm single. So, do you have a girlfriend?"

Without any expression she answered. "How could you tell? Yeah I have a girlfriend. She's away at school right now. We've been together for two years."

That shocked him, he didn't know what to say. He was just joking, but now he had the dumb look. Then she burst out laughing. She couldn't hold it any longer. She was laughing and pointing her finger.

"Oh my God, you should see your face. I got you good."

"Okay, okay, you got me. It wasn't that funny."

"Oh yes it was, you're only saying that 'cause I'm the one laughing." He loved that she was witty too.

"Okay, let me try this again. Do you have a boyfriend?"

"No."

"Is that by choice or by chance?"

She looked as if she had to think about that before she answered.

"I had a boyfriend, but I broke it off."

"Why, if you don't mind me asking?"

"He was too possessive and abusive. He went to Kettering. He was on the basketball team, Varsity, but got expelled for beating up a teammate. He was too insecure. He accused me of cheating all the time. One time me and my girlfriends were at the mall and I was talking to a guy in my English class. He came out of nowhere, grabbed me by my neck and pushed me against the wall. I was so hurt and embarrassed, my girls had to pull him off me. He called me all kinds of bitches and whores. He used to tell me that if he ever caught me cheating on him he would kill both of us."

When we first started dating I had a lot of friends, guys and girls, but I had to cut my guy friends off 'cause it had gotten to the point that if he even thought I was looking at a guy he would smack me."

Nipsey's stomach began to tighten from him feeling so queasy from what he was hearing.

"Why did you stay with him?" He could still see the pain in her face as she told her story.

"I was scared to leave, and then one day I just had enough. I couldn't take anymore and broke it off. I've even caught him following me. He's crazy and he scares me.

"Do you really think that he'll hurt somebody?"

"Yup, I told you he's crazy."

Nipsey thought he was paranoid, but after listening to Sonya he knew his instincts were right. His sensei would always tell him to trust his instincts because they'll keep you alive. He first noticed him when he first met Sonya at the fountain. Then he saw him again when they stopped to get some soft pretzels and pop. Now he's glad he never said anything to her. He didn't want to spoil her fun.

"Let's go over here to the Riverwalk and have a seat." He was already going in that direction before he finished speaking.

"Okay."

The sun was going down and as you look out over the water you could see Canada's skyline and with the sun positioned where it was it looked so beautiful. As they sat down he turned toward her slightly so he could peer over her shoulder.

"Yup, there he was." Nipsey thought.

He wasn't hard to miss with his six foot something frame. He had on shorts, an all white tee, and some shell-toe Adidas. He also had a cap pulled down over his eyes.

"Sonya, I have to go to the restroom, will you wait right here for me?" "I promise I'll be right here."

He kissed her on the cheek and as he rose to leave he glanced that way briefly and walked toward the restrooms which were downstairs right by where they were holding the concert. There was a jazz band playing.

"Our stalker follows, but not too close, but he follows, breathe, focus, assess."

With every step Nipsey composed himself. As he went down the stairs he peered around once again.

"Still coming."

When he got in the bathroom he casually checked the stalls.

"Nobody, breathe, remember your training."

He went to the sink, took off his shirt and hung it on the hand dryer, turned and washed his hands. By the time Sonya's ex walked in Nipsey had paper towels drying his hands. Still looking in the mirror, Nipsey eyed him.

"Sonya must've forgotten what I told her?"

"Let's not do this, no one has to get hurt." As Nipsey spoke he showed no emotion, calm, Nipsey spoke slowly. "If you don't leave I hope you at least brought a Snickers 'cause you may be here for a while!"

Body loose, senses heightened, and the ex swung. He was clumsy though. Still facing the mirror, Nipsey took a step back, grabbed his arm, pulled him off balance, spun backwards bringing his elbow up at the same time striking him at the base of the skull. He went to sleep. As he fell into the sink Nipsey spun back around in one swift move, took the wrist of the hand he was still holding, twisted it, he landed on the floor. While he was still holding the wrist standing over him he brought the side of his hand down in a chopping manner across the bridge of his nose, he never woke up.

Nipsey washed his hands again, put his shirt on and exited the restroom. All of this took less than five minutes. As Nipsey was making his way back to where he left Sonya he noticed she was turned around looking for him and when their eyes met they both smiled. She got up and met him halfway.

"Are you hungry, Nipsey ?"

"You know, as a matter of fact I'm starving. That pretzel was nothing."

"Good, let me buy you something to eat." She was pulling his hand leading him to a concession where they were grilling all types of stuff.

"You don't have to do that, I have money."

"Well hold on to it, and the next time we see each other you can feed me.

Deal?"

"Deal."

They sat and ate and talked for about fifteen minutes and there was some sort of confusion. Then the loudspeakers came on.

"This is DPD we need everyone to please leave the Plaza in an orderly fashion, we have an emergency. The festival is now over. Thank you for your cooperation."

"I wonder what's going on." Sonya was saying while grabbing her food.

"Maybe I need to meet back up with my ride. Can I have your number?" he asked as they were making their way through the crowd.

"Sure. Thank you for listening to me run my mouth all day. I really had fun."

"That's cool. I had fun listening to you all day. I'm a good listener." She kissed him on the cheek and left.

Everyone was already at the van when Nipsey arrived. Everyone was standing around talking about the commotion and hating they had to leave early. Sister Constantine was frantically trying to make sure no one got left. A couple of guys had seen Nipsey with Sonya throughout the day and were picking at him and a few were trying to be nosy, but they knew how far to go with Nipsey so he just humored them. After Sister Constantine had counted for the eighth time she was ready to go.

Later that night Nipsey was laying in his bed unable to sleep. He just couldn't get over the euphoric feeling he felt today. For a minute it was as if he had stepped outside his body and was watching himself. He had never felt anything even remotely close to what he felt, even now as he lay there anxious, but anxious for what exactly he didn't know. But what he did know was that Sonya's ex will never hurt anyone again.

CHAPTER 7

Monday morning Nipsey made it a point to go see Sister Burke. She was surprised to see him.

"Nipsey, what do I owe this pleasure?"

"I wanted to talk to you about what's gonna happen to me after I graduate."

"Well son, what do you want to happen to you?"

"What are my options?"

"Nipsey, your grades are very good, you would have no problem getting into a good school, or we can assist you getting into a halfway house. You could go to the military or you could even start looking for a job and find an apartment. So you do have options. Look son, at the end of the day ultimately the decision is up to you. But whatever you decide, make sure it's something you really want to do. You have so much potential and if it's something you really want to do you'll be successful. That's one of the keys to success. Do you understand my son?"

"Yes ma'am."

"Nipsey, let me ask you a question. How would you feel about seeing your mom after all this time?"

The look he had was different from the one he had when he first came, it was no longer any fear in his eyes.

"Sister. I love my mother, always have, even though I was scared of her, and I hope one day we're able to sit down and reconcile. Then she can help me understand how she was able to do the things she did to us."

"What about your sister and brother?"

"My sister will always be my best friend no matter where we are and I will lay down my life for her. I have to go now Sister Burke."

"I understand son." There was that nod again. She didn't push, she let him end the conversation there.

"Nipsey, you are a special young man, and you are in control of your future. I'm here for you son."

"Thank you, Sister. I'll let you know what I decide."

"Okay, Nipsey. I know you will make the right decision."

Over the next few weeks Nipsey's time was divided between

weapons training at the dojo and spending time with Sonya. They had become an item and had enjoyed each other a great deal. He began to confide in her about his training, his sister, St. Francis, as well as the abuse that he endured before he ran away. It was as if they were kindred spirits.

One Friday evening, after he had finished for the day at the dojo, he and Sonya were walking toward her car. She had started picking him up every evening after he was done.

"Nipsey, I thought we could go over to Belle Isle this evening and have a picnic. I brought some food."

Belle Isle is an island in the Detroit River about three miles long and one mile wide, laid out with parkland, hiking trails, and sports facilities. It even has a conservatory and an aquarium. The only access to the island is a bridge.

"That sounds cool, I've worked up an appetite."

"You know, some detective came to see me today" she said while pulling off.

"Oh yeah, what did you do?"

"I didn't do anything. They came to ask me when was the last time I had seen or talked to Ronald."

"Who's Ronald?" he was looking straight ahead.

"He's my ex I told you about."

Nipsey never knew his name cause she only referred to him as her ex. She had his full attention now though.

"Why did they want to know that?"

"Because they found his body."

"Are you serious?" He was feigning surprise now.

"Where did they find him?"

"Get this, they found him at Hart Plaza the same weekend as the Jazz

Festival. I think that is what all the excitement was when we had to leave."

"Did they say what happened to him?"

"They don't really know. It was on the news and everything."

Young black males in the inner city of Detroit died all the time and it never made the news. The only reason this had was because it was right downtown at what's considered a tourist attraction and generates major revenue for the already "economic stricken" city.

"They asked me if I knew anyone who might have wanted to hurt him. I told them no." They were pulling into the parking lot on Belle Isle. "I told them the last time I had seen him was maybe a week or so before the Festival. They told me if I thought of anything that may help them to give them a call and gave me a card."

They found a picnic table, spread a tablecloth out and began to set the food out.

"So, what are we having dimples?"

"I made us some club sandwiches with turkey, ham, bacon, lettuce, tomato and Provolone cheese and I toasted the bread. You have either mayo or Miracle Whip, and either mustard or Dijon."

"Oh really?"

"Yep! Hold on, that's not all your girl got you. I made some potato salad too. I brought some Ruffles and made some Kool-Aid, grape and lemonade mixed."

"Oh man! Not the Kool-Aid" he said rubbing his hands together. She had even brought handi-wipes and plastic ware.

"You thought of everything, didn't you?" with his mouth full of chips. "I'm liking this, no, I'm loving this!"

He stood up, leaned across the table and kissed her passionately. She took her hand and fanned herself.

"Whew!"

"Baby, I've been thinking about going to talk to a recruiter" he shared in between bites.

"For what?" She was looking directly in his eyes.

"I think I want to go to the military."

"For what?"

"I'm hoping I can make it to Special Forces."

"What about me Nipsey?"

"We can still be together."

"What if something happens to you?"

"Don't think like that."

"But I just found you." He saw the sadness in her face.

"I am not leaving you. I want to try and make something of myself and

I want you to be with me. Can you do that?"

"If you want me to."

"I want you to."

She smiled and said, "I'll be focused on my studies anyway, so I'll stay busy. And plus, during my breaks I'll come to visit you if I can."

"Trust me, we'll be alright babe, God sent you to me and I'll always be here for you." She smiled even bigger when he said that.

It started to rain so they packed up and headed to the car. Once inside they sat and talked for a while. The rain was really coming down now and you couldn't see anything. She put her hand on his head, leaned over and kissed him. As he kissed her back she crawled over and sat on his lap facing him. When she felt the rise in his pants she became even more aroused. Before you knew it she was releasing him from his pants so she could feel his passion inside her.

As she was releasing him he was removing her panties from under her skirt. When they were both free she lowered herself slowly until he was completely buried in her. She began to ride him with slow, deliberate strokes. He caressed her breast firmly as he looked into her eyes. And as he looked, all he saw was love and as their rhythm began to reach its peak; they kissed and held each other and rode the wave of ecstasy until they stopped quivering.

They cleaned themselves with wet wipes.

"We should have used protection." He was serious.

"I'm on the pill baby." Then as an afterthought, she asked: "You don't have anything, do you?"

"It's too late to ask me that. Now you already got it." "Boy, quit playing!" She punched him.

"No, seriously though, you were my first."

She smiled slyly. "Well, I'm gonna be your last and you're gonna be my last."

"How do you know I'm gonna keep letting you take advantage of me?"

"Oh, you're mad 'cause I popped that cherry, and you didn't put up much of a fight." "Oh yeah, maybe because you were too busy putting your tongue down my throat." He laughed. He was on cloud nine.

CHAPTER 8

The School year was in full swing and Nipsey still hadn't called Angel, so he decided to go call.

"Knock. Knock." Sister Burke opened the door.

"Nipsey, you're becoming a regular. How are you?" He smiled.

"I'm fine ma'am, how are you?"

"I'm fine, thanks for asking."

"Sister, I was hoping I could use the phone."

"Of course Nipsey, I need to go and see Sister Alicia anyway, so you can have a little privacy."

He really loved these Sisters, he would miss them when he left.

The phone rang three times when grandma answered.

"Hello!"

"Hello, grandma."

"Lord have mercy, is that you Nipsey?"

"Yes ma'am."

"Child, why you ain't done called before now?"

He smiled to himself. He loved the way she spoke, always motherly, with concern and much love. He could also tell she was smoking, which she wasn't supposed to be doing because she was on oxygen, but she refused to quit.

"I don't know grandma, I guess I've been so busy with my studies I just haven't had a chance."

"You not giving them nuns over there no problems are you?"

"No, ma'am."

"How you doing in that school they have over there?"

"I'm doing good grandma. You know this is my last year?"

"Lord child, bless your heart. I'm so proud of you."

"Thank you, grandma." Just talking to grandma made him miss being there even more.

"So, how have you been doing grandma?"

"Well baby, I'm not doing so well. They got me on this darn medicine and now I have to sleep in one of those hospital beds with the rails on the side so grandma won't fall and hurt herself, and it's in the living room. But I guess I need to count my blessings and not complain 'cause I'm still here."

Nipsey knew that she was sickly but he had no idea how bad or from what. It saddened him because he felt that even though she gave her life to God, that God wasn't holding up His end of the bargain.

"I'm sorry, I hope you feel better."

"Child, don't you be sorry. I believe in the Lord, like it say in Psalms 28:7, *The Lord is my strength and my shield; my heart trusted in him, and I am helped; therefore my heart greatly rejoices, and with my song I will praise him.* Baby, when it is time for me to go I will rejoice because He is calling me home and you should rejoice because you will know I'm in a better place."

"Yes, ma'am."

"Well baby, I know you want to talk to your sister but she gone off with that boy Brett she been seeing. She gone be upset she missed your call."

"That's okay grandma, at least I got to talk to you."

"Well, I'm glad I got to talk to you too baby."

"I'll call Angel back another time grandma. Just tell her I called and I love her."

"Okay, baby."

"I love you too, grandma."

"I love you too, baby. You take care of yourself now, okay?"

"I will grandma. Bye."

For the first time since he'd been there he saw Sister Alicia coming and that was cause she was coming from the opposite direction. She was walking with her hands behind her back looking as if she was in deep thought, but when she saw him her countenance changed back to as he always saw her, full of sincerity and love.

"How are we this morning, Nipsey?" Standing in front of him now with her hands still behind her back as were his.

"I'm doing well Sister, but I don't know how you're doing. That would make me psychic, wouldn't it?"

She gave him an inquisitive look and Nipsey recognized it for what it was, so he elaborated.

"You asked how we were doing Sister." Before he finished she cut him off, she understood, so now it was her turn to enlighten him.

"Nipsey, you are a child of God and God said: *When you come into the land that the Lord God has given you, you shall not learn to follow the abominations of those nations.*"

"Why did I get her started?" Nipsey regretted testing her as soon as he did it.

She continued. *"There shall not be found among you anyone who makes his son or daughter pass through the fire, or one who practices witchcraft, or a soothsayer, or one who interprets omens, or a sorcerer,* or one who conjures spells, or a medium, or a spiritist, or one who calls up the dead. For all these things are an abomination to the Lord and because of these abominations, the Lord your God drives them out from before you."

This is God's law Nipsey, so for me to call you or even think of you as a psychic would be an abomination and you're far from that. You may be dealing with things that you don't quite understand, but you're a special young man and God has a plan for you." There's that knowing smile and nod that's so prevalent with all the sisters.

"Yes, Sister Alicia." He began to wonder how she always knew what to say.

"Sister, I'm planning on going to talk to a recruiter. Do you think that would be a good idea?"

"I don't know. What do you think?"

"I think I want to go to the army, but I want to be in 'Special Forces'."

The look of approval that came across her face told him what he needed to know.

"I'm sure you can do whatever you put your mind to and I support you wholeheartedly. I'm proud of how far you've come."

"Thank you Sister." He began to walk off and stopped. "And I mean for everything."

She stopped and looked as if she was looking through him.

"I know my son, but I'm only the vessel in which God uses to show you that you are loved."

He didn't know what to say, so he nodded and walked off.

The next week Nipsey went to talk to a recruiter. He hadn't gone there with the full intention to sign up, but he took the A.S.V.A.B.

"With your test scores Mr. Hussle your options are unlimited. You could definitely be considered for SF but I can't sign you up for that. You have to be chosen to be a part of SF. But let me get you signed up and we'll go from there. We can get your physical out of the way today and wait for your background check to come back and you're in."

"Alright, let's do it." Nipsey said with every expectation to succeed.

"I'll keep in touch Nipsey and if I can help you with anything make sure you call me anytime. I'm here to help."

"Okay Cory, thanks." Nipsey said while shaking his hand even though he really didn't care for Cory, he actually thought he was arrogant and cocky. He also gave him the impression that he looked at all black kids the same because at one point in their conversation

Nipsey felt as if Cory thought he was another street kid or something because he went into this whole spiel about how he too was from a broken home and used drugs to escape the reality of his existence. Nipsey disregarded all of it.

As Nipsey was leaving he was reading the brochures he had gotten from Cory when he heard his name.

"Nipsey."

Before he even looked he was grinning from ear to ear because that voice was like music to his ears. He put his hand up to block the glare of the sun. Then he saw her.

She was wearing a sun dress that tied in the back. It was white with cherry blossoms on it and came just above her knee. She wore open-toed sandals that tied up around her ankles. She wore her hair down around her shoulders curly and she had on shades. Standing there with the sun cascading on her Nipsey swore he was seeing an angel. He was standing there with a smile on his face but hadn't spoke.

"Nipsey, what's wrong?"

"Nothing, can I just admire your beauty?"

"You're so sweet. I love you." She walked over and hugged and kissed him.

"I love you too baby. How did you know I was here?" "I'm stalking you." He thought that was funny.

"When you're stalking someone, I don't think you're supposed to let the person you're stalking see you. So I don't think you're doing a good job!" "Well I guess I have to work on that."

"You skipping class today?" He asked while walking to her car.

"I left early. I had to take some papers over to Wayne State so I decided to stop by St. Francis to see you, but Sister Cohen said you had signed out and this is where it said you were coming. So, I decided to see if I could catch you."

Sister Cohen was the first person you see when you come through the door of St. Francis. You have to talk to her to see anyone; kids, administration, anybody. It didn't matter, if you didn't have proper identification you didn't make it past Sister Cohen and she is not to be messed with. He wasn't surprised that she told Sonya where he was. She loved Sonya.

She would always say: "You remind me of my grand-baby." She would hold up a picture with a young black girl and a white guy. They looked happy holding a mixed baby girl with big brown eyes and long curly hair. They must have been at Disney World cause they were standing next to Snow White. Sonya agreed that she looked like she could be her little sister.

"So, what's up, where do you want to go?" He asked.

"You want to go downtown and get something to eat in Greektown?"

"That's cool. I can get me a gyro."

Greektown was a little section downtown where all the eateries, boutiques, and bars were Greek inspired.

She turned her nose up and said: "A gyro? Who eats lamb with yogurt sauce, yuck!"

"Actually, it is lamb and beef. And don't knock it until you try it."

"Well, I won't be knocking it 'cause I'm not trying it. Give me a good old fashioned hamburger, fries, a lemonade and I'm good."

It was after lunch so traffic flowed smoothly, and when they got downtown there wasn't much hustle and bustle, so they were able to find a parking spot fairly easily. They still parked a block away so they could walk and talk.

With her shades on the top of her head now to keep her hair from blowing in her face, she asked: "How did it go?"

"I signed up."

"Are you serious? Just like that? I thought you were gonna wait!" Her words were falling over each other coming out.

"Yeah, I know. I hadn't planned on it, but when Cory started laying out all my options, I was impressed and had heard and seen all I needed to."

"So, when do you leave?"

"After I graduate."

"I hope you don't forget about me Nipsey."

"Look at me Sonya. How can I do that? You're gonna be the mother of my children and my wife. I love you, and I'm coming home to you no matter what I have to do!"

"How long are you gonna be gone?"

"I signed for four years and hopefully I get chosen to try out for Special Forces and become a Ranger."

"If you wanted to be a Ranger you could have told me and I would have bought you a black outfit and you could have been The Black Ranger. Then I would have my own Power Ranger."

He knew she was okay with everything because she was joking. She thought that was funny.

"Oh really? You got jokes? You know that was corny, right? And just think, I was gonna come home on leave and write as much as possible, but now I may have to reconsider."

She stopped laughing and tried to look serious.

"Boy, don't play. You know I almost got this stalking thing down, and don't make me go get no kryptonite. You know that's a Power Ranger's weakness." He cracked up.

"Kryptonite works on Superman silly."

"Well, what's a Ranger's weakness?"

"You expect me to tell you that? You're a stalker!"

As they were turning the corner going into Greektown, "Boom", two guys ran right into them. They didn't know what was going on. Sonya hit the ground hard and cried out. Nipsey reacted instantly. While he was stumbling he reached out and grabbed one of the guys' shoulders and spun him around. The other one bolted.

He saw Sonya getting up off the ground out of his peripheral and became insensated. Without a word he thrust his hand forward and hit the guy in his larynx. He fell backwards holding his throat. He couldn't speak or catch his breath. As he was falling, Nipsey kicked the inside of his knee. He would walk with a limp for the rest of his life.

"Nipsey baby, it's okay. There's the police." She touched his arm. It was like he woke up out of a trance.

"Are you okay, baby? Are you hurt?" She was looking at him in amazement. She couldn't believe what she had just seen. The way he went from zero to one hundred in zero point two seconds.

"I'm not hurt baby, I'm okay. Look." She was pointing at a cop in uniform and a man dressed casually.

Nipsey looked back at the guy on the ground for the first time. Everything had happened so fast he didn't notice the gun he had tucked in his waistband. When the cops made it to where they were they wasted no time putting handcuffs on the guy on the ground, even though he wouldn't be going anywhere anytime soon. The guy that was with the cop approached Nipsey and Sonya.

"Are y'all alright?"

"I just scraped my arm, but I'll be okay." Sonya was rubbing her arm as she spoke.

"My name is Detective McMillan." He stuck his hand out. Nipsey shook it but didn't say anything.

"Can I ask your name young man?"

"Nipsey Hussle."

"Are you okay, Mr. Hussle?"

"Yes sir."

"And your name ma'am?"

"My name is Sonya Foster."

"Mac, we're gonna need an ambulance for this one, his leg is broken and they may have to have a look at his throat." The cop interrupted.

"This is Officer Johnson, did you call for one yet?" He said all in one breath.

"Yes, sir."

"Good, I'll see you when I'm done." Turning back to Nipsey.

"That was some fancy moves young man. Can I ask where you learned to move like that?"

Nipsey could smell coffee on his breath as he spoke. He looked like he just crawled out of bed. His shirt and tie were cheap and looked like some of the ones you see in Walmart on one of those tables with the shirt and tie sold together. The shirt sleeves were rolled midway up his arm and the tie hung haphazardly around his neck. His badge was attached to his belt and his loafers were old but had that look of comfort. You could tell that he was seasoned, not just by the gray mustache and receding hairline but by the patience in which he assessed the situation, with keen eyes and a slow assured tone that projected control and tact.

"I take a self-defense class." Nipsey responded modestly. "Well, it paid off."

The EMT's arrived and were looking the guy over.

"We're gonna have to transport him to the emergency room, he's in pretty bad shape." McMillan looked from the EMT's back to Nipsey with a look that said his last statement had just been confirmed.

"Johnson, get down to the hospital and I'll finish up here, and what's that?"

"It's a 9mm Ruger, fully loaded."

"Secure it, log it and I'll see you at the station."

"Alright Lieutenant."

"Mr. Hussle, just between you and I, if they hadn't run into either one of you they would have gotten away. So, thanks." Nipsey nodded. "Did either of you see which way the other one went?" "No" they answered in unison.

"Did either of you see what happened?" He asked while scribbling something on a pad he produced from his shirt pocket with a pen.

"No" again in unison. Then Nipsey added: "All I know is we were coming around the corner and out of nowhere they ran into us, but I thought they were trying to hurt us so I reacted."

"Yeah, I see that. What did you do?"

"I caught him in the throat and kicked his leg." He was trying to minimize it as much as possible because of Sonya's vibe.

"That's all huh?" McMillan said, mocking Nipsey.

"Man, I'm getting too old for this. You can't even have a decent meal in the city anymore."

McMillan and Johnson just so happened to be having lunch in Greektown at a bar & grill that they frequented. He had just sat down sipping on his coffee when they saw a group of young men through the window in a heated discussion. Then they observed one of the guys punch another one and he went down. Johnson saw it first.

"Lieu, did you see that? Look!" As Johnson was saying it he was moving toward the door. By the time McMillan made it to the door Johnson was already in pursuit. Everyone had scattered.

He yelled back: "I'm on the gun Lieu!"

"I'm right behind you!"

"Well you better come on old man, you're gonna miss the party!"

"Just save something for me."

McMillan hated to run. That's why he loved being a detective. And after being a beat cop for seven years and a detective for fifteen, he felt like his running days were over.

"There he is Lieu!"

"I see him. That sonofabitch is fast!"

"Don't worry Lieu, I got em." Johnson was gaining momentum.

Before Johnson could catch him he made a wrong turn. McMillan slowed down and watched it unfold. He ran into a couple and the young lady fell hard, but her friend moved with such proficiency that McMillan knew that the guy wasn't going anywhere. Johnson watched in awe.

"So, do y'all live close by?

Sonya spoke first. "Yes, I stay over off Jefferson and E. Grand Blvd."

"I'm wondering why you look so familiar Ms. Foster. Have you been in any trouble before?" "No sir."

"Where do you stay Mr. Hussle?"

"I stay at St. Francis."

Taking notes again, then he stopped writing, folded his arms and tapped the notepad against his temple as if conjuring up a thought. Then it hit him, pointing at her with his notepad.

"Hart Plaza" he said a little too loudly. Then he began flipping through his notepad.

"Here it is, right here. Ronald Parker. He was your ex right? You stay on

Charlevoix St."

"Yes, sir."

"You don't remember me? I came and talked to you a few months ago." He didn't recognize her of course when he spoke with her, she had on a cheerleading outfit and her hair was in a ponytail. She had just come in from practice.

"Oh yeah, I remember you now," she said glancing at Nipsey . He caught it. "Did you find out what happened to Ronald?"

"No, not yet, but we're working on it. Well, I guess we're done here. I'm sorry for all this. And Ms. Foster, have that arm looked at."

"It'll be okay, Thank you."

"You still want a good ol' hamburger and fries?" Nipsey asked apprehensively. He was really concerned about how he reacted in front of her.

"No, I'm not really hungry now, can we go?"

"I'm sorry. Let's go then. Do you want to have your arm looked at?"

"No, I'm fine. "

"Well, you can just drop me off at the dojo."

"Okay."

Neither one spoke on the ride back. Sonya was processing what she had seen. She was taken aback by the whole thing. She had never seen Nipsey like that before. He was someone else and she didn't know if she liked that person. The look he had when she touched his arm was frightening to say the least. It kinda reminded her of the look she had seen in Ronald's eyes too many times before.

Even though Nipsey was trying to lighten the mood by asking if she still wanted to eat, he knew before he asked that Sonya was astounded at how he responded to the situation. He knew he lost control and she was feeling a certain kind of way because while McMillan was asking them questions he caught her giving him sideways glances. But the thing that really messed with Nipsey's head was the fact that he wanted to kill that guy and if Sonya wasn't there he would've.

Pulling up in front of the dojo, Nipsey asked her, "You sure you're alright?"

"Yeah, I just don't like violence, it shook me up."

"I'm sorry baby, I thought they were trying to hurt us and as long as we're together no one will ever do that to you. I love you."

"I love you too, Nipsey. It's not you. I know you were trying to protect me and thank you. It's just ... I don't know ... it scares me."

"I understand. Why don't you go home and put something on that arm and I'll talk to you later, okay?"

"Okay. I'm sorry if I seem distant."

They kissed and he got out and walked into the dojo. He wasn't in there ten minutes when he decided to try and walk off that anxious feeling.

CHAPTER 9

Detective Lieutenant Randall McMillan was sitting at his desk going over his notes and talking to his partner Leroy Cox. "Roy" as McMillan called him, who was about 6'3", 240 lbs., and of African descent. He was athletically built and soft spoken, but very serious when it came to his job. He grew up in the inner city.

Roy was a junior police cadet. It was something his mom got him started in. It was to keep him off the streets when he was young and it worked. It worked so well he never had a problem in the neighborhood because when he got out of school he would go straight to the precinct and stay there until about 6:30 pm, learning cadences and line formations, some minor laws and a few other things that would help him if he decided to go to the academy, which he did. Every evening one of the officers would drive him home. It was usually the Captain since the program was his pet project and he dealt directly with the children. He took special interest in Roy because he was a good kid and adamant about becoming a cop one day. Every time you saw Roy he was with an officer or doing some type of project given to him by the Captain.

Roy had been married for seven years and he felt he was going through the "seven-year itch." If he wasn't spending too much time at work he was bringing his work home. Susan, his wife, was ready to start a family. She knew her maternal clock was ticking and with her and Roy being thirty-three she wanted to start now, especially since she had been reading all kinds of parenting info and found out that after thirty-three the risk of having kids with birth defects was greater.

He knew she was right but he was focused on his career. He was a sergeant but still didn't feel like he made enough to start a family. He wanted to make sure when he did start a family they wouldn't want for anything. No matter how unrealistic it sounded, he just wished she understood his position. He planned on talking to McMillan to get his opinion, he had been married for thirty years with no kids and it works for him.

McMillan and Roy had been working together for six years. They were good friends and respected each other's investigative practices. Roy was a lot more unrelenting and by the book, very thorough, making sure all "i's" are dotted and "t's" crossed. "Mac," as Roy calls him, is more laid back, easy going and sympathetic to other people's plights. They complimented each other nicely. They didn't have to play "good cop, bad cop" because they really were so to speak.

"Roy, you remember the ex-girlfriend from the Parker case?"

"Yeah, what about her?"

"The collar me and Johnson made today, well, the guy who she was with took him down. The idiot ran into them."

"You mean literally?"

"Yeah."

"What happened?"

"It was impressive, you would've had to be there."

"And your point?"

He reminded me of you, only better looking and a lot smaller, but he had the same intensity."

"So, did you check him out?"

"For what, getting ran into and keeping me from having to run another mile?"

Mac was smiling but he knew Roy was serious, he always was. They had been on that case for a few months with no leads and the case was going cold.

"Was he the guy she was at the festival with?" Roy smelled a lead.

"I don't know, he may have been the guy she met there."

"Have you talked to the girlfriends yet?" Mac asked as he read his notes.

"Yeah, but they pretty much said the same thing, they thought he was an asshole. Lieu, I'm telling you, no one really liked him. He was popular because he could play ball and he was the leading scorer. When he beat up his teammate for saying something about his girlfriend he was expelled and arrested. He put the other guy in the hospital. I got a hold of his juvie record. It just showed the one incident. He was only there for the night and was released to his parents in the morning with a summons to appear in court for assault charges, of which he received probation. He transferred to a new school and didn't seem to have any enemies. He did have a slight attitude but kept it in check well enough to play ball. He stayed to himself you know, new school and all, but he got along with his teammates well."

"Did he have a new girlfriend over there?"

"Well, from what I gather, he was still dating Ms. Foster, at least that is what he lead his team to believe."

"Evidently Roy, he didn't get the memo, 'cause she said they had broken up before he transferred. In fact, after she had found out about the altercation he had, she said she got fed up and dumped him because he was so jealous. She feared he was going to end up really hurting her. He even roughed her up a few times."

"That sounds like motive to me Mac."

"So what Roy, she hired a professional to take him out downtown on one of the busiest nights of the year?"

"Stranger things have happened. Did she tell anyone about the abuse?"

Mac knew where Roy was going, but he figured he would just humor him.

"She said after they broke up he didn't put his hands on her anymore. She said she thought he was following her a few times but she chalked it up to coincidence and didn't think there was any cause for alarm."

"This guy she was with today, did he know Mr. Parker?" Roy was still pushing.

"I didn't get that from him while I talked to Ms. Foster. He seemed pretty neutral."

"What was your impression of him then?"

"Actually, he was really composed. It was like that whole situation today didn't phase him. He answered my questions, didn't evade, and was really cooperative. Ms. Foster on the other hand, was frazzled. I caught her giving Mr. Hussle some disapproving looks. If I had to guess, I would say it was because of the whole situation. She was real uncomfortable, but tried to put up a good front."

"Mac, it's just hard for me to believe that out of all the people coming and going at that festival, no one saw anything."

"It's not that no one saw anything, it's just no one knew what it was they were looking at. Look, let's just stick to what we do know, something will break. By the way, wasn't there a print at the scene?"

"It wasn't enough to get any kind of a match."

"What did the coroner's investigator say about the placement of the body?"

Roy was looking through the reports he had in front of him. He found the coroner's report and tossed it across the desk while he was speaking.

"He believed it was positioned that way because the victim was killed right there and the time of death corroborates that as well because if he had been killed anywhere else and brought there the perp would have been seen carrying the body there. He wasn't a little guy and you would have to be pretty strong to do that or have an accomplice. From the crime scene photos it's hard to tell if or what type of struggle there was in the restroom because everything is concrete and there was minimal blood at the scene, in fact, the only blood at the scene was found coming from the victim's nasal passage and it had dried with no signs that it had been wiped."

"My thing is this Roy. The way the kid was killed and the level of skill used, listen to this." He was reading the report. *"The cause of death was brain hemorrhaging caused by blunt force trauma to the bridge of the nose and shattering it, causing bone fragments to shoot into the brain. He also had a contusion to the back of the cranium at the top of the spine which may have rendered him unconscious or out of it.* Just enough to be subdued. He also had a fractured ulna and wrist which meant this was all up close, personal and quick," closing the file and tossing it back to Roy.

"It's just too clean Roy, not one piece of evidence. What was this kid into or did he walk into something he wasn't supposed to? I'll tell you this, whatever it was, we need to figure it out before the chief has my ass in a sling."

"Mac, can I ask you something totally unrelated?"

"Can it wait? I really need to get this report done so I can get out of here.

It's Thursday."

"Oh yeah, that's right. Date Night with the misses, right?"

"Yeah, we're going across the bridge to Windsor to this beautiful Italian restaurant, right there on Riverside Drive W., on the water. They have the best Manicotti I've ever tasted. We have reservations for 8 pm." He was saying all this while rubbing his hands together and licking his lips.

Johnson was at his desk. He had the guy booked and in a holding cell when Mac found him.

"So what do we have Johnson?"

"Lieu, we have a Daniel Flemmings, aka Big Mike. It seems Big Mike hasn't been a good boy. He has two priors, one for felony possession of crack and assault with a dangerous weapon. He did five years on the latter and been out for two years. He said he found the gun somewhere, so I charged him with possession of a firearm. And since we never caught the guy he assaulted the only other thing I can charge him with is fleeing and eluding. I sent the weapon over to ballistics to check for bodies."

"Sounds good to me. Hold off on getting him to the magistrate for his bond as long as you can. That's for making me run."

Johnson laughed. "You got it Lieu. Anything else you need sir?"

"Just put your report on my desk and I'll take care of it."
"Yes sir."

Mac knew he needed to be working, but he had made a commitment with his wife years ago when they were going through a rough patch in their marriage. During those periods Mac had become so consumed with his work that he neglected his wife completely. He'd work from sun up to sun down and usually when he got off work his wife would already be asleep. She had given up waiting up for him a long time ago.

Even though she didn't wait up anymore she still cooked every night. He would come in and get his plate she would have for him out of the oven and go to sleep on the couch so he wouldn't wake her. He loved and respected his wife but he didn't think she understood his working so hard and part of the reason was because she came from money and lived off a trust fund. She didn't have the work ethic that Mac was instilled with. That didn't negate the fact that Pam was a philanthropist and wanted to help any and everyone but Mac didn't look at that as work. He felt as though he could think of a lot better things to do with his money. But that was also one of the reasons he loved Pam so much, because she had a big heart.

Little did Mac know during that time that he was being consumed his marriage was becoming disjointed. It all came to a head one day when Mac came to one of her charitable events unannounced. As he navigated his way toward a few of his and his wife's friends, he observed his wife laughing and talking off to the side away from everyone.

The first thing he noticed was the hand around her waist as she threw her beautiful blond mane back as she laughed. Then the subtle way she flirted with her eyes as this young handsome doctor, he found out later, leaned over and whispered something in her ear. As they turned to leave his first impulse was to run over and punch the guy in the face, pull his gun on him and tell him if he ever looked at his wife again he would kill him. But instead he stayed back and followed them to the parking lot. As they approached the Mercedes she received for a wedding present, she turned and they kissed passionately. At that point Mac ran from behind the column he had been watching from, They saw him too late. He punched him in the eye. Pam screamed.

"Randall, what are you doing?"

"What the hell you mean what am I doing. What are you doing?. Who the fuck is this, you're having an affair?" All of his words came out in a rush.

When he said "affair" the doctor looked at Pam and back at Mac and said: "Affair? Where's your ring?" Starting to get up now. "You mean to tell me you're married?"

Mac hit him again. "Shut up! Nobody asked you nothing yet." He fell again.

"Stop that!" Pam yelled with her hands up to her face covering her mouth.

"Yeah Pam, where is your ring?" Mac said while grabbing her hand.

"Patrick, I'm sorry." Tears falling now.

Patrick was on the ground again, quiet now, looking up shaking his head with his hand covering his nose trying to stop the bleeding.

"Randall, please calm down."

"Calm down?! Calm down?" "I'll show you calm down!"

He pulled up his pants leg to reveal his ankle holster, pulled the little six shot revolver out and pointed it at Patrick.

"Oh my God, Randall no! Randall no, please don't!"

She hugged him, crying uncontrollable now. Patrick was pleading for his life with his hands extended to block whatever was to come next.

When she latched onto Mac, tears began to run down his face and he started to lower his gun. Patrick took that opportunity to get away and she began to explain herself.

"Randall, please listen." She said softly in his ear while still holding him. "I'm sorry. I didn't mean to hurt you. I love you. I just … I just made a mistake."

He looked her in the eyes and asked: "Have you slept with him?"

"Honey, just listen."

"No! Answer my question."

"Let me explain sweetheart."

"I'm gonna ask you one more time, have you slept with him?" Her tears were replaced with anger now.

"Yes! Is that what you want to hear?"

It was like he was hit in the chest by a sledgehammer. He walked over to the Mercedes, put his back against it and slid to the ground. He put his head in his hands and wept. He wept for the pain he felt in his heart, for the confusion he felt in his mind and because of the love he had for his wife. That wouldn't allow him to leave her for her indiscretion.

She went over and sat beside him, put her arm around his shoulders and they cried together. She cried for the damage she knew she caused her marriage, for the pain she caused this wonderful man that had loved her from the first day they met, and she cried for Patrick and the pain she caused him. The more she cried the more she realized that she was glad to be getting all this out in the open. She knew she didn't love Patrick, she loved her husband. She just didn't know how to break if off with Patrick, and even though this situation had reached its boiling point, she breathed a sigh of relief that she didn't have to sneak around anymore.

All the rest of that day and night they talked. She told him how she felt neglected and how he didn't show interest in her charities and Patrick did. She also told him how she met Patrick at "Shoes for School," a charity she founded to help low income families with shoes for each new school year for their kids. Patrick had been one of her donors and afterwards one of her biggest supporters for whatever cause she was pursuing by using his influences in the medical field to get donations. And he was accessible. She said that is how it happened, it wasn't planned, it just happened.

She wanted to end it but she loved the attention. He always made her feel beautiful or as she would say, "Like the most beautiful woman in the world."

In response Mac said, "I promise we're gonna get through this. I'm gonna be here for you no matter what. But you have to talk to me, I will listen. We're gonna start having "Date Night" every Thursday, but our main focus will be communication and whatever is going on in our life, it doesn't warrant infidelity. So this one is on both of us."

CHAPTER 10

The feeling Nipsey had when he awoke the next morning was indescribable. As he rose up he swung his feet over the side of the bed and put his feet on the floor. He still had his clothes on.

"That's strange." He thought to himself.

So instead of getting up he sat there for a few moments and tried to collect his thoughts. For some reason it was a kind of blur.

"What's wrong with me?"

He stood and stretched, then he walked to the center of the room. As he was about to sit on the floor Samuel began to stir. He sat down and folded his legs under himself. He placed his hands on his thighs palms up. Just as he was about to close his eyes Samuel called his name.

"Nip. What's up dude, you alright?"

Nipsey looked but didn't speak. Samuel mumbled something and rolled over.

Nipsey began to meditate for the next thirty minutes. When he reopened his eyes he felt calm and centered and yesterday was clear now. He remembered going up W. 5th St., the setting of the sun, the dagger he still had in a sheath around his ankle, the sickness he felt in his stomach before it happened and the smell of the blood when it was over.

The weight of the dagger around his ankle began to weigh on his mind. He knew that if anyone saw him with it he would be in trouble because there was a "no tolerance" policy for weapons, you go directly to jail. The

dagger was his he just never removed any of his weapons from the dojo. He had a total of ten weapons that he had mastered and owned. They were presents from his sensei for mastering them.

He knew he had to get his dagger back to the dojo so he showered, got dressed quickly and headed for the door. He figured he would jog around to the dojo and be back before his first class.

While on his way to sign out, Sister Alicia called his name from behind him. She had appeared out of nowhere.

"Nipsey, going somewhere?"

When he turned and looked at her his heart skipped a beat. He already felt like she knew everything.

"Yes, ma'am."

"It's kind of early, don't you think?"

"Yes, ma'am. I thought I'd take an early morning jog to work out some kinks.

"So, no class today?"

"Yes ma'am, I'll be back in plenty of time."

"You don't seem like yourself this morning son, is everything alright?"

"I didn't sleep well for some reason."

"I've been told when you can't sleep at night and you toss and turn the devil's at your door."

He had no clue what that meant but he knew it had to be some underlying message, but at this moment he couldn't wrap his mind around it and he didn't really feel like standing there having her elaborate either. So he humbly listened and tried not to give her any reason to hold him up longer than she had to, but she did anyway.

"Nipsey, when was the last time you talked to your sister?" That caught his attention.

"I don't know Sister, I've wrote her a few times, why do you ask?"

"She's called a few times wanting to see you, but since you haven't been to see Sister Burke she hasn't had the opportunity to tell you."

He began to feel elated. "Thank you Sister."

She noticed his smile and she couldn't help but smile herself. She loved to see him smile, because when he did it lit up the whole room and that was one of the few times you could tell how he felt.

"She really loves you Nipsey, don't take that for granted."

"I don't. I've just been busy; mentally, dealing with the next stage of my life and physically preparing for it. I may go and see her this weekend. I really miss her."

"Well, in any case, call her anyway, okay?"

"Okay."

She started walking off and with her back to him she halfway turned back looking over her shoulder and said: "It's still dark out, be careful on your jog and have a blessed day."

Nipsey was off. His jog to the dojo and back was uneventful and relaxing, almost therapeutic with the sun not being up and the morning dew still glistening on the grass being able to be seen by the moon's rays. The morning air was cool and crisp which made the sweat-suit he had on a warm welcome. If you didn't know any better you would almost think it was the beginning of winter instead of autumn.

His jog gave him time to reflect on his actions and who he was becoming confounded him because he knew he had a deep seeded hatred for people who gained pleasure in other people's pain, but he also wondered if that made him a bad person and if he killed every bad person he came in contact with would that really be helping anybody besides himself. He knew his time was short at St. Francis and in a way he felt safer there than he had felt anywhere in a long time. The thought of having to leave both saddened and scared him. Then there was Sonya, whom he loved. But could he share his deepest fears with her or anyone else for that matter? He would have to dig deeper to come up with these answers.

He never realized how many issues he was dealing with subconsciously until his run, and he couldn't believe the relief he felt now that he had things in the right perspective instead of being jumbled up in his mind.

Nipsey had made up his mind to get Angel to sign him out for the weekend. So, after racking his brains with trigonometric ratios, Law of Sines and Cosines, and trying to figure out how to compute any triangle he was ready to unwind, call her, tell her his plans for the weekend and let her know that he had to have contact info and someone to sign him out.

When she heard his voice she started crying. It had been almost four years since she heard his voice.

"Hey fat head girl!"

"Who is this?"

"Who does it sound like?"

"Nipsey, is that you?" An octave higher now.

"What's up, sis?"

"Heeeey boy, I miss you soooo much!" Now over the top and crying. "I'm so glad you called, when you coming to see us?"

"Well, that's one of the reasons I'm calling, to see if you can get grandma or your dad to come and sponsor me for the weekend. That's if grandma will let me stay."

"Boy, you know grandma will let you stay, but Imma have to get daddy to come and sign you out because grandma don't leave the house too much 'cause she's been too sick and with her being on oxygen and needing help to use the bathroom sometimes, that would be best."

"Is grandma getting worse?"

"It's not that she's really getting worse, it's just that she's not getting any better. And then I'm scared sometimes that she might blow herself up."

"Why do you say that?"

"Because you know she ain't supposed to be smoking while on oxygen, but she does anyway."

'Why don't you just take them from her?"

"I do, but she'll hide some and whenever I leave, she'll smoke them."

He knew she was telling the truth cause he remembered hearing her smoke the last time he called and Angel wasn't there.

"Nipsey, you wouldn't believe it. She's a trip. Then she'll get mad at me and say I don't love her and cry and everything."

As she was saying that he could hear grandma in the background saying: "Don't you be telling that boy that 'cause if he thinks that he's gonna come over here and keep me from smoking he might as well stay over there with them nuns 'cause he's got another thing coming!"

While he was laughing he heard Angel say, "Grandma, you need to stop."

Then grandma said, "I bet if I was smoking them funny cigarettes you be smoking it would be OK, or them stinking cigars with that plastic tip on it."

"I'm not sick either grandma. Tell her Nipsey."

He knew not to get into that conversation.

"Did you call me Nipsey, 'cause my name is Wes!" Angel laughed.

"What he say?" Grandma asked.

"He's talking about his name not being Nipsey, but Wes." Grandma liked that. She started laughing.

"That's right Mr. Wes, 'cause if you coming over here, you better stay out her mess." Now she was laughing at herself.

"You know what you want to do when you get here Nipsey?"

"I don't know. What's going on?"

"You know they still have them parties on the weekend and me and my girls be in there. You want to go with us?"

"We'll see. I'll bring something to wear just in case."

"What time you want us to come get you?"

"My last class is over at 2:00, so any time after that."

"Okay, I'm getting ready to go over Tina's. Mrs. Wilson cooked and she fixed me and grandma a plate."

Tina was Angel's best friend who stayed two houses down with her grandmother, Mrs. Wilson whom had been living on Cooper since everyone were kids, and like everyone else on the block, they loved grandma and Angel.

"Tell Tina I said *what's up,* and I guess I'll see y'all Friday."
"Alright Nipsey, I love you."
"Love you too, sis. Kiss grandma for me."
"I will. Bye-bye."

CHAPTER 11

"Nip!"

Samuel was calling him from the other end of the hall as he left Sister Burke's office. He hadn't seen him since this morning. Since he wasn't quite himself he thought it would only be right that he waited for him to catch up.

"Nip what's up, you feeling better?"

"Yeah, I'm alright, sorry about this morning, I wasn't feeling too well."

"Where you go so early?"

"I went for a jog. I had to unwind and work some things out I had on my mind, but I'm alright. So, what's up?"

Nipsey knew Samuel was asking out of true concern so he didn't mind, because the whole time he has been there, Samuel has been nothing but a friend and he really liked him.

"I'm on my way down to the lobby to wait for my girlfriend. Why don't you let me introduce you to her. I think you'll like her."

"I don't know Samuel."

"Come on dude. Don't be so antisocial."

"Alright, let's go."

"So Nip, you decide what you want to do after you graduate?"

"I'm going to the military. I signed up for four years."

"Really? I didn't know that. That's cool. My parents said I can go on a trip before I go to college next fall."

"So, where are you planning on going?"

"I don't know. I was thinking about Europe, but everyone goes to Europe, so maybe I'll go to Cairo to see the pyramids in the Egyptian city of Giza, not really Cairo, but near there. You know where I'm talking about?"

"Of course, they're one of the seven wonders of the world. I've always been fascinated by them."

"Hey Nip, why don't you come with me? I'm sure I can get my parents to let you come. They'll pay for it, all you have to do is get a passport and I can help you with the application if you want."

"Naw, I don't think I could let you do that for me, that's too much, but thanks for asking. No one has ever offered me anything like that before." "It's alright Nip, if you change your mind let me know."

"Alright, I will."

That really made Nipsey feel good that Samuel would offer something of the magnitude.

As they were walking into the lobby Nipsey saw a beautiful young lady. She was absolutely breathtaking. Her short Halle Berry style cut really complimented her high cheekbones and slender face. She had some of the most beautiful eyes he had ever seen on a female. They were like a greenish, grayish color with perfectly arched eyebrows with a tiny mole under her left eye. Her lips were full and pouty with a perfect cleft in her chin. The light brown blouse she had on went perfect with her pecan complexion, buttoned up to two buttons from the top showing just enough cleavage to look conservative. She had on a thin tie, also brown in color just a little darker, which was tied in a Windsor knot loosely hung just below the second button. The blouse didn't quite cover all of her belly. It laid just below her belly button where you could see her waist chain connected to her navel ring which hung over the top of her mid-thigh high brown, white and checkered skirt. Her legs were toned with pecan stockings and three or four inch heels, the same color as her tie. She was stunning.

Nipsey tapped Samuel and nodded in her direction.

"I wonder who that sista's looking for?"

"Yeah, she's beautiful, ain't she?" Samuel's statement surprised him.

"Oh yeah Samuel, you like sistas?"

"I like women, Nip."

As she turned and saw them coming she smiled. Nipsey grinned from ear to ear. As he got ready to speak she said, "Hey baby!" Nipsey looked at Samuel and Samuel smiled at him.

"Close your mouth Nip, I'd like you to meet Sabrina. Hey, baby."

"Hey, baby!" She said while wrapping her arms around his neck and kissing him.

"Baby, this is Nipsey. I call him Nip."

"Your roommate, Nip?"

"That's the one."

"You be talking about me Samuel?" Nipsey was somewhat surprised.

"Yeah." Samuel answered with a smirk.

"Well, at least you're honest."

"Hi Nip, nice to meet you. Samuel does talk about you, but it's all good."

"I'm sorry I can't say the same about you." He was looking at Samuel sideways.

"I understand he don't usually tell people he has a black girlfriend 'cause some people don't believe in that."

Now Nipsey was offended, and Samuel could tell when he spoke.

"Wait a minute Samuel, you know I'm not like that, we're friends, I don't see color."

"I'm sorry Nip, we don't discuss race, so you know I didn't think about it and I'm so used to keeping that part of my life to myself. My bad Nip, no offense."

Nipsey couldn't believe it, he misjudged Samuel again.

"It's alright Nip, I get that look all the time, I'm used to it."

"My bad Samuel. You never cease to amaze me. Nice to meet you Sabrina. How long have y'all been dating?"

While she responded she was looking at Samuel instead of Nipsey

"Since elementary, we grew up in the same neighborhood."

"Are you serious?"

"Yep. This my baby," looking at Samuel still.

"Nipsey, we're going to the movies, you want to come?" she asked.

"Yeah, come on dude."

"What are y'all going to see?"

"We don't know. We usually pick one when we get there," Samuel said looking at her now.

"Alright, I guess so. I'm not doing anything."

"Good, let's go." She was pulling Samuel by the hand.

Going out the door Nipsey was shaking his head to himself as he looked at Samuel. He was in dark contrast to Sabrina, with his black Polo jeans, black Polo tee, black Doc Martens, his jet black hair, and an all black Movado watch with some black Onyx in his ears. They seemed to be in love which made Nipsey smile. He was genuinely happy for Samuel.

When they got outside and Nipsey saw the Range Rover he whistled to himself. When she heard him she said, "Yeah, this is the new toy my daddy got me for my birthday."

"This is nice," Nipsey said while rubbing the leather and admiring how soft it was.

On the drive to the AMC theater Sabrina began to ask Nipsey about himself, but she got as far as where he was from and if he had a girlfriend before he steered the conversation back on them after he answered which she was more than happy to divulge. He started by asking if she was still in school.

"No, I graduated last year. I went to Cass Tech and graduated early."

Cass Tech was one of the few advanced high schools in the city. Nipsey knew she had to be smart cause you had to maintain a high GPA to stay enrolled there. She continued without being asked. "I work for my daddy…" Samuel cut her off.

"Yeah, she's a daddy's girl." "So! You're a momma's boy." She was quick witted.

"So, what do you do for your dad?"

"I'm like an intern, but I get paid. I'm like a paralegal, my dad's a judge. Sometimes we bump heads 'cause he knows I want to be a defense attorney, but he supports whatever I want to do."

"Yeah, my baby's gonna be a lawyer. I like the fact that she's gonna look out for the little guy," Samuel said proudly.

"Thank you baby, but it's not that I just want to look out for the little guy. I believe that everyone deserves to receive "due process of the law." Sometimes in the inner city the local law enforcement conveniently forgets that. So one day I want to own one of the premier law firms in America, you know like Johnny Cochran. I'll donate so many hours to "pro bono" work each year."

"So, like I said, she's gonna look out for the little guy." Samuel had her with that and she couldn't deny it.

"You're right I guess baby, maybe it was how simplistic you made it sound, but you're right."

"It's alright baby, I got you."

Nipsey was impressed with how passionate she was. Samuel interrupted his thought when he told Sabrina Nipsey was going to the military.

"Really? What Branch?"

"The Army."

"So, what if a war breaks out?"

"I hadn't thought about that, but I guess if I have to go I'll do what I have to do."

Her next statement shouldn't have surprised him, but it did.

"What about your girlfriend, did you think about her? Y'all must not love each other. I think anyone who goes to fight in a war is crazy, especially if they leave their wives and babies home to worry constantly. It's sad how many of our young men, not much older than us, never make it home."

Nipsey could see the movie theater up ahead and was glad because it sounded like she was getting ready to go off on a tangent.

"I can understand your position and I respect it, but I plan to use the military as a catalyst. I don't have the financial backing to start no business and this way I get to go to school for free and learn a skill."

"I'm sorry Nipsey , I didn't mean to demonize your ambitions. I talk too much. Baby, why didn't you tell me to shut up?"

"Would you have?"

"Yeah, if I would have known I was making Nipsey uncomfortable." Nipsey felt she must have sensed his agitation.

"I'm not uncomfortable. It's okay."

"Yeah baby, he's not uncomfortable so shut up."

She looked at Samuel and instantly he knew he shouldn't have said that.

"Don't be telling me to shut up, who you think you're talking to Samuel?

Don't make me slap you."

Samuel changed the subject, but she still gave him the evil eye.

As they pulled into the parking lot they could see it was packed. They circled the lot trying to find a close enough space with little success, so they parked at the back of the lot closer to the street. When Samuel saw the movie *Dead Presidents* was playing he got excited.

Before they even exited the vehicle he remarked: "We got to see *Dead Presidents.*" Sabrina agreed. Nipsey didn't really care, but when he saw that the movie didn't start for another forty-five minutes he asked: "So, what are we gonna do for forty-five minutes?" Sabrina got back in the SUV.

"Where you going?" Nipsey was asking.

"I'm gonna roll a joint."

"A joint?"

"Yeah, let's smoke some weed."

"Baby, he don't smoke." Samuel said while hopping back in also.

"Oh, I'm sorry Nipsey ."

"It's okay, but y'all go ahead. I'll stay out here."

She rolled the window up and said: "He's kind of a square."

"He's alright though, he works out, jogs, and stuff like that, but he's a cool dude. I'm kinda surprised he came, he usually stays to himself, so don't give him a hard time."

"I won't. I like him. I wish I could have met his girlfriend. I bet she's pretty, cause he's cute. Have you seen her?"

"Yeah, she's pretty."

When Sabrina was through rolling up the joint she handed it to Samuel. He tapped on the window to get Nipsey's attention. When

Nipsey looked, Samuel held up the joint, made a gesture toward it and smiled. Nipsey smiled and shook his head. Samuel lit it, took a deep pull and handed it to Sabrina. He held the smoke for a few seconds, rolled down the window, blew the smoke out and asked Nipsey .

"Nip, have you ever smoked before?"

"Naw, it's just not my thing, my temple isn't for that."

He heard Sabrina yell from the other side: "You don't know what you're missing. This is some killa."

"Well, you can have mine."

"Thank you. I appreciate it. I owe you one." She said then smiled, that wily smile.

"Samuel, where did you find her, she's a live wire?"

Before Samuel could respond she said: "I know, that's why my baby loves me so much. Ain't that right baby?"

"I'll love you more if you pass the joint." She giggled and passed it.

Nipsey smiled cause he thought they were like an extension of one other. He thought that was cool. It made him think about Sonya and the fact that he hadn't talked to her in a few days. He was missing her. "Y'all know y'all crazy, right?"

"Nip, you the one standing in the cold sober, what do you think baby.

Who seems crazier?"

They burst out laughing and in unison said, "Not us."

Nipsey could tell they were already high. He hit the side of the Range Rover.

"We have fifteen minutes, let's go!"

"Sir, yes sir!"

Samuel was acting like a soldier, saluting and everything while he and Sabrina were laughing at everything the other one said.

When Nipsey looked again to see what was taking so long. He saw her putting on some lotion and Samuel was spraying on some cologne. Then they got out and went to the ticket booth. There was a short wait, but they didn't mind, they were too busy laughing and enjoying themselves.

While they were talking, Nipsey noticed three guys a few spaces back ogling Sabrina. He knew they were talking about her because one of them was talking loud enough to be heard.

He started out, "Look at shorty with the checkered skirt."

His friends were like, "Damn, she's fine!"

The short one with all the gold on said: "Yeah, that's my speed."

He looked like he could be a Mr. T look-a-like with all his gold. He was about 5'5". He and Sabrina looked to be about the same height, minus her heels. He had on an Adidas sweat suit with some shell toes. His waves were perfect and he was light skinned with a baby face.

The other two didn't look as flamboyant and they clearly weren't as boisterous either. He was definitely trying to get Sabrina's attention, and if Samuel knew it he didn't let on to the fact.

Nipsey casually stepped to the outside on the other side of Sabrina.

"This is on me. Pay for it Sabrina." He was handing her the money.

"Thanks Nipsey."

When she stepped up to the window, Nipsey stepped over next to Samuel so they were both directly behind her, shielding her without letting on to what he was doing. When the three saw that they automatically assumed she was with him.

"Oh, she with that chump!" The one that was a little taller than Nipsey said.

He was charcoal black, he had on some blue jeans and a hoodie, some boots and not as many chains as the short one had on. The third one looked like he could be his brother. He was maybe a shade lighter and he had gold teeth for days. He had braids, some baggy jeans, a tee shirt with Bob Marley on it and some Reeboks.

Nipsey didn't say anything, he held the door for Samuel and Sabrina. As he started through the door, a young lady was coming out so he stepped to the side and held the door for her. Before he proceeded through the door, he glanced back to see all three looking in his direction. He caught up to Samuel and Sabrina at the snack counter loading up on junk.

"Nip, you want something?" Samuel asked while licking the butter from his fingers.

"Yeah, let me get a bottle of Evian water and some Good & Plenty."

While he waited for them, he kept an eye on the door for the three guys. As they were coming through the door, Nipsey, Sabrina, and Samuel were leaving the counter. Sabrina just happened to look in their direction and Golden Mouth made eye contact and smiled. She smiled back and then put her arm around Samuel's waist as they began to go into the designated theater with Nipsey walking in front now. Still very much aware of the guy's presence because they didn't stop at the snack counter and they were now behind them in what seemed like seconds.

As soon as they were in earshot of Samuel and Sabrina the guy with the braids said, "Couldn't find a real man shorty?"

Without even turning around but loud enough for them to hear, "I got a real man right here!"

Then the short one chimed in.

"You need a man that can take care of you." He pulled out a wad of money and flashed it.

Nipsey was walking next to Samuel. When Samuel looked at Nipsey, he smirked. Nipsey didn't know what to expect so he didn't say anything. Samuel grabbed Sabrina as they approached the door, took her hand, stopped mid stride, held it above her head and said, "Take a spin baby." As she spun Samuel said, "Looks like I do a pretty good job!"

Sabrina kissed him and Samuel grinned at the guys and at Nipsey. Nipsey smiled back. As he watched he thought they were hilarious. The guy was offended now and didn't know what to say, so he lashed out.

"Broke punk ass white boy, I'll buy you and that bitch!" He pulled out a wad of money and they all laughed.

"Who you calling ..." Sabrina was saying as Samuel cut her off.

"Hold on baby. What's that?"

He was looking at the money the guy pulled out and was laughing. Sabrina started to laugh too. Nipsey laughed cause they laughed. Samuel started looking at his watch and was speaking at the same time.

"You know what, you couldn't afford her. How much you got there, about a thousand? I'll tell you what." Looking at his watch again. "Here, take this. This is that new Movado, it runs no less than fifteen hundred, but mine was a little more because of the black diamond. Take it and go buy something else to play with, cause she's taken!"

He nonchalantly tossed the watch. Nipsey watched it land in front of the guys and couldn't believe what he was hearing and seeing Samuel do.

They laughed and walked into the theater.

The short guy's ego was bruised. He couldn't believe how that played out either, he was infuriated. He picked up the watch and threw it against the door that was shutting behind Samuel, Nipsey and Sabrina. They were still laughing as they found their seats. They sat on the left side of the theater close to the wall, while Nipsey sat in the seat closest to the wall.

"Man, y'all are nuts." Nipsey was saying still shaking his head.

Sabrina kissed Samuel tenderly without saying anything, and when they stopped kissing Samuel said: "I know baby, I love you too."

"Can y'all get a room?"

They were having a good time when Nipsey thought he felt

something. He thought something hit his ear. He touched his ear to see if a bug or something was on him but he didn't feel anything. So he waved his hand like he was fanning a fly in case one was flying around and kept watching the movie. Then he saw it. A piece of popcorn hit Samuel on his head. He looked at Nipsey with questioning eyes. Nipsey shrugged. Then Nipsey saw another piece and at the same time, out of his peripheral, he saw an arm raise and appear to be throwing something. Then he knew what it was.

Trouble.

Samuel looked past Nipsey to his right and saw the three guys from earlier laughing and making a scene. Even though it was dark, Nipsey could still see the anger in Samuel's eyes.

"Let's try and ignore them, maybe they'll chill out." Nipsey said.

So he agreed and they tried to get back to the movie. Sabrina was oblivious to what had happened. She was really into the movie until a piece of ice hit her on the side of her face. Nipsey knew instantly there would be no talking to her, so he prepared for the worst.

Sabrina became furious. It was like someone had turned on a switch, especially when she saw the direction Nipsey and Samuel were glaring in. When she saw how hysterically they were laughing at her. She calmly took her shoe off and flung it in their direction.

"Bam!"

It found its mark. It was so dark he never saw it coming. It hit golden mouth right in the mouth.

"Look baby, I got him!" She was besides herself.

"Now, I bet you ain't laughing now. Laugh at that!"

Right then the lights came on and as Samuel, Sabrina and Nipsey were getting up they saw some ushers and security guards coming in their direction. Nipsey looked at Golden Mouth, his mouth was bleeding. Sabrina was animated now, screaming and yelling, and when she noticed his mouth bleeding she put her hand over her mouth and pointed in their direction, making fun of golden mouth.

"Now, that's what you get. Now you got rose gold. Now that shit in your mouth may be worth something. And I better get my shoe back!"

Nipsey couldn't believe how much heart she had. Samuel was trying to calm her down while security was telling them to leave. Nipsey finally grabbed Sabrina by her arm.

"Come on, let's go!"

"Let me go Nipsey, I ain't going nowhere without my shoe!" One of the ushers went to find her shoe. "Just a minute, here you go ma'am." She took it and put it on.

"Thank you." She flashed the usher an unexpected smile.

The three guys were being led out by security. They were pretty calm considering.

On their way to the vehicle, Nipsey couldn't help but check his surroundings to make sure they weren't in any immediate danger, but when they got close to the Range a burgundy Cadillac pulled up in front of the Range to a screeching halt. Everyone stopped and nervously looked to see what was happening. The doors swung open. The three guys began to get out of the car. Nipsey noticed Sabrina trying to make it to the Range around the back of the Cadillac, but Golden Mouth got out of the back of the car and stopped her by stepping in front of her.

"You have a big mouth to be so fine," he said while stroking her face.

Samuel was moving in that direction, but before he could make it the one with the braids came around the front of the car and stepped up to Samuel and hit him in the jaw so hard it sounded like it broke. Samuel hit the ground. Nipsey started to move and in two steps he was in front of the guy with the braids. Without a second thought he kicked him in his temple. Nipsey swung around and swept his legs from under him. When his head hit the ground he was knocked unconscious. The short one ran in Nipsey's direction. He caught his arm as he swung and brought it around over his right shoulder and in one motion, squatted and flipped him over. When he stood back up he was standing over him. Nipsey brought a closed fist down across his jaw and knocked him out.

While that was happening Samuel had gotten back up and rushed Golden Mouth. They both hit the ground. Samuel was on top of him throwing punches and out of nowhere, Sabrina went over and started kicking him in the groin over and over. He started screaming in pain. Samuel got off of him and had to pull Sabrina away. The whole time she was yelling obscenities at him. Samuel was trying to calm her down.

"Baby, it's over. Come on. It's over!"

"Pick her up Samuel, we need to go."

He picked her up and carried her to the Range, but not before she got one last kick in. Nipsey started for the back door of the Range.

"Who's gonna move that piece of shit so we can go?" Sabrina said putting her vehicle in reverse.

"I got it baby."

Samuel jumped in the Cadillac and moved it out of the way, got out, left it running and ran back to the Range Rover.

Nipsey couldn't believe what just happened. Samuel's jaw had swollen slightly, but other than that he was fine. Sabrina was still amped. She was talking a mile a minute. Nipsey was pumped as well, but he was quiet. He didn't want anyone to know how good he really felt inside. He stared out the window and listened to Samuel and Sabrina.

Samuel turned halfway around and said, "Damn, Nip! You're really a badass. Can you start teaching me how to move like that?"

"Yeah Bruce Leroy, teach my baby some of that, whatever it was!" She added and laughed.

"You teach him, you did alright yourself."

"Yeah, I did alright." She was making a muscle.

"Yeah baby, you did good. Thanks for helping me."

"You know I always got your back."

CHAPTER 12

When Derrick woke up around 10 a.m. he was in a great mood. He felt his life couldn't be any better. He had a good job selling vacuums, making good money. He was one of the best salesmen there, so he pretty much made his own hours. He felt he had left home at the perfect time. Nipsey had been at St. Francis for about a year. Lauren's drug habit had become unbearable, She never cooked, cleaned or even went shopping. Angel and Derrick were left to fend for themselves, day in and day out.

Derrick had said "enough was enough" when one day he came home and found his TV and some of his clothes were missing. He could remember that day like it was yesterday.

"Lauren."

He always called her by her name. He was trying to get her attention through her room door.

"Lauren, where's my shit?"

He was the only one who spoke to her like that. After he had gotten so big he stopped fearing her and started despising her.

"Boy, don't be yelling at me. What the fuck are you talking about?" She was yelling back through the door.

"My TV's gone, you don't got it?"

"Why the fuck would I have your TV?"

"Well, it's gone. And some of my clothes are too.

"Well, what do you want me to do? You know you should have your door locked!"

"If you came out of this room sometimes and check all these damn crackheads you got all over the house I wouldn't have to worry about this shit!"

"You know what Derrick, this is my fucking house and if you don't like what the fuck I do in my house, you can get the fuck out!"

"You know what Lauren, you're right, fuck you with your crackhead ass. I'm getting the fuck out of here!"

He kicked her door, went and packed his things, called Aubrey and left when she came and got him. He hadn't spoken to her since.

He had been dating Aubrey about two years. She was six years older than him, he was 18 at the time. Her son Ronnie was three when they met. Aubrey worked for a temp service as a secretary, when she could get work.

When she had met Derrick he was a junior salesman. Her house was one of the ones in the neighborhood he was training in, going door to door selling vacuums. They had hit it off immediately. She couldn't afford one of the fifteen hundred dollar vacuums he was selling, but she did let him know that she was interested in him. They exchanged numbers and began seeing each other exclusively.

In the two years they had been dating, Derrick had become one of the top salespeople in the company making good money. Everyone automatically assumed that since he was younger than Aubrey and they were living in her house, that he was living off her. In reality, she was dependent upon him.

Not long before Derrick moved in with her and her son, she had lost her permanent job with the City of Detroit as a Transcriber. She had been laid off with an empty promise of being called back. With Derrick making the money that he was, Aubrey looked at him as her savior for being there when she needed him.

From the time Derrick moved in, he began to show who he really was. Controlling, demanding, abusive, and a sexual deviant. He felt since he was the one making the money that things should go like he said. He had no problem making her or Ronnie follow his rules. Every chance he got he reminded her that if it wasn't for him, her and her son would be out on the street.

When it came to sex, if he wanted to have some, whether she wanted to or not, he was having sex with her. Aubrey used to think it was something wrong with him cause he was fascinated with anal sex. She loved having

sex with him but when she refused to let him penetrate her anally he held her down and forced her anyway. She would cry and beg him to stop but he wouldn't until he satisfied himself.

Even with all the things he put her through, she was blinded by love. Blinded to the point that when Ronnie told her that Derrick had touched him she wouldn't believe him. She told him that he was confused. That he didn't know what he was talking about. She couldn't bring herself to believe Derrick would ever do anything like that.

Derrick really had her brainwashed. She told him what Ronnie said. As he was laying in the bed he rewound the conversation they had the night before.

"Teddy Bear," she called him that because of his size. "Ronnie told me something today. It's nothing for you to worry about but I still thought you should know."

She was making sure she didn't say anything to set him off.

"What was it?"

"He said you touched him on his privates."

When she saw the change in his demeanor, she added.

"Now don't worry, I told him he must be mistaken. He was saying that in school they told him if someone touches him that he should tell his parents or someone at the school."

This last part scared him. He knew if he told someone at school, social services, the police or both would be at their door.

"What's wrong with that boy Aubrey? We were playing a video game and he was sitting on my lap like this. Let me show you!"

He pulled her on his lap with her back against his chest. She giggled and said, "I know you wouldn't do nothing like that."

"Hold on, I don't want you to have any doubt!"

He wrapped his arms around her to show her where his hands laid. They laid in between her crotch. Then he started moving his fingers to simulate a controller. She was looking down at his hands, but she was no longer thinking about what Ronnie had said. She was more focused on the heat on the back of her neck. The friction that her behind and his penis were causing as she was moving around on his lap. Feeling his arms embracing her. Waiting to feel more. Anticipating more.

She became intoxicated with desire. Her head began to sway invitingly, exposing her neck. She began to grind subtly on his penis. He picked up on those little nuances instantly and began to kiss and suck on her neck. He met her subtle grind with his own. He picked her up, laid her back on the bed, and allowed his tongue to take her where she wanted to go. He knew he had her body and mind.

The Marathon Continues   *Eugene L. Weems*

CHAPTER 13

When McMillan arrived on the scene, there was a crowd of people standing around the crime scene outside the yellow police tape.

"Excuse me. Excuse me." He said making his way through the onlookers.

A patrol officer was standing just inside the tape when he got to it. The officer held the tape for Mac. Upon entering, he asked the officer, whose name he couldn't pronounce when he looked at his name tag. His name was Vzral.

Mac didn't know the young officer, so he just said, "Officer, my name is Detective McMillan, Homicide. I'm from the twelfth precinct. Who made the call?"

"It was anonymous. People around here don't talk to the cops too fast."

He walked toward the body where another officer was talking to the CSI.

The officer acknowledged him as soon as he stepped up.

"Mac, how's it going?"

"Well, it depends on what you have for me. How have you been McDougal?"

"Pretty good Mac. I've just gotten here myself so I don't have any particulars as of yet." They were both from the twelfth precinct.

"McDougal can you get these people out of here? And how about getting me a couple of officers to canvas the area."

He was gesturing with his hands while pulling out some rubber gloves to put on.

He got a good look at the victim, then turned to the CSI whom he knew.

"Hey Sam." Short for Samantha. She was kneeling down over the body.

"Hey Lieu, looks like our friend here had a bad night."

"Looks that way, doesn't it? What do we have here Sam?"

"Well Lieu, white male, 43 years old, 5'9" tall, roughly 180 lbs. Here's his driver's license. His name's Trevor Scott. He lived in Southfield.

"What the hell were you doing over here, Trevor? Predominantly black neighborhood, drugs, and street walkers." Mac was brainstorming to himself out loud.

"I don't see a wedding ring Lieu, so maybe he was looking for a little action."

"I guess he got more action than he was looking for!"

"I don't know Lieu."

"Tell me what you do know Sam."

"Okay. I know the body hasn't been moved. His pants were pulled down before death, but the penis was removed postmortem."

"How can you tell that?" He was leaning over Sam watching as she pointed out her finding.

"Because, if it had been removed before, there would have been blood everywhere." She was still pointing with the pen.

"Why would blood have been everywhere?"

"It's basic Anatomy 101. When your penis becomes erect it's pumped with blood. If it was removed in that state, it would have squirted everywhere. Now, if you look here, the blood has settled beneath him between his legs. That leads me to believe that he wasn't moving. And you see where his hands are placed?"

"Yeah, out to the side."

"That's right, away from the body. If he had been alive he would have been cupping where his penis was, trying not to bleed to death. It's human instinct."

"How did he die, Sam?"

"On the surface I could not tell you without an autopsy, but if I had to guess I would say a broken neck. The contusions were not life threatening."

Mac's stomach started doing flips due to the whole area smelling of blood and excreta.

"How long have you been here Sam?"

"Maybe two hours."

"Aren't you almost done?"

She was gently moving the body. She was very professional and you could tell she still loved her job and had not become jaded.

"Yeah, I'll be done after I finish with the pictures, and get everything tagged."

"Good, I want to get some lab guys in here before it rains. With so much debris in this alley they're gonna need time to work. I'm not trying to rush you."

"I understand, Lieu."

"Who would do something like this?" He was talking more to himself than anyone else.

"Do you have a time of death?" Mac said as he looked around as if he was looking for someone.

"Let's see here." She was looking at her notes. "From the temperature I would have to say in the last twelve hours, plus rigor has come and gone. See how relaxed the body is? Flaccidity of death is pretty much expected."

"McDougal." Mac was calling him back over. "Get the DMV and find out if he has a registered vehicle. I know he didn't walk here from Southfield, and if he has one put out a Bolo for it. When and if it's found, I don't want it touched until forensics get through. Then have it towed to the station."

"You got it, Mac."

Mac started to leave when he saw Sam pull the man's crumpled jeans high enough to search his front pockets. She pulled out some keys with a Ford symbol on them.

"Bingo! Just what I was looking for. Tag them and let me have them. McDougal, get over here. I'll bet you $200 to a doughnut that these will fit that nice looking Mustang I passed down the street on my way here." He was holding up the keys. "Let's go." He said while tossing the keys in the air and waving McDougal on. "Thanks Sam, I'll see you later. Tell Doc to notify me when he has the cause of death."

"Will do Lieu, glad I could be of service." She said as she was turning back to the victim.

Mac and McDougal wasted no time making it back to where Mac had seen the car. They noticed the Mustang's window was down on the passenger side as they approached. Mac went to the side of the car that had the window down and looked in, making sure not to touch anything. He observed how nothing seemed out of place.

McDougal was on the other side peering through the windows. Mac took the keys he had gotten from Sam and inserted one into the lock and turned. He could hear the lock pop. He smiled and looked at McDougal.

"Cancel that Bolo and get forensics down here. Tell them we have the vic's car." He was talking to McDougal across the top of the car.

He locked it, stepped back and began to look on the ground.

"What are you looking for, Lieu?"

"Anything that will begin to tell me a story. Come here and look at this window, and tell me what you see."

"Nothing Lieu, what am I looking for, or should I say, what am I missing?"

"That's right, nothing. Nothing out of place. There's no sign of a struggle, nothing."

"So, what do you think happened?"

Still looking for anything, he said, "I don't know, but whatever happened, it didn't happen right here."

McDougal looked up and down the street and asked, "Do you think he could have been with someone? Think they lured him into the alley and robbed and mutilated his body?"

Mac was halfway listening to him. He never answered his question. He was deep in thought looking at the window. He walked back up on the window and asked, "You see how only this window is rolled down?"

"Yeah. You think someone was sitting on the passenger side?"

"No, I think he was talking to someone on the sidewalk as he drove, then pulled over."

"A prostitute would be my guess, Lieu."

"Mine too. Look, stay here until the techies get here. Make sure they go over this with a fine toothed comb. Tell them to make sure they pay special attention to the passenger side of the car. I want every street walker questioned, then I want them questioned again. Maybe one of them serviced him. Maybe he refused to pay, and their pimp worked him over. Maybe one of them talked to him. Get me something to work with."

"Okay Lieu, I'm on it."

Mac began walking back to his car and almost as an afterthought he yelled over his shoulder and said, "Get that area taped off all the way to the building from the car."

"Yes, sir." McDougal was already taping it off.

CHAPTER 14

Nipsey was sitting in Sister Alicia's office. She had wanted to talk to him before he left for the weekend. He was curious to find out what she wanted to talk to him about. She rarely called him into her office.

"Nipsey, I know your time here is getting shorter by the day. I wanted to talk to you about your mother, she has been calling every week for the past month."

This wasn't the conversation he wanted to have right now. It was totally unexpected.

"Is that why Sister Burke asked me if I thought about her?" He had wondered why all of a sudden Sister Burke was talking about her.

"That was part of the reason my son."

"What's the other part?"

"We feel you have some unresolved issues that really need to be dealt with. I am not a psychologist by a long shot, but I have been doing this long enough to know that unresolved issues become burdens."

He felt like he wanted to crawl inside a box and hide. Hide from the visions he has when he thinks about Lauren. Hide from the monster inside him that yearns to be released when he thinks about Derrick, and every other person who receives joy from other people's misery.

He had went to another place inside himself when he heard her speak again.

"Look son, one thing that we will never be able to do is change the past. I know what you have been through. The pain that it has caused you. Even the things we haven't discussed."

"Sister, since you know about the things we haven't discussed, how do I ... you know, face it?"

"Nipsey, listen. Don't allow your past to define you. If you allow the hate and fear to consume you, there will be no room for healing and forgiveness. The only way to face it is let it out. Talk about it. Open up to someone you feel you can trust. Someone that only has your best interest at heart."

He was looking down. His vulnerability began to show and he knew it, but he still took everything in. His heart became heavy. He knew he could learn to forgive Lauren, but he didn't know if he would ever heal from the pain Derrick had caused him. One thing was for certain. There would be no forgiveness for him. The more he thought about it the angrier he became.

When he spoke this time the words that came out were laced with pain, anger, and confusion he had been carrying around for so long.

"Sister, I feel like he hurt me down to my soul. I wasn't always like this.

It's like my DNA has been changed, and now I'm different."

There it was, he finally said it out loud. Even though she had known all along, Nipsey had never opened up to that extent. Now that he has, her heart cried out for him. She prayed that she had been wrong this whole time. Her heart cried out, because as much as she wished she could take away all of his pain, she couldn't.

With tears blurring his vision when he looked at her he asked. "Will he ever be punished?"

"That's not for me to say my son, you have to let go and let God..."

"If God was gonna help me, he would have when all that bad stuff was happening to me. I've let God long enough, now it's my turn to help myself."

The tears were gone now. He was looking her directly in her eyes with all seriousness. A chill went down her spine when he said that. It was the coldness in his voice, and how he abruptly ended the conversation.

"Sister, I need to go get ready. Is that okay?"

"Sure, Nipsey. Let me leave you with this. Hatred stirs up strifes, but love covers all sins. Have a good weekend my son."

"Yes, ma'am."

Nipsey had already had his bag packed for the weekend. He had his weekend pass from Sister Burke and was waiting in the lobby, for Angel and her dad to get there. He was a little apprehensive. Only because his nerves were getting the best of him. He hadn't been around anyone remotely close to being family in a long time. He was also anxious because the last time he saw Angel he was a scared and timid young man. He wasn't so little anymore and the only thing he was scared of now was what he would do to anybody that crossed his path with bad intentions.

While Nipsey was waiting, Samuel came walking into the lobby smiling.

"What are you smiling for?"

Nipsey was smiling even before he found out why. He saw Samuel in a whole different light since the incident at the movies.

"What's up, Nip! So today's the big day, huh?"

"Yeah, they're on their way."

"How do you feel? Are you nervous?"

"I guess I'm a little nervous."

"Yeah, I know what you mean. When I first started going back home for the weekends, I didn't know what to expect. I didn't know if my family would look at me different. I worried if my family would accept me now that they really understood me better."

"So, did they? Did you feel alienated at all in the beginning?"

"No, not really. They kinda went out of their way to make me feel comfortable. I understood it for what it was. I knew they loved me and wanted me home. I had also learned in counseling that as long as we communicated we would be able to work through our differences. Nip, can I ask you a personal question?"

"Go ahead."

"Well, I hear you talk about your sister, but I never hear you talk about your mom. Is she still living? And if she is, do you talk to her?"

Nipsey wasn't prepared for that question, and Samuel picked up on it as soon as the words came out of his mouth. He didn't know if he had crossed the line or not so he said, "I'm sorry Nip, I didn't mean to pry."

"It's okay, Samuel. I guess I don't speak about her because I don't have fond memories of living with her. At one point in my life I was terrified of her. It's crazy Samuel, because I try to remember the happy times, and don't get me wrong, there were some. It's just that the bad ones have seemed to wipe the good ones away.

"When I was young there were only a few instances where I remember her being truly happy. She was very abusive, verbally and physically, and sometimes mean as hell."

Now Samuel understood why he never talked about his home life. Samuel actually felt guilty for feeling lucky to not have had parents like that. His problems paled in comparison.

"She tried to kill me before Samuel."

"You mean literally, Nip?" Samuel was astonished.

"Yeah, she tried to drown me in the bathtub and my grandmother came in and saved me."

Nipsey was full of emotion talking about it, but it was different than how he felt when he was talking to Sister Alicia. The pain wasn't so intense. He didn't understand it, so he continued.

"The confusing part to me was, after she was finished beating me she would act like she really loved me, and say she was sorry. She would say, *You know you shouldn't make me mad like that.* It was like she had two people in her, and you could never be sure which one of them you were dealing with."

"Wow, Nip! I would have never guessed something like that happened to you. I'm sorry to hear that dude. I don't think I could talk to my parents if either one of them had done that to me."

Samuel felt for Nipsey, he would never look at him the same again.

"I haven't talked to her either, Samuel. She's called here a few times, but I'm not ready to talk to her. You know, the funny thing is that I love her, and hate her at the same time. You know what I mean?"

"Yeah, I think so. I felt that way about my parents at one point. I felt like they didn't love me 'cause I was different, and I hated them for that. But I still loved them because they were my parents. You mean something like that, right?"

"That's exactly what I mean. You alright Samuel. You're a good friend, thanks man. I've never told anyone any of this."

"That's okay, Nip. Thanks for allowing me to be a friend. I'm always here for you, Bruce Leroy. You alright too! Look Nip, I got to get ready for my parents to get here. I hope you have a good weekend."

"Thanks man, you too."

The entrance door opened and in walked Sonya. Nipsey's heart almost leapt out of his chest. She didn't see him right away because of where he was sitting. He could see the door, but you couldn't see him. So as she was signing in he hid behind a column inside the lobby so as she walked in he grabbed her arm. She screamed and yelled.

"Boy, what's wrong with you!"

He was bent over laughing so hard. She started hitting him on his arm.

He was holding his chest now trying to pull himself together.

Sonya was laughing too. She was so happy to see him. She grabbed him, pulled him close and kissed him.

"Hey stranger, why haven't you called me?" She asked with a pouty look on her face.

"To tell the truth, I got the impression that you weren't too happy with me when you dropped me off. You really didn't have much to say to me, so I thought I would give you some time. I really didn't know what to do or say to make you feel better because I didn't know what you were feeling."

"I'm sorry Nipsey, it's just I had never seen you like that before and it scared me to see that side of you."

"I understand baby, but there's no way I was gonna stand there and let anything happen to you. I would die first. You're all I have, you have made me whole and have given me even more purpose in life. What if something had happened to you, how would you have felt then? You know I've been hurt in one way or another all my life, but those days are over. No one will ever hurt me or someone I love as long as I'm breathing ever again. If I'm wrong for feeling like this then so be it. If I can't protect you, the love of my life, my future wife, and the mother of my children, you might as well leave me now, because I am not that guy and never will be."

As he finished saying this he stepped back and spread his arms in a way as to ask if she was staying, or if she was going. She instantly closed the distance between them, and embraced him. She laid her head on his shoulder. She couldn't bear the thought of losing him, he was good for her and she knew it. He was different than most guys she met, and she felt safe with him. She really loved him, and she knew in her heart he would never do anything to hurt her. The fact that he was smart, and good looking was just a plus.

"Baby, I'm not going anywhere. I want the same thing you want. I love you. Thank you for being patient with me and thank you for protecting me."

"I promise you Sonya, I will always be here for you."

"Now, why were you down here?"

"I'm glad you showed up, because now you can meet my sister."

"She's coming here, Nipsey?" She was excited for him.

"Yeah, I'm going to grandma's for the weekend. She and her dad are coming to sign me out."

"Where does your grandma stay?"

"She stays on Cooper, between Barker and Chapin, off Warren. Do you know where that is?"

"Is that down by Cadillac Ave?"

"Yes, Cadillac Ave. is a few streets over."

"Isn't there a 4H over there somewhere?"

"Yeah, it's on Barker and McClellan right around the corner from grandma's house. We used to go to the 4H everyday when we were kids and school was out. We would get those free lunches they used to give out every day at 12."

As he was finishing his statement, in walked Angel and her dad. She had grown since last he saw her. She was taller than he was now. He almost didn't recognize her, but she recognized him immediately and ran over to him yelling his name with a big smile on her face.

"Oh my God boy, look at you, you look so good! I've missed you so much!"

Sonya watched from the side as they hugged. The love they had for each other was evident. Tears began to run down her face, she was so happy for Nipsey. She felt that with all that Nipsey had been through he deserved to be happy like that all the time. Her heart was overjoyed. She began to feel guilty for acting the way she did after what happened downtown.

After a few minutes, Lou walked over.

"What's up, Nipsey?"

He didn't hug him. He knew Nipsey never really liked to be touched by men. He just shook his hand and pat him on his back.

"Hey Lou, how's it going?"

"You know me, I'm doing me."

"Same ol' Lou I see!" Nipsey said while shaking his head.

"Don't he look good, daddy?" Angel could barely contain herself.

"Yeah, you look good, Nipsey. It's good to see you. How have you been?"

"I've been good. But hold on y'all." He was directing their attention in Sonya's direction.

In the midst of the excitement he had almost forgotten about her. He reached his hand out to her. She grasped it.

"Lou, Angel, this is Sonya, my girlfriend." She was next to him now.

"It's so nice to finally meet y'all." She put her hand out so Angel could shake it.

Instead of shaking it, Angel grabbed her and gave her a hug. That surprised Sonya. She wasn't expecting that.

"You're so pretty, y'all look good together." She was looking Sonya in the face. Sonya blushed.

"Thank you. I think we look good together too."

Lou was ready to go so he started to head for the door. He asked Sonya, "Are you coming with us sweetheart? You're more than welcome."

"No, I'm sorry I can't. My mom and I are having a girls day today. I just stopped for a few minutes to see Nipsey, but if it's okay with y'all, maybe I can come by tomorrow?"

"You can come over anytime you want. Then maybe we can hang out and get to know each other." Angel assured her.

"Just call and I'll give you the directions, okay baby?" Nipsey told her.

"Okay, I'll talk to you tomorrow." She was saying as they walked to her car.

Lou ran back inside to sign Nipsey out. Nipsey and Angel began to catch up. For the first time since she got there he noticed her hair.

"What happened to your hair?" he said and rubbed his hand through it vigorously.

"Boy, don't be doing that. I'm doing my Anita Baker thing."

Anita Baker was from Detroit, and a lot of young ladies emulated her style. Angel was no different, she made sure she kept up with the latest fads.

"So, what have you been up to sis?"

"You know I been chillin' with my girls. I told you I still be hitting the JuJu, and taking care of grandma. She got it set up where I get her checks now to take care of her. They give her enough to pay someone to come in and attend to her, but instead I do it so she gives me the money. She did have daddy's girlfriend doing it, but she was stealing grandma's money."

Lou gave her a crazy look when he heard her say that. "Daddy, don't be looking at me like that. You know she was!"

Lou opened his mouth to say something but Angel put her hand up, sucked her teeth and said, "But anyway Nipsey, sometimes grandma didn't even get bathed for days. She made me so mad. Since grandma has to wear adult diapers, she really needed someone who cared about her well-being. And since I wasn't working, who else would be better than me? It worked out great. You know I love grandma and with me doing everything I know it'll always be done."

"Lou, do you still work for the city?"

"Nah Nipsey, I had to let that go."

"If you had to let that go means they fired your ass for getting high on the job then, you're right, you had to let that go!" Angel was rolling her eyes.

"You know what? Your ass gone be walking you keep fucking with me!"

"Yeah, you may be right, but it'll only be to the phone booth."

"So, what are you doing now, Lou?" Nipsey was trying to keep this from blowing up.

"I told you, I'm doing me."

Angel cut her eyes at Nipsey. He knew what that meant. He shook his head for her not to say nothing. He remembered in her letter she said they were stealing everything they could.

Nipsey did have love for Lou. Even though he wasn't his father, everything he did for Angel he did for him. Those were some of the good times that Nipsey remembered. When Lauren was married to him, he would take him and his sister to Barnum & Bailey Circus every year. They went to the Ice Capades as well as to see the Harlem

Globetrotters. They always had so much fun. They had some of the best Christmases Nipsey could remember.

Lou made good money back in those days, and he took care of them. The only problem Nipsey really had with Lou was that he used to beat on Lauren. He would do it in front of them. They never knew why, but the pain he caused her was evident after a while. She would have black eyes. Patches of her hair would be pulled out, and sometimes when she moved a certain way she would wince in pain.

When she had enough, one day while Lou was at work, she packed up as much as she could, took Angel and Nipsey and left. They ended up at the house of one of her girlfriend's and her family. But Lou was like a drug to her cause after she had managed to move away from grandma's house she still had a relationship with him. She really loved him. He was all she really had at that point in her life, so she attached herself to him and put up with the abuse in hopes that she could make him change. In reality she was wrong, because it didn't matter where he moved to, he was there and when he got mad they ended up fighting. Even though they still had a sexual relationship, Lou was sleeping with someone else. He had another son that no one even knew about until the boy was grown.

"So sis, when was the last time you spoke to ma?" She had been on his mind since she had been calling.

"I really can't remember, but you know I still talk to Pam right? She said she hadn't seen her since the fire."

"Fire! What fire?"

"Pam said one day she was outside playing with her baby and saw smoke coming from ma's bedroom window. She said she knew ma was home and she didn't have any company because there was no cars parked in front of the house except hers."

Angel knew Pam couldn't be wrong, she lived across the street. She had been living there a lot longer than most families on the block. She went to school with Derrick, and had a crush on him. So, she had been in and out of Lauren's house a numerous amount of times. She knew who slept in each of the rooms, and where they were located. Pam always liked Angel, even though she was older than her. She befriended her, and they've kept in touch ever since.

Lauren's room was upstairs in the front of the house above the living room. If you look out her bedroom windows you would be looking down on the street. There were four windows, and there were two pine trees sitting right in front of the house in close proximity. They were as tall as the house. Even with the trees being directly in front of two of her windows, there were four windows, so if you really wanted to see in you could if her curtains were open.

"Pam said she took her baby in the house, and went over and knocked on the door. All of a sudden, while she was knocking, she heard a window break. She ran off the porch and back across the street. When she turned back and looked she saw ma breaking out her bedroom window. As she broke out the window you could see flames behind her.

"She said ma was screaming, and yelling for someone to call the fire department. So, she ran in the house and got her cordless phone. When she came back out, ma was climbing out onto the roof. She said there was so much black smoke you could barely see ma on the roof. While she was on the phone with the fire department, she saw her jump onto one of the trees. Pam screamed. She didn't think she was going to make it. It scared her. She made it though. She said she could tell she was in bad shape, cause she was choking. That's when Pam's dad and brother came out. They had been watching from inside the house. They ran over to help her.

They positioned themselves under the tree and told her to climb down. If she fell they were going to catch her. Before they knew it, she had jumped. They tried to catch her, but she went through their arms and hit the ground. They broke her fall though. She said she don't think she hit the ground that hard.

When the fire department got there they put some oxygen on her, a neck brace, and put her in the ambulance. After they took her, Pam didn't know what happened to her. She never called to say thank you, or to let them know if she was alright. They called the hospital, but they refused to give them any info because they weren't immediate family."

What no one knew was, as soon as Lauren felt well enough to leave, she checked herself out of the hospital. She went to stay with an old boyfriend. She was scared the police was gonna be looking for her because of the drugs she had in the house.

She had been smoking crack when she knocked over a whole bottle of alcohol. She also knocked over a wick she had lit smoking with, which in turn started a fire. It spread so rapidly that she couldn't put it out fast enough. The fire was in between her and the door and the smoke was overtaking her fast. She did the only thing she felt would save her life. She went through the window but the window wouldn't go all the way up. Those windows had never been lifted high enough for a body to fit through.

She tried to lift each one. With the smoke becoming more toxic and thicker by the minute, she began to choke and panic. Her only recourse was to break the window. She snatched the curtains off the window, took the curtain rod and broke the window. When she had gotten enough glass cleaned out, she climbed out onto the roof, still choking and blinded completely by the smoke. Which would explain why she jumped the way she did. With the heat from the fire at her back, the fumes from the smoke and being overcome by it, panic set in. She was disoriented. Self preservation kicked in, and her actions became more impulsive than calculated.

When they pulled up in front of Perry's Drugs, Angel hopped out.

"Come on Nipsey. I need some blacks and shells. You need anything?" "No, I'm good."

"Daddy probably has to get something to drink. You know he's an alcoholic!"

Nipsey didn't know if she was joking or what because she could be so sarcastic at times.

"He be drinking like that?"

"Yeah, he make me sick too. Sometimes when he drinks he gets stupid. He be hitting on my girls sounding all stupid. They know he be drunk, so most of the time they laugh it off."

"What do grandma say?"

"What can she say? She tell him to leave us alone, but that's like talking to a wall. He be talking all crazy to grandma sometimes. He really be trippin'. He already don't pay no bills. Staying in her house, and eating up all the food. He's an ungrateful ass!"

She was tired of dealing with Lou. All grandma asks of them is that they respect her, keep her house clean, and be there for her when she needs them. Lou didn't do any of those things.

While Angel was paying for her stuff, Lou came to the counter with five 40 ounce bottles of Old English. She looked at Nipsey. She didn't have to say anything. Nipsey already knew what she was thinking. He shook his head, and walked out of the store with Angel on his heels.

"This is gonna be an interesting weekend." He was thinking to himself as they got back in the car.

"So, what do you want to do this weekend?" she interrupted his thoughts.

"I don't know. I'm with you. So, what's up. You got anything planned?"

"No, not really. Let's sit back and chill this evening. I want you to meet Brett, my boyfriend. You know grandma can't wait to see you, so we can spend some time with her too. And tomorrow hopefully I can get to know

Sonya better. Then we can hit the JuJu tomorrow night if you want."

"Oh yeah, that'll be cool. I brought something to wear."

"Nipsey, do you remember Kenny and DeAndre?"

"Yeah, what's up with them?"

"They usually go with us. They the jit kings around here. They be having them girls going crazy. They be killin' 'em."

The jit was the most popular dance in Detroit. If you could jit, you could dance.

As they were pulling up to the house, a feeling of nostalgia overcame him. That warm feeling that he used to always feel when he came to grandma's house was ever present. It felt so good to him, all he could do was smile and relish in the moment. Angel saw the look on his face. She could only imagine what he was feeling.

"I missed you, Nipsey. I'm so happy you're here. We're gonna have so much fun. Come on, let's go in, grandma's waiting."

Angel ran upstairs while Nipsey and Lou followed. On their way up the stairs someone yelled Lou's name. She was a dark skinned female, about 5'6". She had on a head scarf with these tight acid washed jeans and a tank top with a windbreaker.

"Hold on, Nipsey. I want you to meet someone. That's my lady, Sue." He held Nipsey up by grabbing his arm.

"Nah! I'm good Lou." He yanked his arm free and kept moving.

"Nipsey! Here, take this up for me. I'll be up later."

"Nah, that's alright, you got it." Nipsey went up the stairs.

As quiet as kept, he was feeling some kind of way towards Lou. He couldn't believe how Angel said he treated his mother. He just didn't say anything.

On his way up the stairs he heard Lou yell up behind him. "Yo ass gone act like that, after I came all the way to the Westside to get you. That's okay, I got you!"

Nipsey stopped, turned around, and went back down the stairs.

"I want you to understand something, Lou. I really do appreciate you for coming to get me, but don't think for one minute that because you did that I owe you. Don't think you're gonna use me in any kind of way and please watch how you talk to me, because I would hate to misconstrue anything you say as a threat."

Nipsey didn't wait for a response. He turned and walked off. Before Lou could say anything, Nipsey had closed the door behind him.

When Nipsey walked through the living room door, the first person he saw was grandma. She was sitting in her lift chair. That was the only chair she sat in. She needed help to get up and down, so the chair made that possible to do it on her own because it was controlled remotely. It was also made like a recliner, so she was comfortable.

"Hey, grandma!"

"Hey baby, come give grandma a kiss! We missed you around here."

"Thank you grandma, I missed y'all too."

"Stand over there in the dining room, and let me see you!"

"Okay, grandma."

"Chile, you're turning out to be a handsome young man. I was worried there for a while. I remember you running around here looking like one of those little things. What do you call them little bitty monkeys them rich folk be having?"

"Grandma, what are you talking about?" Angel asked as she chuckled.

"You talking about a spider monkey, grandma?"

"That's it!"

Angel was on the floor now. Nipsey thought it was funny too. She embarrassed him though, and the wry smile she had on her face told him she knew it.

"Nipsey, you have a girlfriend or are you becoming a monk?"

"Nah, grandma. I got a girlfriend."

"She's pretty too grandma, I got to meet her. She was with him when we got there."

"You'll get to meet her tomorrow grandma. She would have come today, but she had some things to do with her mom."

He knew grandma wanted to meet her so he wanted to assure her before she asked.

"How long them nuns let you out for? When you gotta go back?"

"I'm going back Sunday."

"Well, you behave yourself while you're around here. I don't want no mess."

"Yes, ma'am."

"You hungry?"

"No, ma'am."

"Well you get hungry. Here Angel, come get this key, and go in the freezer and let him get something out. And be a sweetheart, and fix something to eat."

"Key? What key?" Nipsey was puzzled.

As Angel got up to get the key she began to tell him about it.

"Grandma had to get me and Brett to get a chain and lock to lock up the freezer. Daddy and his girlfriend would come in here and steal the food so we just keep it locked all the time. When we get hungry or I have to just fix grandma something, I'll go get something out."

Nipsey shook his head and changed the subject. He didn't want to spoil the mood.

"How have you been grandma?"

"Well baby, I'm doing okay I guess. That one right there (pointing at Angel) takes good care of me. I don't know what I would do without her. Now, if I can stop her from smoking all them weeds, that would be great."

Angel put her hands on her hips and said, "Oh no you didn't! If you stop trying to blow us up with them cigarettes, I promise I'll quit smoking my weeds. How about that?"

"Oh yeah, that sounds pretty good. Let me think about it. Umm. No!

Now get out of here, I need a cigarette."

"Come on Nipsey, let's go to my room, I want to show you something." Grandma stopped him.

"Nipsey honey, do you smoke?"

"No, ma'am."

"Well, that's good. Don't stay around that one too long, she'll have you believing that them weeds are medicine."

"That's okay grandma, at least back here he don't have to worry about catching cancer from all that second hand smoke!"

"Oh, you just a smart little thing, huh? Well guess what?"

Angel smiled and looked at Nipsey. She knew grandma had to have the last word.

"What?"

"I know what both of y'all got to worry about, and that's getting hungry!

Who got the key?"

"Ooh grandma, that's a low blow!"

"Little girl, I always told you there's no such thing as a fair fight!" Nipsey was laughing. He couldn't believe how much alike they were.

"Okay grandma, you win," Angel conceded.

"I know baby. Now get out of here!"

When you walked through the dining room to go to the kitchen, there was a door that swung both ways.

"Nipsey, make sure you close the door."

Walking in her room, the first thing he saw was pictures of all shapes and sizes covering one of her walls. They were a collage of her life as it was. She watched him go over the pictures. She began telling him who was who and where they were taken. Most of the people he knew.

"That's Brett right there. That's my baby. We been together for two years," pointing at the pictures her and Brett took together.

"Oh yeah, where's he from? I've never seen him around here. Do I know him?"

"I don't think so, he didn't grow up around here. You know his cousin though. You remember Sean from around the corner on McClellen?"

"You talking about Sean with the messed up leg?"

"Yeah, that's him. You know he's gone now? He got a scholarship to go to OSU. You know he had to come let everyone know. I met Brett then. He moved in after Sean left. He moved in to help his grandmother. He's so sweet. He's 20 and a manager at White Castle. He'll be going to WCCC next semester. He's good to me Nipsey. I hope you will like him. Grandma loves him."

"What about Lou? What do he think about him?"

"He like him, but I don't care if he like him or not! So, what's up with you Nipsey ? How long are you gonna stay at St. Francis?"

"Well, at the end of the second semester, I'll have enough credits to graduate. I planned on going to the army. I don't think I'm gonna go right away.

I think I may wait till the fall."

"Boy, stop playing! You going to the army?"

"Yeah, I already signed up for four years."

She was looking at him intensely to see if he was joking. He didn't give her any indication that he was.

"Oh my God! Why are you just telling me? Were you gonna tell me if I hadn't asked?"

The face Nipsey made told her that was a dumb question.

"Of course I was gonna tell you. I just hadn't gotten around to it. You know I wouldn't leave without telling you."

"You ran away without telling me, and left me at ma's house by myself." That stung him in his heart. He never knew she felt that way.

"I'm sorry sis, but I had to go. You know what she used to do to me. There was no way you could have come with me. I didn't even have anywhere to go. I just ran and wasn't thinking. It wasn't planned."

"I know Nipsey, I was just mad cause I was alone, and Derrick didn't care about anyone but himself. Stuff had gotten real bad for a while. She stopped buying food, and a couple of times the power was cut off.

"She acted like she didn't want me to come to grandma's. I think she knew if I came that I wasn't gonna want to come back. When I got in contact with grandma she didn't want me to go back. Grandma was gonna call the police, but daddy convinced her not to. Don't ask me why." Her mood had become gloomy. She rolled a joint to lift it.

CHAPTER 15

Kenny walked in. He lived directly across the street. He and Angel were real close friends. He and his family only lived on Cooper for about six years. The only new family to move on Cooper as far back as Nipsey could remember.

"What's up, Chicken?"

That's what the people who grew up around there called her. Even though Kenny didn't grow up around there he took to calling her that as a joke cause he thought it was funny.

"What's up, Kenny?"

He stretched out on Angel's bed.

"What's up, Nipsey ? Long time, no see."

"Yeah, it has Kenny. How you been?"

"I'm good. Pass that joint Chicken, and roll this up!"

Nipsey began to feel uncomfortable. He took Angel smoking a joint, but now they were getting ready to smoke a blunt. That would be entirely too much, so he got up and went into the kitchen and sat at the table. Kenny took notice.

"What, you not smoking?"

"Nah, I don't smoke. I have to keep a clear head at all times. I'm not stopping y'all though, go ahead."

"What, you a monk now?"

"Nah, just more conscious of what I put in my body."

"Yeah, I'm more conscious of what I put in my body, too. That's why I don't smoke that dirt weed and just smoke that skunk!" They all started to laugh.

"Are you going to the JuJu tomorrow? You know me and DeAndre gone be getting our jit on."

"I'm thinking about it."

"Oh, he's going, even if I have to drag him!"

The hallway door swung open and in walked Lou with someone Nipsey didn't know, and with him sitting at the kitchen table he saw them first. Angel caught the look on Nipsey's face and yelled out, "Who's that?"

Lou and the guy kept walking without answering. When they neared the door Nipsey stood up and said: "Y'all can't hear?"

Everyone was surprised at his reaction. They just watched, and no one said anything.

"Look who I found!" Lou said.

"Hey, baby!" Angel jumped up and into Brett's arms. She lit up. That's when Nipsey recognized him from the pictures.

Lou turned toward Nipsey and said, "What, you on guard duty out this motherfucker?"

"Daddy, shut up! Brett, this my brother, Nipsey." She introduced Brett before Nipsey could respond to Lou's snide remark.

"Nice to meet you, Nipsey. Angel talks about you all the time. How long you gonna be here?"

"For the weekend. It's nice to meet you too."

Nipsey took in everything about him in less than a minute. From his 6'7" height to the Puma sweat suit he had on. To the way he slightly tilted his head to the right when he looked at Angel. He was about two shades lighter than Angel which gave him a caramel complexion. His hair was wavy, and he was carrying a basketball.

"I was on my way to the 4H to shoot some hoops. I thought I would stop by and see you for a minute."

"I'm glad you did. I wanted you to meet my brother anyway. Here, you want to hit the blunt?"

"Nah, I'm alright. You know I don't like to smoke before I shoot. What's up, Kenny? I didn't even see you over there."

"I'm chillin,' B. I'm getting ready to take Kanesha to the movies, and get her some gym shoes. You know she's got a shoe fetish!"

"Yeah, I know. She got it from you, but check out these Air Max. These are those new Bo Jackson's." He stuck out his foot.

"Damn! They fresh. Where you cop those?" Kenny sat up.

"Out at Southland Mall the other day. Angel didn't show you them joints I got her?"

Kenny had a surprised look on his face.

"Oh yeah, Chicken! You holding out on me?"

"I was gonna show you tomorrow night."

Nipsey poured salt into the wound by saying, "I'm glad I brought something fresh to wear."

Kenny gave them a derisive look as he started to get up to leave.

"I'm out. I'll holla later."

Everybody knew he was going to get something fresh for the party tomorrow night.

"Nipsey, you want to go shoot some ball?"

He didn't really like to play basketball, but he did want to get to know Brett, so he agreed.

Nipsey changed clothes. As they were leaving, Tina, Rina, and

Yolanda were coming up the sidewalk. When they saw Nipsey, they all said in unison, "Heeey Nipsey!"

Tina was the first to step up and give him a hug, then Rina, and Yolanda. They were all smiling from ear to ear and flirting. Tina was the first to say something as well.

"Damn boy! You look good. Angel told me you were coming for the weekend. Where are you going?" He was flattered.

"Thanks, Tina. You look good too. What's up with you? How's your grandmother?"

"I know I look good."

She stepped back and did a little turn like she was on the catwalk. She did look good. Her and Angel could pass for sisters, in fact they called themselves sisters. The only difference in the two was that Tina had a nose ring and she wore her hair down around her shoulders.

"My grandma alright. She sitting on the porch talking to my uncle. You still haven't told me where you are going, and when you're coming back." She had Nipsey blushing.

"We going to the 4H to shoot some ball, and yes, I'm coming back!"

"Well, I guess I'll talk to you when you get back."

Rina and Yolanda finally got a chance to speak. Tina had turned, and walked up the stairs with a little extra sway in her hips. She nonchalantly threw her hand up and said. "Oh! Hey Brett."

"Come on Nipsey, let's go!" He didn't speak back to Tina.

Nipsey spoke to Yolanda and Rina briefly, and kept going. He couldn't believe how he had the biggest crush on Tina for the longest time. Now she was flirting with him.

"It's too late now, Tina. You can't touch Sonya." He was thinking to himself. He hated he had to wait till tomorrow to see her, but he was glad he had the chance to talk to her before he left.

"So Brett, my sister told me you plan to go to WCCC next semester?"

"Yeah, I want to play ball, but with my grand's not doing so good, I felt it would be better to stay with her instead of trying to go out of state. That way, I can still play ball and take a few classes. When grand's gets better, I'll transfer as many credits as I can to Michigan State. Grand's gonna help me pay for it. Plus, I make good money, so I'm saving too."

"So, how you like the neighborhood?"

"It's cool. And with me dating Angel, I meet a lot of people. She knows everybody.

"Yeah, grandma has been living around here all our lives. We lived over here full-time for a while. Then when we moved we would come over throughout the week and stay on the weekends. We went to Marxhausen

Elementary when we lived over here."

"So, I hear you think you can ball?"

"I know I can ball! I'm breaking ankles out here!"

Nipsey saw a light come on when he spoke about his game. You could see he was passionate about it.

"So, are you gonna try and play when you get to Michigan State?"

"Yeah, I could've had a scholarship. I wasn't focused on my studies, so my grades fell. For a scholarship from Michigan State, not only do you have to be able to ball, but your grades have to be right."

"When do you graduate, Nipsey ?"

"By the end of the second semester I'll have all my credits, so I'll be done."

"So, what are your plans?"

"I'm going to the military."

"Do Angel know?"

"Yeah, I told her today."

They made it to the 4H. When they walked in a game was already being played. Brett asked who was next. Nipsey knew a few of the guys there. He noticed how they all wanted Brett to play on their team. He was glad cause he didn't want to play anyway. He took a seat and watched like everyone else. Even though he knew most of the people there, he still chose to sit all the way at the top of the bleachers with his back against the wall.

CHAPTER 16

After Ronnie told Aubrey that Derrick was touching him, Derrick became even more confident that he could get away with whatever he wanted. So, it was no surprise that when he took Ronnie to the park and played with him, that he continued to playfully fondle Ronnie. At one point, Ronnie stopped, and had a look of concern on his face. When Derrick saw it, he began to try and delve into Ronnie's mind to see what he was thinking or feeling.

"Ronnie, is something wrong?" Derrick feigned a look of concern.

"No, I know you didn't mean it!"

"Didn't mean what?"

"My mommy told me that if you touch my privates that you don't mean to hurt me, and it's not bad so I don't have to tell my teachers."

"Ronnie, come here." He was aroused now. "Here, sit right here." He sat on his lap. "Now, you know I love you, right?"

"Yes, I know you love me and mommy!"

"You know I will never do anything to hurt you, right?"

"Yes, I know that."

"You know that if you ever tell anyone that I touched you or anything like that, they will take you from me and mommy?"

Ronnie's countenance changed instantly from the fear of being taken away.

"You don't want to be taken away, do you?"

"You mean I won't ever be able to see you and mommy again?" A tear rolled down his cheek.

"Well, as long as you don't tell anyone about anything we do you won't have to worry about that."

Derrick was so excited that his manipulation was working that he prematurely ejaculated on himself.

"Here, give me a hug. Don't worry, we not gonna let anyone come and take you away. I promise, okay?"

"Okay."

Ronnie began to feel better. He was believing everything Derrick was saying.

"Listen Ronnie, if you don't tell anyone, I promise I'll take you to get candy and ice cream anytime you want."

"Really? Can we get some today?"

"Sure can, but remember what I said now!"

"I will!"

He sat him back on the ground.

"Now gone back and play a little longer and when we leave we'll go and get some candy."

"No, I want ice cream!"

"Okay, we'll go get ice cream." "Yea!" He ran off.

Derrick wanted to take some time to get himself together.

By the time they made it back home, Aubrey was already there.

"Hey baby, I'm glad you're home."

"Hey Teddy Bear, what's up?"

"Make Ronnie watch TV and meet me in the bedroom."

He couldn't wait to get home. All he could think about was what he wanted to do to Ronnie. The overwhelming compulsion was so great that he took Aubrey instead. She wondered what had come over him and why he was so aggressive when he took her, but she didn't complain. She loved it. If she had known what he was thinking about while he was taking her from the back, she would've laid down and died.

She assumed it was the love they shared between them that made him please her the way he did; but when she became sore and wanted him to stop, he got mad. So in order to placate him, she orally satisfied him until her jaws were beginning to lock and he was spent.

"Teddy Bear, what's gotten into you?" She was laying across his lap exhaustingly.

"I thought about you all day, that's all. Is that okay? He was smiling.

She thought he was smiling because of her, but in reality he was smiling because she was so naive.

"Well, you need to think about me more often." She was smiling seductively. "So, how was y'all trip to the park?"

"It was wonderful. I took him for some ice cream afterwards."

"I love you, Teddy Bear. I don't know what I'd do without you!"

"I know, baby. Can you fix something to eat?"

"Okay, baby. I'm gonna take a shower first."

By the time she got out of the shower Derrick was asleep. She got dressed and quietly left the room to go check on Ronnie and cook.

"Hey Ronnie, mommy missed you today. Did you have fun?"

"Yeah mommy! I got ice cream too." He said without taking his eyes off the TV.

"Oh yeah, what kind?"

"It was orange, green and another color too mommy but I can't remember!"

"Umm, that sounds good. Did you save mommy some?"

"Nope! I ate it all before it melted." He was still looking at the TV.

"So what all did you do today?"

"I played with Derrick at the park, and don't worry mommy, I'm not gonna tell you nothing to make you worry!"

"What do you mean, baby? Did somebody tell you not to tell me something?"

"Only stuff to make you worry!"

"Ronnie look at me!" She gently turned his face towards hers to look him in the eyes.

"You listen to me now. The only time I'm gonna worry is if you don't tell me something. Do you understand me? Don't you ever let anyone tell you not to tell me something. I don't care what it is, I won't get mad at you!" Her antennas were up now. She felt something wasn't right.

"Okay mommy. I just don't want anyone to come take me away if I tell you when Derrick touches me!"

"Wait a minute! Wait a minute! What you say? Did…" Before she finished she looked toward the bedroom to make sure the door was still closed.

"Did Derrick tell you not to tell me something?"

"He didn't say not to tell you something, he said nobody. He said he will give me candy and ice cream if I didn't tell nobody!"

"Wait a minute! What in the hell does that mean?"

"Look sweetheart." Looking towards the room again. "I'm your mommy, you tell me everything. Don't ever be scared to talk to me. You don't have to tell Derrick you're gonna tell me, just tell me, okay?"

"Okay mommy. Will I still get candy and ice cream?"

"Whenever you want baby. Whenever you want!"

She grabbed him, hugged him tight and kissed his forehead.

"Mommy loves you, baby!"

"I love you too, mommy."

"Are you hungry? Mommy's gonna cook."

"Yeah, can I have ravioli?"

"Sure, baby."

When she walked into the kitchen she had a myriad of thoughts and emotions. She silently prayed that Ronnie really was confused. One thing was for certain, she would get to the bottom of whatever it was that Derrick was trying to keep from her, and if it in any way harms her son.

CHAPTER 17

When Mac made it to the office, Roy was already there.

"Roy, how long have you been here?"

"Let's see. It's 9:00. For about an hour and a half. So much for an early start, huh Lieu?" He was sitting in Mac's chair.

"Don't bust my balls. I had a long night. This new case…" Roy cut him off.

"Anything I can do, Lieu?"

"I don't know, it's too early. I haven't got my wits about me yet." He was feeling groggy from too much wine at dinner.

"That's alright, Lieu. I just been going over what we have on the Parker case. I thought maybe I would follow up with Ms. Foster to see if I can shake anything new loose."

"Roy, let's slow down. I haven't even had my coffee yet. That's probably why it sounds like you're speaking Mandarin."

"Okay Mac, get yourself together and I'll wait for you."

"So, why are you still sitting in my chair then? Go get me some coffee."

"Oh, sorry about that Mac. You take it black, right?"

"That's okay, Roy. Yeah, black and thanks!"

Mac didn't want to let on that he was worried about the progress of the case. With no new leads and the captain breathing down his neck for results, the pressure was really getting to him. Especially since this new case had been dropped in his lap.

"Here you go, Mac."

"Thanks, Roy. I'm gonna need you to take the lead on the Parker case. I got a call from the Captain this weekend chewing my ass out. He needs something to take to the mayor. He's in an uproar because we don't have any suspects yet. It wouldn't be so bad if this was your "run of the mill" homicide."

"Wait a minute, Mac! We never get pressured by the mayor to solve the murder of a young black male. So when you say "run of the mill" are you referring to black-on-black crime that's rampant in our neighborhoods that rarely gets solved?"

"Roy, come on, you know as well as I do that if this hadn't happened when we had hundreds of people from everywhere, including Canada here, the Captain wouldn't be on my ass. You know it's not me, so let's not play the race card this morning!"

"I'm with you Mac, no offense."

"It's alright. Look, we need to see if we can track down the young man Mr. Parker had the altercation with."

"The one on the basketball team, right?" Roy was searching his notes.

"What was his name, Mac?"

Mac was looking through his notes as well.

"Here, I have it right here! It was Harper, Chris Harper." Roy said when he saw Mac couldn't find it.

"Do you have an address there as well?" Mac was writing in his pad now.

"No, not yet."

"We need to get on that then!"

Mac had just finished speaking when McDougal walked up handing him some files.

"Thanks, McDougal. I take it this is from the Scot case?"

"That's it, Lieu."

"Alright, I'll call you if I need you. Wait a second. Has the Doc sent anything yet?"

"No, sir. He said it may take a while. He's kinda busy."

"Alright McDougal, keep me posted."

"Will do, Lieu."

"Is it bad, Mac?"

"Bad isn't the word I'd use to describe it."

He tossed some crime scene photos on the desk.

"Did they find a murder weapon?" Roy asked with a disgusted look on his face, from what he saw in the photos.

"Not that I know of. This was ugly. Up close and personal."

"Do you think it could be the same perp?" Roy was still looking at the pictures while he was speaking.

"It's hard to say right now without some more evidence and what the Doc may have. While I'm waiting for my autopsy report and coroner's report I want to go out to the Parker kid's house to talk to the parents with you. There's no sense in sitting around here doing nothing."

On their way out the door Roy asked, "What about the kid Ms. Foster met at the festival. Do you think he may have known the victim?"

"I thought about that, especially after I saw the way he moved when we approached that perp in Greektown. I just can't see the connection. Maybe if they went to school together or stayed in the same neighborhood. They had never even seen each other before then, so I've ruled him out."

Turning off Woodward on Grandriver Ave. Mac was in deep thought. He had a nagging feeling that the Scot case and Parker case were connected in some kind of way. Mac was so deep in thought he vaguely heard Roy.

"Mac!"

"Yeah?"

"Where do they live?"

"On Indiana."

"You know this Kentucky, Indiana's the next street over!"

"You sure you're alright Mac?"

"Yeah, just thinking about this new case."

"Well look, I think we should think twice before we rule out that guy. What's his name? Hussle."

"Alright, you handle it." He was still contemplating, not really paying attention.

Roy and Mac were pulling up the same time a man and a woman were. They recognized them to be the parents of Ronald Parker. As they were getting out of their unmarked car, Roy called out.

"Mr. and Mrs. Parker, can we have a word please?"

They waited while Mac and Roy grabbed their suit jackets and put them on.

"Ma'am. Sir. Do you remember us? I'm Sgt. Leroy Cox and this here is Lieutenant Randall McMillan. You spoke to us downtown when your son was killed."

The parkers had went downtown to identify the body. They spoke at that time, but not in depth. Mrs. Parker was in no condition to be talking, so Mr. Parker wanted to get her home.

"Sergeant. Lieutenant." Mr. Parker spoke with a nod. "How can we help you? Have you found out who killed our son?"

Mac could tell that the grieving process was over, or so it seemed. Mr. Parker wanted answers now. Roy took the lead.

"Mr. Parker, first I would like to offer our condolences once again. I was hoping to ask a few questions?"

"About what?"

"We were following a few leads, and were hoping you could shed some light on a few things?"

Roy could see where Ronald had gotten his height from. Even though Roy was tall, Mr. Parker appeared to be towering over him. He figured he probably played basketball in high school.

"Go ahead. I'm listening!"

Mac still hadn't spoken. He was observing how Mr. Parker was becoming more hostile by the minute.

"Sir, did Ronald have any problems with anybody in the neighborhood? Do you know of anyone who may have wanted to hurt him?"

Mr. Parker became indignant. "Wait a minute! What's your name? Fox or Cox?"

"It's Cox, sir."

"Whatever! You mean to tell me you don't even have a suspect? What the fuck is going on?"

Roy told himself to empathize with them and keep his composure.

"Sir, we have a few people we are looking into, but nothing concrete has panned out."

"I bet if this was some white kid this shit would've panned out! Don't you think that if I knew anyone who wanted to hurt my son that they would've been the first person I went to see?"

"I understand sir. I'm sorry, but we are doing everything we can…" Mac interrupted Roy. He had heard enough.

"Mr. Parker, I understand your frustration. I have been on this job for almost twenty-three years. Roy, you have been on the force for how long now?"

"Almost eight."

"Okay, almost eight years. We didn't take these jobs only to protect white people. Quite frankly, I take offense to those implications! We're gonna do all we can to find out who did this to your family, but we need all the help we can get. I know this is a slow process, but it's the process. It may not be a perfect process, but it works.

"Now, if you feel the need to take your frustrations out on someone, then so be it! But only so long as you help us catch your son's killer, and that's by giving us your cooperation!"

Mrs. Parker had been standing slightly to the side and behind her husband quietly listening up to this point. She knew her husband could be very forthcoming. His attitude was sometimes misconstrued as mean and insensitive, but in reality this was how he was dealing with his grief. This was his only son.

Mrs. Parker stepped up and placed her hand on the back of her husband's neck. It was as if she had put a cold compress there. He looked at her. The tenderness and love between them was unmistakable. She didn't have to say anything. He turned and went into the house without saying anything else.

"Mr. McMillan, please excuse my husband. He's been having a hard time dealing with all this."

"No need to apologize ma'am. I truly understand. We just have a few questions." Mac let Roy finish his questioning.

"Ma'am, the young man your son had a confrontation with in school. Do you or your husband know him?"

"We knew him from being on the team with our son, but not personally.

I don't think my son hung out with him."

"Do you think your son had any enemies?"

"Not that I know of."

"Do you know if your son went to the festival with anyone that day, ma'am?"

"No, since my son been on probation he didn't hang with too many people. Mr. Cox, you have to understand. My son was a good kid, but he was bullied when he was younger. His dad taught him how to fight, so he could be kinda intimidating at times. Then he started fighting in school. It wasn't that he started things, but he finished them. That's what his dad taught him to do."

"After he was placed on probation and started to go to this other school he seemed to be getting it together. I think the counseling was working." "Counseling, ma'am?" Roy asked, still taking notes.

"Yes, my husband is a truck driver so he's on the road weeks at a time. For some reason, Ron had a problem talking to me about certain things, so the probation officer recommended he talk to a counselor. That's one of the main reasons my husband is having a hard time. He feels as though he didn't spend enough time with Ron, that he failed as a father."

Mac could tell that statement weighed heavy on her heart and mind, because the way she looked down as she spoke the words was as if she was struggling with the realization of the truth. When she looked back up into Mac and Roy's eyes she knew her thoughts and demeanor betrayed her.

"I know my husband would've been here if he could've. He would've done more if his job wasn't so demanding. He's a good man."

Her thoughts betrayed her once again. She felt the need to defend her husband. Mac knew very well that she was convincing herself more than them. As her tears began to moisten her cheeks, Mac sympathized with her. He placed his hand on her shoulder.

"Mrs. Parker, you done all you could do to be good parents. This isn't either of your faults. Your son was the victim of a senseless crime, and I promise we're gonna do everything in our power to bring the perpetrator to justice!"

Roy finished up his questions, and told her he would be in touch, thanked her and then they left.

"Thanks, Mac."

"For what, Roy?"

Mac was looking straight ahead as Roy drove. He was going over everything in his head as he did with everything. He could feel the pain that family felt good, so he could only imagine.

"I was really starting to get frustrated. Thanks, again."

"Roy, sometimes you have to take a different approach. Compassion is always good when dealing with emotional parents, but with a parent like Mr. Parker you have to be a little more assertive. If you don't, you'll be going round for round with him. So don't sweat it."

"I'm gonna go over to the school to see what I can get on the kid Chris Harper. You wanna ride along or can I drop you somewhere?" Roy asked, glad Mac came.

"Yeah, you can drop me at my car. I got a few things I need to do pertaining to the Scot case. I need to pound the pavement a little as well. I'll see you later."

On the way to drop Mac off, Roy decided to pick his brain before he got away. Roy knew once Mac became immersed in the Scot case he would have to catch him when he could.

"Mac, do you think it was a coincidence that Ms. Foster and Mr. Parker were at the festival on the same day that he gets killed?"

"I don't know. Maybe he had been following her unbeknownst to her. Remember she did say she had caught him following her before? Maybe he was a victim of an unsuspecting crime. What really bothers me is the lack of physical evidence at the scene."

Mac had been dealing with that aspect of the murder the whole time. He knew without any evidence that there was a good possibility this case could go in the unresolved files. That was the last place he wanted any of his cases to end up.

"Do you think he was into some things his parents had no idea he was into?" Roy was still picking.

"I wouldn't rule out anything at this stage in the game, anything's possible."

"What do we know about the kid he got into it with?" Mac asked, grasping at straws wherever he could.

"Not much. It appears he wasn't as popular as Ronald, but he was well liked among his peers. He was a good ball player and student. His grades were okay. He had a good sense of humor. A couple of Ms. Foster's friends knew him. They say he was always cracking jokes, which is what caused the incident. At least that's what they say the rumor was around school."

"When you get finished at the school maybe you can go out to St. Francis and see what you can find out about the Hussle kid!"

"Yeah, I had planned on doing that. Maybe something will come up." Mac doubted it, but he didn't want to discourage Roy.

"Mac let me ask you something totally unrelated."

"Shoot Roy, what is it?"

"You know Susan has been harping on me to have a child! How did you and Pam do it all these years without having kids? Y'all never wanted kids?"

"Pam and I made a conscious decision not to have kids. I don't want any and she don't want any, so it works out great. Do you want to have kids?"

"Yeah, I guess."

"That's not a concrete answer."

"I mean I do, but not right now."

"Why not? What are you waiting for?"

"I'm waiting for the right time."

"Whose right time, yours or hers? Let me tell you something sergeant. The right time isn't when you decide or she decides, it's when both of you decide together. You see, there can't be any individualism in that decision.

That's your wife, you're her husband. You both have obligations to one another. You are obligated to fulfill her every need, desire and wish. If you don't, she'll find someone else who will. She has those same obligations.

"You need to figure out when is the right time. Sit down and have a serious conversation with a serious timeline that both of you can agree on and stick to the plan. You both have to compromise."

"Thanks, Mac. I guess I need to be a little more sensitive to Susan's maternal clock!"

"Well, only if you want to stay married!"

Getting out of the car, Mac said, "Keep me abreast of things. I'll talk to you later."

Instead of getting in his car, Mac went into the station to see if he could find McDougal. When he found him he was talking to the young officer he had seen at the crime scene.

"McDougal, you get anything from the neighborhood?"

"No Lieu, no one saw anything."

"I'll tell you what, let's me and you go talk to a few people!"

"Okay Lieu, but you may have better luck with Vzral, that's his area." "Okay Vzral, let's go."

McDougal was right. Vzral knew the neighborhood. On the ride over he gave Mac the whole layout, and knowing that he had worked the neighborhood for a few years made Mac glad he had him with him. It made him more confident that he'd come up with some leads. Even though cops didn't fare well in that neighborhood, Vzral had a good rapport with the people around there.

It had been recognized throughout the city that this was a "red light" district so to speak. The Mayor had come to the conclusion a long time ago with the police chief (in one of their back room discussions where they decided that as long as these drug-infested neighborhoods keep their drugs away from their kids it will continue to thrive no doubt) that in order to keep prostitutes contained to one area that consisted of a three mile radius, and not spread to every major thoroughfare throughout the city.

Mac was questioning a trick when she asked him, "So, baby, you gonna be working with V?"

Everyone called him V around there cause no one could pronounce his name.

"For a little while. What's your name?"

"My name is Toni. That's Toni with an 'i'!" She said while popping her gum.

"So, Toni with an 'i', have you heard what happened around the corner a few nights ago?"

"Yeah, I know everything that goes on around here. It's sad that guy died like that."

Then Vzral asked, "Toni, have you seen him before?"

Mac was holding up a picture of the victim's driver's license.

"Let me see. Ooh, he's cute! I wish I had. I may have given him my police discount!" She smiled and winked at Mac.

Mac smiled and thought he would humor her a little to see if he could get her talking more.

"Oh yeah. What's the police discount?"

"Well, today I have a two-for-one special!"

Mac was beginning to turn red. He looked at Vzral. Vzral was smiling and shaking his head. He knew how Toni was. She had been trying to get him ever since he started in the neighborhood. Mac was smiling because he thought she was funny and with her thick Latino accent she sounded like she had just come across the border.

"I'm sure it would've been well worth it." Mac was still smiling.

"You better know it papi!" (*gum popping*)

"So, were you working that night, Toni with an 'i'?"

She liked the way Mac said her name. She smiled, blew a bubble, popped her gum and said. "I don't work that time of night. I be home with my baby ever since that girl got killed a couple years ago. I decided to call it quits no later than 8:00 pm." (*pop, pop, bubble, pop*)

"So which of the girls should I talk to?"

While she was thinking Vzral asked. "Do the little blond that be with

Tracy still work around there?"

"You mean, Casey? Yeah, she may have seen him 'cause he's her type!"

Mac gave Vzral a puzzled look before he asked. "Oh yeah, what type is that?"

"The white type. She only turns tricks for white guys. She says black guys are too big, they be trying to tear her insides up. She says the white guys treat her better and gentler. She thinks Mexicans are nasty, and always want to feed her coke. She hates drugs!" (*bubble, bubble, pop, pop*)

"Thank you, Toni with an 'i'. You've been a lot of help. Here's my card, if you hear anything give me a call."

She took his card and said, "You're welcome, papi." Mac smiled and winked at her.

"Thanks Toni, I'll see you around. You be careful and take care of yourself. This person's still out there. We don't know what he's capable of." Vzral was being sincere.

"Okay, papi. I'm always careful. He don't want to mess with this hot Latina. I'll cut him real quick!"

She made a gesture as if she had a knife and went across her face, neck, and stomach. Then giggled and switched off. (*pop, pop, pop*)

It was nice and cool so Mac and Vzral decided to continue to walk through the neighborhood. They felt it was more personable than driving and less threatening.

When they approached Casey and Tracy they were coming out of the Coney Island. It was the local eatery. It stayed open 24 hours. It was kind of a safe haven for the working girls. They would go there to get warm and a good meal.

The owner looks out for the girls. They can come in and stay as long as they want as long as there is no fighting and they buy something. All the girls loved and respected him. They called him "Poppa." He has owned that establishment for fifteen years. His daughter used to run it with him until she was brutally murdered a couple years ago leaving the restaurant. The police never caught them. He has resented the cops ever since. He treats the girls as if they were his own daughters and doesn't judge them.

Poppa was an easy going, laid back white guy. He wasn't scared to speak his mind. His hair was snow white, and his eyes were a striking clear blue. Everyone says if his hair was black he would be the spitting image of Frank Sinatra. What he lacked in size he made up for with the .45 automatic he kept in a holster on his hip, and best believe if you came around with malicious intent, you'd be sorry because he was a crack shot.

When Mac and V approached the young ladies in front of the restaurant, Poppa was keenly aware. He was watching for any sign of trouble. V spoke with familiarity in his voice.

"Casey, what's up?"

"Oh, hey V, what's up?"

"Tracy, how are you?"

"I'm good, V."

Casey sidled up next to Mac giving him the once over before she said, "Don't be rude V, who's your cute friend, your new partner?"

"You can say that Casey. This is Detective McMillan, we're just talking to a few people about the murder the other night!"

"Y'all need to put some lights down yonder, then maybe somebody can see something!" Tracy's southern drawl was filled with sass.

Vzral just happened to look up through the window of the restaurant right into the eyes of Poppa. He was standing there with a scowl on his face. He started toward the door.

"Shit!" Vzral exclaimed.

"What's wrong, Vzral?" Mac asked.

"Here comes, Poppa!"

Mac was lost on Vzral's discontent.

"Who is he?"

"He owns the restaurant."

Casey began to laugh first. When Tracy saw why Casey laughed she giggled. Poppa opened the door and stepped out onto the sidewalk.

"Sir, my name is Detective McMillan." He put his hand out to be shook. Poppa put his hands in his pockets and said, "No thanks, I don't have any sanitizer!"

Mac didn't pick up on the cynicism behind the gesture, so he proceeded.

"They call you Poppa, right?"

Poppa turned to Vzral like Mac hadn't spoke a word.

"V, don't y'all have real criminals to catch instead of harassing my girls?"

"That's what we're trying to do, Poppa. We're investigating the murder from the other night!"

He knew that Poppa would give any information he had, but only on his terms. That's why he didn't ask for his help. It turned out that he was right cause Poppa offered up a little nugget.

"Let me give you a piece of info V. From what I hear, he was around here trolling for young men."

Mac and Vzral looked at each other, not in surprise, but in revelation.

"So that's why none of the girls serviced him?" Mac deduced.

Mac started to ask another question, but decided against it. He figured since Vzral knew him, he would allow him to handle him.

"Is that all you have for me Poppa?"

"There's a tranny two blocks up that maybe you should talk to. You can't miss her. She wears a long blond wig. There's not too many black women around with blond wigs. She hangs out close to the Blue Moon Hotel."

"One last thing!" He started to walk away but added. "You may want to talk to Ms. Fuentes. She runs a photography studio up the block. She has a security camera outside her shop."

"Thanks a lot, Poppa."

Vzral knew the conversation was over because Poppa turned and walked back into the restaurant without another word. Mac gave Vzral an inquisitive look. Vzral didn't address it just then. He wanted to see if the girls could give him any more information.

"Tracy, you said it's hard to see down there?"

"Yeah, a lot of the girls from that side use that alley just because of that reason. Just to give a quick blow job."

Mac was taken aback by how direct these women were. He liked it too. He knew there was no lying in them, as long as they knew you were only there to help them.

"So ladies, do either of you know the transvestite that Poppa was referring to?" Mac inquired.

"Yeah, everybody knows her. She's a sweetheart. She don't take no shit either!"

Mac smiled when she finished speaking. He loved her sass and she picked up on it. She smiled back. People told her what she knew he was thinking all the time.

"What's her name?" Mac asked while taking notes.

"Her name is Destiny, but we call her Desi. She's always down there too.

She knows everyone and everything that comes through or happens!" Mac remembered Toni said Casey works down there.

"Casey, don't you work down there?"

"Yeah sweetheart, sometimes, but only when there's no money coming through on this side. I didn't see anything though!"

Vzral could tell Mac was comfortable now cause he asked all the questions. Vzral didn't know that actually Mac was becoming impatient. He felt like they were wasting time. He couldn't figure out if no one actually seen anything or were they all just good actors.

"Did either of you see a red Mustang driving around?"

They both looked as if they were trying to remember. Casey was shaking her head as she began to speak. "I don't know. You know how many cars I see in a night? I don't know. Did you see it, Tracy?"

"Oh, you work down there too?"

"Yeah, we use the buddy system. Poppa feels it's safer for us if we stick together, in case something happens to one of us. I didn't see no red Mustang though!"

Vzral was wondering why he didn't know Desi, or even see her before.

He prided himself on knowing most of the young ladies around there.

"How long has Desi worked down there? I don't know her."

Casey smiled like she had a big secret. Vzral looked at her and asked, "So, what's the big secret?"

She decided to clue him in. "V, you remember Brad that used to wear the nose ring?"

"You mean obnoxious, animated Brad? You mean that's...?" Casey was grinning, nodding her head up and down.

"Yep, that's him. He took out the nose ring and started wearing wigs, skimpy clothes and became Destiny, aka Desi. She been that way seven or eight months, right Tracy?"

Tracy was tickled looking at Vzral's expression.

"That's about right!"

"Thanks, girls. Here, take this in case y'all see or hear anything." Mac handed them a card.

On their way back to the car, Mac gave Vzral another questioning look, so before he asked Vzral filled him in.

"Poppa's daughter was killed one night on her way home a couple years ago. They never caught the killer. So ever since then he has had a hatred for the police.

"He has taken it upon himself to know everything that goes on in the neighborhood. It isn't hard either. Everyone goes in there to eat and everyone loves him, so they tell him everything.

"He treats all the girls like his own daughter. He protects them like it too. When it comes to us Lieutenant, he only tells us what he wants us to know, no more, no less. Everyone knows not to ask him anything. If he want you to know something he'll call the station or flag a cop down. He don't serve police in his restaurant. He don't just come out and say it, but it's implied. If you go in there and order something, he's out of that. Let him tell it, he's always out of coffee and he don't sell donuts. Everyone knows he don't serve cops. We usually stay away from there unless it's absolutely necessary. All in all though, he's a good old guy. I like him."

They decided to drive down to the Blue Moon. It was getting late in the evening and cooler. Mac really wanted to get some coffee from the Coney Island but decided against it after the way Poppa treated him. After he learned more about him he was glad he hadn't went in to ask.

Mac felt kinda sorry for the old guy. It must be hard to lose an only child and feel like he has no one. He also admired his strength and drive to keep going in the face of adversity and take a stand and fight to keep these girls safe.

As they were pulling into the Blue Moon they saw Destiny bent over in a car window talking to two occupants. They continued into the parking lot to park. They were exiting the car when they saw the car she was leaning into leaving.

"You boys scared off Desi's money, so I hope y'all coming to spend some, honey!"

"Well, I think I can speak for the both of us. On our salary we couldn't afford you," Mac teased. She smiled and got right to the point.

"How can I help you fellas or are you fellas sightseeing?" She turned to the side and struck a pose.

"My name is Detective McMillan. Do you know Officer Vzral?"

"Yes, Desi knows V."

They looked at each other when she kept referring to herself in the third person. Mac knew this was going to be interesting.

"V, what do I owe the pleasure?"

She was digging in her purse looking for a cigarette.

"We're trying to come up with some information pertaining to the victim that was found in the alley over there. We were hoping you could help us. Anything would be helpful!" Vzral cut to the chase.

"Desi saw this guy driving around that night. I figured he was looking for someone in particular!"

Mac's interest was piqued.

"Why would you assume that?"

"Usually they would stop and talk to a few girls. He would slow down, look and keep going. He would make a block or two and come back."

"Did Desi see him stop and talk to anyone?"

Mac couldn't help himself. He was curious to see the response he would get if he actually addressed the third person, so to speak. Vzral caught on and refrained from laughing.

"Yeah, he stopped and talked to my girlfriend Peaches. She said he told her she had on too much makeup, and he was looking for someone younger!"

"Younger? How much younger?"

"Well honey, she didn't say all that!"

"What direction did she point him in?" Vzral asked.

"Well, most of us boys around here are trannies, down on this end anyway. I think he was looking for just a male prostitute!"

Mac and Vzral looked at each other at the same time, with the same thought in mind.

"Boys!" It was like they had an epiphany at the same time.

"Yeah honey. You boys didn't know on this end is where all the 'trannies,' 'gays,' and 'cross dressers' make their money?"

"Now we do!" Mac said with a hint of accomplishment in his voice.

He looked at Vzral. Vzral knew instinctively what he was thinking but he let him say it anyway.

"That's the reason none of the girls talked to him! They were barking up the wrong tree. Where's your friend now?"

She had just given the investigation new life and Mac was eager to get it going in the right direction.

"She don't come on till later this evening." Mac pulled out a card.

"Can I leave you this card to give to her? Will you tell her to call me as soon as she can?"

"I don't know. Desi has a deal for you! As long as y'all don't come back around scaring off Desi's money I'll do it, deal?" "Deal, Desi!" They both agreed.

CHAPTER 18

Lauren had been out of the hospital for three weeks. She and Sam had been getting high on the regular. Sam was her ex-boyfriend, but they remained friends. Sam genuinely cared for Lauren. Lauren couldn't stand to be around Sam but for so long though. He was clingy and soft, two qualities she couldn't stand in a man. He would do anything for her and Lauren knew it, but she still walked all over him.

It wasn't that she didn't care for him, it was just that she cared about herself more. Lauren had been hurt one way or another all her life by men, so she didn't hold them in high regard. It started with her brothers, then her uncles, and finally the men she sought love and affection from. So the only purpose she had for them was for her own selfish gain, and right now was one of those times, and Sam just happened to be the man she used at this time.

She was still afraid the cops were looking for her so getting high wasn't enjoyable as it once was. Her paranoia wouldn't allow her to relax or even sit down when she was getting high. She couldn't eat or sleep. She had lost ten pounds and her mind started playing tricks on her from lack of nutrients and sleep deprivation.

When she began to feel like she was spiraling out of control again, she said enough is enough. She had to make a change, but this time for good. This isn't how she wanted to die. She wanted her kids to remember her for more than a drug addict.

She began to take a self-evaluation of what she had and who she had become. It amounted to nothing. It sickened her to the point where she couldn't look at herself in the mirror anymore. She had become nothing more than a shell of her former self. It wasn't just the drugs that she needed to deal with, but she also needed to deal with the emotional problems that she had never been able to confront.

She needed help and she knew exactly where to go to get it. During one of her self-loathing, drug induced moments of clarity (If there is such a thing), she had researched rehabilitation clinics. She found one that was perfect to suit her needs in Canada. She learned the facilities in Canada were free. They were away from everybody and everything she knew.

She had been killing herself slowly, but surely for years now, and she finally accepted the fact she was tired of walking around dead on the inside and out.

The Saving Grace Treatment Center was confidential and very efficient. In essence, everything she wanted and more importantly, everything she needed.

She didn't plan to leave. She only knew she had to, and with her impulsive nature anytime was the right time. When that time came she decided not to tell anyone, especially Sam. She didn't need him crying and trying to stop her.

As she began to gather what few things she had, her heart began palpitating. She was stepping out on faith. She didn't know when she would see her kids again. It had already been too long. She was scared, but also determined. She wouldn't let anything stand in her way. She knew the only way she could go forward with her family was to get the help that she needed.

She had her car all loaded up.

"Where are you going?" Sam asked from where he was sitting.

She never responded. She was scared if she discussed it with him that she would give in to her fears, and allow him to talk her out of it. She walked to the front door, opened it and turned to look at Sam. Her eyes said it all. He knew she wouldn't be back. She was gone.

As she drove off in the night she let herself cry for the first time in a long time. It was all the pain and anguish that she had carried around for so long. It was the heartbreak of losing her family the way she had, and the fear of the unknown.

By the time she crossed the bridge into Canada, the last of her tears were drying up. She looked into her rear-view mirror at the skyline of Detroit and silently prayed she would see it again soon.

CHAPTER 19

Nipsey was lost in his thoughts when he heard Brett. "Nipsey, come on man, be on my team!"

"Nah, I'm good. Go ahead." He waved him off.

He had been thinking about his life and where it was going. What he had done and why he had done it. As he went back into meditative thought he picked right back up where he left off.

For some reason, the fact that he killed two people was unimportant. He only felt he did what he had to do. He had disassociated himself from the murders. He wouldn't talk about them. He wouldn't even think about them after he committed them.

"Why did I even kill them? Did they really deserve to die?" He thought about that for a second. "Of course they deserved to die. I've been abused all my life. I've seen people abused just because they couldn't defend themselves or were too scared to. For someone to assert their will on someone because they are too weak to stand up for themselves deserves to die.

"Ronald deserved to die. He was one of those who preyed on the weak, like Sonya. Now that I know more about her life and abuses that she suffered at the hand of her father, which were more mental than physical. Furthermore, lets me know I did the right thing."

Her dad was an alcoholic. When he came home drunk, he and her mom would fight all night. They wouldn't fight in front of her, but she could hear the crashing of the furniture and her mom crying while she hid in her room. The next day they would act like nothing happened. The bruises never lied though.

He had total disregard for Sonya. He would call her all kinds of names. He would tell her she was gonna be just like her mom, a slut. He would even claim Sonya wasn't his daughter. Sonya cried all the time and became a nervous wreck around violence.

She eventually learned to deal with everything by using cheerleading as an outlet. She had been cheerleading ever since she was in middle school. She excelled at it because she devoted all her extra time to it. As long as she didn't have to go home and deal with her dad, she was okay.

What was most disturbing about the whole thing was her mom always defended him. Her mom would tell her she just needed to stop making him mad, or he was stressing about some other nonsense.

Eventually he sobered up. Sonya still hated him. The damage had been done.

Nipsey was still coming to grips with the emotions that he felt when he killed Trevor Scot. It was more of a hatred, and disgust. It was as if he was possessed by something he had never felt. The scariest part was when it was over, and the feeling of nirvana overcame him.

"But why is it, for the first time in my life I truly felt alive when I saw the light extinguished in his eyes? He should've left when I told him I didn't want a ride. Maybe he would still be alive. He deserved to die. He was sick.

"He shouldn't have told me he likes little boys. How soft and innocent they were to him. He shouldn't have told me how he liked taking pictures of them. It's like he was begging me to kill him. All I heard him really saying was how he destroyed kids lives. How he wanted to destroy mine if I would let him.

"Maybe if he hadn't stopped his car, and got out he would still be alive. I don't understand why he felt as though he should walk with me and tell me what he wanted me to do for him.

"He made it so easy. He was so caught up in his obsession that he never saw it coming when I told him okay. He was so excited. That's all he could think about. So as we were passing the alley he suggested we go into it. He said he used it before. When I agreed, he rubbed my arm. That sent me over the edge.

"As we entered the alley he began to play with himself. I felt sick to my stomach. All I could think about was how many kids he may have hurt. Then he leaned against the wall. I knelt down as if to tie my shoe and unsheathed my blade unbeknownst to him. I rose so fast he never had a chance to react. I took my head and as hard as I could struck him under his chin. His hands went to his face immediately. I took the butt of my dagger and hit him in his temple. Dazed and confused, he closed his eyes. When his back hit the wall I hit him in his throat. The noises he made were indecipherable.

"The look in his eyes told me he knew he made a grave mistake and it would be his last. An elbow to the face to break the nose, a twist of the head to snap the neck, and the noises stopped. He slid down the wall. I don't know what possessed me to cut off his penis. It wasn't even something I thought about. I just did it. His pants were already down. I just knew that was the instrument he used to hurt people, so I took it away from him. He would never hurt anyone with that again."

As Nipsey came to terms with what he had done and why, he felt justified. He became more at ease with who he was becoming.

Sitting there he felt exhilarated and self-assured. He was so self-absorbed he didn't hear or see Brett get close to him. It aggravated him momentarily. So when he acknowledged him it was kinda brash. He quickly rebounded though.

"My bad Brett, I really have a headache. Don't pay me no mind."

"Come on, you ready to go?" Brett was saying while wiping sweat with a towel.

"Yeah, I'm kinda hungry. Let's go!"

"So Brett, you going to the JuJu?"

"Nah, I got to work. Plus, I don't like it. I went once but these dudes that was digging your sister tried to start something with me. They pulled guns on me and everything!"

"Do you know who they were?"

"Nah. Angel knew them though. She screamed at them."

"Did she say if they were from around here?"

"Yeah, but I don't remember what they look like. You know how dark it be in there."

"What's up with you and Lou?" Brett had noticed the tension between the two.

"I think since I won't jump when he speaks, he may feel a certain kind of way. I see y'all cool though."

"He alright. He thinks I'm good for your sister. We have never had any bad words."

"I think my main problem with Lou is, as long as I can remember grandma gave him everything. She lived for him. You see how she dotes on Angel?"

"Yeah, she loves that girl."

"Well, that was Lou. Look how he treats her in return. It's sad. I hate it! Grandma has done so much for everyone. I know it hurts her for him to be how he is towards her. She don't deserve that.

"Answer this for me Brett. How is it that everyone loves you except the one person you want to love you?"

"I don't know. That's sad though."

"Brett, I know one thing for sure and that is; you reap what you sow!"

"Yeah, my grand say the same thing about him."

"Oh yeah, your grandma know how he treats grandma?"

"Yeah, grandma be telling grand when she talks to her. Grand don't like him."

Entering the house they heard Lou cursing and yelling. They both took the stairs two at a time to get upstairs. When they opened the door, the first person they saw was grandma. She was looking dismayed. Sometimes Lou was so out of control she didn't know what to expect from him. They saw Lou and Angel standing in the dining room faced off arguing.

Nipsey heard Angel saying, "You know grandma don't want her crackhead ass in here! Why you keep bringing her in here?"

Lou was high. He couldn't stand still. He was sweating profusely and his eyes were the size of silver dollars. He had cotton mouth so bad every time he spoke he had to clear his throat.

"I live here too! Y'all can't tell me who to bring in here!"

Angel was a little pit bull once she was set off and he had set her off.

"I'm not telling you who you can bring in here, grandma is! You don't pay no bills up in here so you don't run shit but your mouth!"

"Who you think you talking to Angel? I'll kick your ass!"

"No you won't either. I'll have your ass fucked up too!"

"Now hold on now! Y'all need to stop all that. Ain't nobody gone do nothing to nobody in here. Lou, I don't know why you keep bringing that child in here. You know she ain't nothing but a thief. Son, you just don't listen to nothing I say no more. What's done happened to you? I 'clare you gonna be the death of me!"

Nipsey just sat down and listened, He knew this wasn't his fight, especially when it came to these three.

"Son, you can find you a nice woman. You know that thang ain't no good. She sleeping with you and everybody else's sons too. Remember son, God said: *For the commandment is a lamp and the law a light; reproofs of instructions are the way of life. To keep you from the evil woman, from flattering tongue of a seductress. Do not lust after her beauty in your heart, nor let her allure you with her eyelids. For by means of a harlot a man is reduced to a crust of bread, and an adulteress will prey upon his precious life.* Now gone and get that thang out of here!"

"But momma, y'all…" She cut him off.

"Now, go on now, and don't bring her through here. Take her back out the door you snuck her in. I don't want to see that mess. And y'all stop all that fighting, y'all giving me a headache!"

He knew he wasn't gonna win this battle. He looked at Angel. She rolled her eyes and gave a little smirk. That enraged him. He grabbed Sue by the arm and went out the back door.

"Now Angel baby, come in here. Now, why you gotta talk like that? Ain't I done taught you better than that?"

"I know grandma, he make me sick. He so disrespectful!"

"You don't think you was being disrespectful talking like that? Them words make you ugly. The word of God says: *A soft answer turns away wrath, but a harsh word stirs up anger. The tongue of the wise uses knowledge rightly, but the mouth of fools pours forth foolishness.* Remember baby, stay above the fray. Don't allow yourself to be drawn into foolishness!"

"Yes, ma'am. I'm sorry grandma."

"That's okay, baby. Now I done worked up an appetite listening to that mess. What are we having for dinner, I'm hungry?"

"I don't know, what do you want?"

"You hungry, boy?" Angel was looking at Nipsey.

"I'm starved! I hope you've learned how to cook. I haven't forgotten how you used to burn water."

"Boy, quit playing. I ain't burn no water!" She hit him on the shoulder.

"Grandma, tell her to keep her feet on the floor!"

Angel's jaw dropped, then she put a scowl on her face. He was really trying to lighten the mood.

"Oh, so you a regular ol' comedian, huh?" She was laughing hard.

"You know I'm just messing with you sis."

She stopped laughing. She grabbed her chest like she was in pain. Her face was contorted. She slid off the edge of the couch and hit the floor. She rolled back and forth. Nipsey had a concerned look on his face.

"What's wrong with her grandma?" He was on his knees leaning over her. "Oh damn boy, you done hit me with your secret weapon!"

He looked at grandma. She could barely contain herself. She saw it coming.

"What secret weapon?"

"Boy, your breath! You almost killed me!" She burst out laughing.

Grandma was laughing so hard she started choking. She was alright though. She had got him good. Her acting was Oscar worthy. He couldn't do anything but laugh. Brett was shaking his head. He leaned down and helped her off the floor.

"Grandma, what do you feel like having for dinner?" Angel asked while gleaming at Nipsey.

"I don't know. How about spaghetti? You still eat spaghetti, don't you

Nipsey?"

"Of course grandma, why you ask me that?"

"You know how y'all young folk is nowadays. You find a new religion and then y'all wanna stop eating pork or you don't eat cereal no more!"

Brett was laughing and Angel was trying to keep from laughing cause she knew she would start in on her.

"Don't y'all know that everything that God put forth for man to eat is good? Y'all better learn how to pray over it and enjoy it!" Brett couldn't take anymore. He decided to leave.

"Grandma, I got to get ready for work. I'll see you tomorrow."

He gave her a kiss, kissed Angel, then shook hands with Nipsey and left. Angel got up and headed to the kitchen before grandma caught her second wind.

"Come on Nipsey, and get the strainer for me!"

She knew she had to save Nipsey, so asking him for his help did just that. Passing Lou's room they saw Lou and Sue had already snuck back in, but it looked as if they were on their way back out. If looks could kill Angel would've been killed cause in the look Sue gave her were definitely daggers. Angel saw it and laughed. Nipsey caught it as well, but didn't say anything. He didn't want to make a bad situation worse and cause any kind of confrontation.

"Daddy, I'm gonna save you some spaghetti I'm cooking. I'll wrap it up and leave it on the stove for you, okay?"

She knew he would be drunk and high when he got back. She liked to make sure he ate. Plus grandma always made sure she cooked enough for him. She loved her daddy, she just didn't like him sometimes.

"Yeah, whatever. You eat it!" He slammed the door behind him.

Angel laughed some more. She went into her room to grab her shoe box top, she had her weed on it. She sat at the table and rolled a joint. Nipsey sat down with her.

"Are you coming for Christmas, Nipsey ?"

"You know I wouldn't miss it for the world! Who's all gonna be here?"

"Maybe a few people from around here. They'll probably be stopping by all day. A few of the ladies grandma used to go to church with, Brett and his grandmother, and Derrick and Aubrey."

Angel was watching Nipsey to gauge how he felt about Derrick coming, but she couldn't read him like she used to. It was strange. He had changed so much.

Every time Nipsey discussed Derrick a chill went through his being. A chill so cold he almost froze in place. He felt himself tremble within. Not with fear, but with hate.

"I have to get a grip. He no longer has any power over me. I control what happens to me!"

The struggle within him made him rely on his training.

He began to breathe steadily and silently to himself. A type of meditation that his sensei taught him to calm himself. Then he thought about something his sensei once said to him about hate.

"Nipseysan, hate is a coward's way of fighting intimidation. You're no longer intimidated by no one. You are in control!"

All these emotions went through him in a matter of a few seconds.

"Can Sonya come?" He asked in control now, and steady.

"What kind of question is that? You know you can bring whoever you want!"

"I'll probably bring Samuel and Sabrina since I'm going with them for

Thanksgiving."

"Is Sonya still gonna come tomorrow?"

"Yeah, if she say she's coming, then she's coming!"

"I'm glad you got to meet her. You're gonna love her!"

"She seemed pretty sweet when I met her."

She was blowing smoke now from her joint. Nipsey was dodging it. He got up to get some water in a futile attempt to get away from the smoke. He leaned against the sink.

"So, when was the last time you talked to Derrick?" He was curious to know what he had been up to.

"He calls here every once in a while with his lying ass!"

Angel was in the full swing of things now making the spaghetti. She moved with grace around the kitchen. She was at home in there.

Angel's next question was so unexpected it stunned him. So much so he had to ask her to repeat it. He needed to make sure he heard her right and it gave him time to compose himself if he had indeed heard her right.

She was back at the table now, sitting across from him and looking straight into his eyes with all seriousness.

"Nipsey, what's up with you and Derrick? Why do you hate him so much?"

The weed had her so uninhibited she had no qualms asking him anything. Even if she hadn't been high she may have asked anyway, cause she knew he wouldn't withhold anything from her if she asked. But, knowing that was a difficult subject for him made it easier.

Nipsey took a couple sips of water.

"Breathe. Steady yourself. She set me up like a pro! Breathe. Steady. Controlled!" He was centered. "Sis, I have never discussed this with anyone.

This doesn't leave this kitchen!"

"I promise I won't say anything to anyone!"

"You may not remember, but when Derrick came back to live with us he started pushing me around. You know he was always bigger than us. He would get mad and start punching on me whenever he felt like it. That's why I tried to stay away from him. Then ma started making him take me with him when he went anywhere. I think he started hating me. I don't know for sure. I'm just assuming, but he treated me like he hated me.

"Then one day, when no one was home except the two of us, he asked me to let him do something."

Nipsey was sweating. He felt as if he was losing control.

"I'm alright. Breathe!" He thought to himself. "I was really scared Angel. He promised me that if I let him he wouldn't beat me up anymore. I said okay. He pulled my pants down and told me to lay down. I laid down for a minute, but when he tried to push into me he hurt me. I told him no and to stop."

Tears were streaming down his face now. It was as if he was reliving it all over again. Angel reached for his shoulder, but as she laid her hand on it, he moved. He put his hand up to stop her. He needed to get it out. He wanted her to know the pain he had been carrying around. He pushed her hand.

"No, don't. I want you to hear this. I'm tired of keeping this in. It has been a burden on me for far too long!" He started where he left off.

"But he didn't stop, he kept saying just lay still. I couldn't, so he held me down and I cried. When I said I was gonna tell, he stopped. He told me he would give me anything I wanted of his if I didn't tell. After I stopped crying, I agreed. I was so confused and hurt. I didn't know what to do."

At that point Nipsey had transformed right before her eyes. She didn't know exactly when it happened, but the person she was looking at wasn't the Nipsey she knew. He had gone from being ashamed to being in pain and now angry.

His eyes were clear. There were no more tears, only anger. A deep rooted anger that one feels when someone or something has been stripped from you. And something had: his innocence, his esteem, his confidence, all his self worth, and most importantly, his identity.

Nipsey focused on his anger and pain in order to finish.

"Angel, this didn't only happen once, but more times than I like to remember. The last time I screamed out, I guess I scared him cause ma was in her room. He promised then, if I didn't tell he wouldn't do it again. I didn't. I ran away instead."

As he continued it was as if he had become calloused from a plethora of emotions. They depleted him. His voice became a monotone, his face was devoid of expression, and his demeanor cold. He had transformed once again, but he didn't stop. He wanted to get it all out. He was afraid if he didn't; if he stopped, he might not finish, and once he did stop he knew he would never speak of it again.

"The worst part of all this is the mental aspect. One point in my life I didn't know who I was or what I was."

"I don't understand Nipsey, what do you mean?"

"Well, I was having, I guess what you would call an identity crisis. I didn't understand what kind of person that made me. I couldn't understand why I didn't fight harder. Then I wondered if because of what happened to me people would think I was gay. I became angry, confused, and scared that he had made me different than everyone else. Eventually, I got over it, but subconsciously I knew I was traumatized."

"So, how are you now? Have you gotten over it?"

"Gotten over it! No. I don't think I will ever get over it, but I have accepted the fact that it happened. I know it wasn't my fault. I realize that he is sick and depraved. He saw that I was weak and took advantage of that."

"Nipsey, I asked if you've gotten over it yet, because I haven't!"

"What do you mean, you knew?"

He was confused. Angel was looking in her lap. When she looked up he saw the tears. The tears she had never allowed herself to cry before. The tears she was shedding for him as well as for herself. He couldn't understand if she knew, why she never said anything.

"I didn't know. He molested me too!"

She was looking at him. Her tears were steady. Nipsey fell back in the chair like the wind had been knocked out of him. He could accept the fact that he withstood the depravities of Derrick, but Angel too?

He didn't know what to say. He just pulled her close and held her until the sobs subsided.

"Sorry sis, I didn't know. Why didn't you say anything?"

"You know ma wouldn't have believed me. You know she treated him better than us!"

She was angry now herself. She lit her joint back up. As she did so, it dawned on him that her coping mechanism was her weed and drink.

She didn't stay angry long. The euphoric feeling of the weed allowed her to hide her emotions better than Nipsey .

"So, why are you inviting him for Christmas?"

"Because, even though I haven't gotten completely over it, I've moved on. And to be truthful, if grandma didn't want me to invite him I can't say I would've because from time to time I still deal with some residual effects.

But for the most part, I've moved on!"

"I wish it was that easy for me. All I want to do is kill him!"

That caught her by surprise. With him having changed so much, she felt in her heart that he would. As they ate and talked Angel had no idea that what she told him may have sealed Derrick's fate.

When Nipsey finally sat back and relaxed he realized how tired he was. He laid on the couch and before he knew it, he was out. Angel left him there. She covered him with a blanket and went to bed. She was emotionally drained.

Nipsey woke to the smell of bacon, and Sonya kissing him on the cheek. "Wow! I must be in heaven!" He marveled when he opened his eyes and saw Sonya looking back at him. "When did you get here?" He was yawning and stretching.

"I got here about 8:30."

"Why didn't you wake me?"

"You looked so sweet and peaceful. Plus I enjoyed watching you sleep."

"Oh, I see you still working on your stalking thing, huh?"

"I told you, I almost got this thing down."

"I see I better keep my eyes on you. How did you find it?"

"When I called this morning Angel gave me the directions. She asked me if I wanted to eat breakfast with y'all. She waited on the front porch for me."

"You see, that's why she my girl. She always got my back. I'm glad you made it. I've missed you. Let me get cleaned up. Come on let's go back here so we don't wake grandma."

He went into the bathroom while she went into the kitchen. Angel was at the table smoking a joint. She had finished cooking and was just relaxing.

"What you doing, girl?"

"I just got through waking Nipsey." She was almost giddy.

"Good cause the food ready. Come on, sit down."

She began helping Angel clean off the table to make room for the plates.

"What are y'all gonna do today?" Angel asked, washing her hands.

"I don't know. Whatever Nipsey wants to do. I just want to chill and to get to know everyone better. I hope that's okay?"

"Well, I'm gonna be chillin' with Brett, he's off today."

She gave Sonya a sly look and smile. Sonya automatically knew what that look meant.

"You and Nipsey can stay around the house if y'all want. Y'all can use the stereo and TV in my room if y'all get tired of grandma. If y'all shut the door, no one will bother you."

When Nipsey walked in whatever Angel was saying went out the window. He was freshly dressed and groomed. Angel observed the light in Sonya's eyes shine when she looked at him. She knew he had become the center of her world.

"Hey, baby!" He kissed her and lifted her out of the chair. "So, what were y'all gossiping about?"

She beamed. "Nothing. We were talking about what we're gonna do today."

"So, what are we doing?" He picked up a piece of bacon and ate it.

"I don't care as long as I'm with you!" still beaming.

"Alright then, that sounds good." He was smiling back at her. Her smile was infectious he couldn't help it.

"Sis, what's up?"

"Boy, you what's up apparently. Look at that girl! You got her nose wide open. What you do to her?" Sonya was blushing now.

"Y'all make a good couple."

"I know, I got good taste!" His ego was inflated.

Even with Nipsey smiling, Angel could still see in his eyes the lingering effects of their conversation. He knew she could see it. In order to keep from having an awkward moment, he sat down next to Sonya and grabbed a plate.

"Let me fix you a plate baby. What do you want?"

"Baby, instead of having to drive all the way over to the dojo I'm gonna go up to the attic and work out for a while. If you want to come and join me, you are more than welcome."

She got excited. She loved to watch him workout.

"I would love to watch you workout. With emphasis on 'watch!' Maybe

I can be your towel girl or something."

"That's not what I meant when I said join me, but I guess that will do.

"Well, what exactly did you mean?" She was flirting now.

"I thought maybe I could teach you a few moves."

"What make you think you need to teach me a few moves? Just because I don't like to fight don't mean I can't. You better ask somebody, I'm from the eastside!"

"Oh yeah, I didn't know that. My bad. Why don't you show me something!"

"Oh, you want to try me, huh?"

She stood up. Nipsey stood up laughing. Angel was looking at her like she was crazy. Sonya put her hands up like a boxer. She started bouncing around. Angel and Nipsey busted out laughing.

"Girl, you look like you got to pee or something!" Angel teased.

Sonya swung at him with a nice cross that got his attention.

"Okay! That was pretty nice." He side stepped her.

"I told you, come on!"

Still bouncing around she threw another one. On instinct Nipsey caught her wrist, bent it down slightly, but not enough to really hurt her though. He pulled her toward him off balance, and as she stumbled toward him, still holding her right wrist with his right hand. He spun in toward her. Now his back was pressed against her chest. He held her arm over his right shoulder, bent slightly downward.

The move was so swift her breath was caught in her throat, cause soon as his back made contact with her chest he brought his elbow back to make contact with her ribcage and the back of his fist came up and stopped at the tip of her nose.

Sonya couldn't move. Not because he had hurt her, but out of amazement. Angel had the same look as Sonya. Sonya couldn't believe she didn't feel anything except for his light grasp of her wrist. She was in awe.

She knew he could move from the incident in Greektown. Somehow this was different. She wasn't in the least bit scared.

"That was a nice punch baby!" He was releasing her wrist and grabbed her around the waist. "But there's always room for improvement." He kissed her. She punched him in the chest.

"Boy! Don't be doing that! You could've hit me or broke something!"

"Damn, boy! What was that?! So that's what you've been learning at the place? How long it took you to learn that? Can you teach me some of that shit?"

Angel was hyped. She wouldn't let him get a word in. The words were tripping over each other coming out of her mouth.

"Sonya, you lucky. He just killed your ass girl! Whaaa!"

She was doing her best impression of Bruce Lee and immolating a kung fu stance. Sonya couldn't help but laugh. He was relieved Sonya didn't freak out. He really didn't know what to expect.

No one had heard Angel as she came up in the attic.

"Whaaa!" She jumped in front of Nipsey as he stretched.

"Girl, you better stop before you hurt yourself. You almost knocked yourself out!"

"Boy, no I didn't!"

"Angel girl you look cute."

"Thank you girl, my baby gonna like this." She was admiring herself in the full-length mirror.

"When are you gonna be back?" He asked without looking up.

"In a little while. Tina and the rest of the girls are coming over so we can get ready for tonight. If you need me call around to Brett's. You remember the number?"

"Yeah."

"Are you okay Sonya? Do you need anything?"

"No, thank you. I think I'm in good hands!"

"Alright, I'll talk to y'all later, and don't be doing it in my bed either!"

Sonya's jaw hit the floor. She looked at Nipsey. He showed no real interest. He was too focused on his breathing.

CHAPTER 20

"Now I'm back to square one!" Roy was saying while walking back to his desk.

"Mac, let me have a few words with you in my office." "Captain." Mac nodded.

"Mac have a seat. I've been going over yours and Roy's reports, and with the similarities in the two cases. I decided to allow a pal of mine who works as a profile analyst for the FBI, to give you a hand. His name is Keith Rivers."

"Captain, with all due respect. We don't need any help. Roy and I have this covered."

"Look Mac, I'm sure you are more than capable to solve this thing but we're not getting any younger, and as bad as my ass is getting chewed out I would still like to have some ass left when I retire. So make it happen! It's not like you'll be working with a rookie, and if it makes you feel any better, he'll only be acting in an advisory capacity.

"Nor yours or Roy's work ethic is in question. These are still your cases, but a fresh pair of eyes may help."

"Yes sir, when can we expect him?"

"He should be here any minute. And Mac, try not to give him a hard time."

"You got it sir. Anything else?"

"Yeah, cut the 'sir' shit Mac! It sounds too condescending. We've been friends too long for that formal bullshit! I just want the powers that be to know that I've exhausted every option at my disposal to get these cases solved."

"I understand Will. I'll do everything I can."

"Thanks, Mac." Mac was already walking out the door. He threw his hand up in acknowledgment.

"So, what's the good news, Mac?" Roy was waiting at Mac's desk when he got there.

"Get your ass out of my chair, that's the good news! And we got some hot shot profiler coming to assist us. So you're on babysitting duty!" He was smiling at Roy's facial expression.

"You're kidding, right? We don't need some know-it-all trying to take over our cases!"

"That's not it at all Roy. Don't look at it like that. Just think of it as having another perspective. To be totally honest with you, I don't like it either, but I have my orders."

While Mac was talking, Captain Williams got his attention and waved him over. He was standing next to a young man in a blazer and slacks. Mac could see a badge hooked to his belt. He assumed this was the guy the Captain was talking about.

Mac thought he looked smug. He was smartly dressed with comfortable shoes.

"Mac, this is Agent Rivers."

"Nice to meet you Rivers. McMillan, but everyone calls me Mac."

"Good to know you Mac. I've heard good things about you."

"Don't believe it. Especially if you heard it from this guy. Come on, let me get you up to speed. This is Leroy Cox. Everyone calls him Roy. Roy, this here is our profiler, Agent Rivers." Roy stood up and shook his hand.

"So how long do we have you for?" Roy asked.

Mac was wondering how long before he would have to pull them apart. He knew his friend, so he just watched.

"Hopefully not long at all. I'm only here as a consultant, to see if your murders are in any way connected. And see if you have more than one unsub."

"What does a profiler do actually?"

"Well, there are three fields to criminal profiling: criminal behavior, crime reconstruction, and forensic which is basically the foundation of criminal profiling."

"Now you can answer my question. What do you do?"

Roy's attitude didn't surprise Rivers at all. He knew how territorial cops were, so he tried to not let Roy get under his skin and kept his composure.

"Actually, I spend the bulk of my time studying; reports, photos, role playing, reconstructing. Which is a form of deductive profiling."

"Well we have a lot of that stuff for you!" Rivers was getting sick of his sarcasm.

"Good, maybe we'll finally get something done!" Rivers shot back.

He was looking Roy directly in the eyes when he did.

"What you say? Who do you think you are?"

"*I* am the same person who walked in here with every intention to put these cases to bed with fellow officers, and not have a pissing contest with some egotistical asshole!"

It had become a match between "wit vs. brawn." Roy stepped forward in River's face, infuriated.

"Roy, calm down now, you started it!" Mac had let it go long enough.

"I'm gonna finish it too!"

"Roy, take a walk. I won't ask you again!" He stormed off.

Rivers was still standing there just as smug as ever. Roy's attitude didn't faze him in the least. Mac liked it. Even though Roy was his friend, his attitude was very volatile and unpredictable. Even scary at times. He liked the way Rivers stood up for himself.

"You have to excuse, Roy. He's like a pit bull when someone comes in his home."

"It's okay Mac, I've seen it before. The sooner he realizes I'm here to help his job and not take it, the better we'll all be."

Roy had calmed down and was back. Before he could say anything Rivers felt it was imperative that he got an understanding with Roy.

"Roy, I have a Master's in Forensic Science. I also know the scientific method of "Deductive Profiling," taught by Brent Turvey. I have also read and studied forty books related to profiling, crime analysis, serial homicide and forensics. I've gathered knowledge from some of the world's most prolific detectives and crime analysis, and I'm here for you to use. I'm not your adversary. We're on the same team. Pick my brain. I've studied all that I have so I can make a difference, and because I don't want status quo to become acceptable. Now, I hope we can move past this and become productive!"

"Rivers, you sound like the man we need. I'm sorry for my actions. Let's start over!" They shook hands.

"So, did y'all see who could piss the furthest?" Mac teased.

"Sorry about that, Mac!"

"Say no more, Roy. Let's get to work!"

Rivers began pulling out files laying them out neatly like he was getting ready to make a presentation.

"Mac, Roy, Captain Williams sent me everything you guys presented to him. So I've had a head start, but I still have a lot to go over." Roy was anxious to see what all those books taught him.

"With what you know so far can you hypothesize for us?"

"Well, for now let's get out to the scene for some reconstruction and role playing."

"Even with the scene being processed already?" Roy was enthralled.

"It makes no difference. It's very important, or a very useful tool to test a theory as to how a crime may have went down, and to set up scenarios that's similar to what may have occurred. Only using facts and not vague guess work."

"Roy, you guys go ahead. I need to look into some things. I'll catch you guys later!"

"Alright, Mac."

"And Rivers, let's catch this sonofabitch!"

"I'm with you, Mac!"

When they arrived at the crime scene, Rivers seemed to have turned into a bloodhound. Anything that wasn't relative to the case seemed to dissipate before your eyes. It was as evident as the nose on his face. As soon as he stepped into the crime scene he was back in his element.

He was standing where the victim and perp once stood in his mind's eyes. Absorbing the environment like he was trying to catch a scent. "Roy, if you look here, the body was here in front of the sink." He was showing Roy the photos.

"Now my first question is what was he doing in here? Did he meet someone down here? Or was someone waiting for him?"

"We know if he met someone down here that would mean he knew the assailant. We've questioned classmates, ex-girlfriend, family, teachers and coach. There's no indication that he may have known the killer."

"Okay then, let's do a little role playing. I'll be the killer, you be the victim. Just for a moment, let's assume I was already in here. Where am I? The most logical place would be the sink, judging by the placement of the body!"

Rivers was pointing and speaking at the same time. As if he had just picked up a scent.

"Okay, I'm at the sink doing what? Looking at my handsome face or washing my hands?"

He stopped in contemplation. He looked like he was looking right through Roy in some type of trance. Roy just watched. He knew his mind was in overdrive. He had read and heard about these profiler guys, but had never seen one in action. He figured it was part of the process.

"So, you're washing your hands. More than likely you just finished using the bathroom."

"The only other viable option would be that you spilled something on yourself."

"Good point Roy, and look there's no visible stains in the photos.

In fact, the scene is relatively clean, minimal blood and even with the contusions they're not as such to suggest any type of weapon was used. What if I was at the sink when you came up behind me, words were exchanged, and a fight ensued?"

Roy could see it as Rivers began to paint the picture. He began to see how his mind worked. It was captivating.

"So, if I'm washing my hands, and you come up behind me, that would explain why both of us were right here at the same time. That would also explain why there's no fingerprints around this area. I'm washing my hands before it happened. There was no need to touch anything."

"Except me, right? They were clicking now. Roy saw it clearly.

"That's right, except you. That screams out skill. No weapon means hand- to-hand. In turn screams out training."

Writing in his notepad Roy asked. "What kind of strength does it take to do that kind of damage without a weapon?"

"It doesn't really require strength, but skill. So I would say someone with a military background or martial arts training. I'm sticking with those two because the autopsy report shows that all breaks, contusions and cause of death are consistent with that sort of training.

I also think we are looking for someone who doesn't panic or crack under pressure. Who is calm and collected."

"Why is that?"

"They didn't panic and run from the scene. If they had, someone would have come forward. This thing has been all over the news and in all of the newspapers. Surely, with the number of people that were in attendance here it would have been virtually impossible not to see anyone acting strangely."

To make sure they were on the same page, Roy took a stab at a possible motive.

"So, are you thinking that there was no motive? That maybe this was something minor that escalated fast and ended just as fast and deadly?"

"Those are my thoughts exactly!"

"Do your thoughts about a motive in this case line up with what you saw in the reports about the other case?"

"Not really, I haven't come up with a motive for that one yet. I had hoped to go over there and with your help see what we can come up with. That's if it's alright with you?"

"That sounds like a plan. Let's do it. Are we through here?"

"Yeah, I think so. The few questions I had have been answered."

"So Rivers, do you ever make it down here for any of the festivals in the summer?"

Roy liked him. He was intrigued by how his mind worked. He decided to try to get to know him better.

"Don't everyone? There's always some hot babes down here and I never miss a Jazz Festival. I'm a big jazz fan."

"Jazz, really?"

"Yeah, I love all the Greats! I grew up on it; Lightnin' Hopkins, Ellington, The Count, Fitzgerald, Armstrong, Washington. You name it, I have it!"

"Wow! There may be some hope for you yet! I took you for more of a

'classical' type of guy."

"Why is that, because I'm white?"

His response shocked Roy.

"Whoa! Whoa! Slow down champ! No, because you seem like a thinker and people like that tend to lean more towards that type of music. Look at Einstein or Hawkins or even Nietzsche! Wow, that's interesting that you would automatically jump to something racial. A little touchy, aren't we? You may want to talk to someone about that, or maybe you should find a book on that too!" Roy was being facetious but trying not to be confrontational.

"I apologize Roy. I get that sometimes from some of my colleagues. It gets under my skin. It's mostly the white guys that give me the most grief because my son is biracial."

Roy understood how he could misconstrue what he said.

"When you say biracial, you mean black?"

"Yeah, my wife and son's mom was black."

"You said, 'was' as in past tense?"

"Yeah, she died from a brain aneurysm six years ago!"

Roy felt like an idiot for prejudging him the more he got to know him, especially since he gave him a hard time.

"I'm sorry to hear that, it must have been hard? You know, single parent and all."

"At first it was. Trying to explain to my son his mom wasn't coming home, and she was in a better place!"

Roy could tell it still weighed heavy on his heart. It made him think about Susan and what she meant to him. What it would do to him if he lost her.

"So, how are things now with you and your boy?"

"They're normalizing. We're taking it one day at a time. The first two years Jack became very combative. So much so I needed to get him some help. So I got us some counseling. I learned that we were both going through an emotional turmoil dealing with the loss of my wife and his mother. The only difference between us were that mine were below the surface.

"I don't think he'll ever be the kid he was before, but like I said, we're taking it one day at a time. And as long as we have each other, we'll make it."

"I wish you the best. If you ever need someone to talk to, unprofessionally that is, you can give me a call."

"Thanks Roy, that's real considerate of you. You know, you're not that bad after all!"

"Oh really, you know I was just thinking the same about you!"

Roy's mind drifted with thoughts of his wife's desire to start a family. The conversation with Rivers had really brought home the fact that he had been selfish. If anything should happen to the one women he loved more than anything, and not get the chance to learn the true meaning of family, he would never forgive himself. His mind was made up. He knew what he had to do.

Roy was so fixated on what he wanted to say to Susan he never heard Rivers calling him.

"Hey buddy, come on back!" He hit him on the shoulder.

"Yeah, I'm here, What's up?"

"Tell me about this Hussle. Is he a potential?"

"It's the new boyfriend. He could be. It's just his proximity to the crime scene. Was it incidental or calculated? So it made me wonder about the veracity of their story which hasn't been sitting right with me!"

"Have they given you any reason to suspect their lying?"

Rivers was trying to ask why he was zeroed in on Nipsey without making him feel like he was scrutinizing him.

"Their story pretty much checked out, but it's just a feeling."

"You know Roy, I've seen a shit load of cases get solved off a hunch. As long as you don't allow it to become your main focus. You'll always be able to see the full picture!"

When they got to the next crime scene Roy made a note of how close to St. Francis it was. He pointed it out to Rivers and he made a mental note as well.

CHAPTER 21

Since Mac knew Roy would be over at the Scot crime scene, he decided to go to St. Francis and have a talk with Nipsey himself.

The first thing he noticed was how peaceful and serene the place was. The neighborhood was unbecoming, but St. Francis seemed to be unaffected by its surroundings.

As Mac entered the main foyer he was taken aback by the whole ambiance of the place. Everything about it seemed to be geared toward making anyone who entered here at ease.

From the bluish red color on the walls to the comfortability of the furniture and it's arrangement, the psychological effect of it all was definitely well thought out.

"Yes sir, may I help you?" Sister Agnes asked from the seat where Sister Cohan usually sits.

"Yes Sister. I'd like to speak with one of your young men. My name is

Lieutenant Randall McMillan, with the DPD!"

"Have a seat officer, and I'll get someone to assist you." He hadn't been seated for a good minute.

"Officer McMillan, my name is Sister Alicia. How may I help you?"

He jumped at the sound of her voice. She startled him. He hadn't heard her walk up.

"Oh! Sister Alicia, nice to meet you." He began to rise, but she stopped him by placing a hand on his shoulder.

"Please, don't get up!"

"Thank you, Sister."

She continued to stand with her hands behind her back.

"Sister, I am here to speak with Nipsey Hussle, if at all possible. He's one of your wards, right?" He was studying her expression. She smiled demurely.

"Officer McMillan, we don't refer to our boys in that manner, and I would prefer if you didn't either!"

"I'm sorry ma'am, I didn't mean anything by it. Does he live here?"

"Yes, he does."

"May I speak with him?"

Her expression never changed. It was so hard to read her.

Especially with her piercing green eyes.

"Did he do something? Is he in some kind of trouble?"

"Oh, no ma'am! I just have a few questions I'd like to ask him. Routine!"

"Well Officer McMillan, police don't routinely come here and question one of our young men, unless they've done something wrong. So there's nothing 'routine' about your presence here!"

Mac knew instinctively that this was the mother hen. The only way he was going to get anywhere with her was to be more forthcoming, but how could he do that without compromising his investigation?"

"Ma'am, have you seen on the news...?"

"No, I haven't!"

"But I haven't finished. I ..."

"I don't watch the news Officer McMillan!" She had cut him off twice. He didn't know if her curt response was indignation or just pious characteristics. He leaned towards the latter.

"Alright, Sister Alicia. I'm just talking to people who were in attendance at the jazz festival a few months ago. I just wanted to know if he had seen anything out of the ordinary? Has he said anything about seeing a scuffle down there?"

He was being as vague as possible.

"If he did see anything like that he would avoid being around it as much as possible. He doesn't like violence." She had just piqued his interest.

"Really!"

"Yes, sir."

"So, am I going to speak with him?"

"No, sir."

"Why is that?"

"First off Mr. McMillan, he isn't in any kind of trouble, and we like to protect our boys from undue stress and worries. Nipsey's a good kid. He has never been in trouble, good grades, and a sweet personality!"

He was beginning to see that he wasn't gonna get anywhere with Sister Alicia.

"So, have you ever seen him in any kind of altercation, verbal or otherwise?"

"No, sir."

"Does he have family?"

"Yes, sir."

"Can you put me in contact with them?"

"No sir, that's confidential. I'm not at liberty to share that information!"

He knew he wasn't gonna get much more, but she had already given him more than enough.

"Sister Alicia, you've been a big help. If I have any more questions can I come back?"

"I'd rather you didn't Officer McMillan. Any and all information about our boys are confidential, and without a court order I am not at liberty to discuss anything concerning them!" She smiled a different smile. More condescending, so he had to ask.

"Ma'am, you could've said that when I first walked in. Why didn't you?"

"Because, if I could've helped in any way, I would've!"

"How could you help without giving any information?"

There was yet another smile. "Mr. McMillan, for my mouth will speak truth; wickedness is an abomination to my lips. All the words of my mouth are with righteousness; they are plain to him who understands, and right to those who find knowledge."

"Sister forgive me, but what do you mean?"

"Mr. McMillan, you came here seeking something, only you and God knows what it was. God put in my heart what to give you. Now it's up to you to discern what that is, and what to do with it!"

"Thank you for your time Sister. If I need anything else, I'll get a court order!"

"Okay, Mr. McMillan. I'm more than confident that you won't need anything else!"

As Mac pondered what she said, he realized she had given him just enough to put to bed any suspicions he may have had of Nipsey . He smiled to himself. He liked her. He knew there was no lying in her, but he still decided to wait to see what Roy had gathered before he cleared him.

Now it was time to find out more about Mr. Trevor Scot and what he may have been doing in the city. The only way he could do that was by taking a ride out to Southfield, and there was no better time like the present.

He drove over to the John C. Lodge Fwy and took it all the way to Southfield. When he pulled up to the two-story brick home, the first thing he noticed was how abandoned it appeared. The curtains were drawn. Newspapers had been piling up, and it was apparent no one had collected the mail in weeks.

Trevor Scot lived in an upscale neighborhood. It was dotted with luxury cars throughout, and the lawns were meticulously manicured.

He began to look around. He noticed how on both sides of the front yard there were bushes strategically placed and trimmed to obstruct the view of any prying eyes. With the house sitting back off the street it was very reclusive. He peered through the windows of the three-car garage and was pleasantly surprised by a beautiful 1967 Ford Mustang Shelby Eleanor. It looked completely restored. Next to it sat a 1968 Chevy Camaro SS 396. Mac had an affinity for antique and classic cars. So he knew what he was looking at.

"Shit, I'm in the wrong line of work! Who the hell is this guy?" He was saying to himself as he rounded the corner headed towards the backyard. He couldn't just look in because of the six foot privacy fence. He went in.

It was the first time Mac had ever seen a swimming pool with a vinyl lining. To his surprise the blinds that were hanging on the glass door were open. You could see through the whole dining room and part of the living room. He decided to try the doors. He knew in these types of neighborhoods doors were left unlocked all the time. When they slid open he smiled to himself. For the life of him he couldn't understand why, when he went to a low-income neighborhood they had attack dogs, alarms, and more guns than the law allows to protect their things. But he comes out to these upscale neighborhoods and he could just walk in.

A gush of cold air hit him in the face unexpectedly. It was like an ice box in there.

"Anybody home? Police department!" He had his gun drawn as he announced his presence. The house was quiet and clean. There was nothing out of place. Making his way further into the house he began turning on lights as he went.

Mac couldn't believe how immaculate the house was. Stepping down into the living room, he stood there for a second taking everything in. There was artwork everywhere. He couldn't tell you by who, but he figured they had to be expensive, or there wouldn't have been track lighting shining on each individual piece from the ceiling. There were pictures everywhere of himself with cars at different car shows. Pictures of him posing with beautiful women and a few men.

"If I had to judge by these pictures I would say he had a good life."

Mac made his way over to two glass doors adjacent to the living room. It appeared to be some type of office. When he tried the doors they seemed to be locked.

"Now why would he lock these doors and not the sliding glass doors? Good thing I know how to pick locks!" He was producing a lock picking kit from his pocket. The lock was fairly simple to jimmy, but that didn't stop Mac from gloating to himself.

"Damn, I still got it!"

The doors slid open in both directions.

"Ahh, what do we have here? Looks like an office. A nice one at that. Let's see what we can find!" Mac was smiling and talking to himself. He knew with all his experience that an 'in home' office could tell a lot about a person. His hobbies, job, address books, and some secrets.

As he surveyed the office, the center of attraction was a huge mahogany desk with matching chairs in front of it. A bookcase was situated behind it. The chairs rested on a Persian rug with a small matching table in between them. It had a small lamp atop. Upon closer inspection the insignia at the base of it read: Tiffany & Co.

Mac perused the bookcase. If he had been an avid reader he would've noticed all the first editions staring back at him, but being unimpressed he turned to the desk. Sitting in the most comfortable chair he had ever sat in, he allowed himself to relax for a few minutes. While he relaxed, he quickly took inventory of what was atop the desk.

"Okay, let's see! Rolodex, lamp, coasters, pictures. Damn, this guy really likes himself! Remote, phone. Come on, give me something!" Nothing looked out of place. He began to rifle the drawers.

"Nothing unusual. Oh, looky here! So you were a financial advisor? And from these documents and this extensive clientele list, a pretty damn good one too! No wonder this guy lived so well, he makes money whether his clients make money or not. Damn, I knew I was in the wrong line of work!"

Mac assumed since he didn't see a television the remote was for the stereo sitting next to the disgusting little sculpture of the naked man with no arms.

"Let's see what type of music you listen to!" He held the remote out towards the stereo and pushed the power button. Nothing happened. He pushed another button. Nothing happened. He looked at the remote and banged it in the palm of his hand.

"Damn, batteries must be dead!" He banged it again, and just started pushing buttons. All of a sudden he heard a faint beep and a humming sound. The bookcase began to move. Mac almost fell out of his chair. It scared him half to death. He was holding his chest and looking around to make sure he was still alone.

He walked through the opening only to find himself in a world so vile and disgusting that he immediately turned around and walked out.

"Oh my God! What...?" He had his hand over his mouth to keep from vomiting.

When he walked in the room the lights automatically came on. He knew the child was dead without even checking. The boy's eyes were open. The freezer-like temperatures had slowed the decomposition process. Now he knew why the house was like an ice box. He was still feeling queasy, but he was fighting through it. The child's throat was cut. He was tied to the four corners of the gurney-like contraption on plastic. He had cuts to his torso. He appeared to be no more than six or seven. A tear rolled down Mac's cheek.

He knew he needed to call Southfield PD, but he wanted to get as much as he could for his investigation. He tried not to touch anything. He took a pen from his pocket and pushed *rewind* on the camera before he pressed *play*. When the picture came into focus he saw another child. You could see and hear Mr. Scot coaching a young girl and boy on what to do. He fast-forwarded to another scene where a boy posed naked. Mac continued to *fast forward* the camera and saw similar acts throughout the tape. He had seen enough.

"This piece of shit is the worst kind of monster! You're lucky you're dead cause I would've killed you myself!"

Mac called Southfield PD. He waited for them outside. When they arrived he gave his statement, made them abreast of the situation and headed back to the city.

He was conflicted with doing his job, and his personal feelings. He was seriously considering letting this case go cold. He didn't think he could go on trying to get justice for that piece of shit without prejudice.

"He already got his justice as far as I'm concerned!" Mac tried to be impartial all of two minutes. "But how could any human being with a heart, and compassion for human life, not feel conflicted?"

"I didn't take this job to protect people like him!"

CHAPTER 22

It was 11:30 pm. Everyone was in the back of the house in Angel's room and kitchen. All her girlfriends. The whole crew was back there passing a blunt around, trying to get blowed before they went to the party.

Kenny walked through the door wearing a fresh pair of all black Adidas Top 10 gym shoes. A pair of black Nautica jeans, with a white linen shirt with a yellow stripe across the front, and a sailboat on the back with Nautica in black lettering across the bottom, and a yellow fleece Nautica pullover to keep the chill off.

All eyes were on him. Angel's girls were sweating him hard. He had some Wild Irish Rose in one hand, some Kool-Aid in the other one, and a blunt behind his ear.

The first thing Angel said was, "Damn boy, you trying to catch tonight, huh!"

"Damn Kenny, you look good!" Kim cosigned. She got up to get a closer look at the thick rope chain he had on. "Can I wear your chain?" She was in gold-digger mode.

Kenny had to admit that Kim was hard to turn down. She was a dark chocolate Filipino, black, and Haitian female. Her eyes were semi-slanted. She had long silky black hair which tonight she was wearing in a ponytail with a pink hair tie. With her having had ran track all her life, she was thick in all the right places. Not an ounce of fat anywhere, except that butt, which was her signature trademark.

Tonight she was wearing black spandex, with a pink stripe on the outside of each leg, with a matching top. Her belly was showing. She had on some pink and black Nike Shox, with some pink ankle socks,

Kenny was cheesing from ear to ear. None of her girls were saying anything.

"Tina, I bet you twenty dollars she get the chain?" Angel whispered.

"Bet, you might as well let me get that!"

Angel saw how Kenny was licking his lips like a salivating dog. She knew that was an easy twenty. She knew how Kenny got down cause they used to date. She knew he was a dog, but what Kenny didn't know was, if he thought he was gonna get some of that, he was gonna have to do a lot more that let her wear a chain.

"I appreciate that Kim. You looking good your damn self!" He was feeling himself.

"Oh, you like what you see?" She dropped down to the floor and came back up slow with her butt stuck out against his crotch. His hand went automatically to her butt like they had a mind of their own. She stood there with her back to him, looking back over her shoulder using her butt muscles to make her cheeks bounce up and down.

"Damn girl, you keep doing that I might have to buy you your own chain, damn!"

Angel cut her eyes at Tina. Tina saw her. Kenny was still rubbing on her butt when she looked down.

"Damn boy, look like you was happy to see me too!" Her not having on any panties had Kenny reeling. Angel and Tina looked at each other. Angel grinned at her. She knew Kim was gonna get that chain.

Kim boldly put her hand on Kenny's erection and smiled mischievously. With her other hand she removed his chain from off his neck. He never said a word. She looked down at his bulging pants and patted him.

"I'll see you later!" She said as she turned and walked off.

Angel was gloating. Tina was mad.

"Damn Kenny, you made me lose my money. You a sucker!" Tina blurted out.

"That's your fault baby girl. You know to always bet on black!" He smirked and lit his blunt.

"I should've put this ass on you, maybe I could've gotten them Adidas!" He choked on his blunt.

"You don't have enough ass for them!" Everybody laughed.

"Boy, don't play!"

"Nah, I'm just fucking with you. I would've given you the chain too. Besides, it's fake anyway! You think I'm gonna wear my real shit to the JuJu?" He winked at Angel.

They started laughing again, but this time at Kim. She was a good sport though. She laughed at herself. She knew it was all love.

"Nipsey, you ready?" Tina asked, all smiles.

He ran his hands over his waves, rubbed his face and brushed some imaginary lint off his shirt and said. "You tell me!"

Sonya smiled but didn't say nothing. She had noticed how all evening Tina had been trying to keep Nipsey's attention. She let it go cause he hadn't paid her no mind.

Nipsey was dressed comfortable. He had on a pair of Eddie Bauer corduroys, tan in color. A white tank top with a buttoned down Eddie

Bauer short sleeve shirt, speckled with its signature Mallard ducks throughout. He had on a dark brown braided belt with matching Eddie Bauer shoes. He wanted to be loose, but comfortable and cool. He knew how congested the party would be. He was wearing the buttoned down open and had a washcloth draped over his shoulder. He was ready.

Angel was beaming. She was so happy he was there.

"Yeah, I see you haven't forgot how to dress!" Tina was shooting daggers at Sonya as she spoke.

Sonya caught them and added. "Yeah, you sure do baby. You look good enough to eat!" She was walking towards him. When she had gotten to him she grabbed him. "Come here, let me taste!" She pulled him by his shirt into her. They were locked in an intimate embrace kissing. He lifted her. She interlocked her legs around his waist. She heard Tina smack her lips.

"Get a room!"

He lowered her back on the floor.

"Damn baby, you taste better than you look!" She didn't have to turn and look cause she knew everyone was burning a hole in her back, and she loved it.

"I see you're marking your territory?"

Her eyes said it all. She didn't even have to answer.

"Boom!"

The hallway door slammed into the wall. In walked Lou with Sue in tow. He wasn't even in the kitchen good enough before he started talking.

"Uh oh, y'all didn't invite us to the party?" He took Sue by the hand and spun her around to the sound of the music. "What y'all got to drink?" Yolanda held up the Wild Irish Rose mixed with Kool-Aid. Angel's glare spoke volumes.

"Damn, I knew I should've left! Now here go his begging ass. He get on my nerves!" She was thinking to herself and rolling her eyes. She loved her daddy, but that didn't change the fact that he was a pain.

"Here daddy, you want some of this blunt?" Angel was trying to be pleasant despite how she felt. As he walked past Sonya he stopped.

"Hey cutie, what's your name?" With her hair down and the glasses he didn't recognize her.

"Come on daddy and get the blunt!" Angel was trying to run interference before he said something stupid.

"Alright, alright, I'm coming!" He waved her off but didn't move.

"I'm Sonya. I met you yesterday, remember?"

"Oh yeah, damn you're beautiful!" He was taking Sonya's hand and kissing it. Nipsey just watched. As Lou went to get the blunt from Angel he added, "So Sonya, you must be a square? You fucking the one!"

"What you think baby, a square beats a fiend any day?" Nipsey countered before Angel could intervene.

"I bet you ain't never had yo ass whooped by no fiend?" He was grandstanding now, but Nipsey didn't respond. He knew Lou was probably high so he let it be.

"Daddy, don't come in here with that bullshit. What, you trying to blow my high?" Kim was serious and everyone knew it. "Just get you a glass and get you some of this ghetto juice!" She was holding up what they were drinking.

"Yeah, bet, let me get some of that!" He walked over to the sink. He reached above Nipsey into the cabinets to get a cup. In the process he elbowed Nipsey in the head. Not too hard, just hard enough to make it look like an accident. No one saw it except Sonya. She casually walked over to where everyone else was sitting around the table cause she was unsure what Nipsey might do.

"Lou... you know what, don't worry about it. You good!" Nipsey knew what Lou was trying to do but he wouldn't bite. But the look he gave Lou was unmistakable. Lou was smiling.

"Lou, get me a glass too!" Sue was holding her hand out.

"What you need a glass for, Sue?" The sarcasm was dripping off Tina's lips.

"I thought I could get something to drink!"

"You better get your dusty ass out of here! You know grandma don't want your ass in here anyway, you lucky I don't whoop your ass!"

Tina was dead serious. She hated Sue. One day her grandma paid Sue to go to the store. She was in the middle of cooking and no one else was home. She saw Sue sitting on grandma's porch. She asked her to walk to the store. She gave her twenty-five dollars. Five was for her going, and told her to make sure she brought her the change from the twenty. Mrs. Wilson didn't see her anymore until later that night. She didn't have what she sent her for either.

She made some excuse about how she lost the money, and didn't come and tell her cause she knew Mrs. Wilson wouldn't believe her. Which was a mistake cause Mrs. Wilson told Tina what Sue had done.

Tina had been looking for her when her cousin Trey told her that he saw Sue around the corner in the joint smoking crack. Tina was livid, so when she finally did see Sue she was coming from the opposite direction up the block. It was two days later.

When Sue noticed Tina coming in her direction with a smile on her face, she was relieved.

"Hey Tina girl, what's up?"

Tina was still a few feet away.

"Hey Sue, you looking all cute today!"

"Thank You." They were in front of each other now.

"Tina I wanted..."

"Bam!" Tina punched Sue right in the mouth.

"Now bitch, you won't be sucking on that glass dick today! That's for taking my grandma money, you dusty bitch!"

Sue took off running. Tina wasn't running after her.

"Bitch, you better get my grandmother her money, and every day you don't have it, I'm going to punch your ass in the mouth!"

When Sue had made it far enough away she stopped running. Still holding her mouth she yelled back at Tina.

"Tina, you didn't have to hit me!"

"Yes I did. You didn't have to take that money. Trey told me you smoked it up. Now you better get it back or I'm gonna keep getting that mouth!"

Everyone knew Tina meant everything she said. The only reason she wasn't getting hit in the mouth right now is because they were all in grandma's house, and you don't fight in grandma's house. Nobody!

"Damn Tina, you don't have to talk to my baby like that!"

"Daddy, don't start. You know what she did!"

He knew how Tina felt about her family, which included Angel, so he knew it would be a waste of time to say anything, so he just followed Sue out.

"Hey y'all, let's get ready to go. I'm ready to get my dance on. Come on Sonya, you going with us!" Angel was grabbing her by her waist pulling her along. Sonya looked over her shoulder, and as if Angel read her mind she added, "You'll see him later."

We don't ever leave together. All the girls go and all the guys go together. Trust me, we all end up together at the party, and we always leave the party together. Unless someone decides to leave with someone else. Then you come tell one of us who you're leaving with."

"You're in good hands baby. I'll see you in a little bit." Nipsey gave a little reassurance of his own.

"Come on Nipsey, let's be out. I have to get some shells. I don't like buying them at the party, they charge a dollar a piece for them."

They sold everything at the JuJu: plates, shells, even 40 ounces. They had a dice room, a tunk room and a couple of bedrooms. It was a two-family flat, so it was more than big enough to accommodate everyone and everything that took place there.

Which store do you want to walk to Kenny?"

"Let's go to the gas station up on Warren. It's the closest one open this time of night." He was admiring himself in the mirror.

"Well, come on, let's go. You act like a female!"

"You know I got to look good for the honeys!"

The neighborhood was abuzz with activity, as it always was on the weekend. The JuJu was so popular that people came from all over the city, but it was the people in the neighborhood that made it happen. It was their party, their hood, and even though people came from all over, the neighborhood stuck together, no matter how much they fought among themselves. The hood was funny like that. So if you thought you were gonna come over there, start trouble and leave, you had another thing coming.

"So, Kenny, how has things been for you and Kanesha since your mom passed?"

"It's been cool. I really miss mom though. Kanesha lives with dad legally, but she stays over here most of the time cause mom left both of us the house. I pretty much take care of her. Then with her school being over here dad just let her stay."

"Look up!"

Nipsey was making him aware. Kenny had been rolling a blunt while he was walking, so he wasn't paying attention to what was in front of him. When he looked up he recognized who it was and went back to rolling his blunt.

"You know you need to come back and stay. You know we all miss you."

"I appreciate that Kenny, but I have other plans right now. You know I miss y'all too."

"Other plans like what?"

"The military. I like the idea of contributing to something worthwhile."

"You're a better man than I am. The only thing I'm doing worthwhile is taking care of the people I love. I'm definitely not going to fight for a country where I'm a second class citizen, and not afforded the same opportunity as everyone else!" He blew smoke in Nipsey's direction to put emphasis on what he said.

"Yeah, yeah, I've heard it all before but I need to do this. This is the best chance I have to pursue a career..." He didn't get a chance to finish.

"Ha! Ha! Ha! Stop it! You're killing me!" He was laughing uncontrollably. Nipsey knew he was high. He laughed also, just from watching Kenny.

"Man, you need to stop that shit. I'm gonna be all I can be! Sir, yes sir!" Kenny said mockingly.

He was imitating the commercials he had seen. It made Nipsey laugh much harder as he took it on the chin.

"Oh, you got jokes?"

"Don't lie. You know that shit was funny!" "Okay, you got that." Nipsey agreed.

"No, seriously though. Don't forget where you come from and come home!"

Before they even entered the store Nipsey could see how busy it was looking through the windows. He knew some of the people that had grown up around there. He also took notice to how Kenny's demeanor changed. He couldn't put his finger on what he was seeing, but he knew he saw something in him that wasn't right.

He began to observe everything and everyone in the store instead of asking Kenny if anything was wrong. He followed Kenny's eyes to see if he could gage the situation. When his eyes fell on the four guys, he knew they were the reason for the distress. Out of the four, he knew two. They were brothers and trouble. They used to be the neighborhood bullies.

When Chris and Cotton saw them, they started in their direction.

"Fucking cowards!" Kenny mumbled under his breath.

"Damn! Is that you Nipsey? I almost didn't recognize you. What's up?"

Nipsey never got a chance to respond to Kenny's remark, so there was no smile from him. He was feeding off of Kenny's vibe. He was laser focused on everyone around.

"What's up, Cotton?" Chris didn't speak. Nipsey could feel the tension as he gave him a head nod.

"What's up, Kenny? I see you clean as always." Kenny didn't acknowledge him.

He was preoccupied with getting what he needed or so it seemed. As he turned around he gave a discourteous nod and headed towards the door. Nipsey knew it was time to go.

"Alright Chris. Alright Cotton. Y'all going to the party?" He was trying to be cordial.

"You know we don't miss it. We'll get up!"

On the walk to the party Kenny wasn't his talkative self. Nipsey couldn't take it anymore so he decided to see what he could pull out of him.

"Alright Kenny, let's have it!"

"Have what?" His flippant response surprised Nipsey.

"Let's not do this, you know what!"

"Leave it alone Nipsey. If you don't know, maybe it's not meant for you to know!"

Now, Nipsey's radar went off.

"Hold on. What do you mean? Was someone supposed to tell me something?"

"Look, if I tell you something, you have to promise not to say anything."

"I can't promise that, and you can't ask me not to, especially if it has something to do with grandma, my sister or even someone close to us."

"You're right, but I'm asking because I was asked not to tell anyone. I gave my word and Angel will never forgive me."

"Oh, you're going to tell me, because if you think you're gonna make it home or anywhere else before you do, you have another thing coming!" Nipsey was thinking this looking Kenny directly in his eyes and even though it was dark his expression left nothing to the imagination. So, Kenny began to explain.

"One weekend last summer we went to the JuJu. Everybody was having a good time. After a while I noticed I hadn't seen Angel in awhile, and that was unlike her. I began to search the party for her. Tina told me she went upstairs with Chris. I didn't think anything of it because she been knowing his whole family her whole life. So I went back to chillin'. When it was time to go no one had seen her. Everyone got worried. I found Chris downstairs shooting dice. He said she didn't feel good and left. So we left. When I went by grandma's to check on her she was in her room in bed with the covers pulled over her head. I called her name, but she didn't answer. So I left her alone. The next day she called me and told me to come across the street so she could tell me something."

Nipsey listened intently, without interrupting. He didn't want to miss a thing.

"She was in her room when I got over there. It was like she had been in a battle. I couldn't believe it. She looked bad. She told me she was upstairs at the party in a room with Chris. They were smoking and kickin' it, when he kissed her. She said she let him at first, but when she told him she couldn't because she was with Brett, he got mad. He smacked her and said she was playing games.

"She said she got up to leave. When she did, he grabbed her by the throat and choke slammed her on the bed. She couldn't scream. She was in shock and terrified of what he may do to her. She knew he had killed someone before from the rumors. At first she hadn't believed them, but seeing him like this put her in fear for her life.

"After he raped her, he left her in the room. She said she just had to get out of there. So she didn't say anything to anyone. She just went home, took a bath, crawled in the bed, and cried."

There were no words to describe how Nipsey was feeling. He was no longer looking at Kenny. He was looking down at the ground fighting off the anxiousness that permeated his soul.

"I can't believe this, we've known Chris forever. I knew they were capable of doing a lot of things, but that, and to Angel? Why didn't she tell anyone or call the police?"

"I asked her that. She said she thought it was her fault. She didn't think anyone would believe her. She was ashamed."

Nipsey was still shaking his head in disbelief.

"Don't they still stay on Cooper, down at the other end, close to Gratiot?" Nipsey asked.

"Yeah, they stay with their uncle in that big white house on the corner."

Nipsey was already formulating a plan. Then, Kenny added, "Their uncle is a jitney over at the Farmer Jack on Harper. He drive that old ass yellow station wagon."

Nipsey made his mind up not to talk to Angel. He would deal with Chris when the time was right.

"How often do you see him since that happened?" Nipsey asked.

"I see him all the time. He be hustling around on Pennsylvania."

"How is it that he is still walking around here after killing somebody, and doing that to females?"

"What, have you been gone too long? What, you forgot how it goes down in the hood? You know don't nobody tell shit around here. We got to live around here. If someone tells on him and he goes to jail, they still have to deal with his family!"

Nipsey thought about that for a minute. And the fact that the same code they used to live by would be the same code that facilitates Chris' demise made him not so anxious. He thought about something his sensei said.

"Nipseysan, when going into battle the one with the most advantage prevails in the end. So if your enemy doesn't know he's an enemy, who has the advantage? Never show your hand too soon, and never allow your emotions to dictate your actions. With patience and planning the right time to strike will always reveal itself."

"Nipsey!" "Nipsey!" He had heard Kenny, but he hadn't heard him.

"Why are you yelling, Kenny?" "Damn, you act like you can't hear!"

"I heard you." Nipsey lied.

"You should've said something. I thought you done went crazy. I was gonna leave your ass right here!"

"What are you talking about?"

"Look, we talking, it's dark. No one's out here and your ass just black out. This the part in the movie where a muthafucka dies. In this movie though, it won't be me! Look, don't tell Angel…" Nipsey held his hand up to stop him.

"I give you my word, I won't, and I appreciate you telling me."

When Kenny and Nipsey got to the party it was in full swing. The girls were already there and everyone was enjoying themselves. Including Sonya, she looked right at home amongst Angel and her girls.

While she was talking, her eyes swept the room constantly. When they landed on Nipsey, everyone knew it. Her smile gave her away. Nipsey nudged Kenny, and nodded in the girl's direction.

"I'm not going over there. Ain't nothing over there for me. I'm going this way. I'm trying to get my freak on!" Kenny was pointing in the opposite direction. Nipsey decided to go with him, and let the girls do their own thing. Plus, he wanted to see who he could see.

CHAPTER 23

As Roy pulled into the driveway of his home, he could see Susan sitting on the couch. He sat there for a few seconds just looking trying to come up with the right words to express how he felt. In the process his mind drifted back to the first time he met her coming out of the dry cleaners. He thought she was stunning. As it turned out, he had blocked her in with his cruiser. When he came out she was sitting in her car waiting patiently.

"Excuse me, ma'am." He was tapping on her window. She hadn't noticed him walk up. She was busy reading something in her lap. "Are you waiting for me?" Turning on the charm.

"As a matter of fact I am. You're blocking me and making me late for a meeting!"

The fact that she never smiled and looked him in his eyes as she spoke was kind of intimidating. His heart actually started beating faster. He wanted to apologize and move his car but her beauty captivated him, so he poured on the charm even thicker.

"I'm sorry, ma'am. If you don't say anything, I won't give you a ticket."

"Give me a ticket for what?"

"You do know it's against the law to have anything on or in your vehicle that may distract other drivers?"

"What are you talking about?" She was aggravated now.

"There's no way I could have operated my vehicle safely if I saw you in the next lane." Finally she smiled.

"Wow, that was so corny. How long did it take you to come up with that?

And I know you're not holding me up for that lame ass line!"

"First off, actually I free-styled that. So it didn't take me long at all. Secondly, yes, I did hit you with that lame ass line, but you gotta give a brother props for trying!" He was showing all thirty twos.

"Well, if I was you, I wouldn't quit my day job. Oh, wait a minute, yes I would, cause I hate cops!"

Just that quick the dynamics of the conversation changed. Along with the smile on his face. He knew he didn't have a chance, but to walk away defeated was not an option. And to walk away leaving her with that impression was definitely not an option. Unfortunately the look on his face betrayed him, but he rebounded beautifully.

"That's kind of ironic, isn't it? Considering the first call you make when you need help is to the *cops*!" Now it was her expression that showed how he had cut her with his words.

That was unexpected. Now she knew that the same attitude she projected towards cops that tried to get to know her would be futile. She liked that but she still wasn't gonna make it easy.

"Okay, you have a point. Why don't you help me now, and move that piece of trash out of my way before I call a real cop!"

"You know what? You're tough, but I'm not intimidated by your beauty. I know you may come across guys that can't stand toe to toe with you. I understand that. Look at your beautiful eyes. So beautiful if someone looks into them for too long, you'll have them under your spell. They also say; I'm independent, strong, and proud. Your skin is flawless and smooth, but also healthy. The lack of make-up and natural hairstyle says you're confident and comfortable in your skin. So, of course they would feel inadequate. But to me it's alluring."

She was impressed. He had her full attention and her captivation was evident in this new gaze and smile. So he continued.

"From your weight, muscle tone, and voluptuous... I'm just gonna say curves to be on the safe side, say you care about yourself."

"So, is that all Officer?"

"As a matter of fact, no. I see you have on a navy blue pants suit and a gray one in your cleaners bag, with subtle heels. Your hair's pulled back and your glasses compliment the ensemble. Which screams; business, intelligence, and I want to be taken seriously. So to sum it up for you, I love a beautiful, strong, and confident black woman. One who's not afraid to go after what she wants, and who's not afraid to speak her mind."

She was speechless for the moment, but her actions spoke louder than any of her words. She handed him her card and pointed at his cruiser. Before she rolled up her window she asked him his name. He understood the gesture. He won. She conceded, and accepted the fact.

"Yes, this is Susan Hawkins speaking." She had answered the phone on the first ring. This was really the first time Roy had the opportunity to call in two weeks.

"Susan, this is Leroy Cox. How are you?"

"I'm fine thank you. Mr. Cox, what can I do for you?"

"All business I see." He was trying to tread lightly. He knew how she could be.

"Excuse me. Do I know you?"

"Oh, I'm sorry. You don't remember me. I'm the guy who blocked you in at the cleaners!"

"Oh yeah, the cop!"

The way she said that made him think about the day he met her.

"Yeah, the cop. Thought I made a lasting impression?" His ego was bruised.

"Yes, it was a lasting impression, but it lasted three days, not two weeks!"

"Ouch. Don't be so mean!"

"Trust me, you haven't seen mean!"

"Well, that's a relief. I don't know if I could handle that."

"That's kind of disappointing to hear. I didn't take you for the type of man that doubts his capabilities!"

"Damn, she's sharp!" He thought before he responded.

"If I didn't have doubts I'd be overconfident. A man that's overconfident doesn't have a full grasp on reality. He also doesn't accept shortcomings well. So to doubt is to be realistic!"

She loved the way he wouldn't give in, but he wouldn't be winning this round.

"So, be as though I'm working, did you call to try and impede my progress once again or what?"

"Since you put it that way, yes and no. *Yes* because it seems I'm becoming good at that, and *no* because those weren't my intentions. I was actually calling to see if you would go to dinner with me?"

"No, I will not!" He wasn't prepared for that.

"Why not?"

"Because dinner is so cliché and played out. Why don't you try to be a little more original. So if you think of something else give me a call. But right now I need to get back to work!" She paused for effect and allowed her victory to sink in.

"Okay, I respect that, but let me ask one question. Are there any limits to what you will or will not do?"

"That's a fair question. I'm pretty open minded, so use your imagination. I have faith in you."

"It's good to know there may be hope for me after all!"

She was glad she hadn't discouraged him. That said a lot about his character. After he hung up he had to calm himself. It was comical how she made his heart rate spike.

Roy was so zoned out he never saw Susan walk up. She was tapping on the window.

"Leroy, is something wrong? Why are you sitting there like that?" He opened the car door and got out.

"I'm sorry honey. I was daydreaming about the first time we met, and our first date. You remember that?"

"How could I forget? Who goes to pick plums and take them to homeless shelters on a first date?"

"I told you to dress comfortable and you liked it!"

"I did like it. We had fun. Especially when you fell trying to act like Tarzan. That was so funny. You hit the ground hard. You lost ten cool points for that."

"That's okay. I got them back later that evening when I cooked that roasted duck and almonds with that almond glaze."

"Yeah, I can't lie, that was good. You surprised me. That was a wonderful night."

They were looking at each other full of love and admiration. He decided to seize the opportunity and make her even happier.

"Come on, let's sit up here on the porch. I came home to talk to you about something."

"Is something wrong? Did something happen?" She was full of nervous excitement.

She never knew what to expect from him, and that's just how she liked it.

"Look, we both have been working hard. You've made partner. I'm doing okay at the department. I don't see any reason to keep putting off adding a new addition to our family."

The look she had was like what he was saying wasn't registering.

"What, you want to get a dog baby?"

The levity in her question was to be expected. Especially with how adamant he'd been about not being ready to have kids.

"No, I don't want a dog. I think we should have a baby!"

"Don't be playing Leroy, unless you're trying to stay at your momma's for the next month!"

"Well, you know I'm not trying to do that, so I guess I'm serious. It's just, life is too short to be worried about the perfect time. I already have a perfect woman, what else do I need?"

Her stomach was doing flips for a few reasons. First off, she was elated. This had been a long time in coming. Then she was relieved. She had stopped taking her birth control a couple months ago, and now she wouldn't have to tell him. And the third and final reason was, she was already pregnant and had been dreading the day she had to tell him.

"Hold that thought baby, let me get the phone." She dashed in the house. "Baby, it's Mac!"

When Roy got the phone he knew immediately something was wrong. Mac got right to the point.

"Roy, I need to talk to you. It's important, but I'd rather do it face to face!"

"Alright Lieu, I'm on my way back to the…"

"No, stay there, I'm coming over. Tell Susan to have some of that lemonade for me!"

"You got it. Is everything alright?"

"Yeah, I'll see you in a minute!"

Roy didn't know what to make of Mac's erratic behavior, and the look on his face alerted Susan to the fact something wasn't right.

"Baby, what's wrong?"

"Nothing honey. I was just thinking about something. Will you make some lemonade? Mac's on his way over."

"Is everything alright baby? Is Mac okay?"

She knew it was unusual for Mac to come by during work hours, so she decided to wait for a better time to talk about her being pregnant. Whatever was going on had to be important because Roy tried to never bring his work home. He liked to keep his home life and work separate.

He didn't even hang out with the guys he worked with. The fact that Susan still didn't like police played a major role. She has always asserted that the police force was akin to every other gang in America, they just operated under the guise of the law. She truly hated the fact that Roy had bought into that veneer of brotherhood. She loved her man though. She just prayed that he would see through the facade before he ended up getting hurt or even worse, killed. And the fact that she was a defense attorney with one of the most prominent firms in Detroit didn't sit well with the department.

When Mac came through the door Roy couldn't exactly tell by just looking at him if something was wrong but as he began to speak it became apparent.

"Roy, there has been a development in the Scot case!" Roy stopped him by holding up his hand.

"Susan, I'm using your office! Bring Mac some of that lemonade please.

Alright Lieu, what's up?" Roy was closing the door to the office.

"I went out to the victim's residence and you won't believe what I stumbled on!" He began to recount what he had found.

Roy listened intently. He knew all of it disturbed Mac. He and Mac had investigated some ghastly crimes, but somehow this affected him differently this time.

"Roy, I need you to listen carefully!"

"I'm with you Mac, shoot!"

"We need to bury this case!" He was looking at Roy with unwavering eyes.

"Hold on, what do you mean *bury*?" The earnestness of what Mac said had Roy perplexed. He couldn't believe what he was hearing.

"Exactly what I said, *bury*. Allow to go cold. Throw in Lake Erie. I don't care what happens to it. It just needs to go away!"

As Mac was talking, Roy's life flashed before his eyes. His career was over, his marriage may survive, but he would never be able to do what he loved to do again. He may even go to jail for obstruction.

"Mac, have you lost your mind? I'm gonna act like I didn't hear any of that!"

"I don't care if you put earplugs in, the fact still remains Roy. That was someone's baby. You didn't have to see the little faces on those kids. I've never seen anything so sick in my life. I know what you're going to say, save it! Don't talk to me about justice. What about justice for them?"

Roy knew that even though he would try and sway Mac's decision, it would be useless. Mac was implacable, but nevertheless he still had to try.

"We still have a job to do, as banal as that may sound. This is what we signed up for. Don't do this Mac!" Roy struck a nerve.

"Let me tell you something. I didn't sign up for that. I signed up to protect and serve those who can't protect themselves!"

"Mac, you're gonna retire soon, I'm not. I do this to make a difference just like you. If we did that, we wouldn't be any better than the person who killed him. We would be taking the law into our own hands. We would become judge, jury, and executioner!"

"Come on, we've been friends for how long now? I know you. So don't act like you're that naive. Your wife's a defense attorney for crying out loud. She puts scum back on the street every day. Don't get me wrong. I still love her, but don't give me that integrity bullshit!"

"Damn Mac, don't do this to me!" Roy was thinking to himself and shaking his head.

"Look Roy, you don't have to do anything. Just have my back if questions are asked, I'll take care of the rest. Cases go unsolved all the time. No one will suspect anything, but if you start to have doubts and need an incentive, go look at my report!"

"Mac, you're my friend, but don't ever ask me to do this again. And as bad as I hate to admit it, much to my chagrin, I agree with you."

"You got it. Thanks man." Mac said with a sigh of relief.

If he hadn't convinced Roy he had already made it up in his mind to do whatever it takes to make this case disappear.

"Now, since we have that out of the way. What do you have on the Parker case? Did you and Rivers come up with a workable motive?"

"We went over to the scene and put our heads together. We were gonna get together with you and go over our findings. So how do you want to handle it?"

"That's fine, we can still do that. After I receive his criminal profile and whatever else you guys have. I'll ensure Rivers that we're gonna introduce his findings into our investigative strategy. Since he's on lone he shouldn't be a problem or have to worry about him snooping around.

"Trust me Roy, it shouldn't be a problem making this disappear. I have a few friends in the right places that can get forgetful."

Roy began to wonder if this was the first time Mac had ever done this. It was just too easy for him. He questioned if he really knew Mac at all.

"Mac, let me ask you something. What if I had said no?"

"Then I would've had to kill you." There was no grin or smirk. The weightiness of his words struck a chord with Roy. "Let's just say, I never doubted your loyalties." He smiled. "Come on Roy, lighten up, I was just joking!" Roy wasn't so sure. Mac pat him on the back as they left the office.

When they got to the precinct Rivers was already there at Mac's desk using the phone. He saw Mac and Roy enter so he finished his call and waited for them to get to Mac's desk. Looking at Mac's face it looked as if it had a scowl. Rivers wondered why.

"Agent Rivers, can I get you anything else?"

Rivers had a confused look on his face. Roy was trying not to laugh.

"What do you mean?

"I see you've made yourself comfortable. You're on my phone and have your papers all over my desk. I was just wondering if I could be of further use?"

"Sorry about that Mac, I was just going over my hypothesis." He was gathering his things trying to get out of the way.

"So let's have it!" Mac said as he took his seat.

"From what we gathered from both crime scenes, this perp is an anger-retaliatory killer who was in and out of the scene in a matter of minutes. Very efficient and effective.

Mac looked at Roy with a puzzled look on his face.

"Rivers, I think maybe you should elaborate for us. I think you may have lost Mac." Roy had heard a lot of this already, so it was more for Mac's benefit than his.

"Well, an anger-retaliatory killer is an individual who kills out of anger, and or in retaliation for some past transgression. A lot of the time it's not premeditated, mostly impulsive. They don't have to know the victim. They could've observed the victim committing and unacceptable act or anything they may deem offensive."

He had Mac's full attention. He hung onto every word. This is what he did. This is what he knew. You could tell this is what he lived for. He was prepared for the next question before Mac even asked it.

"So which is it, anger or retaliation?"

"I would have to say both cases, though similar, reflect escalating anger and violence."

Roy was looking at Mac again.

"Lieu, what are you thinking?"

"To tell the truth Roy, I felt it was anger that may have fueled this individual. That's why there was no workable motive and the more I think about it Roy, the more I think maybe you were right!"

"Right about what?"

"It's nothing, just a hunch." Roy knew not to dig any deeper. He knew in due time Mac would let him in on whatever it was.

CHAPTER 24

Making his way through the party Nipsey heard someone calling his name. Even with the hypnotic beat of the strobe lights it was still too dark to make out who the person was until he was right up on him.

"Deon! Man, what's up? Long time, no see!"

"Damn! Look what the cat drug in, my little brother! Aw man, come here! What's up Nipsey? How have you been?"

Nipsey was excited to see someone he really considered family. He had been knowing Deon all his life.

"How's grandma? I've been busy so I haven't been to see her in a few weeks."

"She's still grandma. How's your family?"

"Everybody's good."

"Damn, I see you been eating your Wheaties!"

"Yeah, I've been drinking a lot of milk too. It don't look like you're missing any meals, and it looks like you getting a little money too!" Nipsey took notice of his jewels and his clothes.

"Yeah, I'm eating a little bit." The double entendre wasn't lost on Nipsey .

"Why didn't Chicken tell me you were staying back over this way? What's up with you?"

Deon knew his situation. He and his family used to live below grandma for as long as Nipsey could remember. He had two brothers and two sisters. They were pretty much an extended family.

Grandma and Deon's mom, Mrs. Godwin, were like sisters, with grandma being the eldest. Anytime Nipsey stayed over to grandma's, Deon and Nipsey were inseparable. Even when they fought they still remained friends, and they did fight. Together and each other.

Nipsey hadn't seen them since they moved. After Deon's older sister died from pneumonia and his brother Dewight got killed, they moved. Too much tragedy had struck their family. As much as Mrs. Godwin wanted to stay, she couldn't. She wanted a new start. So with the money she had been saving all the years working as a nurse, she did just that and bought a house. But that didn't change the fact that they would always be family.

"So, do you live over this way?" Nipsey asked, trying to catch up.

"You know, after we moved I couldn't stay away. I don't live over here, but I stay over here. This is my hood." Deon had his arms outstretched for emphasis.

Out of nowhere, Angel ran up and punched Deon.

"Boy, what's up? Oh, you wasn't gonna come and find your girl?"

"Come on, you know better than that! Don't every time I come through I come find you?"

"Okay, I was just checking!" She put her arm around Nipsey's shoulders.

"You see who I got with me? Kissing him on the cheek.

"Angel, get off me. You know you reek of weed!"

"Well, that's good. Maybe you'll get a contact and relax!"

Deon was laughing at Nipsey. He knew Angel was high. He had saw her smoking with her girls.

"Angel, let me holla' at my dog!" He was kissing her on the cheek.

"Alright. I know when I'm not wanted." She rolled her eyes and walked off.

"Come on Nipsey, let's catch a corner. We have some catching up to do."

Before they could make it five feet a dude Nipsey didn't know came over and whispered something in Deon's ear. He abruptly stopped and gestured towards the door to two guys who appeared to be watching his every move.

"Nipsey, get my number from your sister. I have something to handle. We need to catch up though. If you need anything you better not hesitate to ask. Oh yeah, you know you don't ever have to pay for anything in here, right?"

"I do now." He gave Nipsey a wink.

Watching him leave Nipsey saw three dudes fall in step behind him out of nowhere. Before he had time to process his interaction with Deon and what he saw Sonya stepped in his path with a brilliant smile.

"Hey baby, I know you're gonna dance with me?" She was pulling him off to the side.

He leaned against the wall while Sonya danced on him. She began gyrating her hips in a seductive manner, which had him intoxicated. She knew he was under her spell. The effect she was having on him was evident by the hardness in his pants. She reveled in the fact.

The next morning Nipsey was up before the sun for his run. He couldn't help but feel that this would always be his favorite time of day. It always allowed him to reflect and put things in perspective. This morning was no different.

As his mind became in tune with his body, his run became effortless. His mind became lucid. He began to think of how much he missed everyone around there and the love he felt since he had been back in the neighborhood. It was home and it felt like it. He thought about moving in with grandma. He knew he could and Angel wanted him to, but he didn't want to become a burden. He knew he could get a job to help out but then he would have to put up with Lou. There was no way he could stay under the same roof as him without killing him or at least breaking something.

Nipsey's train of thought went to Chris and ultimately what he was going to do to him. When he realized this would be something he had to plan, for some reason he became enamored with the ideal. He felt like his skin was tingling.

Subconsciously he had already began to formulate a plan. As he navigated his way through the neighborhood he made his way around to Hurlbut St. where the Johnson's corner store was located across from the joint Chris was selling out of. He committed everything he saw to memory. He knew he had to be patient and wait for the right time to present itself, and not allow his emotions to dictate his actions.

By the time he made it back everyone was up. Sonya and Angel were cooking breakfast and talking like they've known each other for years.

After everyone ate they sat around and talked. Nipsey decided he didn't want to prolong the inevitable and prepared to head back.

"Well sis, I really enjoyed myself."

"Me too Angel." Sonya agreed with him.

"When you coming back baby?" Grandma asked.

"Can I stay next weekend grandma?"

"Well baby, maybe not next week. You got to give me time to miss you again, and since you don't know the answer to that question I think you may have hit your big ol' head so you may need to rest!"

He gave her a hug and a kiss. Sonya did the same.

"It was nice meeting you grandma. I'm gonna come visit you, okay? So we can sit down and watch your husband."

Sonya was talking about Matlock. Grandma called him her white husband. She never missed an episode.

"Okay, sweetheart. It was nice to meet you too. You make sure you do that."

"It was good to see you, Nipsey. You know we love you and miss you." Angel was getting sad. Almost to the point of tears as she spoke. She hugged him tight.

"Alright sis, chill out with all that. You act like you're never gonna see me again. You'll see me more often now, okay?"

"I better!"
"You will, I promise."
"Bye, Angel. I love you girl. I'll call you!"
"Alright Sonya, Take care of him!"
"I will."

When Sonya dropped Nipsey off, the first person he saw was Sister Alicia.

"Nipsey, welcome back!"

"Thank you, Sister."

"How was your weekend, young man?"

"It was great!"

The way she was looking at him made him feel like she knew everything he had done. He felt uncomfortable.

Even though he liked being with his family this place was his fortress of solitude. He missed it while he was gone. Maybe it was the peace and tranquility that engulfed him.

"Hey Nip!" Samuel was coming up the hall with a huge smile on his face.

"Go ahead Nipsey, and after you get settled in come see me!"

"Okay, Sister." He was thankful for the intrusion, and Samuel knew it because as he turned to greet Samuel, his facial expression said it all.

"Samuel, how nice it is to see you. I hear you had and interesting weekend?"

"Shit! I should've kept walking." Samuel was kicking himself.

"Yes Sister, I had a nice weekend."

"Well good, let's go to my office and talk about it!" Before he could respond she turned and walked off.

To his annoyance he followed as if on cue. Nipsey silently hunched his shoulders and smiled. As if she had eyes in the back of her head she said. "I'm looking forward to seeing you shortly, Nipsey. So try not to go too far dear!"

In a mockingly fashion Samuel silently put his hand over his mouth to mute his laughter and tease Nipsey.

"So Samuel, I hear you went fishing this weekend?"

"Yeah, we went to St. Clair Shores. Do you know where that is?"

"Yes, I'm a little familiar. If I'm not mistaken, it's close to Warren, Michigan, right?"

"Yeah, that's it." The tone in his voice revealed his annoyance. She paid it no mind.

"So how was it? Catch many fish?"

"No, not really. We talked a lot."

"You make it sound unfortunate. That was good, right?"

"I guess."

"Well, maybe I should have asked if you made any progress as far as your differences are concerned?"

"I guess. I think we're in a good place right now." He was wondering where all of this was leading. She already knew how his relationship with his parents had progressed. He's known her long enough to know there was an ulterior motive.

"So, who all went?"

"Just me and my dad."

"So, did you have a discussion about returning home and what would happen if you did?"

"Yes, ma'am. I'm ready to go. I'll stay for awhile and go to college in the fall."

"So, are you planning to quit smoking before you begin class?"

There it was. Her motive. She struck him dumbfounded. He had no idea she had known about his smoking.

"Look son, the signs are all too clear. No one told me. That guilty look on your face just confirmed my suspicions!"

He smiled. He liked the way she just played him. He had to admit it was pretty smooth. He couldn't lie, so he caved.

"I had planned on it. I don't smoke a lot, just every once in a while when I'm feeling a little stressed."

"My son, you're a smart young man. I believe in your capabilities and your drive. You have showed me so much since you've been here. Now, I don't condone anything that defiles the temple. The spirit of God will not and can not reside in an unclean vessel. Don't hinder your blessings my son.

"Plus, how can you reach your full potential if you're not in control of all you faculties?"

"This is what I get for coming in here high and thinking no one would know it!" He scolded himself.

He'd rather get cursed out by Sabrina than sit there. This was torture for him. He felt like she knew he was high now and was trying to talk to him until it was gone.

"When you came here you were looking for acceptance. You felt alienated. You wanted to be loved for who you were and to be given a chance. To show that you were more than some misguided teenager.

Now that you have that chance, don't squander it!"

"I won't, Sister. I really am focused on my future. I really do understand." "So, how's Sabrina doing?" She asked changing the subject.

The light in his eyes became bright as they always did when anyone mentioned her name.

"She's fine. She was accepted at Harvard Law. We're gonna go together."

"That's wonderful, Samuel!"

"The only thing I'm worried about Sister is us growing apart. College is way different than being here. I don't know. Maybe I'm scared she will meet someone"

"All of us have insecurities my son, but when you rest in the Lord, all things work together for good for those who love God."

"I guess you're right Sister. If it's meant to be, it will be."

"That's right son. Worry about what's important in your life and let God worry about the rest."

"I guess that goes back to what you always tell us. Let go and let God!"

"See, I knew you've been listening. Now, let's pray my words take root like in the parable of the sower. I've enjoyed your company Samuel. Keep up the good work. Remember, I'm not here to judge, but to help guide you in the right direction. Our doors are always open for all of you!"

"Thank you, Sister."

"Have a good day, Samuel."

"Nipseysan, quiet your spirit. Feel the energy all around you. Allow your Chi to flow freely." Nipsey's sensei was speaking while Nipsey sat on the floor blindfolded. "Listen my son; anticipate, react, do not hesitate. In a moment's notice anything can transpire!" He swung in a chopping motion and caught Nipsey on the side of the head. "You not focused Nipseysan!"

"I'm sorry sensei!"

"Sorry not good. Sorry cannot protect you or save life!"

Nipsey could hear the frustration in his sensei's voice. He was caught slipping. He had become almost entranced listening to his voice.

"Kung Fu is a way of life Nipseysan. It can be anything. It means to master one's actions. It's goal is to attain enlightenment and you only attain enlightenment when you have mastered your life, and everything in it. It is possible my son." His words were smooth with no variation in his tone, hypnotic. "Calm can be your friend or your enemy. Friend because you're controlled, and devoid of emotion. Enemy because it can be disguised to make you feel complacent!" He swung a second time in the same fashion.

Nipsey heard the slight movement of his clothing and the distinctive sound of a foot pivoting on the floor. He anticipated the move by leaning back all the way to the floor still in his seated position. He reacted by using his leg to block the blow and he didn't hesitate when he countered with a kick to the midsection of his sensei that missed. His sensei was too swift. Nipsey sat back up again with his legs crossed.

"Nipseysan, better. But, you lack intensity and quickness. When striking from a seated position you must use more force and speed to be effective. Don't be so quick to showcase what you know. Most of the time a good defense is your best offense. Up!" Nipsey sprung to his feet. He took a defensive stance.

Still blindfolded, Nipsey turned his head slightly to best pick up any sound or movement. His sensei lunged forward, but Nipsey was ready. He barely moved. He pivoted left and used sensei's momentum against him by slightly pushing him with his left hand on the back of his left shoulder. Allowing his Chi to redirect his anxious energy to propel sensei right on past.

Sensei was moved by how skilled Nipsey had become. The push was light as a feather. If sensei hadn't taught him he wouldn't have detected the light touch. He wouldn't even had known what had happened.

As Nipsey rounded the corner to his room, he was not in the least surprised to see Sister Alicia coming up the hall, as if she strategically timed his return to intercept him.

"Nipsey, what a coincidence. It's amazing how the Father places you in the right place at the right time. Just so you can receive whatever it is he feels necessary for you to have!"

She had caught him at the right time. He was always more receptive after an intense training.

"Nipsey, you know if and when we discuss anything it goes no further than these walls?" She was gesturing towards the wall with both hands.

"Yes sister, I understand, but I already know that."

"I'm glad because you know a detective came by while you were away!

Do you have any idea why?"

"No, ma'am." They sat down on a bench in the hall.

He knew instinctively that this conversation would be serious even before the first words came out of her mouth. He was prepared to listen.

"My child, you're leaving here soon. You may come here for any type of help, but I want you to always remember, every decision you make should have a purpose." He was absorbing every word she spoke.

"How do I know if my purpose is right?"

"I would pray that purpose would be to serve God. He bestowed His grace and mercy upon you, so everything you do should glorify Him!"

"What if it doesn't seem right to anyone else?"

"What you do my son is between you and the Father. He alone knows your heart and your true intentions. It's for him alone to judge, not man. I know every decision you make won't be the right one or even an easy one, but whenever you come to that fork in the road lean not to thine own understanding. There's a helper with you always."

He loved the way she spoke in a way that always seemed to comfort him and reassure him at the same time.

"Nipsey, I have something to attend to. It's always a pleasure speaking with you. I'll talk to you soon."

"Thank you, Sister."

"May God be with you my son."

"And also with you Sister."

CHAPTER 25

Sue and Lou were downstairs in grandma's house. No one had lived down there since the Godwin's had moved. They would sneak down there to smoke crack and whatever else they chose to do. Lou was peeping out the window through the blinds. Sue was sitting on the couch naked.

"Sue, put your damn clothes on. Ain't nothing crawling on you!" He was whispering.

"It is I'm telling you, I feel them. They're little bugs!" She was rubbing and looking at her arms and legs.

"How you know its little bugs if you can't see them?"

"I don't have to see them, I feel them!"

"Just hit that shit and pass it. You fucking up my high wit that looking for bugs and shit!" She passed him the stem.

He was so paranoid he couldn't stop peeping out the window long enough to hit it.

"Are you sure you got the right key while you was giving him head?" He passed the stem back.

"Come on daddy, you know I got that fire head. I had time to take it off the ring and everything!"

"That's my girl. Now pass that stem back so we can go. And get off that damn floor. Ain't shit down there!"

By the time they got through getting high it was already late in the evening. When they made it around to CJ's stash spot they went around to the back door. Lou broke the window and helped Sue up through it. Then he climbed in behind her. He was moving fast.

"Come on Sue, we ain't got all night!" It was pitch black. She couldn't see so she was moving slow. "What room is it?" He was whispering.

His heart felt like it was about to come out of his chest. He knew if they got caught, they were dead.

"It's upstairs on the left." She was next to him now.

When they entered the room everything was just as Sue had described it. The mattress was on the floor. A throw rug was on the floor next to it. There were dingy curtains hung on the windows. The dresser had a mirror attached to the back with a candle on it and a few miscellaneous items scattered atop.

"You sure it's under that rug?"

She sucked her teeth and didn't answer. She lifted the rug and began to remove the floor slats. When she was done a safe was exposed. Much to Lou's delight.

"Here, let me try the key you stole!" He inserted the key into the lock and turned it once.

"Click."

Before he even opened it Sue was bouncing around. That click was all she needed to hear.

"See daddy, I told you!" She was popping her collar and gloating.

"Yeah baby, you did good. Let's get this shit and get out of here!"

He pulled a bag out of his pocket and began to empty the safe. After they removed everything from the safe, they placed everything back as they found it.

Back at the house Lou was salivating at the four and a half ounces of cocaine. They had a digital scale and after they counted all the cash it totaled to seventy thousand dollars.

"Damn baby, you see what we got?"

"Yeah daddy, I did good, huh?"

He got up and picked her up and swung her around. For her to see Lou as happy as he was made it all worthwhile. She loved Lou and would do anything for him, even if it meant putting her life at stake.

Their elation only lasted a short time because now Lou was scared. They had just stolen from some real killers.

"Lou, nobody saw us. Stop looking out that window before someone see you peeping!"

"Shut up. Put something on that stem. I'm trying to go to the moon!"

"Alright daddy. Give me something to break some off with. This shit hard!"

"Find a nail or something," he was saying while looking around on the floor. "Here you go baby. Use this brick and nail!" He had a loose brick from the wall and a nail.

"Damn daddy, this shit stank!" She was covering her nose as she tried to break some off.

"Let me see baby. You taking too long!"

When he saw the crystallized flakes and realized it was in powder form he stopped breaking it off.

"Shit! This shit is powder. I can't smoke this. We got to find someone to cook this shit up for us. Then we gonna party. Look, you stay down here. I'm gonna go upstairs and take care of something. Then we gonna bounce. First, let's hit a few lines though!"

After they hit a few lines he darted upstairs. The first thing he did was go sit on the toilet. When he got done he took grandma some money.

"Here momma, take this!" He was handing her five thousand dollars.

"Now son, what you done went and did? Where you get that money from?"

"Momma, I ain't done nothing. Just take it and give Angel this!"

It was another five thousand.

"Now son, I don't know what you done went and did, but Lord knows I don't want nothing to happen to me and my grandbaby over your mess. So you just go on and take that mess on out of here!"

"Damn, momma!" He snatched the money and headed to Angel's room.

She wasn't there so he left it on her stereo. As he began to leave grandma stopped him.

"Look here son. For the love of money is the root of all kinds of evil. If you took that kind of money from somebody, you're gonna bring all kinds of evil down on this house. You want something to happen to your old momma and daughter?"

"Momma, I ain't did nothing. You trippin'!"

"Son, I love you. You need to get right with the Lord before it's too late!"

"I gotta go momma. I love you!"

He stormed out the house. Grandma's spirit was grieved. She felt uneasy in her heart of hearts. She knew this was gonna end badly for someone. She prayed it wouldn't be her son or Angel.

Lou and Sue had parked on Pennsylvania. It was the next street over so no one would know they had been there. The last thing he wanted to do was get his momma or daughter involved. They left out the back and cut through the alley, then through someone's backyard, which was the same way they came.

When they were out of the neighborhood, Lou began to feel a little more at ease and confident that they had got away.

"Sue, we did it. We out this muthafucka. We ain't going back either. When we get to Eight Mile Road, we gonna get a room. You can call your girl Diane to bring her shit so she can cook this shit up!"

When Sue called Diane she was more than willing to cook up the dope. There was no way she would've turned them down, especially since she was getting paid. She was a hustler. If there was some money to be gotten, she wanted it.

"Hurry up and get here. We'll pay for your cab, but don't tell no one where you're going!"

Sue didn't want to take any chances of anyone from the hood finding out where they were.

"Okay girl, I'm on my way. I have to stop and get some B-12, I got everything else."

"Alright, we'll see you when you get here."

The call had went exactly how Sue hoped it would. Now the only thing left to do was wait. While they waited they ordered some porn and snorted some more.

"Daddy, hurry up and come out that bathroom so I can get some of that dick. You know this shit got me horny as hell!"

"Alright, baby. You know that powder make me have to use the bathroom!"

"Well hurry up before Di get here!" She was sweating while taking off her clothes.

When she was completely naked she laid back on the bed and began to masturbate.

"Damn baby, hurry up. I'm starting without you. This pussy good and wet too!"

Lou loved when she teased him. He loved her sex game too. He had never met someone so uninhibited in his life. Even though he tried not to show it, he was hooked. She knew she had him though. She just pretended she didn't know.

By the time he came out of the bathroom she was already working on her second orgasm. The first thing Lou did when he saw her lying there with her legs agape, was proceed to bury his face between her thighs. She loved when he did that. She could've sworn he had the fastest tongue on the eastside. She was right too, because before she knew it he had made her orgasm two more times.

"Damn daddy, hold on, stop for a minute!" She was pushing his head back, to no avail.

It was too late, he was devouring her.

"Oh my God! Baby, baby, please!" She was shaking uncontrollably.

He was in beast mode. Sucking on her clitoris and sticking his finger in her anus. Almost like magic he was on top of her penetrating her. She was so gone she couldn't remember when he started.

"Fuck me, daddy! Here, put both my legs up on your shoulders. Yeah, like that. Faster daddy, faster. Umm, that's it!"

"You like that baby?" He was in overdrive, filling her to capacity.

"Yeah, daddy. I love it. I love you. Umm... Give it to me daddy!"

He loved the way she talked. It drove him mad, and she loved the way he continuously stroked her and played with her clitoris at the same time.

"Here daddy, let me turn over. Fuck me from the back. Hard baby. Spank my ass daddy. Yeah, that's it!" He was impaling her relentlessly. Spank that ass daddy. Yeah, that's it. Harder daddy!" She was driving him crazy with her demands.

"Boom, Boom, Boom." He almost fell on the floor.

His heart felt like it was about to explode. It was a mixture of the cocaine and the sudden banging on the door. He grabbed his .38 automatic out of his bag and got behind the door. He motioned her to get on the floor.

"Damn daddy, why you stop like that? You know that's that bitch, Di. You could've waited till I came again. I hate when you get like that!"

"Shut up and get the door. Make sure she by herself too!" She was grumbling as she put on her panties and bra.

She peered out the window and yanked it open.

"Damn, bitch! Why you banging on the door like The Big Four?"

"Hey, bitch. All that damn noise you were making I didn't think you could hear me!" Lou made no attempts to conceal himself.

When she got all the way in the room, he startled her when she closed the door. He hadn't moved from behind it.

"Damn Lou, what the fuck? Put that shit up before you hurt somebody with that shit!" The smile she gave him told him she wasn't talking about the gun.

Sue picked up on it as well.

"Heel, bitch. Go have a seat!" She gave Lou his pants and took the gun. "You didn't tell no one you were coming here, did you?" They were looking her in the face for any signs of deception. They saw none.

"Y'all don't have to worry about that. I told y'all I wouldn't. Y'all need to chill the fuck out!"

She decided to go ahead and get started before they pissed her off.

When she finished cooking the dope in the microwave they had five and a half round cookie shaped pieces that were hard as stone.

"Beautiful. Just beautiful!" Lou was saying on his way to the bathroom.

"Let 'em dry for a while. This gonna be that fire! I can't wait to try it. I brought me some weed too!" Diane was appreciating her work.

She felt like an artist that had just completed a masterpiece.

"Where y'all get all that dope from?"

"We bought it. You know I got this white boy I be tricking with." She lowered her voice like she didn't want Lou to hear.

"For real girl? He must really like you."

"You know I be putting this pussy on him. Plus, when I swallow that dick he can't take it. He be talking about *I ain't never going home*. I hit his safe the other day and he had all this money. You know I got him!" They started slapping high five.

"Come on, let's get high!" Lou said coming out the bathroom.

"I know you're gonna take care of me, ain't you Lou?"

"Say no more, I got you." He pulled out a wad of cash and her eyes got wide as saucers.

"Damn Lou, you rollin', ain't you?" She was taking the two thousand dollar bills he was handing her.

He smiled with an inflated ego. When he gave her one of the cookies she thought he was joking.

"All this is mine Lou?" She was looking at Sue at the same time.

"Yeah, Rodger used to look out for me. So, yeah." Sue added, "Yeah girl. That's also so you will forget you ever saw any of this. He may go to the police!" Sue was selling her story.

"What you talking about girl? What money? Sue who?"

"That's what I'm talking about." Lou was satisfied with her response.

"Thanks Di," Sue said while putting a piece of crack on her stem.

When CJ came out of his joint he was furious. He couldn't recall when the last time he had seen his key. He had a sickening feeling something wasn't right.

"Meka, look in the console and see if my key in there!"

Meka had been waiting in the car still feeling the effects of a long night of drinking and smoking at the club with CJ. Yet and still CJ had her up at the crack of dawn.

"I don't see it."

"Shit! Where the fuck is my key? Come in here and help me look for it!"

"Aw, babe. I don't want to go in that piece of shit. It stank in there!" She said with pleading eyes.

"It's a joint, what the fuck you expect? Come on, I can't find the key to my safe."

When she heard *safe*, she knew it would behoove her to just do like he said.

The house was musky, not as bad as she expected, but musky all the same. She covered her nose as she looked around. She had never been in there, and she was glad of it. The house was sparsely furnished with a piece of couch and coffee table in the living room. The walls were soiled with only God knows what. The kitchen had a microwave, a table, a stove and a few dishes.

As she ascended the stairs she heard CJ cursing. When she entered the room, he was pulling back a rug. That's when she saw the safe after he removed the slats for the first time. She was in awe, and lying there next to it was a key.

"Oh shit! Here it go." His stomach was churning. "How in the fuck it get under here?" He quickly opened the safe.

When he looked inside it was as if the air was sucked from his lungs. He sat down on the floor, staring into space.

"What's up, babe?" Meka knew that look all too well.

Something wasn't right. She treaded lightly. She knew CJ's temper could go from zero to a hundred in zero point two seconds.

"It's all gone. Everything's gone!" Meka didn't speak, she just watched. "Who the fuck got my shit? Fuck! Fuck! Fuck!" He was screaming now.

He was pacing back and forth talking to himself. He was so mad he couldn't think straight.

"How much was it, babe?"

"About a big boy and seventy thousand. Fuck! Fuck! How the fuck I let this happen?"

"Did you leave your key somewhere baby?"

"Come on, let's go!" He never answered her.

He knew he could've left it any number of places When he gets high, he gets reckless. He mentally tried to trace his steps.

"You drive, I need to think!" He was getting in on the passenger side. "Somebody gonna pay for this shit. Shoot me over to the joint on Hurlbut, and I'll talk to you later!"

She knew until he got to the bottom of this things would be tense. She was happy to drop him off. When he got there, people were in and out.

"Yo! Everybody in the house, now. Tell them bitches to bounce. Tony, come here!"

It had never been that quiet in there before. By the tone in his voice everyone knew he meant business.

"Yo cuz, I need you to hit the street and see if anybody has come into some work or spending money. People that ain't normally getting money!" Tony was puzzled.

"Why, what's up?"

"Somebody hit the stash spot."

"You bullshitting! When?"

"I don't fucking know! Either last night or early this morning. They got the bread I was supposed to hit Big Man off with."

"Get the fuck outta here! I thought you were gonna hit him off last night?"

"I know, I know. I got fucked up and kicked it with Meka. That's why I'm up so early. I was gonna hit him off this morning."

"Do he know?"

"Hell no! He ain't gonna know either. We gonna handle this shit. You know how he is!"

"Alright, I got you. I'll holla at you later." Tony had heard enough.

"Look Green Eyes, if you find out anything, get at me. Don't do nothing. Just get at me!"

"Alright cuz, I got you."

"For real. Don't do nothing. Just get at me. We gonna make an example out of these muthafuckas!"

"Damn cuz, I'm not gonna do nothing. Just chill, I got you."

If CJ knew he could trust anybody, it was his cousin Tony. Even though Tony was a live wire he was embedded in the streets. He was respected by everyone. If he was on your team, he was loyal.

Major dudes wanted him on their team. Dudes that were getting way more money than CJ. But family meant everything to him, and the one thing everyone knew about Tony is he was a killer. If you crossed anyone he loved, those green eyes would be the last thing you saw. People were misled by his baby face and good looks and he used that to his advantage. He would put them at ease with his charm and good looks. If he was coming to kill you, you would never know it because he came with a smile.

"Y'all check this out." CJ was addressing everyone that was left. "I want everybody to be on their toes. If y'all see or hear anything out of the ordinary, handle it. Nobody come with any shorts. Look, I'm gonna pay y'all but y'all got to give me a few extra days. Something came up. I got y'all though, and I'm gonna throw y'all something extra but I need all four of y'all to buckle down and get this money.

"Chris and Cotton, y'all gonna work this joint and Norm, you and Black go over to the one on Mt. Elliot St. How much y'all got right now?" They all had a total of seven thousand. "Shit!" he thought to himself.

He was gonna have to go into his personal stash to cover the four birds he was fronted.

"Alright, who got the keys to the whip?" Chris gave him the keys. "When y'all get through with what y'all got left, holla at me. I'll hit y'all off with something else."

The only way CJ would be able to get all the money he owed was to take the seven thousand and the thirty thousand in his personal stash and get some more work. The only problem was, he couldn't go to Big Man without his sixty thousand. So he needed to find someone else to cop from without him knowing. If he found out he would think that CJ was taking his money and trying to flip it without him knowing it.

Big Man was so well respected. It was gonna be hard to keep anything from him. He was known throughout the city by most of the hustlers but they only knew him by *Big Man*. His government was well guarded because even though he was young he made the right connections and had a few business ventures. He made it a point to keep his illegal business away from his legal business.

CHAPTER 26

When Meka made it to Trina's house she was relieved and ready to relax. Being around CJ when something has happened was stressful. To be able to sit back and smoke some weed with her girl was a welcomed relief.

Trina was sitting on her porch talking to Wade and Dee Dee. She knew them because they went to Kettering High School together. She didn't want to be chillin' with them today, especially with CJ on the warpath. That's all she needed was for him to ride past or for Tony to come by and see her chillin'.

When Trina saw her pull up she walked down to the curb.

"Hey, girl. What you doing?"

"I just came by to kick it for a while. Hey, Wade. Hey, Dee Dee. Girl, CJ fixin' to be on the warpath. You got any L's?"

"We just rolled the last one."

"Well, you know I wanna stay for a while, but you know I can't get caught chillin' and smoking with them."

"I know what you mean girl. Let me go lock my door and we can ride and get some L's. I'll just tell them I'll talk to them later." Trina knew how Tony and CJ was so Meka didn't get no argument from her.

"Hey y'all, Imma ride with my girl. Imma talk to y'all later. Wade, let me get some of that Christmas Tree so I can smoke with Meka!"

"Naw Rina, I'm good. Imma pass on that. She won't be putting them soup coolers on none of this shit here!"

She looked him straight in his eyes with a seductive look, put her hands on her hips and the next words that fell out of her mouth almost knocked him over.

"See. That's why your ass ain't never gonna get none of this pussy. Your ass too cheap!"

"Oh shit!" Dee Dee was clowning him laughing hysterically.

"Oh yeah, that's how you're coming Meka? You know I was just playing!" He was reaching inside his underwear to get a sack of weed.

He handed her some lime green buds. They had to be some of the prettiest buds she had ever seen. She pinched him on the cheek and ran up the steps to lock her door.

"Thank you, Wade. You so sweet. You still not getting none of this good pussy though!" She giggled and ran down to the car.

"Damn dog, you a sucker. She get you every time!"

"That's okay, I'm wearing her down. You can't talk though fool. I may not be hitting that shit but every duck get you every time. Look how Renee be gripping your grain, and Shannon be hitting them pockets like you a slot machine. Fool, I need to put a sticker across your forehead that say *jackpot,* because your ass be kicking!"

"Aww, why you had to go there? That's cold!"

"I'm just fucking with you. You still my dog!" They gave each other some dap. Then Dee Dee added, "You still a sucker though!"

Wade laughed with him because he knew he was right. He had a weakness for Trina, with her 36-24-36 frame; her full lips, chocolate complexion, and her sassy attitude. He thought she was so beautiful. He had been feeling that way since they were kids.

He knew he was in competition with Tony but he didn't care. She really liked Tony and for the life of him Wade didn't know why. Tony was hardened by his environment, whereas Wade strived to get out. Even though he smoked weed he was going to U of D and was very smart with great potential. He sold weed strictly to pay for his tuition.

When Meka and Trina returned to the house they were still there chillin' and talking.

"Damn, I told y'all fools I'll talk to y'all later. Why y'all still on my porch?"

"Well, it is later and you talking to us now. So, what's up?"

"Please boy, just because you hang around Wade don't make you smart so get the hell off my porch and I'll see y'all later!"

She poked Dee Dee in the head as they went around them into the house.

When they got situated in the house Meka began filling Trina in on what she knew.

"You know that man had me in that joint early this morning looking for some damn key?"

"Key to what?"

"His safe."

Trina's eyes got big.

"Girl, stop playing. He lost his key?"

"Yeah, but we found it under the rug. When he opened it he looked like he wanted to lay down and die. Girl, everything was gone!" Trina choked on some smoke when she heard that.

"Here, pass that while you over there choking and shit. Yeah, everything was gone!"

"Stop it! Girl, somebody gonna die over that. How much they take?"

"Seventy."

Trina choked again.

"Seventy what? Thousand?"

"Yep."

"Get out!"

"Yeah, so until CJ handle his business I can't spend no money."

"That's okay, I got you. If you need anything, just let me know."

"I appreciate that girl, but I'll be alright. You know I still got my rainy day money. That's why every time he gives me money I put some up without him knowing it." They gave each other a high five.

"That's right girl. Don't be no fool. You see what happened to my cousin.

Now look at her ass, staying up in my shit!"

"Oh yeah, that's right. Where is Diane? How she doing?"

"She alright. She didn't come home last night. I don't know where she's at."

"So, is she still holding Rodger down? That's messed up he got all that time. They were trying to rob him!"

"Yeah Meka, but he shot them guys even after they threw his money and jewelry down and tried to run. The court say since they were running away it wasn't self defense, it was murder."

"That's still messed up. I remember seeing a little something about it on the news. What happened to all that money he had?"

"Di used most of it to pay for his lawyer. Then he had a 1 million dollar bond. Whatever was left, Di used to try and live on. She even sold the rest of his drugs, but after he got sentenced no one really trusted her enough to sell her any more. The word on the street was that she was trying to set somebody up to get him out."

"Was she Trina?"

"Bitch, please! She was trying to live and since Rodger had taught her all about the game she tried to get it on for herself. You know how the streets is. When they start talking, everybody listens. It don't even have to be true."

"Damn, I didn't know it was like that. I feel bad for her."

"Yeah, I do too. That's why I let her stay here until she figure something out."

"So, you still messing with Tony, girl?"

"Yeah, but he get on my nerves sometimes, acting all crazy and shit!" "Is he still with Toya?"

"Yeah, but I don't care. As long as he keep my pockets fat, and keep giving me that good dick!"

"Girl, you crazy. Y'all deserve each other."

Trina knew that Meka didn't approve of what she was doing with Tony, especially since Toya was Meka's first cousin. But she always made it a point not to insert herself into Trina's sordid affairs, no matter how scandalous.

She wasn't really in love with Tony, it was more like *in lust*. The relationship was built more out of necessity. To accumulate what she could before she moved on to who she really wanted to be with. Someone who she felt had more promise and who wasn't married to the streets like Tony. Someone who would take her away from all the sex, drugs, and death that plagued Detroit.

CHAPTER 27

The Scot case was going cold fast. Mac couldn't have been happier. Roy on the other hand was conflicted. If there was anything that resembled a lead, Mac would bury it, or he just wouldn't follow up. It was working out just as he'd hoped. He knew Roy was having difficulty with the whole thing.

He felt like the two cases were connected. So to bury one would also mean to bury the other one, unless something broke the case wide open. He wanted more than anything to get justice for the Parkers. Mrs. Parker made it tough. She refused to sit idly by and wait. She vowed to keep her son's murder on everyone's mind. Roy did all he could to keep the case active but their desks were being weighed down with other cases that were being neglected.

"Rivers, I really appreciate all your expertise. Even though the case's at a standstill, what progress we have made will help a great deal." Rivers was packing up his belongings.

His time there was over. He had done all that he could and needed to get back to his headquarters. Mac was subtly pushing him along. Mac believed if he stayed he just may crack the case and he couldn't have that. He had done too much to make it go away.

Rivers felt like these cases weren't getting the attention they deserved, almost like they were being swept under the rug but without any concrete evidence to corroborate his suspicion. That's all it was, suspicion. Even with Mac's investigative practices becoming more and more lackadaisical and less intuitive, there was still nothing he could do.

"I'm sorry I couldn't be of more help, but if I come up with anything pertaining to either case I won't hesitate to pick up the phone."

"Rivers, you've done a great job. You have nothing to be sorry for. We've just exhausted all of our leads for right now, but until something falls into our laps there's nothing we can do." Mac was being sincere.

He had never done anything to hinder an investigation. He hated to see all Rivers' work go in vain.

"Alright Mac, tell Roy I will be taking him up on his offer. He'll know what I'm talking about. It has been a pleasure to work with the both of you. Make sure you guys keep in touch and keep me abreast of your progress."

CHAPTER 28

Angel hadn't been home for a few days. Kenny had been keeping an eye on grandma for the most part, but when he had something to do, Tina took over. They did that when she and Brett wanted to spend some time together. This way grandma was never alone.

Grandma wasted no time telling her about Lou and the money when she came in. When she went to her room and saw the money for herself, her blood instantly began to boil. Just like grandma, she knew nothing good would come out of her having it.

She called Kenny. The tone in her voice alerted him to something being wrong. Before Angel even had the phone on the hook good enough he was coming up the stairs.

"Hey, grandma." He walked over and kissed her on the cheek.

"Hey, baby. How you?"

"I'm good."

"That's good, baby. How's that little girl?" She was referring to his little sister.

"She good grandma."

"Well, make sure you tell her to come see her grandma. I don't know why that child haven't already been to see me. Tell her she better get her tail over here before I have to come looking for her!"

"Hey Angel, what's up?" She was sitting on the couch with the stack of money sitting next to her.

"You seen my daddy?"

"No, why?" She tossed the money at him. "What's this?"

"I don't know. I'm trying to find out. Grandma said he came in here acting all funny with wads of money. I guess since she wouldn't take any of it when he tried to give it to her he left it in my room. I don't want it either, there's no telling who he stole that money from, count it. That's not a little bit of money so he must have a whole bunch, and ain't no telling where he is!"

Kenny didn't know what to say. From the looks on their faces he knew they were worried.

"Damn, Angel! What do you want to do?"

"I don't know. I need to find him and Sue. I know she in it too. Before they get themselves hurt, or we get drug into something that has nothing to do with us. Can you call Greg and see what he can find out?"

Kenny didn't hustle, but a lot of his friends did and Greg was one of them. He didn't work for anyone and everyone knew him. He kept his ear to the street so if anyone could find out anything it would be him.

"I got you, Angel. As soon as I hear something, I'll let you know. Just be careful and don't tell anyone else. And don't spend any of it either!"

"Boy, get out of here. I ain't stupid!"

"Well, I don't know. You know your wig looking kind of busted right now. I just don't want you to go around to Shay's and get it whipped!" "Oh, you funny, huh!" Grandma was amused.

"Yeah baby, he got you. That head is looking kind of nappy in the back!"

"Grandma, don't be saying that!" She got up to go to her room. "Grandma, you know them baby curls. Don't be trying to act funny. Kenny, you know I got you, right? That's okay!"

When Diane finally got home, she had bags from where she had been shopping. She handed Trina two bags.

"Thanks Di. What's these?" Opening the shoe boxes. "Damn girl, you didn't have to do this. These are two hundred dollars!"

"Yes I did. You been looking out for me!" She was walking around in the six inch heels she had gotten for herself.

Then she gave Trina five hundred dollars. Even with what she had spent and what she gave Trina she was still sitting pretty because she had sold almost all the dope she had.

None of this seemed out of the ordinary to Trina. She knew how much of a hustler Diane was so she didn't even think to ask her where she had gotten any of it from.

"I'm gonna go take a bath, cuz. You're welcome! You know since my boo went to prison you been there for me!"

While she was in the bathroom she rolled her a joint and mixed some of the crack she saved just for that purpose. She made sure she turned on the exhaust before she relaxed in the tub while she smoked her *Judy fly*, because if Trina suspected her favorite cousin smoked crack and was smoking it in her bathroom, she would be devastated.

When she finally emerged from the bathroom the distinctive smell of Christmas Tree wafted in her direction.

"Damn, Trina! You wasn't gonna offer me none of that good-good you smoking?"

"Well bitch, if you wasn't so busy acting like yo ass was in a Calgon commercial, you could've had some!"

"You know a bitch can't be walking around with her pocketbook all smelly!"

"Yo, pocketbook. Bitch, please! What you ten years old?"

"Bitch, shut up! You remember how mama used to tell us that when we were little?"

"Yeah, I remember how she used to stay on us about not letting boys touch our pocketbooks. I miss Auntie Ann!" As soon as the words left Trina's lips, she regretted it.

She knew Diane was still taking the death of her mother real hard and the fact that they never caught who hit her head on made it that much harder to find closure.

Whoever it was, they were driving a stolen car being chased by the police. Her mother was driving down a one way street, when the stolen Chevy Nova came careening around the corner going the wrong way and hit the little Peugeot head on. It was engulfed in flames in a matter of minutes. Pinned under the dashboard, the police did everything they could to rescue Ann until they were fought back by the flames.

By the time the fire was extinguished she was already dead. There was nothing anyone could do to bring her back.

That day changed Diane's life dramatically. The one person she knew would always have her back was gone. She compensated by clinging to Rodger who worshiped the ground she walked on. Even though she loved her Rodger, the pain of losing her mother was almost crippling. She began to self-destruct behind the scene.

It started when one of her girlfriends gave her a blunt laced with crack, and she liked it. She liked not having to dwell on the pain. Even with smoking *Judy Flies*, she began learning all she could from Rodger. She had made up her mind that no matter what, if something was to happen and she ended up alone, she would know how to take care of herself.

Rodger never knew she was stealing some of the dope he gave her to stash, and she never took too much where he would miss it. Just enough to get high. She never allowed her smoking to get out of control or that would have been the least of her worries.

Now things were at their worst. Rodger's gone. She's living with her cousin and still smoking, but she had made up her mind. After all the dope she had was gone she was gonna pick up the pieces of her life and move forward. The few thousand she had would be her start.

When Deon received the call from Donnie he knew something was amiss. Everyone knew not to call him at his club. He told Donnie to meet him at a little diner not far from there on Michigan Ave. that he frequented.

When he saw Donnie he was dressed as flamboyant as always. It made him glad that too many didn't see them together. He hated unwarranted attention. Just being seen with him would raise suspicion in the wrong people.

Donnie's reputation preceded him as being a major drug dealer but no one could prove it. The fact that he was a young white guy driving around in a Maserati wasn't unusual. Especially when your parents owned luxury car dealerships throughout the city, and was part of the corrupt political infrastructure in Detroit.

"Donnie, what's up?"

"Mr. Godwin, nice to see you." He always called Deon by his government name.

He felt calling him Big Man made him look more like a thug than a business associate. So he refused to call him that.

"Have a seat. Can I get you something to drink?" Deon motioned to the empty seat across from him.

"No, thank you. I haven't had lunch yet."

"So, what's up? What's so important?" Deon wanted to get right to it.

"Well, it seems one of your people reached out to me, and inquired about a few of my automobiles!"

"Oh, really?"

"Yes."

"What did you tell them?"

"You know me. I know you have a dealership that you use exclusively. I found it kind of odd that any of your people would contact me for anything. So I told them to let me see what I have on my lot in that price range. I really wanted to see if everything was everything with you!"

Even though Donnie was very ostentatious, he was definitely all business and he knew how to conduct it in public. From what Deon garnered from their conversation someone approached Donnie about purchasing a couple kilos for a certain price. He told them he would get back to them.

"How did they contact you? Better yet, how did they know I refer people to you?"

"Oh, I don't even think they know we are associates. Just so happens one of my clients that uses my rental service is friends with him. He vouched for him. When he brought him by for a meet and greet I recognized him. You brought him by and he purchased a BMW, but if you remember, he never came in my office. The young lady did all the paperwork. Her name was Tameka Cobb."

Deon couldn't believe what he was hearing.

"Are you sure?"

"Positive!"

"Okay. How much did he say he had to spend?"

"Something like thirty."

"Oh yeah! Okay, make a deal with him but get your cleaning service to clean everything up nice and pretty for him afterwards!"

A smile came over Donnie's face. He could see the wheels turning as Deon spoke. He didn't know what the outcome would be, but if Deon needed his services they were at his disposal. He couldn't understand why Deon wanted him to send his squad to take the dope back afterwards. He didn't care either. His loyalties lie with Deon.

"Are the automobiles to be delivered or what?"

"Really, to tell the truth Donnie, my garage is full."

"Say no more!" Donnie knew that meant Deon didn't want the dope, only the money.

"Now, Mr. Godwin, this is what I need you to do for me. I'm having an all-white pajama and lingerie party the weekend of Thanksgiving, and I need some entertainment!"

Deon's strip club doubled as an escort service.

"How many and what flavor?"

"About fifteen in total, and what part of all-white party did you not understand? No offense. No worries though. When I have my all-black party on New Year's, I'll make it worth your while!"

"No offense taken Donnie. I'll take care of it. But you know these ladies still must be tipped?"

"Come on. Don't insult me. How long have you provided ladies for me and my associates?"

"Alright. The initial fee for all the ladies is on me."

"Thanks, friend."

"No, thank you Donnie. Loyalty is a hard thing to come by in our business!"

As they stood, they shook hands. The meeting was over. Before Donnie could get out the door Deon could hear him tell one of his guys to set up the meet with CJ.

That night CJ didn't tell anyone where he was going when he took off in his car. When he pulled up on Lakeview it was relatively quiet.

He felt he was one step closer to getting Deon's money but in the back of his mind he was counting the minutes till he found out who robbed him.

"As he got out the car he put his gun in the small of his back. He grabbed a little grocery bag to put the kilos in. He had been instructed to enter the second building on the right. Go to the first floor, second door on the right and give the young lady the money. After she makes the call, go upstairs, second door on the right and get the product.

Everything went smooth. As he pulled off Lakeview and made a right on Mack, he stopped at a 7 Eleven. The whole time he never noticed the blue, 4 door Caprice with tinted windows following him. As he parked in front of the store, the Caprice parked on the street running down the side of the store.

When he exited the store, and before the door even closed all the way behind him, he heard a sound he knew all too well.

"Click, Click."

Then he felt the barrel of the Mac II pressed against his temple. The voice was low and controlled. There was no rushing. No yelling. No chaos. That's what scared him the most.

"Don't look at me, and put your hands down!" The voice said calmly. "Come this way!" Another voice in the shadows said.

He was being ushered to the side of the store where there wasn't much light.

"Look, you can have everything!"

He knew he should've brought Green Eyes with him. They wouldn't have ever got the drop on him. He thought about reaching for his gun, but he knew that would be futile.

"Shut up, we know we can have everything. Thanks, anyway." Just the tone in his voice infuriated CJ.

He wished he yelled or something. Only one spoke. The other one held the gun to his head. There was no playing in him. CJ knew they meant business.

The voice removed the gun from his back, took his keys, and relieved him of his wallet and the money he had left.

"Look, that's all I got. Just take it and let me go. I won't call the police!" They laughed at that.

The voice handed his partner CJ's car keys. He still didn't speak. He only moved with purpose.

"Okay, this what's gonna happen. My friend's gonna search your car to see if we can find any goodies. Then, we're gonna throw the keys over in that vacant lot, and you can make it out alive. Then, there's door number two. You can take your chances and try me, and I can leave you leaking right here. So, what's it gonna be?"

CJ didn't respond. He hung his head in defeat.

"Good boy!" He was patting CJ on the head with his gun. "Here, take your wallet. We don't need it."

When the silent one returned he had the grocery bag with the two kilos in it along with the Mac 10 CJ had under the seat. He threw the keys and got in the Caprice.

"We appreciate you not making us kill you. Now go get yo shit and get the fuck on. The next time you get caught over here you may not be so lucky!" He got in the Caprice and they peeled out.

CJ was pissed to the highest level of pissivity. He couldn't believe his luck. He had no idea that this was all by design. After he found his keys, he sat in his car for a few minutes banging his head against the steering wheel.

Now, the only thing he could do was tell Big Man, but he would hold off and pray Tony came up with a name.

"Sonya, are you sad about Leroy leaving to go to the Army?"

From the moment Sonya met Sabrina she had been calling Nipsey *Leroy*. She figured it was some inside joke between them. She never asked, she just went with it.

"Yeah, I'm gonna miss him. I'll get to see him after basic though. I'll be okay."

"You know what? I hate to see someone as special as Leroy sacrificing his life to go fight for a racist ass country like America!"

Sonya wasn't expecting that. She didn't know where Sabrina was going with that. She was curious to see though. She challenged her.

"I don't see it like that. What's sad to me is, how some of our young men choose not to take advantage of the opportunity this government affords them. Instead they turn to the streets.

"Riddle me this. If you can't afford to go to college, and you can't get a good job without a college education, every time someone looks at you it's as a statistic for lack of these things. So, they're not willing to take a chance on you because they feel you would be more of a liability than a asset. What are you to do as a young black man?"

"Wow, there's some passion in there!" Sabrina said. That was a side Sabrina hadn't seen.

From the time Samuel, Nipsey, Sonya, and herself arrived at Royal's Skating Rink, Sonya hadn't said much. She didn't know how to take Sonya. Now that she got a rise out of her she liked it.

Before Sabrina could respond Samuel came speeding out of nowhere from behind them sliding sideways with his skates making a loud screeching sound. He scared Sabrina and made her lose her already unstable balance which everyone got a kick out of, and changed the mood between Sabrina and Sonya.

"Samuel, stop playing! You gonna make me break my ankle on these damn things!" He was still grinning.

"You need some help beautiful?" A light-skinned guy asked with total disregard for Samuel helping her.

"I got her. We appreciate you asking!"

"I wasn't talking to you, white boy!"

"Wow! You just couldn't wait to show us how ignorant you are, huh? Now we know. You can move along now. My man got this!" She was shooing him away with her hand.

Sonya loved it. Now she understood what Nipsey had been telling her about Sabrina. She loved her candor and sharp as a knife wit.

"Fuck you, bitch!"

"Oh, look baby. Did I hurt him big ego? Now him have to overcompensate by using him big words. Aw, poor thing. Let me give him a hug!"

"Yeah, go ahead baby, give him a hug!" He was humiliated.

She reached out to give him a hug. He backed away as if she was contagious and rolled off shaking his head.

"Crazy, bitch!" She heard him mumble under his breath.

Sonya looked on in total astonishment. They were cracking up.

"Girl, you crazy. Both of you. You're my hero!" Sonya was being genuine.

She loved the strength Sabrina exuded. By the time Nipsey rolled up they were through laughing about the situation. He had seen the whole thing. He could only imagine what was said. He knew Sabrina and Samuel could take care of themselves. He excused himself to go call Angel.

Angel answered the phone on the first ring.

"What's up, sis?"

"I was hoping you were Greg calling. He supposed to be calling when he find daddy."

"Why, is something wrong?"

"I don't know, maybe I'm just trippin'. He came in here with all this money!"

"How much money?"

"Nipsey, he left ten thousand dollars in my room. He tried to give grandma some, but you know how she is about anything he bring in here!" When she said *ten thousand* the hair on the back of his neck stood up.

"Is there anything I can do?"

"No. Maybe I'm overreacting. I doubt it, but until we find out something what can we do?"

"Well, if you need me, I'm there."

"I know. Where are you?"

"I'm at Royals with Samuel and his girl and Sonya. That's why you hear all the music."

"Tell Sonya I said, hey. Tell her to call me so we can hang out."

"Alright, sis. Remember if you need me call me or leave a message for me."

"Okay, Nipsey. You know I will. I love you."

"Love you too, sis."

When he got back to the table Sabrina was spewing her radical political views. A conversation he didn't want to have.

"Samuel, are we still on for Thanksgiving?" He was thinking of anything to change the subject.

"I'm glad you asked, Nip. My parents decided to go on a cruise so we may have to come up with other plans."

"That's cool. We can all go to my grandma's if y'all want to?"

"I appreciate that, Nip. That sounds good to me, or we can go over to my uncle's. He would love to have us."

"Let's just play it by ear. But whatever we decide, let's do it together." Nipsey looked at everyone. They all agreed.

"Well, well. It's amazing who you see when you venture out. I need to get out more often!"

"Deon, what's up? What are you doing here?" Nipsey was shocked to see him.

When he looked at Deon there were two guys standing in the distance watching. He wondered who they were. They seemed to be on guard. As they hugged, Deon noticed Nipsey had picked up on them.

"They're okay, Nipsey. They're just a couple of associates. They're just not too social. That's a keen eye you have there!"

"You can never be too careful. Come on and meet my girl and my friends. This is my girl Sonya, my friend Samuel, and his girl Sabrina."

"Nice to meet all of y'all. I'm Deon. Nipsey's like my little brother. We kinda grew up together!"

"Nice to meet you Deon." Sabrina was the first to speak. "So, how do you *kinda* grow up with someone?"

He smiled a slow deliberate smile.

"Nipsey didn't actually stay with grandma as much as Angel, but he did stay most weekends and holidays. So he kinda lived over there and with me being older, I looked at him as being my little brother. So we kinda grew up together. Does that answer your question?"

"I guess that makes sense."

He turned his attention back to Nipsey. Before he could say anything though, two little girls ran up asking for quarters.

"Deon, you have kids?"

"I might as well. These two precious little girls are Camilla and Cameron. They're my nieces. They're the best part of who I am."

As Nipsey looked into his eyes the love he had for them was ever present anytime he looked at them.

"Okay, hold on. First I want y'all to stand still and meet your uncle Nipsey!"

"Aww, Uncle Deon. Somebody gonna get our machine!" Whining in unison enhanced the more than obvious twin characteristics they possessed.

"Okay, okay, wait a minute! What if someone did get the game, then what?"

They looked at each other, then back at him, and in unison once again, they hunched their shoulders.

"We don't know what will happen!" With an inquisitive look on their faces.

"Then you'll just have to wait. Your time would come again, so why rush?"

"Oh, we not in no rush, Uncle Deon. We just don't want to wait. Do we Cam Cam?"

"Nope, we want to play now!"

He knew he wasn't gonna win with them tag-teaming him. He gave in as always. He allowed himself to be dragged over to the game.

"Come on Uncle Nipsey, you can play too!"

"Well, who's gonna pay for Uncle Nipsey, Cam Cam?"

"You are Uncle Deon. That's what family is for, right?" He threw his hands up in defeat.

"Hey little ladies, can I borrow Uncle Deon for a minute, and I'll pay for the games? As soon as we're done we'll come and play!"

"Okay, Uncle Nipsey."

"What's up, Nipsey?" Nipsey became serious. "Did you hear about what Chris did to Angel?"

"What are you talking about? You mean CJ's cousin Chris?"

"Yeah, that Chris!"

He began telling him about that fateful night. By the time they had finished talking a plan had been hashed.

CHAPTER 29

When Roy took the message from McDougal he got on the phone immediately. He called Mac against his better judgment. He knew every time he talked about the Scot case Mac was less than enthused about following any kind of lead. Since Mac was the lead detective on the case Roy couldn't just take it upon himself to follow up on anything having to do with the case.

The next message Roy received was from his wife. She needed him to stop by the house whenever he got the chance. He decided to meet with Mac first.

Mac was in his driveway kissing his wife through the window of her car as she began to pull out. She waved at Roy as she passed.

"Roy, what's so important this couldn't wait until I got to the office?" "There's a development!"

"Are you gonna tell me or are you gonna drag this out as long as you can?"

"Alright, don't get your panties in a wad!" Roy was stoked.

"I got a message from McDougal. It seems a photo studio three doors down on the opposite side of the street from where the victim was found, the owner just happened to be reviewing some old footage from her security feed and guess what shows up?"

"Don't tell me. Our vic?"

"And our suspect!" Roy finished it before Mac could.

"Okay, let's go see what we have."

"My thoughts exactly." Roy assented.

The tension between the two on the way to the studio was thick. It made Roy uncomfortable. Mac felt Roy's vibe and tried to ease the tension.

"Roy, thanks for having my back. I know how you feel about all of this. It really means a lot."

Roy stayed silent because secretly he had his doubts from day one, he just didn't know how to tell Mac that he was going to the Captain.

Upon entering the studio, they encountered a young, vibrant, and from the sound of it, Hispanic woman.

"Buenas Tardes, Caballeros."

"I'm sorry ma'am, we don't speak Spanish." Roy said.

"I'm sorry. Habit. I said *Good afternoon, gentlemen!*"

"Good afternoon, ma'am. My name is Sgt. Leroy Cox and this is

Lieutenant Randall McMillan."

"Yes, yes, nice to meet you. The man I speak to tell me you come by!" She was vigorously shaking their hands. She was very animated.

"Yes, ma'am. We're investigating a murder. You called and said you may have some footage." Roy was pointing at one of her security cameras.

"Hay, Dios mio! I hear about that. Como triste. I'm sorry. I say, *That's so sad*. Follow me!"

"If I may ask Mrs...?" She stopped Roy before he could finish.

"No Mrs., only Ms. Fuentes!" She was wagging her finger from side to side as if to scold him.

Mac smirked. She was almost comical.

"Please forgive me. Why did it take you so long to contact someone? It's been three months!"

"I busy all the time. How do you say, *viejas*? You know, going all the time for work?"

"Travels!" Mac interjected.

"Yes, that's it. Travel?" She repeated it as if she was trying to commit it to memory.

"So, I no here all the time. No one break in so don't check all the time. I check yesterday because I need to, how you say, aww, *borrar*? You know, clean off?"

"You mean *erase*!" It was Roy who helped this time.

"Yes, thank you. That's it, erase." They could tell it made her happy they understood her. "Yes, I need to erase to make space for new footage. So I watch. I remembered alley from news program. I see that gringo with the black guy. See right there!" She was pointing at the screen.

"Mac, that's them! We got him Mac! Is that who I think it is?"

Mac was looking at the person on the tape. He couldn't believe what he saw. Everything was caught right there on tape. He didn't say anything. He didn't want to give Roy the satisfaction in saying, I told you so."

"Ms. Fuentes, may we have this?" Mac wanted to make sure he had the tape in his possession, so he could figure out what to do with it.

"Sure, un momento." She handed him the tape.

"Thank you, ma'am. This is a big help!"

"De nada. Anytime."

Leaving the studio, Mac was in deep thought. Roy knew what he was thinking. Roy decided right then that he owed it to Mac to let him know his intentions.

"Mac, we need to talk."

"What is it Roy?"

"It's about everything that is going on with this case. I can't do it. I feel like I am compromising my morals, values, integrity and everything else I grew up believing in. I just can't continue to do that!"

"Pull over, Roy. Let's talk about this."

They pulled over in a random neighborhood off Joy Rd. and Dexter Ave.

"Roy, I understand your position, but we've already embarked on this journey."

"I know Mac. I made a mistake. I should've never agreed to any of this. After looking at the tape, I realized the only way I'm gonna get closure for the Parkers is by locking the Hussle kid up. He's our guy in the Scot case as well as the Parker's. I'm also going to IAD and telling them everything, and maybe I can salvage what's left of my career!"

"Roy, you're going to Internal Affairs! You're gonna break the code like that? You go to IAD and say what? We've lost evidence on purpose? For what, a fucking pedophile? You're gonna destroy my career to save yours. Is that what you're saying?"

"Mac, we're better than this!"

"Fuck you, Roy! That kid's a fucking hero if you ask me, and without this tape all you have is circumstantial evidence!" He felt betrayed.

If Roy went to IAD that would be the end of Mac's career. Every case he'd ever worked on would be scrutinized. His pension, gone. His reputation, tarnished. The possibility of him going to jail would be more than likely. He wouldn't allow any of that.

"I'm sorry, Mac. I have to think about my future. I'm trying to start a family!"

"It's all about you. You're gonna rat me out? Go ahead, tell them. That kid will be alright because you have nothing on him, and if you think you're gonna get this tape, you better think twice! How do you think you're gonna prove that I've destroyed evidence? It's your word against mine. Who do you think they're gonna believe, me or your black ass?"

"Mac, give me the tape and this conversation is over!"

Mac had struck a nerve. The implication that they wouldn't believe him because he was black and Mac was white didn't go unnoticed. The sad part was Roy knew there was truth in Mac's words. He knew he had to have the tape.

"Mac, give me the tape!" He tried to snatch it from Mac's hand.

Mac pulled back and spit in his face.

"You fucking rat! You're a fucking disgrace!"

Before Roy knew it he was punching Mac in the face. He was delirious with rage. When Mac fell Roy jumped on top of him pummeling him with blow after blow. It took everything in Mac to protect himself from the onslaught. Roy was too strong, too big, and too skilled. When he stopped, Mac's face was bloody and bruised.

Roy got up, took the tape and kicked him in the ribs. To add insult to injury, Roy spit back in his face. He turned and began to walk towards the car. In mid stride, he stopped.

"Click." It was the unmistakable sound of a gun cocking.

He slowly turned around to see Mac holding a little six shot .32 he had retrieved from his ankle holster.

"What are you gonna do with that?"

The last thing Roy ever heard again were the three shots that rang out. All three were center mass. Susan would never get the chance to tell him that she was pregnant.

Mac took that tape and got on the radio.

"Shots fired! Shots fired! Officer down! Need assistance now! Three suspects, two black, one white. Can't pursue, performing CPR on Sgt. Cox."

CHAPTER 30

Lou and Sue were relaxing. Their money was getting low and they were trying to figure out what to do about getting some more. They had been hustling hard. They had sold all the dope they had left after they were through partying.

After they had started getting a taste for the good life, Lou decided that was how he wanted to live. He was tired of being treated like dirt. They decided to go cold turkey and kick their habit. It didn't take a lot of convincing for Sue because it didn't matter to her one way or another. Whatever Lou wanted to do, she was down. She would go to the end of the earth for him.

They had bought a new car and rented a townhouse off Livernois on Dix St. in a real nice complex.

"Baby, you know we're gonna have to stay on the grind if we want to continue to live like this!"

"Daddy, I know, but we don't have to go back to the neighborhood. What if somebody is looking for us?" She was scared.

She knew if anyone knew what they had done there would be a death sentence hanging over their head. If she was high she wouldn't have cared, but having not been high for over a day now she began to see clearly. Lou on the other hand was on another high. A money high, and had no intentions of coming down. Whatever he had to do to stay that way, he would do.

With what they had spent at the hotel, the townhouse, car, furniture, clothes and even a little jewelry, they had already spent close to forty-five thousand.

While Sue put on her clothes, she overheard Lou on the phone talking to someone. She didn't know who, but she knew it was someone from the neighborhood because he told them to meet him at the Johnson's Family store.

"Look baby, I'm gonna drop you off at your mama house. When I get this work, Imma come get you. Okay, baby?"

"Okay, daddy. You just be careful!"

"I got my burner. Don't worry. I'll be okay!"

Lou had thought it through. If no one figured out what he and Sue had done he would be able to cop and go grind at Francine's. He figured this would be his first step in changing his image because instead of being a fiend, he would be serving the fiends. He was determined to be taken serious. He had to take it easy though and not move too fast. He couldn't give himself away. So when he called Green Eyes and he hadn't found out, he was in the clear.

When Tony got the call from Lou he didn't think twice about selling him the four and a half ounces of crack. Especially since he knew Lou didn't have a clue as to how much it cost. So he had no problem charging him four thousand, when he could've easily got it for thirty-five hundred. Since Lou had convinced him that he was coping for a white guy he knew Tony knew Lou really didn't care how much it cost. Tony figured that Lou was going to cheat the white guy anyway.

While Lou was sitting in his car waiting for Tony his nerves started getting the best of him. His stomach started cramping. He had to use the bathroom. He left his car running and went behind the vacant house next to the store. Even with it being cold, he took a dump. When he came out Tony was parked next to his car.

"Green Eyes. Here I go!"

"Fuck, what you doing over there, Lou? Who back there?" He was reaching for his gun.

"I had to piss. Damn! You too paranoid. Chill out!"

"Muthafucka, you chill out! Ain't no such thing as too paranoid!"

Lou got back in his car. Tony had backed in next to it unknowingly.

"Muthafucka! Who car is that?"

"This my shit! I traded my other one in." He had the black Pontiac 6000 detailed and it was spotless.

"Get the fuck outta here! That ain't your shit!" He didn't give credence to anything Lou said. "Where the money?"

"Here you go. Four thousand, right?"

"What I say muthafucka? It all better be here too!"

It was really eating Lou up the way Green Eyes talked to him. He was tired of being treated like that. He wished he could just kill him, but he was scared. He vowed to himself that all that would change.

After Tony gave him the dope, Lou reached out to give Tony some dap.

"Muthafucka! Didn't you say you just got through pissing? Nasty muthafucka!" He peeled off with a disgusted look on his face.

Lou went and picked Sue up. He tried to look normal and composed, but having so much dope again made him feel awkward and uncomfortable. Even though he hadn't smoked any he was still a junkie. So having it in his possession still made him have to use the bathroom. He fought the urge until the feeling passed. He was determined to stay clean. To help fight his urges he went to Francine's and got on his grind. He figured if he sold the dope fast enough the temptation to smoke wouldn't be so tempting.

The only downside to Lou and Sue's plan was, when anyone comes into the hood getting money, short stopping customers. Everyone knows, especially if you are from around the hood and unfortunately that's what they were doing. It was unintentional, but by them looking out for the smokers they normally got high with, word spread like wildfire. So what it was, and what it appeared to be were two totally different things, but the adverse reaction would ultimately be the same if news reached certain people.

"Greg, what's up?"
"You know I'm doing me, Kenny." "Have you heard anything?
"Yeah, I heard from one of my people that both your people over at Fran's. They said they're getting their grind on. Let me ask you a question though, Kenny! If they get down like y'all say, where they get all that work from?"
"I don't know. You mean they grinding like that?"
"That's what I heard anyway and check this. Word is CJ got robbed. Somebody went up in his stash spot and hit his safe. You don't think they had nothing to do with that, do you?"
"Damn, Greg! For real? Man, I don't know. When you hear that?" Kenny's antennas were fully extended now.
"I heard that a couple days ago!"
"I don't know, Gee. I hope they didn't have nothing to do with that shit!
Let me go holla at Angel. I appreciate that!"
"No problem. If you need me, you know where to find me!"
On his way to holla at Angel he couldn't help but worry.
"If that's CJ's money they spending ain't no telling what he'll do!" He thought to himself.
He made a detour and went by Trina's to see if she could get at her boy Wade for some weed. When he got there, much to his dismay, Tony was there chillin' on the porch with Trina and Diane. He thought this would be a good time to see if any of the rumors were true.
"Green Eyes, what's up?"
"Kenny, what you doing in this neck of the woods?"
"Trina, Di, how y'all doing? I just stopped by to see if Trina could holla at her boy Wade for me. I need some good?"

"Alright Kenny, I got you. Let me go call him!"

Kenny needed to be tactful when it came to dealing with Tony because even though Tony was high, he was very sagacious.

"I haven't seen you around lately, Green Eyes. What's up?"

"I been trying to get this money, that's all! Where your girl Angel and that little clique of hers?"

"You know how she do. She probably somewhere with her man or getting lit with her girls."

"I saw her dad a couple days ago. Or maybe it was yesterday!"

"Oh yeah? Where you see him?"

"In a whip he said was his, buying dope for somebody at the store."

Kenny wasn't getting anywhere playing it like he was, so he chose a more direct approach.

"I heard what happened to your cousin!"

"Yeah, somebody fucked up! They robbed the wrong muthafucka!"

He gave no indication that he believed Lou and Sue had anything to do with it.

"They didn't get a lot, did they?" He knew he was pushing it, but he needed to know how bad it was.

"It was about a big boy and seventy."

"Damn, that's fucked up!" Kenny was really in shock.

"Yeah, but we gonna body them muthafuckas!"

Even though Tony hadn't put two and two together, it didn't take much for Diane to put it together. Before Kenny and Tony finished talking Diane excused herself and told them she would see them later. She knew if Sue and Lou were back in the neighborhood and had some dope, it was only one place they could be and that was Francine's.

She had to know for sure if what she suspected was true. She had to confront them, so she would know what she had to do to cover her own ass. If anyone found out that she helped them by cooking up CJ's dope there wouldn't be anywhere she could hide from their wrath.

By the time Kenny made it to grandma's, Nipsey had arrived. He and Sonya were in Angel's room getting filled in on what was going on. That's why when Kenny walked in all eyes were on him expectantly.

When Kenny had finished relaying what he had heard, Nipsey became enraged. You couldn't tell by just looking at him. He listened and didn't speak. Angel on the other hand was crying. This was a bad situation. All she was concerned about was grandma's safety.

"Kenny, come on. Let's go!" Kenny already knew where they were going. "I'll be back soon, baby!" Sonya was busy comforting Angel.

The gravity of the situation eluded her. She did know not to ask Nipsey any questions. She saw how his demeanor changed, and the look in his eyes; she had seen it before, but this time it was mixed with something else. Something she hadn't seen before. Worry.

"We'll be back, grandma." Nipsey was saying as they were walking out the door.

"Okay, baby. You better put something on your head, it's kind of windy out there. Y'all gonna mess around and catch the death of pneumonia out there!"

"Okay, grandma." They both said at the same time while simultaneously closing the door.

When they turned on Belvidere St. they heard someone screaming and yelling. Looking up the block, they couldn't quite make out the words, but they could see clearly who it was. Lou and Diane were standing over Sue as she lay on the ground.

"You stupid, bitch! How you gonna get me involved in your bullshit?

I oughta stomp a mud hole in your ass!"

"Bitch, ain't nobody beg you to do nothing!" Lou said, trying to defend Sue who wasn't saying anything while she was holding her eye.

"Shut your punk ass up, Lou! What you gonna do? I'll have you fucked up. You know who I am! I don't give a fuck about neither one of you crackhead muthafuckas!"

"Bitch! Don't act like you don't be smoking. You ain't no better than us. You ain't been shit since Rodger been in prison. The only difference between you and us is your ass a closet smoker!" His truth hurt her.

He couldn't have hurt her any worse if he had smacked her. She went to swing at him and missed, lost her footing and hit the ground hard. The fact that there were a few people standing around added insult to injury.

She started to cry. Not from any physical pain, but all the emotional baggage she had been carrying around. Everything from her man leaving her to fend for herself, to trying to hide the fact she was getting high.

"That's okay, punk ass! I got you. You gonna regret this shit. You and your bitch!" She was brushing herself off.

She didn't want to look up and reveal the shame that was evident on her face. By the time she did look up Lou had grabbed Sue and disappeared.

She began to mumble to herself and walked off.

Throughout the whole ordeal, Nipsey and Kenny stood off in the distance and observed the whole thing.

"Nipsey, what we doing?"

"I didn't want anyone to think we were with them. Come on, let's get back to the house!"

When Nipsey and Kenny made it back, Lou and Sue had already made it back. He anticipated Lou still being amped from his confrontation with Diane. Instead, he looked defeated. He seemed different. Nipsey just couldn't put his finger on it.

"Lou, hold up!" He was situating things in the car. "We know what y'all did to CJ and before someone gets hurt y'all need to try and make it right!"

Before Lou even opened his mouth, Nipsey recognized the look of defiance in his eyes.

"I don't know what you're talking about, and get out of my way!" Lou took a step forward. Nipsey took a step back and extended his arm to halt Lou's progress, making sure he didn't touch him.

"Look Lou, no one knows but us, and from the looks of it, Diane. If you know Diane, after that scene went down the way that it did, we won't be the only ones for long. You know how CJ and his cousins get down. So if you care about anyone other than yourself, make this right!"

They say, "The eyes are the gateway to the soul," and if there's any truth to that, then Lou's soul was as cold as ice. It was as if the drugs had eaten through the very existence of his soul. Seeing this sent a chill down Nipsey's spine. The kind of chill that tells you there's only one way this can end.

That tore at Nipsey's heart strings. He looked from one to the other. When he looked in Sue's eyes they were in stark contrast to Lou's. Fear and anxiety resonated there. He decided to play on that. To persuade her to use the love Lou felt for her against him.

Lou brushed on past Nipsey when he and Sue went into the house. Grandma was asleep and everyone had left.

"Sue, bring your ass on before somebody sees us. Damn! I knew I should've left your ass at home!"

"Don't be rushing me! You make me sick with that shit! It ain't like nobody don't know where to come looking for your ass, and with that ugly ass car out there, you ain't hiding!"

"Shut the fuck up and come on! If you wouldn't have called that bitch Diane we wouldn't have to worry about shit!"

"Oh, so it's my fault now?"

When he was leaving he made sure not to wake grandma. He kissed her and as he done so, he felt a pang in his heart. Even though he didn't treat grandma as he should've, he loved his momma, and she loved him too. For anything to happen to her would devastate him. He couldn't stay and be the cause of that. He had made his mind up, he had to get himself together.

When they made it to the Edsel Ford Fwy., they took it to I-94 towards their townhouse. A tear rolled down his cheek. He knew there was no turning back. Sue affectionately touched his hand but didn't speak. She knew this was a hard choice for him, and she didn't want to make it no harder.

Soon as CJ answered the phone and heard Deon's voice he languished. This wasn't a call he was expecting the night before Thanksgiving. Deon never called unless it was important.

"CJ, it has come to my attention that we have mutual associates!"

CJ's head began to hurt.

"Who do you mean?"

"Are you planning on doing your own thing without giving me a courtesy call, or even paying me my money? Especially with how much I've done for you!"

"Hold on. What are you talking about?"

CJ realized it didn't matter what he said. Deon wasn't hearing it, so he patiently listened. He knew somehow he had found out about him buying the dope. He couldn't help but wonder if he knew about him getting robbed, and if he did, why hasn't he said anything?

"This is what's gonna happen. You're gonna come see me tonight! This way we can get an understanding and there's no misconceptions."

"Click." The line was dead.

CJ made up his mind that if push came to shove, they would kill Deon.

After Deon hung up the phone he sat back and reflected on what he had just set into motion, and the conversation that ultimately changed the dynamic of their relationship.

That conversation took place the day Nipsey was at the skating rink. When Nipsey started talking he never questioned the source because he remembered back to a night when CJ, Tony, Chris, and

Cotton were all at his club.

"CJ, you remember that bitch I told you I fucked at the party, and how I did her?"

"Yeah, I remember. I been wanting to hit that for a long time. Next time we need to hit that bitch together!"

"Yeah, maybe we'll do that. I told that bitch I'll hit that pussy whenever I want to, and she better not say nothing! Shit, who she gonna tell anyway, her crackhead ass daddy? Or her bitch ass man?"

They were laughing and talking like that shit was cool. Deon wasn't in the conversation, he was busy talking business. They never said a name either, so he didn't get into the conversation. He also didn't have a clue who they were talking about. If he had known, none of them would've left alive that night.

The fact that CJ knew Angel, and what she meant to Deon, let him know that he needed to distance himself from them, and there was no better time like the present. It made it a lot easier to come up with a plan with Nipsey.

When Nipsey found out what Deon really did and how major he was he knew his plan would work. But, Nipsey didn't think he could come to terms with what Deon did.

"You mean to tell me you supplying everyone over there? Everyone works for you? Even at the JuJu?"

"Not everyone."

Nipsey was in awe. He had no idea Deon was doing it like that.

"For how long? How many people know?"

"For a while now. Only the people I do business with knows, and Angel, and now you!"

"You mean to tell me all the drugs, and guns, and no telling what else, are all you?"

"Nipsey, don't be so dramatic! I sell drugs. I have nothing to do with the rest!"

"Is that what you tell yourself to sleep at night? We grew up around there. We know everybody. We used to go next door and play every day at the Benson's. Now they are dead, and their kids are on dope! Look at the twins, on drugs! Look at Roscoe on the corner, your drugs!

"We used to walk into any house on the block. No one locked their doors. Now look at the neighborhood, people don't even want to sit on their porches. You say you *only* sell drugs. One is a catalyst for the rest."

As Deon listened to Nipsey drum on, he couldn't believe how

passionate he was. He couldn't believe how much of an enigma Nipsey was.

"If I didn't sell it to them, someone else would. It might as well be me!"

"Oh yeah, how many times you practice that in the mirror?"

"Look, I'm sorry about what happened to Chicken! What do you need me to do? Whatever it is, you got it! But let's not turn this shit around on me. I know you're family, and you're right; but regardless of that, I am who I am and that won't change!"

The more Deon thought about CJ and his cousins the more disgusted he became. He thought it was ironic how things turned out, because now the robbery became a part of a bigger plan.

CHAPTER 31

As she turned on Hwy. 400, she knew there was no turning back. She instinctively rubbed her specially made *two year chip* she wore around her neck that her sponsor gave her. She was gonna miss Tina. She had become one of her biggest supporters throughout her struggles from day one. She never gave up on her. Lauren promised her that she would return as soon as she made things right with her family, and anybody else she had wronged.

This was part of her recovery she hadn't completed, and she was determined to do so. She felt this would complete her. Make her whole again. That's something she never thought she would see again, because when she landed on Canada's soil she was broken; spiritually, physically, and emotionally.

When she got to Toronto, she didn't think she would make it. She knew no one, and had no one. The first day she was at the treatment center she met Tina. She had thirty days clean already and was proud of it. Lauren felt like God was looking out for her because she took to Lauren right away. It was what she saw in Lauren, a reflection of herself from when she first arrived at *Saving Grace Treatment Center*. Even though Tina was from the suburbs, they were from the same world and Lauren loved her.

In the time Lauren was there, she never missed a meeting or a social skills workshop. She was adamant about working her steps, by herself or with anyone who needed help working theirs. After she got her six month chip she became an *In-House Resident Counselor*. When she got her one year chip she moved out, and found herself a place in the Richmond Hills area outside Toronto; where she enrolled in school to become a social worker and treatment counselor. By the time she had two years clean she was working with at risk youth, doing meetings, holiday workshops, and sponsoring addicts. Her plate was full.

Tina was like a proud mother through it all. They went to church every Sunday, and that's where she told her.

"Tina, I'm almost three years clean now and I still feel incomplete. I need to set things right with my family, even if they hate me. They need to know who I am now, and that no matter what I'm still their mother. That even though I'll always be an addict, I'll still lay down my life for them!"

"Lauren, if that's what you need to do to continue to heal, then by all means do that. Remember though, always stay true to your recovery. Never stop working your steps, and this is your home now. Come back home Lauren! Come back home!"

"I will Tina. I love you. You're my sister for life. Thank you for everything!"

Lauren took Hwy. 400 to 401 until she got to Chatham where she got off. She drove a couple of miles to Blenheim, right there on Lake Erie. She parked and got out of her car. Her nerves had her stomach in knots. It wasn't the fact that she thought she would use again. It was that she hadn't seen Nipsey since he had become a ward of the state. And with him not accepting her phone calls, she didn't know what to expect.

She hadn't seen Angel in just as long. She didn't know what she would say to either one of them, or if they would want to see her at all. Seeing Derrick wasn't as nerve wrecking, because he always did his own thing anyway. Nevertheless, she still needed to face him. Her addiction affected him as well. Sitting there looking out over Lake Erie she prayed:

Dear God,

I come to you today in all your glory to ask that you guide me on my journey. Go before me and light my path as you did for the children of Israel. Please build a fiery hedge of protection around me as I seek to reconcile with my children. Comfort me Lord God and let my word glorify you and if I can't find the words, allow the Holy Spirit to give them to me as your word says. Lord God, I pray these things in Christ Jesus' name. Amen."

She continued to sit there and meditate. A calm fell over her that was so immense it felt as if she was actually sitting in God's shadow. She smiled. She knew that no matter what obstacles lay before her, she would succeed.

By the time she made it back to Hwy. 401 towards Windsor she was ready to face her worst fears. As she began to cross the bridge in Windsor, leaving Canada going into Detroit, she unconsciously rubbed her chip as if it was a good luck charm.

Now in Detroit, she made her way over to Washington Blvd. to get a room at the Holiday Inn, so she could call grandma and get some rest.

When grandma answered the phone, Lauren's heart skipped a beat.

"Hey, mama!"

"Hey, darling. Who is this?"

"It's Lauren."

"Who, baby? You gotta speak up, you know grandma old!"

"It's Lauren, mama!"

"Lauren, child, where you been? No one seen you in a month of Sundays. You okay?"

"Yes, ma'am. I'm fine now! I had to go get myself together. I'm clean, and I've been clean for over two years now."

"Well, baby. We can do all things through Christ Jesus. As long as you keep your eyes on him."

"I know mama. How's the kids?"

"Angel around here somewhere, and Nipsey is doing good. You know them nuns take real good care of him. He's fixin' to graduate. He comes for the weekends, and throughout the week. He'll be here tomorrow for Thanksgiving. Now Derrick, he living with some girl, I forget where. He suppose to come too."

"So everyone's gonna be there?"

"I suppose."

"How would you feel if I came?"

"Now baby, you family, ain't none of us perfect. There was only one perfect person, and them kids need to see you. They may not like some of the things you done, but that's okay. You're still their mother. Now it's time to move forward, and the only way that can be done is to come together and settle y'all differences. God will handle the rest."

"Are you gonna tell them I'm coming?"

"I don't know. You just don't worry about that, just come on, you hear?" "Yes, ma'am. And thanks, mama!"

"Don't thank me child, thank God I answered the phone. You know I don't be wanting to be bothered when my husband on the TV!"

"Okay, mama."

When Diane reached the joint, Chris was the only one there. She really didn't want to talk to him. She thought he was disgusting and didn't like the way he leered at her. He made her feel like she was walking around naked.

"Chris, where's CJ?"

He picked up the contempt in her tone immediately, so instead of trying to get in her pants he became serious.

"Why? What's up?"

"Because I need to talk to him."

"Well, he not here."

"I can see that. Where is everyone?"

"Damn Di, you asking a lot of questions! You want me to give him a message?" He had grown tired of her attitude.

"Just tell him or Tony I need to talk to him. It's important."

Before Nipsey left, Sister Burke had paged him to her office. When he walked in the overwhelming smell of potpourri invaded his senses. She and Sister Alicia were both present. The mood was somber.

"Y'all need to see me sisters?"

Sister Burke began. "Since you have all the credits you need to obtain your diploma, plus you'll be eighteen soon, we have some decisions to make. As hard as it is for me to inform you of this, you must know. Under the guidelines of Child Protective Services for wards of the state, once a child reaches the age of eighteen he is no longer a ward of the state. Therefore, he can no longer reside here under our care."

Sister Alicia's eyes were watering as Sister Burke went over the provisions.

"I don't mean to sound so formal son, I just need you to understand it's not our call. It's the politics of the system that regulates our funding."

"In actuality, it's a leash Nipsey. If we pull too hard, we choke ourselves! In other words, our funding goes away, and there's far too many children who need us!" Sister Alicia was speaking from the heart.

She was emotional, and made him emotional, but he tried to keep it in check.

"I understand Sisters. I'm ready. Y'all have done so much for me. You have been like mothers to me, and I will never forget you. I'm ready!"

Sister Alicia let loose the floodgates. Her tears began to puddle on the desk in front of her. She tried to compose herself before she spoke again.

"Nipsey my son, there are some things we can still do for you, like get you into a halfway house, give you vouchers for clothes and you can still come here for counseling. We love you son, and we only want the best for you!"

"I know Sister Alicia. I'll be fine."

"Son, we will always keep you in our prayers, and I know God isn't through with you yet."

As Sister Alicia finished speaking, he looked into her eyes and saw that all too familiar look, like she could see into his soul! Like she knew his innermost secrets.

"Always remember, no matter where your journey may take you, we will always be here for you. This is the start of a new chapter in your life. So as you go, go placidly amidst the noise in haste!"

As Sister Burke finished where Sister Alicia left off, Nipsey's heart began to feel heavy, but those feelings were of no use right now. He didn't need them to cloud his judgment, or dull his senses in light of what needed to be done that evening.

As he left, he tried to refocus his mind on his way to the dojo. His training was uneventful, and much needed to take the edge off. Before he left he took his twenty-five inch Dao and his dagger. Getting into Sonya's car she wondered what that was strapped to his back because it wasn't exposed.

She didn't dwell on it.

"Hey baby, you have a good workout?"

"Yeah, how are you?"

"I'm alright. I wish I didn't have to help my mom though, then we could spend some time together."

He was glad she had to help her mom, because he didn't need her around this evening.

"Don't worry baby, tomorrow's Thanksgiving, and we'll have the whole weekend."

The sun had already began to set as Sonya took the longest way possible to get to grandma's, so she could spend as much time as possible with him. When they pulled up to the house, Nipsey took a deep breath, exhaled, and got out. It was so subtle and quick Sonya never saw it. He walked around to her window and kissed her goodbye.

Soon as Sonya was out of sight he became anxious. So much so he had to take several deep breaths and focus. No one was outside to take notice of him. Instead of going into the house he went down the side of the house toward the backyard where he cut down the alley. He broke into an effortless trot. He cut through another backyard and came out on Pennsylvania. Instead of cutting across Cadillac Ave. to Hurlbut St., he went down Barker St. all the way to Bewick St. He cut through another backyard in an effort to be seen by as few people as possible and came up behind CJ's joint that sat on Hurlbut St.

He came up the side of the house and went in through the front door into the living room. He saw no one, as it should've been, but he heard Chris yell out from the kitchen. He was under the assumption it was one of his people who had came in.

"Who, dat?"

Nipsey never spoke. He took a quick inventory of everything. He knew Chris would be the only one there, because he and Deon had planned it that way.

"I said, who dat? What the fuck, y'all can't hear?" Still no answer.

When he entered the living room his eyes grew to the size of saucers. Nipsey never moved. He stood with his hands resting, interlocked in front of him. Calm. Everything was crystal clear. He followed Chris' eyes to where a gun laid on a coffee table. He was two feet away from it, about the same distance Nipsey was from the table. He looked from Nipsey to the gun, and back to Nipsey and smiled.

"Nipsey, you getting high now? What's up, what you doing here?" Silence. "What the fuck you want?"

"Nothing!"

The one word answer made Chris nervous and antsy. Nipsey could see it, and just like that it happened. Chris lunged for the gun. Nipsey took one step forward, and in the same instance he removed his Dao from his back. With one swing he cut Chris' hand off at the wrist. It was so fast he didn't scream immediately. When what had happened finally registered, and he saw his hand laying on the gun, he screamed, holding his arm. Nipsey closed the distance in two steps, took his Dao, stuck it in between Chris' 6th and 7th ribs, twisted the blade and opened his lungs. As he inhaled, blood filled his lungs. Chris dropped to his knees.

It was as if Nipsey was slicing butter. The blood grooves near the back edge of the blade were etched in for stability, and for allowing air into the wound for a quick pull out. He took total advantage of it because as he was pulling out the Dao, he just as fastly unsheathed his dagger and inserted the blade into Chris' cardiac notch to pierce his heart and end his life.

Nipsey wasted no time. He wiped his blade clean and left. He made his way back the way he came without anyone noticing. He felt exuberated. There was no guilt. There was no remorse. Only a sense of justice.

When Deon told CJ to come to meet with him, he knew Tony and Cotton would be with him. They were two of CJ's closest cousins, and they were killers. He also knew CJ wouldn't feel safe coming to see him alone. So, that left Chris alone.

When they arrived at the club, they were ushered upstairs to Deon's office. CJ didn't know what to expect so he was on edge. He had already decided that he needed to tell Deon the whole situation, but he was still uncertain about what to expect.

"CJ, Tony, Cotton, y'all have a seat!"

Before anyone could even get comfortable, CJ was already talking.

"Look, I need to tell you something! I know you wanted me to have your money by Saturday, but somebody hit my spot. They went in my safe, and got me for everything. Seventy thousand and a big eight. I tried to make that shit up but I got robbed over off, Mack Ave. Shit just ain't been good!"

Now Deon understood, but it was too late. It really didn't matter what CJ said, it wouldn't change how he felt about anything.

"What would you like for me to do, CJ?"

"I need you to give me some more time. I..." Deon cut him off. He held his hand up for him to stop talking.

"More time? I gave you plenty of time. You chose not to tell me the situation, so more time is not an option!"

"Wait a minute, all the fucking business we've done! You gone act like that?" He began to raise his voice.

Deon remained calm. He didn't care about CJ's temper, because he had already made a fatal mistake by sitting directly across from him. Even though it was three of them, he had an equalizer. He had a sawed off double barrel shotgun about a foot and a half from barrel to grip, mounted on the underside of his desk, pointed at CJ's torso. Plus, they were being watched, and listened to by some of Deon's people.

CJ was done. He was tired, stressed, and frustrated.

"You know what? Fuck you!" All three of them stood up at the same time. Deon never moved. "After I pay you, we're done!"

"You promise?"

Deon was in his head.

He wanted CJ to give him a reason to kill him right there, but CJ was too smart. He knew that if he did anything in that club he would get everyone killed. So, no matter how mad he got, he knew to keep it in check. As they were leaving, Deon facetiously wished them a *Happy Thanksgiving*.

CHAPTER 32

"Hey, grandma. It smells good in here!" Nipsey had his nose in the air taking in the aroma.

"Hey, baby. Yeah, that child started cooking for tomorrow."

"Why you lying down? You don't feel good?"

"No, I don't feel so good."

"You need anything?" When he saw her eyes zero in on her cigarettes he regretted asking.

"Yeah baby, hand grandma a cigarette. I been laying in this bed all day!" "I don't think you need to be smoking with that tank on!" She abruptly changed the subject. It was real casual like.

"You know them folks called from over there where you stay?" Her tone was matter of fact.

"I figured they would be calling. I told them you said I could stay here for a while!"

"Oh yeah, that's what you told them? You can't even do like you're asked. I don't know if you can stay here like that, hold on, let's see something.

Baby, hand your grandma a cigarette!"

He smiled. He got the message loud and clear.

"Thank you, baby. You'll be fine. I told them you were home. You can stay as long as you want." She smiled and lit her cigarette.

"Where's Angel, grandma?"

"When she called to check on me she was with that boy, what's his name, Bart?"

"Brett grandma! His name's Brett!"

"That's what I said, child. See, that's what's wrong with kids today. Y'all don't listen to nothing. How you spect to learn anything if you don't listen?"

"Okay grandma. You want something to eat?"

"Baby, Imma get me some shut eye."

"Alright, I'm going to see if I can find my sister. I'm here for the weekend." He kissed her on the forehead.

As he walked around the corner he thought to himself. "At least now I know Deon is still Deon, family, and it was beautiful, but who am I becoming?"

Even though Nipsey had come to terms with who he had become he still felt like his moral compass was shifting.

"God, if I'm wrong please forgive me!"

"Nipsey, what's up?" Brett saw him before he saw them.

They were sitting on the porch. With his being in deep thought, Brett startled him.

"What's up, Brett? Hey, sis."

"Boy, what you doing around here?" She was getting up to meet him.

"I'm here for the weekend. Grandma said you were around here. I see you got the house smelling good."

"Yeah, I'm ready for tomorrow."

"Yeah, I can't wait to get my grub on." Nipsey was rubbing his hands together and licking his lips. "So, have you decided what to do about your daddy?"

"I have the money he left still at home. I'm gonna hold on to it so when one of them come ask me about it I'll give it to them. Maybe that will buy some time to help daddy get the rest."

"Speaking of your daddy. I saw him and Sue at the house. It looked like they were leaving."

"That's okay, I'll talk to him later. I just don't feel like dealing with him right now. I'm so mad at him I don't know what to do!"

"Well look, I'll see you later. I'll be at the house with grandma.

When Green Eyes got to Trina's he had no idea Diane had been looking for him. So it took him by surprise the way they were acting when he just stopped by.

"Damn, Tony! Didn't Chris tell you I was looking for you?"

"Naw, I haven't been over there yet, so I haven't seen him. Why, what's up? Why you trippin'?"

"Look, don't start...!" Diane started but Trina cut her off.

She knew Diane was in a rush to get everything off her chest, but she didn't want him to flip on her.

"Green Eyes, hear my cousin out before you say anything!"

"What y'all talking about? Tell me what the fuck is going on!"

Trina saw he was already getting heated. She gave him a look to say promise. He caught it.

"Alright, I'm good. Just tell me!"

"About a couple weeks ago Sue called me to come and cook some dope for her."

Green Eyes was smoking now so he was a lot calmer.

"So, who's Sue?"

"You know Sue, she wear a headscarf all the time. She fuck with Lou!"

"You mean Lou off Cooper?"

"Yeah, that's him!"

"Okay, and?"

"When I got there, they had all this coke and money. I asked her where they got all that shit from. She told me some bullshit about some white dude who's safe she hit. So I didn't think nothing of it!" She had him now. It was becoming clear, but he didn't say anything. He was waiting to see where this all went. "So I cooked it and they paid me two thousand. They also gave me a cookie. Now I believe he gave me all that to stay quiet. After I started putting two and two together, I realized it had to be CJ's shit!"

"Oh yeah, why you figure that?"

"Because when you came over that day after I got back, I heard you talking about what happened with Kenny. I knew right then."

"Why didn't you say anything before now?" He was still surprisingly calm.

"I wanted to make sure, so I talked to Lou first. When he started trippin, I was sure."

"Damn Di, I wish you had said something that day. I had just sold that muthafucka something! I should've known something when that muthafucka said that whip he was driving was his!" He was trying to keep it together, but he was seething. "That's alright Di, we good. Don't say nothing to nobody else. I mean nobody! Imma handle it."

"I won't Green Eyes, I promise!"

CHAPTER 33

It was Thanksgiving. Sonya had made it. She came with Samuel and Sabrina. Kenny and Kanesha were there along with Brett. The traffic in and out of the house was crazy. It was like that every holiday.

Everyone who knew about the situation gathered in Angel's room except Nipsey, he was on the phone.

"Did everything go as planned?" Deon asked. He hadn't spoke to Nipsey since he killed Chris.

"Yeah, but that's not why I'm calling. I'm calling because we have a problem!"

"What is it?"

"Lou and Sue hit CJ's stash house, and we don't know where they are. I don't know if he knows yet, but when he find out, you know what it is!"

"You're right Nipsey, that is a problem. He told me he got robbed and if he find out who did it, they can cancel Christmas! Listen, don't sweat it, Imma try and handle it. Why you just now telling me?"

"We just found out, and I've been a little busy!" Deon knew what he meant.

"Is Chicken alright?"

"You know how she is about her daddy, and if anything happens to him..., let's just say, I don't want that!"

"Where is she?"

"Let me speak to her."

"Hold up, let me go get her."

"Sis, telephone!"

"Who is it?" She wasn't the only one who wanted to know. Everyone was waiting to see who he said.

"Here, just take it!"

All she got out was *hello*. Deon didn't give her a chance to say anything else.

"Chicken, why your ass didn't call me and tell me what happened? You know we family before any of this street shit!"

"I don't know, I just didn't think about it."

"Look, don't worry about this shit! Imma handle it, okay?"

"You sure?" Angel's concern came through in those two little words.

"What you think?" He reassured her.

Tears began to stream down her cheeks. In between them her words were barely audible.

"I... love..." Sniffle. "Thank... I just... My daddy!" Sniffle. She calmed herself before she finished. "I just don't want anything to happen to my daddy!"

"Just chill, I got you! Save me a plate, I'll be through there in a little bit, and kiss grandma for me!"

"Thank you, Deon." Now she felt she could relax for the first time since this thing had started.

Sonya and Sabrina were crying as well. They didn't know why, they just were.

Angel heard Tina calling her name. Everyone got it together and came out the room. As soon as she stepped out into the hallway there was the looming presence of Derrick.

"Hey Derrick, about time your ass got here!"

"Shut up, Tina!" He hated to see Tina. She had no filter.

"Don't tell me to shut up. Where's your slow ass girlfriend?" All the girls laughed.

"Her name is Aubrey, and she ain't slow with your stupid ass!"

"I can't tell she ain't slow, she sleeping with you!"

Nipsey came into the hallway. Derrick hadn't seen him since he left, and almost didn't recognize him.

"Nipsey, you look good. How you doing?"

"I'm real good, how about you?" The tension was suffocating.

As Nipsey shook his hand all he could think about was how easy it would be to kill him right there. That thought made him smile. He went on to the living room where he saw a young lady who he assumed was the subject of Tina's ridicule.

"Hi, I'm Nipsey."

"Oh, you're Derrick's brother, right? I'm Aubrey."

"That's me. Now who's this little fella?" squatting down in front of Ronnie.

Ronnie didn't speak. He looked kind of timid to Nipsey.

"What's your name, little man?"

Ronnie looked down and didn't respond.

"Come on honey, don't be shy! This is Uncle Nipsey!"

"Yeah little man, it's okay!" Nipsey stuck his hand out for him to shake.

Ronnie reluctantly shook it, and sat back next to Aubrey.

The table was all set. Everyone that was gonna stay picked their spot. Everyone that wasn't fixed a plate for themselves or whomever they came to get one for.

Angel was tired of waiting for Lauren, but grandma insisted she wait.

"Baby, I know she shouldn't be here, but this is a day for family. No matter what your mama has done, she still family. You know if we don't forgive we won't be forgiven, right baby?"

"Yes grandma, I know."

Nipsey went to find Samuel and Sabrina to see what they were doing. Derrick stepped in front of him, and put his hand on his shoulder. It was like he had been hit with 2000 volts of electricity. The way he backpedaled looked as if the jolt from it knocked him back.

Sonya had appeared in the doorway with a dish just in time to hear Nipsey's warning.

"Derrick, if you put your hand on me one more time, I will kill you!"

When Derrick looked him in the eyes there was no doubt he meant it.

Derrick was still cocky though because of his size.

"You ain't gone do shit!" he said challenging Nipsey.

Sonya had walked up next to Nipsey. He looked at her, then he looked back at grandma. She was talking to Ronnie not paying any attention. As he began to move Sonya's voice brought him back.

"Baby, where are we gonna sit?" Her touch seemed to soothe his soul.

He looked at Derrick emotionless and calmly said, "We will have our time!"

He turned to look at Sonya with a smile. What she knew was in his heart she didn't see in his eyes. He had learned to mask that part of him and she knew it. What he couldn't hide was the malice he had in his heart towards Derrick. When he shared his pain with her he also shared his desire to kill him. Even though Nipsey never gave her the impression that he had killed anyone, she knew he was more than capable. So that smile told her he was in control.

"We're gonna sit next to grandma on the other side of the table."

She was still looking in his eyes searching for anything that would tell his true intentions. There was none. The only thing he showed her was the love he had for her.

A few minutes later, Lauren walked through the door. To everyone's surprise, she looked beautiful. Her skin and complexion were flawless. Her hair was cut and styled. She had gained all her weight back. She even looked like she had been working out.

Grandma was the only one who wasn't surprised. Lauren had told her what she had been through. When she gave grandma a kiss, she whispered to her at the same time.

"Thank you for letting me come and believing me!"

Grandma took her face in her hands and said, "Child, don't thank me, thank God. If it wasn't for him, you wouldn't be standing here right now. He is the one who made this all possible. Now go see your kids!" She kissed her on the forehead, and watched as she walked towards the back.

Angel was the first to see her. She smiled. She knew immediately she was clean. Seeing her was bittersweet. She loved the fact that she was clean, but still had reservations about their relationship. She was still willing to hear her out. She went and hugged her as everyone looked on. Angel began to cry as they embraced.

Derrick couldn't believe his eyes. He walked over, hugged her and asked, "Where have you been?"

With tears in her eyes she said, "We'll get to that in a little bit. How have you been?"

"I'm doing good. Guess who's here?"

"I know, where is he?"

Nipsey and Samuel were coming down the hall. When she saw him she couldn't believe how much he had changed.

"Oh my God, look at you!" She had her arms extended so she could hug him.

This wasn't the woman he remembered. It felt strange. He feared her for so long. This was a new feeling to be around her without fear. He didn't quite know what he was feeling. Even with him knowing she was coming the reality of her being there was different than he had it worked out in his mind.

"Lauren, y'all go on back in that kitchen and talk. No sense in putting it off. You got some explaining to do to them kids. Then we can eat."

After she had told them everything from the last time she saw each of them to her re-emergence, it was time to eat. Angel helped grandma to the head of the table. Everyone else took their seat. After grandma prayed, she asked Lauren to cut the turkey and Angel cut the ham.

Everyone was talking and enjoying their food except Ronnie. Something about it bothered Nipsey. Ronnie was alright as long as he was sitting next to his mom, but now he sat in between Aubrey and Derrick. He played with his food absentmindedly. Every time Derrick looked at him he cringed. It wasn't so obvious that everyone noticed, but it was enough for Nipsey to take notice. Then it dawned on him why it bothered him. He saw himself in Ronnie. The signs were plain as day. The subtle way Derrick would rub Ronnie's shoulder. The way he would rub his face as if he was removing food solidified it for him.

The queasiness Nipsey felt in his stomach began to rise up into his throat. He couldn't take it anymore. He abruptly excused himself from the table.

Lauren thought it was her, so did grandma. Angel didn't know either way. Sonya on the other hand knew exactly what it was. She had been watching Nipsey watch Ronnie the whole time and she saw what he did. So, when he got up to go outside, she let him go.

Angel followed him and Lauren followed her. He sat down on the porch. Angel sat on one side, and Lauren sat on the other.

"Nipsey, are you alright?" He didn't know how to respond to Angel's question with Lauren there.

He didn't know if he could or should share what he was feeling with her. The awkwardness of the moment made Lauren uncomfortable. So, before she lost the courage she decided to give them the rest of her truth.

"Since we're out here there's something else I need to tell y'all. I know I was not the best mother by no means, but I was the only kind of mother I knew how to be. No one taught me how to be a mother. The only thing I had to look to was my mother. She abused us mentally and physically.

Now that I think about it, I don't think that woman was even capable of love! I know that's no excuse, but it's my truth and I'm living in it. So, when I abused y'all it was the only way I knew how to show love.

"Now, I know different. It took me becoming an addict and giving my life to God to understand how to truly love, not only myself, but you guys too. If it takes the rest of my life to change y'all perception of me, so be it. I love you guys, and I know change won't come overnight, but I'm asking for a chance!"

Nipsey had never heard her speak like this before. This wasn't the person he was expecting.

"Ma, we love you too and always will. But some emotional scars may never heal like our bodies have!" This was his way of trying to open up.

"I understand that, so maybe we can get some help?"

He was looking down trying not to look in her face for fear that his eyes may reveal things that he wasn't sure he wanted her to know.

Angel saw he was having a hard time getting out what she knew he wanted to say. She looked at him then back at Lauren and said, "What he's trying to say is, Derrick molested us!" She said it as if she was spitting venom.

With the look on Lauren's face, her words carried the desired effect.

"What are you talking about?" She was in disbelief. "Why didn't y'all tell me? When did this happen?" She began to tear up. "Do y'all really think I would've stood for that? I would've done something!" The pain she felt was real and evident.

Not only had she been a failure as a mother, she also allowed one of the worst things unimaginable happen to them under her roof. She was mortified.

"We didn't tell you because we didn't know how to tell you. During that time it was hard to talk to you. I didn't think you loved me like you loved him. I didn't think you would believe me!"

"Do you believe us ma?" Angel needed to know.

"I don't think y'all would lie about something like that. I'm just astonished! I don't know what to do now. What can I do?"

Nipsey put his arm around her shoulder and said, "I don't know ma, but it's okay. I'm better now. I'm stronger, and I forgive you for not being there or not even knowing how to be there. Even though I have issues that I'm dealing with I believe everything will be alright."

She was blown away by how mature he had become. He gave off an air of confidence and control that she hadn't seen before. She also felt something else she couldn't put her finger on and that scared her.

"Since we're talking, you might as well know!" He had to tell her what he saw.

"What is it? What else should I know?"

"I didn't come out here because of you to begin with."

"So, what was it?" There was confusion in Angel's question.

"Ronnie's going through the same thing!" They both looked at him now with questioning eyes. "I can see it in his eyes Angel! Look at the way he clings to Aubrey. Every time Derrick touches him he cringes. He's withdrawn. He don't talk, and I bet he throws some type of tantrum every time he has to be alone with him!"

"How do you know Nipsey?" Lauren asked while trying to wrap her mind around what he was saying.

"I've seen other kids like that. I was like that as well."

Lauren didn't say anything. She didn't know what to say. She got up and went upstairs. She went straight to the bathroom and locked the door.

"Hey baby, everything alright?" Brett saw the look of distress on Lauren's face as he passed her coming down the stairs.

"Oh, hey baby. Yeah, we good." She hadn't heard him come down. After the emotional conversation she just had he was a welcomed sight. "Damn baby, you always show up at the right time!" She got up and hugged and kissed him.

"I was coming down to see if you wanted to walk around the corner with me to take grand this food?"

"Yeah, let me run upstairs and get a blunt. I'll be right back!" On her way upstairs she ran into Sabrina. "Hey girl, where you going?"

"I just want to get some air, it's hot up there!" She was fanning herself.

"You want to walk with me around the corner, we're taking Brett's grandma some food?"

"Sure, why not."

"Okay, I'll be right back." Angel was saying as she ran the rest of the way up the stairs.

As they were leaving Deon pulled up. He was in his white on white Jaguar.

"Hey, Deon, I'll be back!" Angel yelled back.

"Hey, Deon." Sabrina remembered him from Royals.

"What's up Sabrina?" He threw his hand up. Nipsey was just getting ready to go upstairs.

"Deon, what's up?" He was happy to see him.

"I'm good. How is everything?"

"I don't know, you tell me?"

"Everything's good. I talked to CJ and told him not to worry about the money. I told him we were good!"

They were going upstairs.

CHAPTER 34

When Tony got to his cousin's house he was irate.

"Cuz, what's up? Sit down! Why you trippin'?" He was pacing back and forth with his gun in his hand.

It took CJ all of ten minutes to calm him down enough to find out what was going on.

"Alright look, Diane told me that bitch Sue called her to come cook some dope for her and Lou. She said they were throwing all this money around. It was the same time the safe got hit. She said she put it together when she found out we got hit and confronted them. It got ugly!" Before Tony finished, CJ began to feel like a mark.

"Fuck! Sue was there that day. That bitch must've hit me for my keys! Damn, that bitch got me with that old shit! When I pulled my pants down, she hit my pockets while she was topping me off!"

Tony interrupted CJ's train of thought with his next question.

"I still haven't figured out how she got the keys?"

It was no way CJ was gonna admit that he pretty much gave them to her.

"She must've picked them up when I was serving her that day, and I didn't realize it!"

Tony dismissed what CJ said because he really didn't care at this point.

"I went to pick up Chris so we could get that muthafucka Lou, but when I got there..." Tears began to well up in his eyes again. He began to shake his head. "He was dead, cuz! He was dead!"

"What! He was what?" CJ flopped down in a chair. He leaned forward, and put his face in his hands.

"Yeah, I don't know what happened. Nothing was missing. It was blood everywhere! His fucking hand was laying on his gun on the table!"

"What you mean?" CJ had never heard anything like that.

"I mean, they cut his fucking hand off!"

"That muthafucka! We gonna kill that muthafucka and everything he love! He must think he's untouchable! Don't nobody fuck with my family!" Now the roles had reversed. CJ was irate now.

"Who you talking about, cuz?"

"I'm talking about Big Man! He called not too long ago and said, *don't worry about the money, we even now*!"

239

What CJ didn't tell Tony was that Deon also said he would take care of the problem he had himself. As he was telling Tony that, he wasn't thinking straight.

"You think he did that shit?" Tony almost couldn't believe it, but it made sense.

"That's alright cuz, don't even trip. He gonna die! That muthafucka Lou, gonna die! Chris didn't deserve that. He would've gotten his money, fuck him! This is what we're gonna do, first let me call Norm and Big Mike!"

While they waited for Norm and Big Mike to show up, CJ filled Tony in on his plan.

"First, we gonna deal with Lou and that bitch of his!" He was still thinking irrational.

It was a culmination of everything that happened since they hit his safe.

"You bring anymore heat with you?" He was strapping on his shoulder holster.

"Yeah, I got a chopper in the MPV."

"Good, let me check on moms and we out!" He heard Norm and Big Mike's car horn.

As they piled into the MPV, CJ filled Norm and Big Mike in on his plan.

"First, let's stop and get the duct tape." Tony said sliding the van's door closed.

You could see Tony had zoned out. He was all business. He called this his killing zone. They had all seen it before, and they knew to watch out. Anything could happen when he was like that. So when he said something about the duct tape no one was surprised.

When they turned off Warren onto Cooper, CJ saw three figures coming up the street. They couldn't tell who it was. Norm slowed the van down. Tony sat up in his seat straining to see.

"Oh, shit!" Tony got excited. "That's Angel right there!" He was pointing with his gun.

"You sure, Green Eyes?" Big Mike asked squinting.

"Look, that's her fucking man! He the only muthafucka around here that fucking tall!" Tony was on the edge of his seat now.

"Good, we gonna snatch this bitch!" CJ said with malice in his heart.

"Who that bitch they with?" Norm asked.

"I don't give a fuck who she is, let's snatch that bitch too! Norm, pull up on them muthafuckas!"

Norm sped up and swerved all the way up on the sidewalk in front of them. Angel and Sabrina screamed at the same time. When the door slid open on the MPV the first person out was Tony. When Angel looked into his eyes and realized who it was, she could've swore her heart stopped for a brief second.

"Shut the fuck up!" Tony spat.

Big Mike had the chopper pointed at Brett.

"What the fuck y'all want?" Sabrina was screaming as Norm brought her back. She had tried to run.

"Green Eyes!" Angel began.

He cut her off by slapping her so hard she almost blacked out.

"Shut the fuck up! Bitch, where yo daddy and that bitch Sue?"

"I don't know!" She was crying. She knew there was no use. She was more in shock than anything.

"Angel, you know what your daddy did, right?" She didn't respond. "That's okay, you ain't gotta talk, but until we find that muthafucka you gonna stay with us! Put that bitch in the van!" CJ was rather calm as he spoke.

"Imma go ahead and kill this muthafucka right here!" Tony pointed the gun at Brett's head.

Sabrina started screaming. Norm put duct tape over her mouth and put her in the van next to Angel.

"Green Eyes, leave him!" CJ stopped him.

He knew Tony was anxious to kill anybody, he didn't care who.

"Fuck that, cuz!"

Tears began to puddle on the carpet where Angel was laying.

"Green Eyes, come on, let's go!" CJ knew he couldn't make Tony do anything, he just hoped he could keep him under control.

"You lucky muthafucka!" Tony turned and got into the van.

As they began to pull off, he slid the door back open.

"Hey, don't you play basketball?" Brett stayed silent. "Hold up. Stop the van, Norm! Oh, you can't hear?"

He jumped out the van while it was rolling. He aimed his gun at Brett's head.

"Imma ask you one more fucking time!" "Green Eyes, don't do it. Let's go!"

He paid CJ no attention.

"Pussy, don't you play ball?" Cocking his gun now.

"Yeah!" Brett blurted out.

"Good muthafucka! Catch this!"

"Pop! Pop!" He shot him in both knees.

He jumped in the van laughing as they sped off.

"Norm, ride up the block. Let's see if Lou car parked out there!"

As they got close to the house he noticed the white Jag parked in front of it.

"Tony, that's Big Man's car right there! You know what? Let's kill this muthafucka now!" CJ was pulling his bulldog out of its holster.

Angel couldn't see, but from what she heard she knew they were in front of grandma's house. She was terrified of what they would do. She silently prayed.

Before they even got in front of the house the van's doors were open. Everyone jumped out and opened fire on the house. It sounded like a war zone. Tony was shooting the chopper while everyone else had their hand guns. Angel was screaming behind the tape over her mouth while Sabrina was trying to kick a window out.

Tina had just come out of her house making her way up the street when she saw them pull up. She ran and hid on the side of her house. She stayed there until she heard CJ yelling.

"Green Eyes, Mike, let's go! Big Mike, we're gonna take these bitches over to your spot on Chalmers. Let's go!"

Inside there was chaos. A fire had started in the living room where grandma was. One of the bullets had already entered her neck and exited her jaw.

She was bleeding profusely.

Kenny was laying on the floor. He had been hit in the back.

"Come on Deon, help me. We need to get to grandma!" Nipsey was yelling at the top of his lungs.

"Everybody go out the back!" Deon was yelling as they attempted to reach grandma.

"Here, I got Kenny! Y'all get grandma!" Samuel said as he grabbed Kenny by his legs.

He drug him down the hallway to the back door. Kanesha was hysterical.

"Kenny! Kenny! Get up!" She was running alongside of Samuel as he drug Kenny.

The living room was engulfed in flames. One of the two oxygen tanks had exploded.

"Deon, get a blanket! Grandma! Grandma, say something! Deon, come on!" Grandma wasn't being burned, but the fire blocked their path.

Deon grabbed the doorknob to the bathroom door. It was locked.

"What the fuck! Somebody in there?" He was trying to get in there to wet the blankets.

"Boom!" He kicked it in.

Lauren was huddled in the corner scared to come out.

"Deon, come on!" Nipsey was still trying to get to grandma unsuccessfully.

"Lauren! What you doing? The house on fire, you gotta get out of here!" He was running water on the blanket as he spoke, but she didn't move.

"Deon! Deon!" Nipsey sounded frantic.

He couldn't worry about Lauren right now. She wasn't hurt.

"Nipsey, here!" Deon had two blankets.

Nipsey wrapped one around himself and dashed through the fire. He made it to grandma. He wrapped her in the other blanket. He could barely see. His eyes were watering up from the smoke and he could barely breathe.

"Deon, I got her! I'm going out the front!" He didn't want to have to go back through the fire.

"Alright, I'll meet you around front! Put her..."

"Hold on, she's too heavy!" She was non-responsive, so she was dead weight.

The fire was steadily pushing Deon back so he couldn't make it through.

"Hold on, Imma go get another blanket!"

"No! There's no time! Wait a minute!" Nipsey pulled grandma out the chair onto the floor. "I got her, I'm dragging her through! Where you at? I can't see you!"

"Listen to my voice, come this way!" Deon was choking.

He put his hands out into nothingness in hopes of Nipsey finding him. He had stopped guiding him with his voice. He was on his knees choking. Nipsey followed the choking sound.

"I'm right here Deon, where are you?" As he finished speaking he tripped over Deon. "Come on, grab her!" She was heavy. It took all their strength to get her up.

They slowly made their way to the back door.

"Wait, you hear something?" Nipsey asked.

"Help me! Don't leave me!" Lauren had been overtaken by the smoke. Her cries for help were faint and inaudible.

Nipsey tried to listen but he didn't have time because the fire had made it to the hallway and smoke was overtaking them fast. They had to go.

They made it around to the front of the house, The fire department hadn't made it yet.

"Put her in my car! Come on Nipsey, we're taking her to the hospital. Fuck the ambulance!"

"Wait, we gotta take Kenny too!" Nipsey was leaning over Kenny talking to him. "Let him go Kanesha! Let him go, we need to get him to the hospital! I got him. He gonna be alright!"

"Nipsey, hurry up, grandma bleeding bad!" Deon had been pressing the blanket to her face and neck.

"I'm sorry grandma!" Tears were running down Deon's face.

"I'm sorry. You're gonna be alright!"

Nipsey had put Kenny in the car, but not before Kanesha made him promise she could go too. She sat on Nipsey's lap. She was still inconsolable.

No one spoke until they reached Henry Ford Hospital. They pulled up to the emergency room entrance. Nipsey ran in and came back with some nurses and a couple doctors. As they removed grandma and Kenny from the car Kanesha held on to Nipsey. He was apathetic to the whole situation.

They were following the gurneys in when a nurse stopped them.

"I'm sorry, you have to go through that door. If you would just go fill out the necessary paperwork someone will be out shortly to speak with you. We'll do everything we can!"

After the fire department put the fire out, they informed Tina that they had discovered Lauren's body right inside the back door. She had died from smoke inhalation.

CHAPTER 35

"Take them bitches to the basement!" CJ was talking about the basement in the apartment building where they were keeping Sabrina and Angel.

As Norm picked Angel up, her body just collapsed in his arms. She was devastated. There was no fight in her. At this point she didn't care if she lived or died, because she had already assumed the worst about grandma and everyone else who was in the house.

Sabrina was still kicking and screaming though. Big Mike was struggling with her.

"Yo Mike, hold up, I'm tired of this bitch!" Tony snatched the tape off her mouth. Now you need to settle your ass down or this gonna get real painful real fast!" She spit in his face.

"Fuck you! You no good muthafucka!" Tony laughed while wiping his face.

"Mike, let her go! You know what?" He was pulling something out his pocket as he spoke. "I like your spunk!"

Sabrina began to say something, but before she could get anything out.

"Wham!" He broke her jaw with the brass knuckles he pulled from his pocket.

She was knocked out cold. Big Mike caught her body before she hit the floor.

"Now, take that bitch to the basement!" He waved her away nonchalantly.

"CJ! Trevon said he saw Big Man leaving. He said he was taking somebody to the hospital!" Norm had just got off the phone.

"Yo cuz, check it! You know what that mean, right?" Tony read the worry in CJ's face when he asked that.

"Yeah, I know what that means. That means we fucked up because that muthafucka ain't dead, and this shit is about to get real crazy. We need to make him pay for them bitches and get ghost. You know that bitch Angel is like his sister!"

"Yeah, I know. That's why I know he ain't gonna pay us shit! He gonna try and kill us. Period, point blank!"

Tony knew what CJ was saying to be true.

"All we got to do is let that muthafucka know if he want to see her ass alive again, then he gots to pay. This way, when he come to pay we dead his ass, and them bitches too!"

CJ knew without a doubt he had to kill Deon, but he also knew it wasn't gonna be easy.

"Alright, look Norm, get somebody to watch out in the back. We need a couple more people to stay in here. I want somebody out front at all times until this shit is over, and we gonna go get Cotton and some more heat. While we're at it, we'll see if we can set up a meet. I don't want nobody fucking with them bitches downstairs, and everybody stay on their toes!"

"Tina, what's up?"

"I'm glad you called, Nipsey . Your girl and everyone else is here. I need to tell you something too!"

"What is it?"

"When I was on my way back up the street I saw them!"

"You saw who?"

"I saw Green Eyes and CJ shooting." She was becoming emotional. "When they were done, I saw them get back in that van and when they opened the door I saw Angel and Sabrina tied up in there. It was nothing I could do!" Crying now.

"Alright, calm down. It's alright!" The gravity of everything was overwhelming to her. He knew in order to deal with the situation he would have to keep a level head.

"But Nipsey, I couldn't help them! I didn't know what to do! I saw them Nipsey, I saw them! They were laying there in that van! Oh my God!"

She was beside herself.

Nipsey let her go on. He knew if he just listened, in her distress she would tell him all he needed to know.

"I heard him Nipsey ! I heard…"

"What you hear, Tina?"

"I heard him say Big Mike, and I heard him say they were gonna take them over on Chalmers somewhere!"

"Did you hear anything else?"

"No, that's it!"

"Okay Tina, thanks. Just chill. We gonna take care of it. Is Samuel down there with y'all?" He had no doubt Samuel knew the situation.

He just wanted to let him know everything would be alright.

"You talking about your friend?"

"Yeah, the white guy!"

"He left. When I told him what I saw he asked if he could use the phone. Twenty minutes later someone pulled up in a gray Maserati. He told us to tell you he would talk to you soon." That was puzzling to him.

"Why would he leave knowing his girl was just snatched? Something's not right about that." Nipsey pushed those thoughts out of his mind. He had to focus on what to do next.

"Alright Tina, hold it down. If we need you we'll call you. Have y'all talked to the hospital yet?"

"Yeah, and it don't look good for grandma. She's in…"

He stopped her. He didn't want to hear it. If it was too bad, he didn't know if he could take it.

"I'm sorry, Tina. I got to go. I'll talk to you later."

"But Nipsey, I need to tell you something else. It's Lauren."

"Where is she?"

"She… She didn't make it!"

He was stunned. He didn't exactly know what to say.

"What happened?"

"The fire department found her lying inside the house! They said it looked like she was trying to make it out, but didn't make it. I'm sorry!"

He pushed his emotions down.

"Thank you, Tina. I'll talk to you later." That hurt him. Even with all that they had gone through, he loved her.

After their conversation that night he was looking forward to starting over with her. A tear rolled down his cheek.

When he got off the phone, he sat there for a minute. He closed his eyes and began to focus on his breathing.

"Nipsey, what's up?" Deon saw the sadness in Nipsey's eyes.

"They found ma in the house. She was dead!"

"I'm sorry, man. I should've made her get up before I left the bathroom."

"What are you talking about?" Nipsey was confused.

"When I went to get the blankets for grandma, I had to kick the door in because Lauren was in there with the door locked. She was scared. She wouldn't leave out. I told her she needed to go. Damn! I'm sorry man, I should've made sure she got out, but I was busy trying to get grandma. I'm sorry man!"

"Don't, it's not your fault. It's alright. We can't worry about that right now."

He ran down everything Tina had told him.

"You sure she said Chalmers? Over off Jefferson?"

Nipsey was wondering why Deon had a smirk on his face.

"Yeah, I think so. Why?"

"I think we may be in luck, that's all! Did you tell Samuel about his girl?"

"Tina told him. She said after she told him, he left." He recognized that expression on Deon's face. He said, "Yeah, I was thinking the same thing!"

"Did he get scared or something?"

"I don't know. She said he used the phone and twenty minutes later, a

Maserati came and scooped him up!"

"Wait a minute! A Maserati? Did she say what color?"

"She said it was gray. Why?"

"Are you serious? I only know one person in the city with a gray Maserati!"

"Who is that?" Nipsey asked, still confused.

Deon went and grabbed his phone. As he dialed the number Nipsey tried to ask him what was going on. Deon held up one finger as someone answered the other end.

"Mr. Godwin, I was just about to call you. My nephew was just telling me what happened. So, what are we gonna do? They have my niece." "Damn, Donnie! This shit is out of control, we need to end this shit once and for all!"

Donnie agreed wholeheartedly. He wasn't in the business of letting things come back to bite him. Samuel was his favorite nephew and Sabrina has been a part of their family for as long as he could remember.

"I've been on the phone since my nephew told me what happened. This is what I have for you so far. The guy Big Mike has a spot on Chalmers. It's an apartment building. He has management in his pocket so he turns a blind eye to what's going on.

"From what my people can tell, they have people posted on the outside, but they're still serving customers. Now, I don't know how many's on the inside. You need to get someone on the inside to get the layout. I'm gonna send you two of my guys. They know what CJ looks like. They'll do what's needed, and they're good at what they do."

"That's perfect because this is personal. I'm gonna handle this myself!" This was something Deon wouldn't normally do, but under the circumstances he wanted to make sure there were no mistakes.

"Mr. Godwin, there's two ways we can handle this. We can reason with them and everyone walks out alive, or we can kill everything! Since you want to handle this personally, it's your call!"

Before Donnie even laid out the options, Deon already knew the fate of everyone involved. Donnie just wanted to hear him say it. There couldn't be any loose ends that could lead back to him in any way. His family's name was much too important to be associated with common street thugs. That's why he was sending two of his best killers, so there would be no mistakes.

"We're killing everything!" Deon told him with certainty.

"Good my friend. I don't need details, but whatever you may need, just ask. Mr. Godwin, I'm sorry this has happened to your family. I wish you all the luck, Now, is Nipsey there? My nephew would like to speak with him. One last thing, my men are on their way to you. Let's bring those girls home!"

"We will, we will!" He handed the phone to Nipsey.

"When you're done, come to the back."

Deon walked off towards a room in the back of the house.

"Nip, what's up?"

"Samuel!" Nipsey was surprised to hear his voice. "What's going on?

Why did you leave?"

Samuel began to explain who his uncle was and why he left. It was just coincidence that his uncle knew Deon. He had only found that out when he called him for some help.

"Nip, my uncle wanted me to stay here. Get Angel and my girl, Nip! Make them pay for this shit! Be careful man, much love." Nipsey could tell Samuel was in his feelings.

"Alright Samuel, we'll talk when this is over. And Samuel, they're coming home!"

When CJ and Tony told Cotton his brother had been killed, he lost it.

"Look, you need to chill so we can get these muthafuckas!" CJ knew if he couldn't calm him down he may do something irrational and he couldn't have that.

"What we gone do?" Cotton asked, still pacing.

"We gonna set up a meet and make him bring us $100,000. When they show up we gonna kill all of them. Then we're gonna kill them bitches too.

So, go get that other chopper!"

On his way to the back he called over his shoulder.

"CJ, y'all gotta let me kill him! Promise me I can kill him!" He came back into the living room and chambered a round.

"You got it, cuz." CJ really didn't care who killed him as long as he ended up dead.

When they got back to the spot, CJ went downstairs where the girls were. No one had been down there since he and Tony had left. Angel had urinated on herself.

"Look at your ass now, you should've told me where your daddy was!" She never moved. She silently prayed she would live through this.

When CJ got back upstairs Tony was already on the phone with Deon.

"Look muthafucka, you can play games all you want, but if you don't get that money, I'm killing these bitches! Now, you got three hours! Meet us at Chandler Park.

"Let me and Cotton go get this shit cuz, and you stay here. We gonna take the loud bitch with us and leave Angel with y'all. If anything goes wrong, kill her and hunt them muthafuckas down!"

When Deon got the call from Tony, little did Tony know that he aided in the conception of the plan Nipsey came up with. From the information he got from Deon about CJ and his family, he was confident it would work.

"We need to go by the house so I can check on things. Plus, I need to grab a few things. Since we have three hours, let's get started."

Nipsey was saying as Deon strapped on his bulletproof vest.

"Alright, I'll be ready in a second. Go ahead and tell them what's up." Deon was talking about Donnie's guys.

"Bo and Pete, go to the park and kill whoever shows up. If I'm right, it won't be CJ. More than likely he'll send some soldiers, so do what you do. I doubt they're gonna bring the girls, but if they do, cool. Make sure nothing happens to them and get them somewhere safe!"

When Donnie's guys showed up they were prepared for anything. Their guns were equipped with silencers, and they already had their vests on. There was no telling what else they had in their duffel bags and no one asked. They never really said much, but the way they moved spoke of their professionalism.

"While y'all are at the park Deon and myself are going to the apartment building. If everything goes right, we'll meet back up here at the same time."

Deon was surprised at how Nipsey took control, but he still didn't understand how Nipsey intended to kill anyone without a gun. He assumed that's why he said they had to stop by the house to grab something. So he would just wait and see.

When they got to Tina's, everyone was in tears. Nipsey's heart sank before anyone said anything. Tina hugged him tight.

"Nipsey, grandma didn't make it!" She spoke into his ear as she held onto him.

"No!" He tried to break free of her grasp.

Sonya came over and hugged him as well. She never spoke. Everything was happening so fast it was like she was watching a sad movie. All three held on to each other. They wouldn't let him go. He began to weep openly for the first time since he was a kid.

"It's okay baby, let it out!" Sonya said as she wept. They were all overcome with grief, but they continued to hold on.

Deon went out to his car. He felt partially responsible. All the things that Nipsey said to him that day at the skating rink came rushing back. He cried briefly. He knew they had to finish what was started. He would mourn later.

The car horn brought Nipsey back to the reality of things to come.

"I got to go baby. I love you!" He kissed Sonya.

"I know, Nipsey. I love you too!" Sonya didn't want to let go.

"Tina, thank you. I love you!"

"We're here for y'all, Nipsey. Go find my sister!"

Before Nipsey got in the car he went to the house. Fighting back tears as he entered he went into Angel's room. The fire hadn't made it back that far. He grabbed his Dao and dagger. He strapped the broad sword to his back, sheathed his dagger on his hip, and grabbed a contraption that almost looked like a dog muzzle. He pulled up his sleeve and strapped it to his arm. It was light and durable. It was also spring-loaded. He attached a two edged blade to it, so if he thrust his hand forward in a certain manner the blade extended, and it was also retractable.

When he got in the car Deon looked at him like he was crazy. Nipsey knew what he was thinking, but he didn't entertain his ignorance. He really didn't have much to say. He really didn't know how to feel about Deon right now. He was hurting, and all he wanted to do was hurt anybody that had a role in grandma's death, and Angel's and Sabrina's kidnapping.

The Marathon Continues　　　　　　　　　　　　　　　　　　*Eugene L. Weems*

CHAPTER 36

Bo and Pete got to the park forty-five minutes early. Bo dropped Pete off at the restrooms. He hopped out with his duffel bag and somehow climbed atop the twelve foot high structure that housed the restrooms. It was about one hundred yards from where Bo waited for Tony and Cotton.

Pete opened his duffel and pulled out a .223 caliber semi-automatic rifle. He attached his 3x9x40 night vision scope to it. Then pulled out an infrared beam and also attached it. He took his time and moved with precision. He held the gun up and looked through the scope. He dialed in on Bo, lifted the walkie talkie to his mouth and spoke one word.

"Ready!"

Bo lifted his hand straight up in the air over his head. As he looked at it, he saw the distinctive red dot that was a prelude to death. The radio came to life again.

"Ready!"

Bo pulled the duffel bag with the money in it out of the car, and sat it at his feet. He leaned back on the car and waited. They were ready.

When Tony and Cotton entered the park, Tony spotted Bo immediately. He scanned the rest of the park for any signs of movement. Cotton pulled the van up a few feet in front of Bo. Bo was calm and patient. Tony got out first.

"You got something for me?"

Tony had a cockiness that Bo despised. He would enjoy watching him die. He stood up off the car slowly.

"Where's the girls?"

Cotton got out, and snatched Sabrina out the back of the van.

"Where's the other one?" As Bo spoke, Sabrina recognized him. He winked at her when he saw she recognized him.

"I'm supposed to call when I have the money, and she'll be let out." Tony lied.

Cotton walked Sabrina up next to Tony as if on cue. Bo went along with it anyway because they were gonna die regardless.

"Alright, let's get this over with. I'm gonna slide the bag over and you send her!"

Cotton held her at arm's length with his gun aimed at the back of her head. Bo slid the bag half of the way between them. As Tony walked forward. Pete place the red dot on the temple of Cotton. Tony

253

never looked back to see it. He leaned down with his eyes never leaving Bo's. As soon as he gripped the duffel bag, he reached for the gun in his back at the same time.

"Pop!" A single shot rang out.

Cotton's brain sprayed Sabrina.

"Pop!" "Pop!" Pete had shot him in his knees.

Tony never got the chance to reach the grip of his gun. He was on the ground holding his knees.

"Sabrina, come over here!"

She ran to him as he said. He went and stood over Tony. He didn't want him to die quick, he wanted to see him suffer.

"Pop!" "Pop!"

He shot him in the hands. Then he walked over to Sabrina and removed the duct tape. Before the tape hit the ground, she ran and kicked Tony as hard as she could in the face, over and over.

"Let's go little sis!" He was pulling her away.

The radio came to life once again.

"Bo, what mom tell you about playing with your food?"

Without even looking, Bo shot Tony in the face six times.

Instead of pulling up on Chalmers, Nipsey and Deon parked on Ashland, one block over. The ran down the side of someone's house and cut up the alley.

"Nipsey, look, somebody's back there! He must be on post?" Deon was whispering.

"Here, hold this." Nipsey handed Deon his broad sword. "I'll be right back!" He stood up and walked in the backyard.

"Hey muthafucka! What you doing? Get the fuck outta here!"

The guy had his hand on his gun.

"I'm just trying to get a little something." Nipsey was acting like a crackhead, digging in his pockets trying not to make eye contact.

"Take yo crackhead ass around to the front!" The guy didn't feel threatened in the least.

So he never pulled his gun, which was his first mistake. Because when Nipsey was two feet away he closed the last couple feet so quick it was almost a blur. He took his dagger and skillfully inserted it into the guy's ball and socket joint of his right shoulder with so much force it became disjointed and with the slightest movement of the blade after it's insertion he severed all of the seventeen muscles that serve to move the shoulder joint which rendered that arm totally useless.

He knew the guy was right-handed because his hand was still holding the pistol grip tucked in his jeans. As he removed the blade from the shoulder, he grabbed a hold of the left arm, and reinserted it through the back of the guy's hand into his hip joint and left it. He began to scream.

"Shh!"

Nipsey quickly placed his hand over his mouth as he kicked the right knee. It became displaced.

"Where's the girls? Answer and you live!" Nipsey was straddling his chest.

He was leaning down close to his ear as he spoke. Then he slowly removed his hand from his mouth so he could answer.

"She in the basement. Green Eyes took the other one to get the money!" He was trying not to scream.

"Good, now how many is in there?"

Deon was walking up as he began to answer.

"Four, and the two in the front."

"Good job!" Nipsey said while patting his cheek.

As he began to stand he extended the blade from under his sleeve and cut his throat.

"Oh shit! What the fuck!" Deon said a little too loudly he immediately placed his hand over his mouth. He had seen people die, but never like this. "Who the fuck are you? Damn dog, you good. We need to talk after this shit!"

Deon was amazed. Nipsey's eyes looked wild. They were wide open and constantly moving. He was keenly aware of every movement and sound. He only spoke when necessary, and he moved assuredly.

"Come on, there's a fuse box over there. Can you take care of the two in the front?" Nipsey was moving toward the box when he asked.

"Yeah, how do you want to do this?" Deon asked while attaching his silencer.

"When you take care of them come back and I'll cut the power. We'll go in through the basement window and hopefully we'll make it out alive! Since Green Eyes and Cotton took one of the girls maybe that will make things a little easier. Hold on, let me get my dagger. He won't be needing it!"

Deon crept around to the front of the building. He was hoping he could get them before they could get a shot off and wake the whole neighborhood. When he got to the corner of the building, he peeped around the corner. He was in luck. They were huddled together rolling a blunt. He quickly stepped out and unloaded eight shots in rapid succession. When they were on the ground he walked over and shot each one two more times a piece in the head. Then pulled both bodies close to the building and jogged back around to the back.

Nipsey was looking through the basement windows to see if he could see exactly who and where they were in the basement. He spotted Angel just as Deon had rounded the corner.

"Over here!" Nipsey was gesturing and speaking lowly. "Angel's right there!"

Deon tapped on the window.

"Don't do that! She may get anxious and give us away if someone's down there. Look, on three you break the glass and I'm gonna cut the power at the same time. We gotta move fast!"

"Alright, I got you!" Deon positioned himself to kick the window out.

"Three!"

He didn't count, he just said *three* but Deon was on point. He kicked the window out. It turns out it was some type of Plexiglas, so there was no shattering. They scurried through the window. Deon heard Angel's frightened muffled cries from behind the duct tape that was still on her mouth.

After they made sure there was no one in the basement with them, Nipsey called out to her. Mainly so he could make sure he was going in the right direction in the dark.

As soon as the lights went out, CJ opened the door that led out of the apartment.

"Mike, come on! This shit ain't right!"

He and Big Mike were inside the apartment, while Norm and Black were in the hallway.

"Fuck! Norm! Black! Where y'all at?" CJ couldn't see and everything was completely quiet.

"We right here by the basement door!" They knew not to move, especially with how *jumpy* CJ was.

"Y'all go down and make sure ain't nothing wrong!"

Nipsey, Angel, and Deon were on the other side of the door getting ready to come through when they heard the conversation.

"Angel, get behind Deon, and make sure you're on the left side with your back to the wall!"

Just as he finished getting the words out, Norm snatched the door open. He stepped down on the first step with his right leg. Totally blinded by darkness, Nipsey grabbed that leg and pulled it from under him. He fell backwards, sliding down the stairs. As he was falling, his gun went off.

Nipsey crouched down and yelled.

"Shoot Deon, straight up the stairs!"

Simultaneously Nipsey reached down and put his blade through Norm's eye socket into his brain. All his movement ceased. Deon got off four shots dead center of Black's chest. He fell backward into the hallway.

"Norm! Black! Fuck!" CJ was scared for the first time.

Nipsey followed the sound of his voice. He removed his Dao. Moving swiftly in a squatting motion.

"Mike, let's get the fuck out of here!"

Nipsey was close. Deon was right behind him, pulling Angel along the wall so she could keep her bearings coming down the hall.

CJ's breathing was labored from panic setting in.

"I'm right behind you!" Big Mike said tapping CJ on the shoulder. "Alright, let's go!"

As they started out the door they surprised Nipsey and Deon because they came out shooting blindly. It was also smart because with the constant muzzle flash they were able to see plainly. Deon threw Angel on the floor and took two to the chest in the process.

"Ugh! Shit! I'm hit!"

Big Mike saw him fall and put two more in his chest.

"Ugh!"

The vest protected him but it still hurt. Then Angel screamed out. She got hit in the shoulder. Deon crawled over and covered her with his body.

CJ ran for the exit. Big Mike was following firing indiscriminately walking backwards. When Nipsey heard his gun click, he seized the opportunity. He ran full speed at Big Mike and ran his Dao straight through him. The force in which he used carried him right out the window.

"Mike!"

As CJ was going out the door, he turned just in time to see Big Mike go out the window. He took aim at Nipsey as he ran down the stairs. The first bullet hit Nipsey in the shoulder and spun him around. The next two hit him in the back and the last one grazed his neck. He fell and crawled around the corner for cover.

CJ burst through the door leading outside. Nipsey heard more shots, then there was silence. No shots. No Noise. No commotion.

Nothing.

"Boom!"

The door leading outside slammed into the wall. Nipsey ducked back around the corner.

"Angel! Leroy!" Sabrina came running up the stairs yelling. "Angel! Leroy! Y'all alright? Where are y'all?"

Nipsey was sitting on the floor with his back against the wall in pain. Sabrina almost tripped over him as she got to the top of the stairs and turned the corner.

"Sabrina, what are you doing here?"

Bo and Pete was coming up the stairs behind her and answered his question.

"She made us bring her back. She said she wasn't leaving Angel. Even after we told her y'all were coming to get her. She said she had to make sure." While Bo was explaining, Pete and Sabrina was helping Angel and Deon.

"We heard the shots from outside. So we couldn't come in, it was too dark. Then CJ came bursting out the door. Pete put a clip in him, but we need to get out of here now. You hear the siren?"

THE FINAL CHAPTER

It was late spring and things were finally normalizing after everything that had happened. Angel decided to keep the house. She had the living room and dining room renovated. Brett moved in after they got married. His dreams of playing basketball were shattered. They decided that they wanted to make a difference in kids lives. So, they both decided to go back to school to take some child development courses.

Angel had planned to open several learning and development centers around Detroit. She loved kids, and she would do anything to protect them. Not only from the streets, but also from dysfunctional families. That's why when she received a frantic call from Aubrey two months earlier to take Ronnie in, she didn't have to think twice.

It was early May when Angel's phone rang about three in the morning.

Aubrey was on the other end.

"Angel, Oh my God! I'm... Oh my God! I did it! I..." Angel couldn't make sense of anything she was saying.

"Aubrey, girl, calm down! What's wrong?" She was sitting up on the side of the bed now.

"My baby wasn't lying! I saw him! I saw him with my own eyes. I'm sorry,

I didn't know what to do. I'm sorry Angel. I love you!" Angel was up now putting on clothes.

"Aubrey, what happened? Calm down, I'm on my way. Just tell me what happened!"

Aubrey caught her breath and started from the beginning.

"Around Halloween last year Ronnie told me that Derrick was telling him not to tell me things. So I started to think, who tells a kid that? So, I went to one of those spy shops and bought a hidden camera. But I never used it even though Ronnie had told me things before." She was crying again.

Angel wondered where this was going. She listened intently.

"Last week Ronnie came to me and told me Derrick hurt him!"

Angel was on her way down the stairs when she instantly stopped in her tracks. She sat down on the stairs and put her hand over her mouth in anticipation of what she knew Aubrey would say next.

"So I listened this time. I got the camera I had and set it up in

Ronnie's room." The more she talked the more Angel could hear the anger mixed in with her pain. "He hadn't come home yet, so I decided to get the camera to see if it caught anything. Angel, he was on top of my baby! My baby was crying!" She started crying again. Her emotions were all over the place.

"I'm so sorry, Aubrey!" Angel was crying too.

"When he came home I knew he would be tired. So I had sex with him as long as I could, and cooked him something to eat and he went to bed." Angel heard the apprehensiveness in her voice as she stopped talking.

"It's alright. What happened?" Angel coaxed her.

"I'm sorry, Angel. I didn't know what to do. All I could see was him hurting my baby! That's why I couldn't stop stabbing him in his sleep! I'm sorry!" She continued to sob.

"Is he dead, Aubrey?" Angel was in shock, she wasn't expecting that.

"I don't know, I ran out the room. I hope so!" She was angry again.

"Angel, I'm calling the police. I packed Ronnie's things. Promise me you'll take care of him! You're the only person I trust."

"I promise, Aubrey. I'm on my way to get him now. Don't call them until I come get him!"

Angel made another call and raced to Aubrey's. When she walked in Aubrey was sitting on the couch. She had calmed down somewhat. Angel walked over and hugged her.

"Don't worry, we're gonna take care of this. I made a call!" "What are you talking about?" Aubrey was confused.

Bo and Pete walked in. Aubrey was frightened, she didn't know what to expect.

"It's okay."

"Angel, what's going on?"

"This never happened! Say it! Look at me, Aubrey. This never happened!" Angel was looking her in the eyes.

"This never happened!" Aubrey said unconvincingly. "Say it again!"

"This never happened!" More convincing now.

"That's right. "This never happened!" Angel said one last time.

"Angel, the new box spring and mattress will be here within the hour. Have a nice night." Those were the only words Bo spoke the whole time he was there. Then they left and no one ever spoke of it again.

Kenny healed up just fine. Brett convinced him to join his movement, *Sure Fire Youth*. They mentored and traveled all over giving inspirational speeches. Brett even wrote books and designed his own puppets to teach about issues facing today's youth. He also coached basketball in his spare time. The kids loved the puppet show they put on. It became their passion.

Deon donated the building where Angel taught parenting classes. She also ran a day care and held food drives. The building was called *Grandma's House*. Every child was welcomed who needed somewhere to feel safe. There was a memorial set up in front in remembrance of grandma. It read: *This building is dedicated to a woman that dedicated her life to God, children and family, and she will be greatly missed.*

Sabrina still planned to leave for college in the fall. Even after her ordeal she still planned to become a defense attorney. She had to have her jaw wired shut from where Tony broke it, but that didn't stop her from being opinionated. She carried a pad around and wrote everything down. She also took that opportunity to learn sign language.

Samuel on the other hand decided not to go to college. He joined the family business and began to work closely with Donnie. His parents strongly advised against it, but supported him all the same. Donnie helped him open his own luxury car dealership. He no longer dressed in all black and began to take self defense classes as well as frequenting the gun range. He took a special interest in Donnie's business and Donnie welcomed him.

He and Sabrina were still together. For her going away present he gave her an Aston Martin. They planned to get married during her spring break.

By the time anyone made it to the scene, Mac had destroyed the video and came up with a story to cover himself. When he turned in his report it read, "When Sergeant Leroy Cox and myself observed three males, two black and one white, holding a gun on a black male, we exited the vehicle with our guns drawn. The suspects refused to comply to verbal commands to drop their weapons.

"When Sgt. Cox got close enough, he attempted to disarm the black male. I held my gun on the other two. As I began to handcuff the other black male, the white male ran. As I yelled for him to stop the suspect I was handcuffing began to assault me. A fight ensued. Then I heard a shot ring out. Sgt. Cox had been hit.

The remaining two perps ran. I performed CPR, but was unsuccessful in reviving Sgt. Cox. I waited for assistance to arrive."

He went on to add some pertinent information about the perps and his injuries and that was it. A brief investigation took place and Mac was cleared of any wrongdoing and wasn't held liable for Roy's death.

After Roy's funeral, Mac presented Susan with a check. It was from a drive that Pam held in honor of Roy. Susan raised seventy-five thousand dollars and she and Mac matched it with their own seventy-five thousand. It would go for Roy Jr.'s college and for whatever else Susan saw fit.

Mac retired with his full pension not long afterwards. The two cases they were working when Roy died remained unsolved.

After grandma's funeral, Nipsey decided to leave for basic sooner than first planned. Grandma's death devastated him. Everything reminded him of her. Being in the house tormented him. Sonya did what she could to comfort him, but she was worried about his state of mind. He didn't talk much and he was distant. Sometimes late at night she would wake up and he would be sitting at the kitchen table in the dark like he was waiting for something.

This had been going on ever since she moved in. She tried not to worry because she knew it wasn't good for the baby girl she was carrying. She just wished it was something she could do. She prayed that he would come around before she started college and he left for the military.

Then, three days before he was to leave, Deon came by the house. It was the first time Sonya had seen Nipsey smile for some time.

"Nipsey, what's up?" He looked serious but had a smile on his face until Sonya left the room.

Nipsey knew there was only one reason why Deon was there. Nipsey had been waiting for this day since before the funeral.

"Deon, nice to see you." His eyes told Deon not to keep him waiting any longer. So he didn't.

"We found him. He was seen at grandma's grave. We knew once

we put the word out that grandma had passed and he missed the funeral he would go to her grave site. So, my people followed him straight to his house!"

He was talking about Lou and Sue. Nipsey told him to find him. No one had seen either of them since everything had happened. They had stayed clean and was hustling making good money.

Nipsey never told anyone that he had Deon trying to find them, and he never told Deon why he wanted them found. Deon already knew.

"Thank you, Deon. Are you still gonna come and get me to meet up with my recruiter?"

"Yeah, I got you." He said as he was leaving. There was nothing left to be said.

That night was the first night he slept soundly, and didn't sit up and wait and see if Lou would sneak in the house through the back door like he used to.

The day Nipsey was to leave he was up at 4:00 am. He told Deon to come get him at 5:00 am, and he had to meet his recruiter at 7:00 am.

"Baby, you ready?" Sonya asked.

She was sad to see him go. She had no idea he was leaving two hours early.

"Yeah baby, don't cry."

"I can't help it."

He embraced her tightly. Angel was up as well.

"I'll see you sis." As he embraced her his heart began to ache.

The fact that there was no way he could ever tell her what he was about to do pained him.

"You ready?" Deon asked.

"Let's go!" The look Nipsey had, Deon had seen before.

So he knew not to try and engage him in conversation until it was over. When they got off the Edsel Ford Fwy. on Livernois, Nipsey put on his gloves. When they got to Dix St. and the address they had, he got out the car without a word. He entered the house through a window in back of the Townhouse. He took the stairs two at a time. When he entered the room, neither Lou or Sue never moved.

He went to the side of the bed Sue was sleeping on peacefully. She was laying on her back. He ran his blade across her throat with ease and as her life drained from her onto the mattress, Lou never moved. Nipsey quietly moved to the other side of the bed to stand over Lou as he quietly slept.

"Lou!" Nipsey said just above a whisper. "Lou!" He said again.

The sound of a man's voice startled Lou awake. He sat straight up. He looked at Nipsey holding his broad sword down at his side. Then he looked at Sue.

"You didn't have to kill her!" Lou said calmly. He never moved. A lone tear rolled down his cheek. He knew it was over. "Tell Angel I'm sorry! I…"

Nipsey stuck his sword through his mouth with so much force, it came out the back of his head and into his headboard. He had to use two hands to remove it.

As Deon dropped him off, he assured Nipsey that no one would ever know. With the death of Lou and Sue, a chapter in Nipsey's life closed. When he entered the military a new one began. Who knows what type of 'Conflict' he may become embroiled in. Stay tuned.

ABOUT THE AUTHOR

Eugene L. Weems is the bestselling author of *United We Stand, Prison Secrets, America's Most Notorious Gangs, The Other Side of the Mirror, Head Gamez, Bound by Loyalty, Red Beans and Dirty Rice for the Soul, Innocent by Circumstance, Cold as Ice, and The Green Rose.* The former kick boxing champion is a producer, model, philanthropist, and founder of No Question Apparel, Inked Out Beef Books, and co-founder of Vibrant Green for Vibrant Peace. He is from Las Vegas, Nevada.

BOUND BY LOYALTY

COREY 'C-MURDER' MILLER
EUGENE L. WEEMS

The novel that critics across the nation are raving about and people are eager to read.

C-Murder and Weems constructed an elaborate contemporary urban thriller full of twists and false starts. Bound by Loyalty is absolutely chilling and bursting with surprises.

$14.95   278pgs   6x9 Paperback   ISBN: 978-0991238002
Celebrity Spotlight Entertainment, LLC

RED BEANS and DIRTY RICE FOR THE SOUL

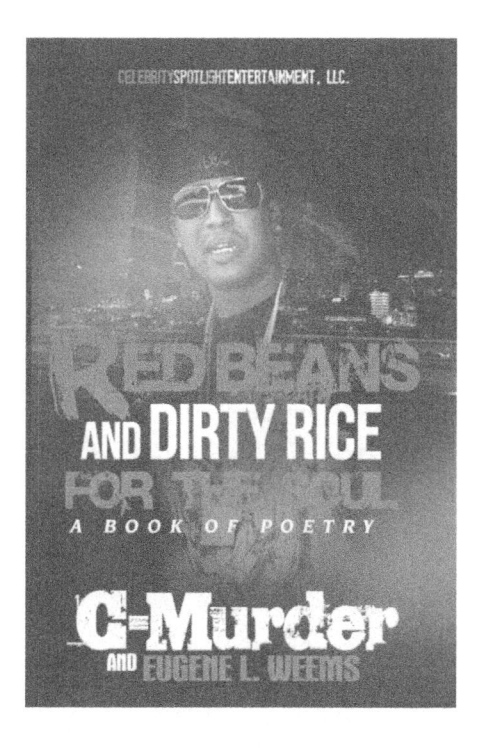

**COREY 'C-MURDER' MILLER
EUGENE L. WEEMS
CLARKE LOWE**

Tread the gutta' life with **C-MURDER** in this gripping compilation of poetry that is deeply rooted in the streets and behind prison walls.

WARNING! May cause a severe reaction or death in people who are square to the game. If an allergic reaction occurs, stop reading and seek emergency counseling from your local priest.

$14.95   103pgs   6x9 Paperback   ISBN: 978-0991238019
Celebrity Spotlight Entertainment, LLC

3 STRIKES

CRUCIFIX

Growing up poor, abused and surrounded by violence, Tito Lopez dreamed of becoming a cop. But as fate would have it, his dreams became a series of nightmares and the treachery of life in the hood overtakes him.

When the water gets too deep, gangsters pull Tito out, embrace him and become his family. Unfortunately, Tito is drawn into a life of crime and gangsterism, which involves the Mexican Mafia and corrupt cops.

This gripping reality takes you on a journey leading to betrayal and a Three Strikes life sentence.

$14.95   187 pgs   6x9 Paperback   ISBN: 978-0-9912380-3-3
Celebrity Spotlight Entertainment, LLC

PRISON SECRETS
2nd EDITION

EUGENE L. WEEMS

Once recognized as a ruthless killer and remorseless criminal, Lyle Menendez remains housed in a maximum security correctional facility with other notorious murderers and gang members. In this level 4 maximum security prison, even one of America's most notorious murderers could be victimized. This novel will unlock the doors to all the prison secrets; weapons manufacturing, drug smuggling, prison rapes, gang politics, officer corruption and much, much more.

$14.95   183 pgs   6x9 Paperback   ISBN: 978-1500934873
Celebrity Spotlight Entertainment, LLC

INNOCENT BY CIRCUMSTANCE

C-MURDER
EUGENE L. WEEMS

The day of his grandmother's death was the day Boo began his quest for survival in the fast-paced, treacherous and wicked streets of Las Vegas, Nevada. The grieving child is forced into hustling, larceny, burglary, robbery and even murder just to maintain the necessities of life. Boo, Jewel and the rest of the kids exact revenge for the brutal crimes committed against them. They find unconditional love, commitment and loyalty within each other and become a family unit.

This action-filled story will surprise the reader with sensitive and all too real situations. A compelling novel with deep, complex characters guilty of horrible crimes...or are they Innocent by Circumstance?

$14.95   202 pgs   6x9 Paperback   ISBN: 978-1503355798
Celebrity Spotlight Entertainment, LLC

THE GREEN ROSE

CLARKE LOWE
& EUGENE WEEMS

MaryAnn is assaulted, but saved from harm by a heroic street-wise stranger. She can't help but be drawn to this brave and charming man. In him, she finds fun, excitement, and security. MaryAnn suggests her best friend Amanda meet her hero's friend Eugene, currently in prison. Sometimes love must be sought in unconventional places. Will they find the deepest, most exotic love of their lives? Will they find the Green Rose?

$14.95   117pgs   6x9 Paperback   ISBN: 978-1503357044
Celebrity Spotlight Entertainment, LLC

EMPIRE COOKIE'S REVENGE

EUGENE WEEMS

Cookie's only mission is to avenge her cousin Bunky's death and take back what is rightfully hers; Empire Entertainment. Scorned and vengeful, she will do whatever it takes to see that everyone who wronged her get what they have coming, even if that means murder.

$14.95   184pgs   6x9 Paperback   ISBN: 978-1515335917
Celebrity Spotlight Entertainment, LLC

LORD 4GIVE ME

**KING TIGER
& EUGENE WEEMS**

Dare to Read!

$14.95   245pgs   6x9 Paperback   ISBN: 978-1091849778
Celebrity Spotlight Entertainment, LLC

Made in the USA
Las Vegas, NV
12 January 2024